MW01258409

# VICTORY OR DEATH

## ALAMO REPRISE

Edith Elizabeth Pollitz

This story is a work of fiction. Except where names of actual persons, living, dead, or, in one case, both, are used, the characters are a figment of the author's overactive imagination. Many places figuring in the narrative are fictional as well, although the setting for most of the story, the Alamo, is very real. Characters associated with the Alamo as employees or reenactors are not based on real personages. Bella the Alamo cat is real and furry. The Alamo fudge sold by the gift shop is very real (and very good). Alas, they do not name their varieties, although, perhaps they should!

Cover art by Wade Dillon. Many thanks to Ned Huthmacher, who provided much assistance for coming up with the cover design.

To the memory of all the incredibly brave souls who were trapped in the Alamo for 13 long days, especially to the soldiers who guarded their fort to the end and fought for that freedom that we so often take for granted, and also to those in all of the years since who have worked to honor, protect, and "Remember the Alamo"!

"The person who has found nothing to die for is not fit to live."

Martin Luther King

# RESURRECTION

The Napoleon of the West smiled as he surveyed the scene of his greatest victory. The dusty plaza of the Alamo compound was littered with dead. Smoke still filled the air. A few bodies were burning. General Antonio Lopez de Santa Anna had finally, after an arduous winter march through the interior of Mexico and a 13-day standoff, made good on his promise to eliminate completely the hated enemy who had caused him so much trouble. He had killed all of them, every man, only, in the chivalry of the day, excepting women, children, and Negroes. The Anglos often looked down their noses at Mexico, and El Presidente bristled with proud anger at these usurpers' fancy that they were somehow superior. One area where Mexico clearly was far ahead of the rough, greedy Americans was on the issue of black slavery. Mexico had done away with it, and that was one of the problems leading to today's hideous event. Americans, mostly Southerners with slaves, had brought them with them illegally when they took up the generous offer of Mexican land in return for promising to become good Mexican citizens and to obey the laws and customs of that country. Travis, the ringleader of the rebels, was a classic example of the problem. Not only was he a slaveholder, rabble-rouser, fanatic, and revolutionary—all criminal offenses, but he was an illegal immigrant on top of that. He had slipped into Mexico and actually managing to get a piece of land for himself after the law of 1830 closed the legal door on foreigners coming in for those purposes. Fine thing in a man who practiced law! Yes, young Travis deserved everything he got and more, as did all those who chose to stick with him. Santa Anna had been planning for Travis' end for a long, long time.

Now, El Presidente wanted to be absolutely sure that his primary quarry was truly dead and would cause him no more trouble. He had asked the alcalde of the town, who would have known many of the so-called "Texians" and certainly their leaders, to identify Travis, Bowie, and Crockett for him. Santa Anna sat on his horse, waiting with some impatience for his aide and the alcalde to return with the needed information. The two men hurried up just as the impatient president/general was getting ready to send someone after them with a threat. They asked which one he wanted to view first. Santa Anna responded quickly: "Travis." The two men led the way, stepping over bodies, and the general followed on his horse. Finally, at the north wall, they stopped, pointing down at a blue-coated figure on his

1

stomach and still clenching a blood-covered sword, his hat on the ground not far from him. There were bayonet wounds in the small of his back and blood permeating the coat. Santa Anna dismounted and stood over the corpse. "Turn him over," he commanded, and the two men quickly complied. The body had been ravaged by a hideous-looking hole in the forehead, above the right eye, a large gash covering the entire right cheek, opening it up, and three bayonet wounds in the left side of his torso, as well as a sword thrust, causing the front of the man's coat to be saturated with blood. He was a tall, slender American with fair skin, thick red hair, and dead, open blue eyes. Santa Anna studied the body of the man who had caused him so many headaches, stooped and dipped his finger into the blood on the forehead, then spoke, as if to the unhearing Travis:

"You were a handsome young man before I did this to you, bright, could have become something. But you chose to become a land pirate, a criminal, a troublemaker, and I had to snuff you out, you and all of your band of misfits and troublemakers. You are gone now, gone to wherever criminals and troublemakers go, God rest your tormented soul. Now I must finally dispose of you for good."

He wiped the blood on his finger across Travis' left cheek, then stood and pulled out his sword, thrusting it into the body's side. The general ordered a special final indignity for the leader of the land pirates, something ignominious in fitting with the actions of the Alamo commander—throw him face down in the fort's latrine, there to remain with the accrued waste and filth of his command forever. Two soldiers lifted the legs of the bloody corpse and dragged it to the latrine, tossing it in, face down, per El Presidente's explicit instructions. They threw the hat and sword in for good measure, no one wanting to bother to take them all the way back to Mexico City, where this victory would likely seem very distant, and hopefully, only a minor prelude to the destruction of the rest of the Texians under Sam Houston to the east. A few shovels of dirt were thrown on top, and Col. William Barret Travis was quickly hidden from the face of the earth. The vast majority of his soldiers would be stripped and burned to erase almost all traces that they ever existed.

Bob Gordon paced back and forth, sniffling and rubbing his head as the dust from the dig penetrated his nostrils and eyes. He had always had severe sinus problems, one reason he took this job at the Alamo years ago. Bob was originally from leafy Pennsylvania, and some of the Keystone State plant species caused excruciating headaches and lots of visits to the allergist.

San Antonio had plants, too, but the varieties did not trigger the same degree of sinus inflammation. Here, generally, he was able to breathe with much less effort. But the students from UTSA's Center for Archaeological Research were testing his sinuses mightily. There had been digs before, and it just seemed to be one of those things that were part of the evolution of what was left of the old mission compound. Almost everything else had been mapped, checked, and rechecked religiously, over the years. But someone got the bright idea that no one had ever definitively pinpointed the latrine, although they knew it was in the vicinity of the livestock pen. And, as with everything at the Alamo, that meant in code the honest-to-God outdoor bathroom facilities used by Davy Crockett and company, not something from some earlier or later era of the long-lived mission. The archaeology center had actually received a federal grant for the dig.

The students were using hand tools trying to scrape at the hard ground, packed for a century or more. A serious piece of machinery had been carefully maneuvered into place early in the morning before the crowds showed up. It carefully scooped up about 18 inches of dirt in a fairly even swath in the area the somewhat contradictory old maps—some in Spanish, indicated was the most likely site for the 19th century restroom. Restrooms had never been the number one priority at the Shrine. Bob could remember that when his family had taken their one "trip out West" to see the Grand Canyon when he was 9, they stopped at the Alamo, only to find what he considered a very primitive excuse for a restroom. Although there had been some improvement since then, the poor facilities were the main thing he "remembered" about the famous fort/church from that trip. Davy Crockett didn't have that much, so it might be tough going to find it.

The initially enthusiastic archaeology students were getting tired with their tedious hand scraping, various ones occasionally stopping, looking around, yawning, mopping a sweaty brow. It was February 19—still technically winter, but the weather could swing quickly and dramatically in the Alamo City, and the winter sun was warming to what was going to be a very warm February day. The students and their professor were hoping that the latrine could be mapped finally and that folks of 1836 might have tossed in some items of archaeological or historical interest along the way. Bob was wearying from watching a process that seemed to go nowhere fast. He headed back to his office underneath the gift shop. Bella, the Alamo's latest cat mascot, stood in the path and looked up at him as he approached the door. He stopped for a quick pet, then headed inside.

Lori Clayton had gotten to "work" early. She was actually only a

3

volunteer, so there was no money whatsoever in this. She played the role of a Texian pioneer woman most days. The 19-year-old had graduated from high school the year before but just missed the requirements for going to UT Austin, probably because she did not apply herself as rigorously as she should have in math and the sciences. Lori loved history, and she effortlessly glided through classes telling of people and events of other times. Not so much anything involving the applied sciences or geometry. Lori was descended from prominent families in early South Carolina, including the Charleston Ravenels. She had been named for a four-times-great-aunt, Lorelei Ravenel Clayton, a girlfriend of Texas General John Bell Hood. The first Lori, a Charleston Southern belle who billed herself as "The Yellow Rose of Texas" in Civil War Atlanta, apparently not aware that the original Yellow Rose was a mulatto, sang in sort of a Confederate version of the USO. The family had an oil painting of Lori I. She was a pretty blonde whose appearance was very similar to Lori II. Lori sometimes thought that she channeled her aunt. She would have to catch herself when she daydreamed of being a time-traveler. She had done her high school community service stint at the Alamo and found that she loved it, continuing to help out as needed at the old mission since. After high school, and while she was waiting for a bolt out of the blue to strike her as to what she should do with her life, somewhat structured half-time volunteering at the Alamo seemed like a way to at least further her interests and add something to a very scant resume.

She had, of her own volition, learned to sew. Her mom, a busy nurse, had not had time to teach her much, but Lori was persistent if anything. She now made historical costumes and sold them at good rates on eBay or to local reenactors, making a smaller profit than would have been expected because the costumes required so much fabric, for her efforts. With her 1800's domestic skills—she also excelled at period cooking, she was popular as a costumed reenactor at Alamo events and with the Texian Association.

Lori picked up Bella, holding her gently, and gave her a few pets before sending her on her way to defend the Alamo against all mice, rats, and other pests that might attack the Shrine. She headed in and down the stairs quickly, running into Bob in her rush.

"So sorry, Mr. Gordon! I didn't mean to mow you down," she apologized.

Bob laughed. "Lori, how many times have I told you, please, just call me Bob! You're fine. If I can't stand up to more than just a brief encounter with a colleague, I should not be working at the Alamo!"

She smiled and continued in her rush to the little cubbyhole where she stuffed her purse and an enormous cup for water—a necessity most days. She straightened her cotton print dress, ran to the restroom to glance in the mirror and check her hair, then put on her "1836 face" and headed out to meet her public. Today Lori was excited as she was going to give a demonstration of pioneer cooking techniques. She headed quickly to her ancient car, not thinking too much about the fact that it would not have been available for the trip to H.E.B., which also would not have been available, in the 1830's. As she opened the trunk to get a sack full of items she would need for the demo, she heard a high squeal from one of the students working on the excavation. There seemed to be a flurry of activity, as several of the other workers stopped what they were doing and stood over the young woman who had made the utterance. Lori, holding her rather heavy sack, walked over to the site, ducking under the rope surrounding the dig, to see what was going on.

"It might be an old shoe . . . can't really tell yet . . . is something black and looks like leather," the archaeologist trainee was saying to the guiding professor, who was now standing over her.

She gently kept working at the dirt. Lori couldn't see anything other than dust but continued to stand, her curiosity up. The archaeology student was adept at her trade, and now more of the black object was becoming visible. It did appear to be the heel of a shoe of some sort.

She turned to the young man next to her. "Rob, if you could get on my left side here," the woman suggested, "we could attack it from both sides. This is going to take forever at the rate I'm going alone."

She moved slightly to the side, and the rest of the team, now all hunched over her, moved slightly to accommodate her shift and Rob's move. Progress increased slightly with two people at the task, and in 15 minutes they clearly had the foot portion of what was apparently a boot uncovered. A gentle nudge indicated that there was something solid inside. With renewed vigor, Rob and his coworker kept uncovering more and more of the lower leg of what was obviously a body. They shifted over again, while another team of two started on the adjacent ground, figuring there was likely to be another boot. Lori continued to stand, transfixed. So far, no one else from the compound had come by, so the work was unhindered by onlookers, but the Alamo opened at 9:00, and the hordes were about to descend on the old mission. The professor realized that and headed for Bob Gordon's office to ask if there was anything that could be used to screen from public view the spot where the students were digging beyond the roping presently strung around the site. Bob hurried out to look, then directed Lori, who was still standing there with an iron skillet in the heavy bag, to find the maintenance man and get some screens put up in a hurry. She did not dawdle, and the screens went up right before the public was permitted on the locked part of the grounds.

Lori edged back inside the screen, standing quietly. The second team had located the other leg and was working diligently on it in close quarters. Rob and the woman who had first spotted the foot were almost up to the top of the boot now, encased in dirt but still formed as if there were flesh inside. Some of the tourists, having heard there was an excavation, were trying to stare through the mesh barricade from a distance, but most went on their way for the usual Alamo tour, having pictures made in front of the ancient church, and buying "stuff" at the gift shop. The worker bees continued, Rob and the woman now getting beyond the knee and going up the leg of the corpse, which was covered with some sort of light-colored clothing, more dirt-hued than anything at this point. Lori looked at her cell phone. She still had 2 hours before she had to demonstrate how to cook cactus over a fire. She sat on the ground and put the sack with its heavy skillet next to her. The students kept inching up the body, exposing the buttocks and up to the waist. At this point, a couple of other students on the perimeter, one on each side, joined in and worked outward trying to find the hands and arms. At the waist, Rob and his partner hit a tangle of blue and red cloth—what turned out to be the tails of a coat and some sort of a sash, which they pulled down in place and kept edging forward. Cuts in the fabric of the coat at the lower base of the center back, surrounded by dried blood, indicated some sort of wounds, likely from 1836 or some other confrontation. The young woman to the left of the main excavation, who had green tips along the lower rim of her blonde hair, stopped, only calling out softly, "Look!"

Everyone stared. A dirt-covered but intact human hand had revealed itself. She touched the hand lightly. "Come on, we've got to free him from this prison!" she stated dramatically, her words in contrast to the softness of her voice.

It all seemed incongruous to Lori, still staring in fascination. Like as if this guy was going to jump up and say, "Gee, thanks for getting me out of the Alamo!" Time was getting short when they finally got to the shoulders and started on the neck and head. It was lunchtime, and Lori was supposed to cook her cactus, but she could not tear herself away. The tourists would just have to wait to see and smell stir-fried cactus.

6

The neck was done in no time, and the students, although now tired and dripping with sweat, were very careful with the head. The man had what appeared to be beautiful red hair, longish, but full of dirt as was everything else. Once "free," as green tip had described, a determination had to be made as to whether to dig around the outline of the body further or try to lift it out of the hole carefully without damaging it. No one wanted to wait any longer, and the guys on the team, along with the professor, positioned themselves around the corpse and pulled it straight up, wrapping their arms underneath it for support, then lifted it above the gravesite and carefully laid it down, still face down, on even ground.

"Well, shall we turn him over?" Rob inquired.

No one said anything. Rob and one other man gently and slowly rotated the body on its back.

It was obviously one of the immortal—although this one looked pretty darn mortal at the moment—defenders from 1836. Battered, bloody, and stained with dirt, it was hard to get a complete idea of what he looked like. There was a gaping hole above the right eye from a gunshot wound, a long slash wound all the way down that side of the face from right below the eye to the jawbone, and numerous stab wounds bunched together on the far left side of the chest, not far below the heart, leaving his clothes drenched in dried blood in that vicinity. He was tall and thin and looked to be very young. The red hair was likely striking, but the dirt, blood, and matted condition made it hard to tell for sure. Open eyes were blue. He was dressed in a coat that had once been blue but was now mostly the dried blood in color, a red military sash, and the filthy, light colored pants and black boots. Everyone just stood and stared.

"Looks like Hell," Rob noted.

"Well, he's been there," the professor responded.

"Probably there now," a Hispanic student responded. She obviously was not fond of Alamo defenders.

Finally, Lori edged forward. "Excuse me, I'm Lori. I work here—have been watching the whole time," she attempted an introduction and excuse for watching the project. "But . . . why is he . . . whole?"

No one answered her. Everyone just continued to stare at the body, even Bob Gordon. Lori did not know much, but instincts told her there was

7

something odd about this—maybe even more odd than the fact that this bizarre event had just occurred. She stepped forward again, knelt down beside the body, and gently held his high collar aside with one hand and put her other hand on his neck to feel for a pulse.

"Oh my God! Call someone! He's got a faint pulse. He's still alive, do something!" she cried. She settled down next to the man, gently cradling the carved-up, pathetic head in her arm.

The professor looked over at Bob Gordon. "Well, Bob, I don't remember a whole lot about what Col. Travis looked like, if they even knew, although I've read an awful lot of stuff on the battle. But I do remember that he had red hair, and I've seen all the movies. Based on the hair, youth, costume, and head wound, I'm wondering if you're going to find yourself answering to a new boss? You may want to polish up your resume!"

"Yeah, right," Bob responded with a little laugh. "'Victory or Death' and all that. This guy, if that's who he is, was defiant and determined then. He may have decided to come back just to beat Santa Anna."

One of the students was already on her cell phone calling 911. She handed the phone to Bob to give the details. It was on speaker, and everyone could hear when the dispatcher asked: "The Alamo? What happened? Did Santa Anna come back and shoot someone?"

"Kind of," Bob responded. "We'll explain when someone gets here, but tell them to hurry!" He scratched his balding head, adjusted his glasses, and sniffled. He was sure the dust was permeating every crevice of his already weakened sinuses.

He handed the phone back to the student and sighed. The anniversary of the reading of Col. Travis' most famous epistle from the doomed fort was in 5 days. In 2013, the state archives had grudgingly allowed the precious original, locked in an airtight, bombproof super-secure container inside a heavily guarded blue truck, out of its vaults and back to the Alamo for the anniversary of the siege. Half of Texas and beyond flocked to see the yellowed paper where the young commander dramatically pled with the Texians and "all Americans in the world" to come to the aid of the doomed garrison. If this mangled, pathetic survivor of the fight were to hang on and actually live for a while, how would that affect the Alamo? Bob was not in the least concerned that a likely brain-dead ghost from the past would create issues for him at work, but he was getting the feeling that things would

8

never be quite the same if a medical miracle could save the relic. And, although the young man met the traditional movie description for the Alamo commander, that was certainly not dispositive. But his costume, youth, and the red hair were certainly indicative. Regardless of who he was, he was clearly a veteran of the fight.

Lori's clothing was no longer presentable even for reenacting the grubby 1830's. Ground-in dirt as well as the dust that permeated everything had discolored her dull rose dress with its large print pattern—the latter all the rage at the time of the battle, at least on the frontier. Her long, yellow-blonde hair was matted and dingy and her face caked with dust .All thoughts of a cactus dinner were long gone. She continued to cradle the defender's head, looking only at him, while Bob, the professor, and the students fidgeted, wiped away sweat, and waited for the ambulance to arrive.

The professor, obviously amused, nodded toward Lori and remarked to Bob in a voice clearly intended to be heard by all, "Amazing isn't it? You read the diary, didn't you? He's still attracting women after all these years!"

Lori looked up in disgust, but she didn't say anything. Bob just laughed quietly. It wasn't long before the siren foretold the arrival of help for the last remaining defender of the Alamo. Lori gently held his head until the ambulance driver and his assistant brought the stretcher and then carefully lifted the still form and strapped him on.

"Any relatives or friends? One person can ride with us if you like."

"Uh, he . . . he . . . doesn't have any relatives or friends," Lori started.

"Huh?"

"We dug him up during the excavation. He's really from 1836—at least we think so. Be very careful. He's got to be fragile, and he may have fallen from the parapet after being shot. They had the guns up on top with dirt piled up in sort of a steep hill below. If he's who we think he is, he would have been up top at the cannon. If so, there may have been broken bones. Who knows how or if they would have healed in all this time," Bob explained.

The ambulance crew had really strange looks on their faces.

"I've got to have my car, but I'll follow you," Lori volunteered, gathering the skirt of her long, dirty dress and heading, at a run, to the vehicle. The sack with the skillet was left leaning against a pecan tree. The professor and Bob, at a more leisurely pace, headed for Bob's car to follow the ambulance.

The San Antonio traffic always seemed awful, but today was particularly bad. Even an ambulance could get stuck in traffic, and this happened twice along the relatively short run to the hospital. Lori had thought to ask which hospital, and she actually got there right before the ambulance. She parked illegally in a handicapped space, hoping no one would check, got out, and was standing to the side of the entrance as the ambulance pulled up and the stretcher was unloaded. She followed as it was hurriedly wheeled inside. No waiting for this kind of emergency. They rolled him on into a slot, Lori continuing in hot pursuit, totally oblivious to the stares of patients and their loved ones at the filthy pioneer lady. As soon as the patient was placed on a bed, nurses started checking vitals and making analyses. One hospital worker crowded into the corner of the small cubicle with a laptop, pulling up and filling in patient data forms. It was obvious that the man could not answer her questions, so she asked Lori.

"Name?"

"I don't know."

"Symptoms?"

"He's unconscious and has all kinds of wounds. You can see them as plain as I can," Lori attempted to answer.

"Why are you with him if you don't know anything about him?" the staffer inquired rather crossly.

"I volunteer at the Alamo. There's an excavation going on there. We found him. We think he's from the battle," Lori responded with a little crossness in her own tired voice.

The woman got off her high horse. "Well, I guess we'll just have to wait and see. No point in asking if he has insurance, I guess?" she looked up with a smile.

"I don't think Blue Cross was selling policies to the Alamo defenders right before Santa Anna showed up," Lori responded. "Considering what happened, they would have been wise not to buy, if they were."

The woman went on her way, after saying that she or someone else would check back for more details for her forms if it became possible to get any of them later, which did not look likely. Meanwhile, someone—Lori had been busy with the woman and not paying attention to the soldier—had stripped off the filthy clothing, only to find the man's body equally filthy. Two young men were attempting a sponge bath of sorts, but there was so much dirt and dried blood that getting the patient truly clean using that method was nearly impossible. He had been hooked up to various monitors, and the two bathers had just finished—or done as much as they could do, when a doctor walked in.

"I'm Dr. Rojas," the man greeted Lori.

"Hi! I'm Lori Clayton. I wish I knew for sure who this gentleman is, but we dug him up at the Alamo today. There have been some educated guesses, but no one is sure."

Rojas replied, "I see. Well, he's in pretty rough shape—no surprise, I guess, considering the outcome of the battle. We're going to take some pictures—CT scan and X-ray. Someone said they thought he might have fallen off the top of the fort when he was hit and wondered if there were broken bones?"

"It's a possibility. They had cannon on platforms on the perimeter of the fort, and if you fell from there, it would be about a 10-foot drop, more of a roll really as they heaped up dirt in a hill," Lori explained.

The doctor attempted a cursory diagnosis. "I would think that anything like that should have healed in place, although it would not be set so may very well have not healed correctly if so. But we'll find out. The head wound is the major concern, needless to say. It's very possible that he will not make it through surgery if we attempt to take the bullet out. And we're talking about the brain. How much, if any, function he will have is a huge question mark. But we are going to scan and get a fix on where the bullet went. If it went in straight and not too far, that's a lot better than if it angled. We're going to take him for tests now. You are welcome to sit and wait here."

"Thank you," Lori said softly.

Bob and the professor, whose name was Tom Ryan, came hurriedly into the emergency room waiting area. They gave a description of Lori, which left no doubt, and were ushered into the small room where she was

11

waiting. She filled them in on what few details she knew. Hospitals were always a waiting game.

Finally, Dr. Rojas returned. "We got the tests, and Dr. Hamilton reviewed them. He's going to do the surgery. He said the bullet did not go in far, and it did go straight. That's good news. If he's from 1836, it's some sort of projectile used by the Mexican Army. Sorry, I don't know anything about what sort of weapons they were using back then. And it's been lodged in his head for 181 years. The right frontal lobe regulates nonverbal communication and negative emotions. That may be better than had it been the left, which tends to the language and verbal skills, as well as positive emotions. But some patients with damage in one area are able to compensate with what's left. Some cannot. And there are all the other wounds. So there's no guarantee."

"Is there ever a guarantee, doctor?" Lori asked meekly.

"No ma'am, actually, there's not. This is an extremely unusual case, and the odds of this patient having a normal outcome are not incredibly high."

"Well, he's already been through the Alamo siege and battle, so I guess he's seen about the worst," Bob ventured.

"Maybe," the doctor cautioned. "But I'm talking situations such as brain dead or not being able to communicate or lack of coordination or not being able to see—could be anything. The brain controls everything."

"But we have to try," Lori said softly.

"Yes, and that's what we're going to do. They're prepping him for the surgery right now."

"How long will it take?" Bob asked.

"Depends on how hard it is to extract the bullet and how much bleeding that causes. The actual extraction won't take too long, but it's all the prep and wrapping up that takes the time. I'm going to say about 3 hours. Dr. Hamilton would have a better timetable, but he's already preparing to do the surgery. He wants to move quickly while the patient's vital signs are as good as they are."

Dr. Rojas headed to his next patient, and Lori, Bob, and Professor Ryan followed the directions of a nurse to the surgical waiting room,

12

stopping at a vending machine for Cokes on the way.

The wait seemed interminable. Bob and Tom Ryan passed much of the time talking about how the Spurs were doing in basketball. Lori rolled her eyes. She hated sports. She kept pulling out and glancing at her cell phone. It had been close to 4 hours and still no word. There was a screen above the desk listing patients and status, but there was no name for this man, so that was not helpful. She had inquired a couple of times, but the only answer she got was that he was still in surgery. She was getting fidgety, to the point that Bob and the professor would turn and stare now and then. Finally, she got up and walked out of the room, down the hall, then back. Her attire limited what she could do without making a scene, and she hated to sit too near anyone with all the dirt and dust she stirred up. She came back in, but no sooner than she had resumed her seat next to Bob and the professor, the attendant called her name. She ran to the desk.

"He's out of surgery. They got the bullet out quickly. That's all I know. The doctor can tell you more. He will be out to confer with you in a minute."

Lori murmured a quick "thank you" and resumed her seat with Bob and the professor. They didn't have long to wait. Dr. Hamilton appeared within 5 minutes, a small, serious-looking man with kindly eyes.

"Are you folks waiting for news of our Alamo soldier?" he asked.

"Yes, we are. I'm Lori Clayton." She pointed to her companions, "Bob Gordon and Tom Ryan."

"Come with me where we can talk in private," the doctor beckoned to a small room off to the side of the large waiting room.

After they were all seated, he started: "I am very optimistic considering just how bad this looked. The ball did not go far, we got it out quickly, and the bleeding was minimal for this kind of situation. But after all, it did go into the brain, so there will be some issues. It was a large projectile—that means more extensive damage as to brain function. We will be doing tests that will give us more clues about that, but right now, we just want him to rest. After 24 hours, the danger from inflammation will decrease—that's the biggest worry in the short run."

"I'm so glad," Lori said with a sigh of relief.

13

The surgeon cautioned, "Keep in mind, he's not anywhere near out of the woods yet. There will be problems of some sort, I'm sure—likely some personality disorders and nonverbal communication issues at the very least. But for the situation, it's looking quite hopeful."

Ryan asked, "Do you have the projectile? I would like to take a look at it so we can see what kind of firearm it came from. Most Mexican troops used the Brown Bess, a holdover from Napoleonic days that Santa Anna was able to buy cheap in bulk. They can make a hole three-quarters of an inch in diameter or larger. Those guns fire a round ball, not a bullet-shaped projectile. There's an alternate theory out there regarding one Alamo defender—and it could be this guy—that he may have shot himself with one of those old pistols they had back then once the situation reached hopeless. If the ball is from a Brown Bess, it will put that one to rest."

"Sure. I will have the blood cleaned off of it and get it to you right now," the doctor offered.

He stepped out and over to the desk quickly and gave instructions to the attendant, who contacted someone in back. Hamilton was back in less than a minute.

"Doc, could you run a DNA test for us? Many of the defender families have DNA on file, and we would like to determine who he is," Bob inquired.

"We already thought of that given the information we had. We've run the test and will have the DNA profile shortly. If I remember correctly, we may have access to the Alamo defender families DNA data. If so, I'll make sure we check for a match as soon as we get his results."

"So where do we go from here?" Lori inquired.

Hamilton raised his eyebrows slightly and sighed. "He will be in intensive care for 24 hours at the very minimum. If we do not see any danger of swelling and all the vitals look good, we will probably be able to put him in a regular room after that. I know this guy doesn't have anyone close to him for obvious reasons, but, if someone wants to stay with him, it's fine. If he does wake up, I think it's going to be very important for someone with steady nerves and a gentle manner to be there. He's going to be in for quite a shock."

Lori quickly volunteered, but only after a brief trip home to shower and get out of the 1836 costume and into some jeans, a comfortable top, and her running shoes. As she readied to head home, she thought to ask for the soldier's clothes with the idea of taking them to a dry cleaner to see if there was any hope for them. After somewhat of a wait, someone came out with two of the standard bags of belongings, the number required for all of the man's regalia. With the soldier in intensive care, Bob and the professor waited for the projectile extracted from the defender's head, then headed to the car and home for the time being.

# REVELATION

"One mystery solved—it's Mexican," Tom Ryan informed Bob. It was 11:00 at night, and Bob had been roused from his bed by the cell phone ringing. His significant other, Leslie, turned but was quickly back asleep.

"Huh? Who is this?" Bob responded sleepily.

"Tom Ryan. Sorry. Did I wake you up?"

"Sort of," Bob tried to soften the reply he had been considering.

"It's just that I thought you would want to know. One Alamo mystery solved—it's a Mexican ball. He didn't shoot himself," Ryan said excitedly.

"You realize that's only important if this guy turns out to be Travis?" Bob yawned.

"I know, I know. But this whole Alamo thing is one myth built on top of another. Unfortunately, if he is Travis, we're not going to find out how Davy died because Travis went first and was on the opposite end of the compound. But if we could get more facts, some of the infighting that goes on about this whole event might calm down," Ryan said hopefully.

"Infighting about the Alamo calm down? With the possibility this is Travis? Oh, come on, Tom—what fantasyland are you coming from?" Bob laughed.

"Ivory tower impractical? Well, maybe so, but in my field, we look for facts, and even this ball may have important implications," he said. "I'll see you tomorrow at the dig. Sorry to wake you."

Bob yawned. "I do appreciate the call, if not so much the time, Tom. See you tomorrow and we can mull this one over further."

As the new day dawned, Bob stopped in at the hospital on his way in to work. Lori, in a cobalt blue sweater and some old jeans, was sitting sideways in a chair next to the patient's bed. She made an attractive 1830's Texian, for folks who found that kind of thing appealing, but she was a beautiful young woman in 21st Century style. Tall and willowy, she had a thin but curvy figure, and huge blue eyes, a small, straight nose, oval face with high cheekbones and a slightly pointed chin, and luxuriant, thick blonde hair. She carried herself well and always wore simple, but stylish and well-fitting clothes, a result of her interest in and research on clothing through the years. She was dozing when Bob came in, but she came to when she heard him enter.

"How's our defender today?" Bob asked. "And how are you holding up?"

"They keep coming in and waking me up, taking his vitals—you know how it is in a hospital," she replied, rubbing her eyes. He nodded. She continued. "All the signs are positive, but he hasn't stirred yet. I met the new doctor who is taking the case from here on out—Roberto Gonzalez. He said something about having an ancestor on the other side! I guess everyone has a stake in this thing if you take it back far enough."

"No animosity toward treating a defender, I presume?" Bob joked.

"None at all. Actually, Dr. Gonzalez seemed interested in that aspect of it—said he's a history buff."

"Any word on whether he's likely to wake up or what damage the wound may have caused?" Bob inquired.

"Not yet. They wanted to give him 24 straight hours without disturbance." She glanced at her cell phone. "Not anywhere near there yet. At that point, the risk of serious swelling apparently goes down quite a bit. They haven't treated all the other wounds yet, and some of them are pretty bad, although the doctor told me that all of this has healed in a manner of speaking, although maybe not quite right. They only evidence they found of broken bones was in the left arm and wrist. If he fell from the parapet when he was shot, he must have landed on that side. Lucky his neck did not snap. The breaks have fused—fortunately pretty well, but I suspect he may have some issues to deal with from it. The way the doctor talked, I don't think they intend to break them again and reset—does not seem that bad."

The door opened, and a middle-aged man with glasses and a high forehead came in.

17

"Roberto Gonzalez," he introduced himself, extending his hand to Bob.

"Bob Gordon—I work at the Alamo," Bob responded with a firm handshake.

Gonzales continued. "I've got some news I think will be of major interest to both of you, and, once it gets out, probably to lots of other people as well. But I would suggest we keep it under wraps just yet as our patient needs some quiet time to get through these first few days. I've asked the folks here who are working with him not to say anything and have arranged for limited contact by staff—only those who need to see the patient. No question, he's Col. Travis. The DNA matched both Sheriff Travis up in Denton County and the other Travis relatives from Texas and Alabama who contributed DNA tests in the past."

Lori and Bob stared at the doctor. They had known this was a likely possibility, but thinking about possibilities and a reality that was this kind of bombshell were two different things. The hesitant volunteer worker who had always addressed her boss as Mr. Gordon had been through a whirlwind in the last 24 hours and had grown into a more adult perspective. And with that came a boldness she had never shown before.

"So, Bob, are you going to polish up your resume like Professor Ryan asked?" she inquired with raised eyebrows.

Bob glanced at the unconscious colonel. "No, not yet. Looks like I've got a little more time," he responded with a smile. He looked at the doctor. "Although based on what I've read about his personality, I can't quite imagine working for Col. Travis." Everyone laughed.

The doctor headed on in his rounds, promising to be back to check on Travis and confer with Lori around 6:00 in the evening.

"I need to run home and do a couple of things. I thought about taking his clothes to the cleaners. They may self-destruct, but something has to be done to get them cleaned up. I'd like to get a couple of hours of sleep if I could. I'll be back well before 6:00 if I leave now."

"Sounds like a plan. Normally, I'd say we should send the clothes for archival preservation, but that takes forever, and it's possible he might wake up and want them, so I guess we can take the risk," Bob said hesitantly. "I'm going on to work. I'm not going to say anything to Tom right yet."

18

Lori rubbed her eyes. She desperately wanted some real sleep, but she had to get the uniform to the cleaners to see if they could try to salvage some of it. She pulled in the parking lot, then sorted through the clothes in the two bags to pick out the items for cleaning. She held out a torn-up bloody shirt and drawers—would try to do something with them at home, and folded the pale yellow—or at least it had been—fancy silk vest, blue coat, red sash, and once-white pants. Bob had read, in fact, had a copy of, Travis' diary and had relayed to Lori all kinds of information from it over time. The diary, which told most of what historians knew about the colonel except for his political and military activities, revealed that, in addition to his addiction to gambling and promiscuity, he was rather a dandy, and definitely a frontier fashion plate—certainly more unusual in a man than in a woman. He ordered cloth and had it made up in the gentlemen's styles of the day. A favorite item seemed to be a style of trousers called by the silly-sounding name pantaloons, which Lori recognized in his white pants. These were distinctive for a very tight fit in the legs with some extra room in the seat so that the wearer could attempt to move around somewhat comfortably. An old British print of the times that Lori had seen in her sewing studies showed a ridiculous-looking English fop all gussied up in a costume that included the silly pants. The man in the picture had dropped a handkerchief, and two other men in more comfortable attire were laughing at him as the pants were so tight he could not bend over to retrieve his hanky. Lori hurried into the cleaners and got quite a look of surprise from the young woman who took her items.

"I volunteer at the Alamo," she explained. Then, realizing that her explanation did not adequately explain all the blood on Travis' clothes, she added, "We had an 1836 wound-dressing exhibition yesterday."

The attendant nodded slightly with a look that said "you're crazy," but she took the items. "Any special instructions?" she grunted.

Lori hated to give anything away so she risked saying no. The clothes would be ready the next day per the sign proudly displayed in the front window. She would attempt to wash out the other items before she took a quick nap at the house. If the colonel did wake up, he would likely be disconcerted about everything if he was functioning, and it would be nice to have his only remaining possessions present if he wanted them.

When she pulled into the driveway, Lori was relieved that her dad and mom had already left for work. Her dad, Robert Clayton, was a military doctor with the rank of major. Starting the next day, he would be off for a week at a conference in Houston. Her mom, Elena, was a nurse in a private doctor's office. Brother Leonard, whom everyone called Len, was 15 and would be at school by now, as would be the youngest member of the family, 9-year-old Victoria, called Vicky. So Lori had the place to herself—great for trying to clean up the rest of the colonel's clothes. She set to that task immediately, using an inordinate amount of Shout on the historical fabrics, unsure whether they would hold up or not. She let them soak in her bathroom sink while she set her alarm for noon and fell on the bed for some much needed rest. She was out immediately. It seemed like no time when the annoying alarm went off. She did not want to miss the latest from the doctor. She spent considerable time and elbow grease on the ancient garments, washing and rewashing them, and hung them over the shower bar in her bathroom to dry. Lori closed the bathroom door, brushed her hair, and grabbed her keys to head back to the hospital. The phone rang as she headed out of her room, locking the door. She had left her cell number with the nurse—she, or someone at the hospital, was calling.

"Yes?" she answered.

"Ms. Clayton?, this is Maria Duarte—the nurse," a voice replied.

"Yes, but please call me Lori. Has there been some change?"

"Not really, but he seems stronger and his eyelids fluttered a bit. We're wondering if he might be going to come to."

"I was headed your way anyway. I'll be there as fast as I can," Lori answered, as she started for her car.

Lori hurried, but the traffic, as always, was what it was. It didn't matter. When she got there, Travis was still unconscious. She looked at him more closely than she had when all the craziness was going on. It was hard to see much of the top of his head, as it was bandaged heavily. The long scar on the same side as the gunshot wound pretty much totaled out any appealing view of that side of his face. The clear blue eyes she remembered were closed now. His face gravitated somewhat toward rounded in shape. He had a rather long, narrow, and very straight nose, and that fair complexion that often comes with red hair. His lips were also rather thin, and his chin was firm and strong. The thick, tousled hair, now that it had been cleaned up, was a gorgeous shade of red. Some redheads almost look artificial, she thought, but Travis' hair, though very red, was a slightly subdued shade that made Lori a bit envious. He wore sideburns in the style of his day. A little bit of stubble was beginning to appear on his face. Travis was very thin— 13 days with limited food at the Alamo might do that to you. His right hand

20

was resting on his chest, with the standard IV and one other needle in it. His hand was long and slender—his fingers were thin, for a man. But they were not thin enough for the famous cat's eye ring that allegedly was given to him by his sweetheart, Rebecca Cummings, long before he entered the Alamo. The story went that Travis, knowing what was about to happen to him, tied the ring to a piece of string or twine and put it around the neck of the baby daughter of another Alamo officer. The women and children in the fort were spared, and the ring went through a number of owners before finally being donated to the Alamo. The colonel either wore it on a string around his neck or it had been resized. She recalled someone on the Alamo staff mentioning that.

Maria had obviously gone to see her other patients, so Lori just sat, staring at the young man from so long ago. Lori was getting fidgety again just sitting there. She got up and paced back and forth a few times, then resumed her seat. Still no Maria or anyone else. Lori had been figuring the 24-hour period from when they got Travis to the hospital, but she thought about it a bit more. It actually would run from the end of surgery, somewhere around 6:00 in the evening—about the time that Gonzalez would come by. Maybe the doctor would take Travis out of the crowded ICU, but likely not, she thought.

Bob and Tom arrived for a quick check shortly after Lori returned. Bob had finally revealed the patient's identity to Tom after swearing him to secrecy.

"No action. I had a slight false alarm when the nurse called as I was leaving for the hospital. She said his eyelids fluttered a bit once, but he's just been lying here since I got back," she reported.

"His color looks a little healthier, in my layman's opinion," Bob ventured. "We do need to think about what to do when he does wake up," he continued. "I wish we could provide a little continuity with the past so he doesn't freak out quite as much as I think I would in a situation like this."

"Continuity? With his immediate past?" Tom inquired. "You've got to be kidding!"

"No, I don't mean a battle and massacre. Gee, Tom, how dumb do you think I am?" Bob feigned exasperation. "Lori, did you get his clothes to the cleaners?"

"Yeah. You should have seen the look the attendant gave me. I told her I worked at the Alamo, but that didn't explain the bloodstains I asked them to try to remove, which was pretty much the whole vest and coat. So I made up something about an 1830's wound dressing demo. She still looked at me like I was insane. I'll go back first thing in the morning to see what they could do. I hesitated to say just how old the clothes were. The stuff really might disintegrate from the cleaning fluid. But I don't know what else we could have done—guess we should have waited and had archival experts take a look, but it's too late now."

"Well, my thoughts on this are that it would be good if he had something recognizable on hand, and the uniform is all he's got left. We could bring it and put it on him if he starts showing signs of awakening."

Lori was getting bold enough to interrupt her boss. "He's got a catheter. Those tight pants will never do in a medical situation. Trust me, I know the history of clothing styles—won't work. The boots would be a nuisance, and, quite frankly all those layers of shirt, vest, and coat and sash. They need to be able to get to his body to do whatever they have to do in a hurry. I'll ask Dr. Gonzalez, but I'm sure that's what he will say."

"I see your point. Well, maybe bring the coat if it doesn't come apart. We could at least slip that on him over the gown," Bob suggested.

"Hospital gown and tailcoat, what a look!" Lori laughed, but she promised to bring the coat first thing in the morning.

"Sound perfect to me," the professor noted. "Think about the major problem with hospital gowns."

Bob and Lori laughed.

The two men headed back to work, and Lori sat for another hour, hoping to catch Maria. Travis still made no motion. Finally, Lori left a note and headed home for a couple of hours. She wanted to be back by 6:00 to hear whatever Gonzalez might have to say. She was relieved that none of her family had been there when she went home earlier and was glad that they weren't home now, as she was determined not to tell them anything yet. Len had a learner's permit, but he was not 16, so he rode home from high school with a friend. Vicky's school was just down the street, so she walked. It was 2:30. She would be home soon. The colonel's belongings that she had washed out were drying nicely in her bathroom. Lori put the alarm on for 3:30 and took another brief nap. She would have to leave early to fight the 5:00 traffic to get back to the hospital by or before 6:00.

The door slamming woke her up before the alarm could go off. It was Vicky, who was calling for her, seeing her car. She turned the alarm off quickly, smoothed her hair, and headed out of the room.

"What are you doing home?" Vicky asked suspiciously.

"Uh, it was a slow day. After all, I'm just a volunteer anyway, and there wasn't anything to do so I came on home." She hoped she was convincing to her sister.

"Well, guess what we did in school today!" Vicky had a self-satisfied look on her face.

Lori didn't say anything—just raised her eyebrows with inquiring eyes.

"I sure am glad you work at the Alamo—gave me a leg up on the other kids. There's an old film—reason I know it's old is the girl's hairstyle was like SO dated, and they actually talked about video stores and watching tapes on VCRs, but it was a cool little film. It was about the Alamo!"

"Oh?" Lori replied. She would have to be careful. Vicky was a very, very perceptive child.

"Yeah. It was sort of—I take that back—it was VERY weird, but the backstory was kind of sweet. This kid is forced to do a book report on something she cares nothing about—one of the guys in the Alamo. She tries to rent a VCR tape on the subject to avoid reading a book on the guy, but the video store is closed, so she's forced to go to the library. The place is actually moldering."

Lori was surprised—she didn't think Vicky knew that word. Her little sister went on:

"They got really hokey and overdone with cobwebs all over the place and a crazy old librarian with a moth-eaten shawl over his clothes. All of that should have been much more subtle," she critiqued the film.

Lori just nodded.

"Anyway, the old guy grudgingly helped her find a book on the subject, but when she opened it, only the first half of the story was there. She went to complain to the librarian, walking past some shelves and found herself at the Alamo with the guns going off and everything."

Lori was staring at her.

"The kid cowered in a corner, and eventually this guy shows up in a goofy-looking Alamo outfit, and, in a Southern drawl, tells her she's safe, that he will take care of her, and takes her to a really large woman inside the church for safekeeping. He heads back out to the battle. The kid is like totally freaked at this point, and she runs back to the librarian to complain about the missing pages and what she had just experienced. He takes that calmly, telling her she's letting her imagination help her see history. Anyway, there's this back and forth where she keeps heading back to the Alamo against her will and pages are filling the rest of the book. Near the end, she has two final confrontations with the Alamo guy. She reads a private letter he wrote to someone taking care of his little boy, and the guy comes in and is indignant about it. He heads out to get killed. She stops him and tells him he obviously does not care about his kid and the kid will hate him if he's going to abandon him to get himself shot for no reason. He tells her something to the effect that there are lots of things worth living for but few worth dying for and that freedom is one of those few things worth dying for. He acts a bit crazy in my view with his determination to get himself killed. He heads out, and there's one final scene where she's out with the bombs going off again looking for him to tell him she was wrong,. He finds her again and takes her to safety. She looks up to him and tells him that the kid will love him after all, and he heads out to die. She returns to the present, and the pages in the book are now complete. It was a biography of the Alamo guy. Saddest thing I've ever seen once you get past the hokey stuff."

"Wow. That's heady stuff for 9-year-olds. But I like the message," Lori said as she gave her sister a hug. She felt she had to ask the question, although she really did not want to, knowing the sad story about the little boy. "Who was the Alamo guy?"

"The Texan leader, Col. Travis. If you could get past the goofy clothes, whoever played him was kind of cute—red hair. Too bad he died."

Lori stammered, "Yes, he has—I mean had—red hair. You're right—too bad he died."

Vicky's green eyes narrowed as she looked at Lori. She was the perfect older sister, but, with the history thing, Lori was always a bit weird.

Lori realized it was getting late, and she gave her sister instructions: "I'm going to grab a bite to eat, then I've got a late meeting with Bob Gordon this evening. Tell Mom not to wait for me on dinner, OK?"

"She's got a late meeting with the doctor after the office closes up. I'm fixing dinner tonight," Vicky said with a shrug. "I'll save some in the fridge for you." Lori had the strangest schedule lately—coming and going at all hours.

Lori headed out to fight the traffic once more. It was getting heavy but as yet no gridlock, and she got to the hospital at 5:45. Bob and Tom had not come, so she settled in to do absolutely nothing except stare at the pale face of the Alamo survivor. It was 6:30 before Dr. Gonzalez finally appeared.

"How's he doing, doctor?" Lori asked as Gonzalez entered the room.

"Very well. We had that brief moment of excitement. I think Maria called you?—when his eyelids fluttered. You haven't seen any motion have you?"

Lori shook her head. "I ran home for a few hours, but no, I haven't seen anything."

"I think we're going to keep him in the ICU overnight. If his vitals hold or get better, we'll probably move him to a room tomorrow morning. It would be great if he would come to—would make everything a lot easier," the doctor wished out loud.

"I've got a question about that, doctor. My boss keeps saying that he thinks it's important to have something from Travis' past here when he wakes up. He asked me to try to get his things from the cleaners and bring that ratty old coat and put it on him. That was his second idea—the first was the whole uniform, but I told him that wouldn't work."

Gonzalez laughed. "Nope. The whole uniform would not work—we've got to be able to work with him! But the coat isn't such a bad idea, assuming it doesn't fall apart when they go to clean it."

"Yeah. I think that may happen. But if it's at all wearable, I'll bring it with me first thing in the morning. I'm going to stay until around 1 in the morning, then head home for another brief nap and a shower. I'll go by the cleaners when they open—fortunately, that's early—and pick up the stuff. I may have to stop by the house again to repair the coat if the seams come apart and it's fixable. Do you think he will come to?"

"There's never any certainty about that. But the signs are looking good. There's very little swelling, and we've got what little there is under control. If he does come to, it likely will be with little warning—it will just happen."

Lori asked, "What would you say to someone from 181 years ago when he wakes up?"

The doctor shrugged. "Welcome to the 21st Century? I really don't know—you are the historian. But we will have to be very gentle with him and tolerant. He will have some function issues. He's likely going to be difficult at times as he's totally unfamiliar with everything. Take all of the blinking lights and machines in this room—he's never seen anything like that. Clothes, particularly ladies' clothes, will be a shock."

"Yeah. This guy was quite a ladies' man. Kept a diary, to which he confided the intimate details of his sex life. I haven't read it, but Bob Gordon has given me lots of specifics."

"Then I suspect he will enjoy the change in fashions!" the doctor laughed.

"Oh, one other thing related to that, doctor. The colonel was apparently very frank in his diary, and he reported one result of his numerous romantic forays. He picked up some venereal disease and was gulping mercury to treat it. Life on the early frontier was often short and always uncertain, even without the Alamo. I suppose he just wanted to have a good time while he could, although I'm certainly not excusing it, of course!"

Gonzalez looked as if he was ready to outright laugh. "Sounds as if Col. Travis was a very, very active gentleman! You know that mercury cure they took made people go nuts if they did it long enough. There was an old saying about it—something to the effect of spending one night with Venus and the rest of your life with Mercury."

Lori couldn't suppress a laugh.

Gonzalez continued. "Well, fortunately, treatment is much easier these days. Antibiotics will take care of it. When he gets out of the ICU, I'll check him out, and we'll get it resolved if it's still an issue. Now, a little advice for you, young lady—take care of yourself. You can't be getting any sleep. The commander of the Alamo may need your services in the future! You have to take care of yourself in order to help someone else." He stared at the colonel and smiled, then headed for his next patient.

Lori had another long, uncomfortable night, sitting sideways in her chair and getting a stiff neck from her position. She had set the cell phone alarm for 1:00 a.m., knowing that would raise questions when she got home if anyone woke up, but it couldn't be helped. She left the motionless colonel for her nighttime ride through the city. Lori knew Gonzalez was right; she had only gotten 3 hours of sleep—at the most. She knew she couldn't keep this up. Bob and Tom were interested, but they were at least as interested in their comfortable beds at home and keeping regular hours. In fairness, they did have paying jobs; she did not. And she wanted to be there for the poor young man who was facing something maybe not as intimidating as the Alamo battle but certainly an unnerving prospect, although he did not yet know that. She turned the lights out as she got to the driveway and parked in front of the house, closing the car door as quietly as she could. The vehicle, a 1999 Chevy Cavalier, was an oft-patched piece of equipment that was all she could afford. The doors did not work right, and the driver-side door was particularly cranky. She walked to the house, unlocked the front door and eased it open, slid in, and slowly eased it shut and locked it. All was dark inside, everyone apparently asleep. She crept past Vicky's bedroom to her own, making it safely to her sanctuary. She set the cell phone alarm on low volume, hoping she would hear it, and was out like a light.

The cell started its annoying beeping, and Lori was halfway disappointed that she did hear it. She did everything else she had to do first, so that the sound of the shower would not wake anyone any earlier than necessary. The ripped-up shirt and drawers had dried nicely, but there were dark, red-brown bloodstains that would not come out except possibly with bleach. She folded the ancient garments and put them in a bag. She turned the water on low and got her very quick rinse-off, not bothering with her hair, then looked in the hallway. Still dark and quiet. She gathered her purse and a bag containing sewing supplies and headed quickly for the kitchen and an energy bar for on the run.

"Lori, is that you?"

She looked over at the table in the nook. There was her mom, sipping coffee in the dark.

"There's plenty of coffee, honey. Come over and sit with me. I haven't really seen you the last few days," her mother said.

"Uh, yeah, well, there's . . . there's been a lot going on at work," Lori struggled to find something that made sense.

"In a volunteer job?" her mother asked gently.

"Believe it or not, yes, honestly, Mom. I'm committed to keep it quiet right now, but you will hear soon. And believe me, when you do, you will see why I've been busy."

Her mother's brow looked furrowed to the point Lori could see in the dim light. Elena Clayton had taught all of her children to be independent but always to think first, act later—a lesson someone else who had entered Lori's life could have benefited from.

"I won't pry, but I'll have to admit, boy, am I curious," her mom said with a grin.

"I know Mom, I know. I promise, as soon as I can, I'll tell you. If you don't mind, don't mention this to the rest of the family right yet. I think Vicky is suspicious of something, and I really can't have this come out right now."

"I can keep a secret, Lori. I can tell you are in a hurry. Go on, honey."

Lori gave her mom a quick kiss on the forehead and ran out the door with her energy bar. There was little traffic this early, and she was at the cleaners in no time. They opened at 6:00, and it was 6:02. She tried to present an air of confidence as she strode into the business. At the counter, she fumbled in her purse and found the cleaning ticket. The clerk was the same short, young woman who had waited on her the day before. She spun the overhead conveyor until she found Lori's order.

"Oh, yeah, I remember you. The weird Alamo threads. There's a note on here from Dave, the owner." She read it: "Worked over an hour on this with some specialty cleaners. Didn't take much of it out. Also, there are cut marks on the left side and lower center back of the coat and vest, and one side seam on the coat is coming loose."

OK, well, that's actually pretty good," Lori said.

"Huh?" the attendant grunted. "I thought you said they just had a medical demo at the Alamo. Would have thought they would use fake blood for that—it probably would come out. I mentioned the demo thing to Dave, and he told me the stains have been in there a lot longer than that—and that they're real blood. That's why the stuff doesn't look any better."

Lori didn't like where the employee was going with her analysis. "They're fine, believe me, at least they're clean. How much do I owe you?" she said hurriedly.

The young woman gave her the bill amount, and Lori paid and got out of there as fast as she could. The clerk was still staring at her as she headed out the door. Lori quickly removed the coat from its hanger and folded it, placing it in her almost-empty sack containing a needle, some thread, and scissors.

There was nothing else to do in the colonel's room, so she determined to mend the old coat. She recalled the fact that the sewing machine was not invented until around the Civil War. Colonel Travis' clothes were all hand-sewn. She fished around her sack and pulled out the coat and found her blue thread with a needle stuck in the spool, as well as her scissors, and was trying to see well enough to mend the cuts from the edged weapons. Fortunately, they were relatively small, although there were seven to mend. Finishing that task, she determined to re-stitch the side seam in the dim light. The sun was just beginning to come up, and she had to squint to see the seam. She was about 2/3 of the way through when she got that uncomfortable feeling that someone was watching her. But no one had come in. In fact, the night shift had pretty much parked it somewhere else, or they were short staffed. Before long it would be time for the shift change. Lori went back to her sewing. The sun was coming up nicely now, and that made the work a little easier. After a few minutes, she looked around, still feeling as if something was off. Finally, she looked at Travis. He was staring in her direction, his eyes now wide open. She dropped the coat and went to his side.

"Hello, can you see me?" she asked softly. "I'm Lori."

He tried to focus on her. "Not too well—vision blurry," he weakly responded in a drawl that was clearly from his native South Carolina.

"Obviously, you can hear me," she replied, moving her hand to cover his right hand, which still lay on his chest. She had to be careful not to disturb the needles in his veins. "Can you tell me who you are? Like I said, I'm Lori—Clayton."

"William Barret Travis," he slowly replied, always preferring his full name. "I can't see very well. Are we still at the Alamo? I don't remember anyone with your name. Only white lady Mrs. Dickinson. The Mexicans . . . they were coming over . . . the wall . . . too many . . . we couldn't stop them. It all went dark," he tried to explain, and tears were running down his face.

"Colonel Travis, you are safe. No, we're not at the Alamo, but we are in Bexar," she remembered to use the name for the town the colonel used in his letters. "I promise you, you are safe here. We're trying to make you well again," she said, wiping the tears from his face with her hand.

"My men . . . the garrison . . . . Where is everyone?" he asked, wide-eyed.

"Oh, Colonel, I wish someone else were here right now to tell you this. Santa Anna overran the Alamo, and he made good on his threat. He killed everyone."

"No! Oh, no!" the young man practically wailed the words. Then, after a pause and more tears, he asked softly in an anguished voice, "Why I am I here? Santa Anna did not even know most of my men. He did know about me—I had been told I was a marked man. Why am I still here?"

She held his hand more tightly. "Uh, well, you weren't. Once the Mexican troops went through the compound, making sure all the defenders were dead, and executing a handful who weren't, they acted like savages, bayoneting and using swords on the dead bodies to mutilate them."

Travis had turned deathly pale and was shaking. Lori put her arms around him and held him. She forced herself to continue.

"You were shot in the forehead, but there's also a slash wound from a sword running down the right side of your face. There are several bayonet stab wounds on your torso and two that are apparently from sword thrusts. We really don't know why they did this—blood lust I guess. It's all part of what is so awful and tragic about the whole Alamo thing. Finally, Santa Anna ordered the bodies of the defenders stripped, stacked, and burned."

Travis' eyes closed, and Lori held him closer.

"The Mexicans buried their own men, but they ran out of space in the cemetery and had to dump the rest of the bodies in the river—that's how many of the enemy y'all took with you," she added that last to try to make it

30

a tiny bit better, although she knew that was really impossible.

"I don't understand. If they burned our bodies, why am I here?" he asked weakly.

"Honestly, we always thought you were burned. There's a casket inside the San Fernando church marked with your name and those of Bowie and Crockett that purports to be your ashes. Truth was, they had no clue whose ashes were whose at the point these were gathered, but, since the three of you were the top men, your names were added."

"But?"

"I know, sorry it's such a longwinded explanation, but there's a lot to it. It's been 181 years since the battle—the year is 2017," she said nervously, knowing that was one more huge shock added to those she had already given him. This time, he just lay there, awake but still.

"We do archaeological digs to find old pottery or foundations showing where buildings were in the past, that sort of thing, now and then. The Alamo is so old and so many people have come through there over the years that historians like to check the ground and try to get ideas of who was there when and what they left behind. About the only thing they had not checked out thoroughly at this point was the exact location of the latrine."

"I can tell you . . . ."

"I bet you can," Lori replied, with the first hint of levity since this awful conversation had started. "But you weren't here to tell us when someone decided to start digging to see if they could find it. They did find it, and imagine their surprise when they found the heel of a boot. They carefully unearthed you, face down in what had been the latrine. Apparently, Santa Anna thought that was even more of an insult than burning, and he admitted his especial hatred for you. We rushed you to this big, modern hospital in the city that you would not believe, and they performed brain surgery to extract the ball. You are very weak and frail, but you are doing very, very well. We didn't know if or when you would come to. I am so happy . . . ." She didn't finish the sentence, just hugged him tightly. He tried to stare at her but could not really focus.

Finally, Travis fell asleep again, and Lori gently released her hold and went to her chair. She picked up the coat and hurriedly finished the seam.

The colonel might be wanting the garment before long. She wanted so desperately to get the last bit of work done on the coat that she forgot to tell any of the medical personnel about the experience with Travis, but she remembered it as soon as she stuffed the repaired garment in her bag. She walked to the door and looked around—no one in sight, so she sat down again, waiting. That was the problem with hospitals—hurry up and wait. Finally, she started to doze, but was awakened when the door opened.

"Lori, hello!" It was Dr. Gonzalez on his rounds.

"Hi, doctor! Have I got news for you," she said in a quiet voice so as not to disturb Travis. "He woke up. He's asleep now, but I was trying to repair a seam on his coat when I felt like someone was watching me. I finally looked at him, and his eyes were open and he was looking toward me. Turns out he's having some trouble focusing and seeing clearly, but he can see something—not sure how much."

"That doesn't really surprise me with the head wound," the doctor said. "We'll have to check it, but that may be something that just has to right itself given a little time. Did the two of you actually talk?"

"Oh, yeah. Big time. Of course, he thought we were at the Alamo, and he was confused that someone named Lori Clayton would be there as he said the only white woman he recalled was Mrs. Dickinson. That's true, she was the only one in the compound. I had to go through the whole thing with him—lots of tears and sadness, devastation really. I have a feeling there's going to be a lot more of that."

"Yes. I'm sure there will be. We're going to have to be strong for him. He's a tough young man, obviously, but this is too much for anyone to process. He will need a lot of help, a lot of help." The doctor shook his head.

"I held him, I wiped away the tears, I hugged him, and I tried to be as soft and gentle as I could be telling him of ghastly things. I hope he will forgive me." She lowered her head and sighed.

"I don't think he will hold it against you once he sorts everything out—and understands, to the extent anyone can comprehend this," the doctor replied kindly. "I'm going to check his stats—was already planning to move him to a private room today. No question now—he's ready."

The doctor fiddled with some of the machines, wrote something on a notepad, put his pen in the pocket of his white coat, said goodbye, and headed to his next patient. It wasn't long before attendants showed up to move the colonel to his new quarters. He was still asleep and oblivious to everything that was going on, likely a good thing. But, at some point, Lori knew he was going to have to wake up for good and face a Mt. Everest of changes. Then she thought to herself, he probably had no clue where that is.

As she followed the attendants and their charge to the new room, she noted a big, stocky Texas Ranger positioned at the door. He tipped his hat to her. She quickly learned that cleared medical personnel and herself were the only people to be allowed in the room. Even Bob and Tom were banned for now. The news was out that an Alamo defender had been unearthed, no surprise since one or more of the students working on the project surely told someone. The news media and public via social media were going crazy over it, although no one had been able to find out who it was or any other details. For the time being, Dr. Gonzalez obviously thought the restrictions were crucial for his patient. It put an extra burden on Lori, being the only nonmedical person with permission to enter the room, but she wanted to be there for the young man from so long ago, tiring though the sitting was.

# EPISTLE

Lori could not stay there 24/7, and she did take a few hours to go home since the colonel seemed to be sleeping soundly. She stopped by the Alamo, briefly telling Bob about Travis awakening, their conversation, and his eyesight, all behind closed doors. Bob was all in a tizzy, as the Travis letter ceremony was coming up in 3 days. A few years before, one of Travis' distant relations, also named William Travis, read the colonel's famous letter from the Alamo. This man was a county sheriff in Texas and had been one of the family DNA donors. Since then, a reenactor performed the duty, but the most likely candidate was out of the country this year. Bob had fished around trying to find a replacement, to no avail. He wasn't about to get up there in a costume and do it himself, and the balding, bespectacled, and heavy 58-year old would have looked ridiculous had he had the courage. He was almost getting whiny about it telling Lori about the predicament.

"I've got an idea," she said calmly.

"This thing is in 3 days—3 days. What's your idea? I'm open to anything at this point. Maybe we should just cancel it, I don't know."

"What about the real Travis?" she inquired firmly.

"What? You said he woke up long enough for you to tell him that the Alamo fell and it's 2017, then promptly collapsed again. You can't take someone who has just had brain surgery, stand him up there in front of a crowd, and ask him to make a speech. Lori! I thought you had more sense!"

She twisted her mouth. "Yeah, I know it's a long-shot, but he's improving rapidly."

"We can't wait around on this. If we go ahead with the ceremony and don't have someone to read the thing. . . . "

"I'm sure the DRT will send someone if you ask them if there's really no one else," Lori suggested.

"Have some society lady get up there and read the Travis letter? Have you gone loco?" he was apparently on the verge of a panic attack at this point.

"All I'm saying is the perfect person to read the letter is here—we just need a little more time to see if it will work. Fortunately, it's very brief, and someone could hold him up or he could do it seated," she kept thinking out loud.

"I thought you said he was having vision issues?"

"He is, but I bet he knows that thing by heart. He wrote it, and he had all those days in the Alamo to think about it," she replied. "Don't panic yet. It may work out. Otherwise, just call the DRT and let one of the ladies get the thrill of a lifetime. They know the Alamo story backwards and forwards."

"Not in a Travis costume, I hope."

"No, not in a Travis costume. For God's sake, Bob, if it comes to that, I'll read it— can't be that hard. I won't wear a Travis costume either, but I could lend a little credence with my frontier dress."

"Deal," he said in resignation. "I know you're in a hurry to get home and get some rest, Lori, but, if you've got just a minute, I've got one more thing I would like to ask you."

"Sure," she said.

"Your dedication to history is obvious. We're still waiting for that cactus meal, but I realize everything has been wild lately. I'd like to sign you on as a permanent employee, half-time, which is about what you've been doing as a volunteer, with the idea of working it up to full-time in time." He smiled at her. "I know you've got another obligation eating into your time right now, anyway."

Lori beamed. "Bob, I could hug you—in fact, I think I will!" She put her arms around the shoulders of the gentle man who obviously really cared about this place but who sometimes seemed a bit bewildered when things started going crazy, as they certainly had lately.

He looked up at her. "I take that as a yes?"

She nodded. "I will have to be in and out on what at least has been a

35

sort of odd schedule right now, if that's OK? I guess this is silly, but I really care about the colonel—want to help him as much as I can."

"That's been obvious since we found him," Bob laughed. "Like Tom said, after 181 years, the guy is still a babe magnet—of course, Tom didn't use those words!"

Some women would have been offended, but Lori laughed. "Maybe so. I do think he's kind of cute in an Alamo sort of way. And don't worry about the letter ceremony. I'm going to work on my pick for the job."

Lori went home, ate dinner with her mom and Vicky, and actually slept in her own bed that night, much to the relief of her concerned mother, who knew not to pry but was wondering how long the mystery and Lori's involvement in it would go on. Major Clayton had left for his medical conference, and Elena had not bothered to tell her husband about the strange goings on with their daughter, figuring whatever it was would have blown over by the time he was back next week. Len was hanging out with a couple of friends from school as of late, the Montoyas' sweet and quiet son, Andres, and Andres' pal Ciro and was sleeping over that evening. Vicky had told her mom about the Alamo film at school. The Montoyas' daughter, Juana, was her teacher and had picked this out for her class, despite her family's Mexican heritage. Elena privately hoped that Vicky did not get the same history bug that had sent Lori off on some of her sometimes impractical adventures, although she did usually land on her feet.

"Oh, no, it's 8 a.m.," a panicked Lori looked at the clock. She had been out since shortly after she got home and had dinner, some 12 hours—making up for some lost sleep. She hurriedly showered and washed her hair, not bothering to dry it, pulled on jeans and a red top, and ran for the kitchen and the incredibly handy energy bars. Everyone was gone. The kids were in school, and Elena was at work. Good, Lori thought—no explaining to do to anyone. She had checked her phone, and there were no calls from Maria, Dr. Gonzalez, or anyone else at the hospital. Thoughts kept running through her mind. Surely the poor colonel had awoken again during all this time, and there was no one there. She jumped in the car, probably going too fast. At least rush hour was over. She imagined that Bob was getting even more antsy about the letter ceremony. It had always been second fiddle, albeit important, to the big March 6 ceremony, but it had become a bigger deal since the 2013 loan of the original letter to the Alamo for the period encompassing the siege. It was now February 22—2 days to go until someone had to read that letter. It was too late to cancel at this point. She pulled into a parking space and raced to Travis' room. All the rush was for nothing. He still lay motionless, asleep. Of course, if he had awakened earlier, it was possible no one would have known. She waited until Maria showed up—she was on duty this day.

"No ma'am, I have not seen any indication of movement on his part. He's in exactly the same position he was in when you left and has been each time I've checked on him—about every 2 hours."

"Thanks, Maria," Lori said quietly. She wished she could be as serene and calm as the nurse. Disappointment was beginning to set in. She was in hope that he really had come to for good yesterday when he did rally and she had to tell him what had happened since he last walked the earth. But that had been dashed when he went back to sleep. His color looked good, and Maria had said all the vitals were normal, but his eyes were closed.

"Colonel? Can you hear me? It's Lori. We talked yesterday," she leaned over him and talked softly in his ear.

He moved his head slightly and his eyes opened.

"Lori?" he said slowly.

"Yes. Do you remember talking with me?"

He turned his head toward her and tried to focus on her. "Yes. Something about digging me up and lots of time going by?"

"Yes," she said softly. "But it's OK. I'm here with you. How are your eyes today?"

He was fully awake now, and it was all coming back to him. He answered in the slow drawl, "Still blurry, but I think they're a little clearer than they were yesterday."

"That's wonderful. You are going to be all right. They are taking very good care of you here," she tried to sound comforting.

At that moment, Dr. Gonzalez came in. Both of them turned at his entrance.

"Colonel! You are awake!" Gonzalez exclaimed in surprise.

"Who are you?" Travis asked quietly.

37

"I'm Dr. Gonzalez. I'm your physician here. You are doing very well—much better than we expected or hoped . . . ."

"Are you Mexican?"

"My family was, way back. But I'm an American—we've been American for three generations," Gonzalez answered. Lori was relieved that the doctor seemed not at all offended by the question and answered Travis gently and carefully.

"Oh, good. I don't want any of Santa Anna's adherents treating me," came the response.

"Not to worry, Colonel, that won't be a problem," Gonzalez replied with a grin at Lori.

"Do you think you could eat something?" the doctor asked the colonel.

"I could try," he answered.

"I'm not sure what folks were eating in 1836—we may not have it here," the doctor hesitated.

"I don't really want what we were eating if y'all have something else," Travis replied quickly. "It had reached a point where what we had wasn't too good."

Again, the doctor and Lori exchanged glances.

"Have you ever had scrambled or fried eggs?" the doctor queried, and knowing the answer to his next question, went ahead and asked, "And grits, with lots of butter, and biscuits and bacon?"

"Yes sir. I would love to have some of all of those!" the hungry Texian responded. After all, he had not eaten since March 5, 1836.

"I'll have them send it right away," Gonzalez said. "After you eat something, I think it's about time we try to get you up a little bit, try sitting, and maybe even standing with someone steadying you," the doctor informed him. "How are your eyes doing today?"

"Still can't see too many details, doctor. But I think they're a little better than they were yesterday," Travis answered.

"That's good. I am going to order a brain scan to be sure everything is functioning OK, and there are a couple of tests I want to do relating to your vision," the doctor explained.

Travis didn't have a clue what he was talking about, so he just stared at the hazy form of the doctor.

Gonzalez realized he was talking gibberish to the young man. "Don't worry. There's nothing to it. It's all routine these days. It will just let me know if there's something more or else I need to do to get you up and over to the Alamo or whatever you want to do in this wonderful second chance, Colonel."

"I hope it's wonderful, sir," Travis said softly, and, Lori thought, somewhat doubtfully.

The doctor went on, and within 15 minutes a full Southern breakfast was brought to the hungry Texian. Lori moved the position on the bed, unnerving Travis at first, as he did not know a bed could do that. She apologized for the surprise. She reminded herself—she would have to be cognizant of each little thing. Everything that was routine to her was likely new to him—except the basics, like eating.

"Do you want me to feed you, or do you think you can do it yourself?" she asked.

"Let me try. I hate to have a lady sit and feed me. Doesn't seem right somehow," came the decidedly old-fashioned answer.

"Whatever you like," Lori answered sweetly.

Travis had never seen food like this before—nor smelled anything that smelled this good. Lori didn't bother to tell him that hospital food was not known for its quality or taste, although the breakfast did look good. And she knew that folks in 1836, even when not penned up to die in the Alamo, ate things like cactus or a steady diet of pork and corn.

He was a little shaky, but the tray was close enough that he could see what was on it, and he managed to get the food to his mouth quite well. Lori opened the prepackaged items. The colonel particularly savored the grits and bacon—and the coffee. He asked if he could have a second cup. Lori ran to the desk and gave them the additional order. She would have to remember to pick up one of the black "Victory or Death"—Travis' slogan from his famous letters—coffee mugs with his picture on it for the colonel next time she was at the Alamo gift shop.

When she got back, she knew she wanted to ask him a question that would seem perfectly normal today, but 1800's propriety was sometimes rather stiff and formal, so she was not sure how he would take it. She decided to go ahead.

"You know everyone is going to call you 'colonel,' because that's your rank and you are famous as the Alamo commander, but is that what people you . . . you knew . . . in the 1830's . . . called you?"

"The military men did, of course, and many men I knew in legal and political circles as well—we were called by our titles, yes. But, if you mean family and very close friends," and he stopped and looked as if he might tear up, then regained his composure quickly, "No. They just called me by my name."

"William? Bill?"

"Actually, I was nicknamed Buck as a boy. It stuck with me. That's what close acquaintances called me."

"Buck Travis! Oh my gosh. Even if there had never been an Alamo, that is such a Texas-sounding name!"

He looked pleased and proud as he put the last spoonful of grits in his mouth.

She hesitantly asked, "Would you mind . . . I know you don't really know me . . . if I called you Buck? 'Colonel' seems so formal, and I'm just not a very formal person. But I will do whichever you prefer."

His blue eyes tried to focus on her. "No ma'am, if it pleases you, by all means, Buck it is!"

When he was finished eating, Travis dozed for a while. His appetite was excellent, but the effort expended in eating tired him. Lori had a rather long stint just sitting again. After a couple of hours, a physical therapist, who introduced himself as Marco, came in with another staffer, apparently an assistant—a rather muscular young woman.

"We're here to see if the patient feels like sitting up and doing some

40

exercises, or maybe even trying to stand?" Marco asked.

Lori nudged Buck. He turned their way and half sat up. Still half asleep, he only said "Huh?"

"These folks are here to help you sit and maybe stand up. Want to try it?" Lori tried to sound enthusiastic.

Buck rubbed his eyes. His vision was getting better, and, at least as far as he knew, the doctor had not given him anything to improve it. But things were still kind of blurry. He nodded in the direction of Marco and the young woman.

They came over to the bed, lowered it slightly—at least Travis was prepared for the strange movements of the contraption this time, and carefully lifted him around and swung him over so that his legs were hanging over the bed. He sat there for a few moments, with one of them holding onto him on each side. Finally the woman moved away. He continued to sit erect. Marco let go, and Travis wavered. Marco quickly resumed his hold, keeping him upright for about 5 minutes.

"Are you doing all right? Let me know if you are tired and want to lie down," he said to the colonel.

Travis did not understand the therapy routine at all. In his day, you just lived or died when you were sick, and that was about it. He tried to follow the therapist's directions, and he answered that he was fine sitting there.

"Do you want to try to stand?" Marco asked.

Travis nodded, and the woman came to his other side. The two therapists hoisted the tall young man to his feet. Travis stood, a bit unsteadily, then attempted to take a step. Marco saw what he was doing and stepped forward with him. He continued, wavering slightly, resolved to walk. He made it to door, then started feeling very weak, and they got him back to the bed quickly. He was out almost immediately.

"Determined guy, isn't he? What happened to him?" Marco asked Lori.

"Uh . . . military . . . combat," Lori answered.

"Don't they usually treat them at the military facilities?" Marco asked.

"Yes, yes, they do, but . . . this head wound was something where they specifically wanted Dr. Hamilton to do the surgery, so they sent him here," Lori covered.

"I see. Well, we'll be back tomorrow morning early to let him try it again," Marco said. "Nice meeting both of you." The young woman waved.

Before long it was mealtime again. This time one of the options was fried chicken with corn and okra. The colonel seemed delighted with the hospital food. The Southern dishes were likely the reason for that. As he was finishing up, Lori got her sack and pulled out his coat.

"I mended this for you—there were the . . . ," Lori hesitated, "cuts from the bayonets and swords, and one of the side seams was coming apart. We washed it,"—she didn't try to explain dry cleaning to him—"but the bloodstains wouldn't all come out. Even so, I thought you might like to have something of yours?" She handed the coat to him.

He looked in her direction, making out her face but hazily. "Thank you. I guess I don't have much of anything left now," he said softly, lowering his head and wiping away an errant tear. "I did always try to present a respectable appearance . . . before . . . ." he trailed off.

"I've got the rest of your clothes in my . . . ," she almost said "car" but stopped herself, "in a bag at home. I washed them out, too. And your hat and sword are waiting for you at the Alamo when you are strong enough," she paused before she continued—would someone who had been through something so awful really want to go back?—but went ahead and finished, "to return to the fort."

"I've got to get back—have been away too long. If I can walk, I think they will let me out of here. Don't get me wrong, they have been very kind, but my place is at the Alamo!"

That was the answer to that. She nodded, not knowing how well he could see the motion, then helped the colonel put on his blue coat, the right side draped over his shoulder because of the tubes running to his veins. She felt certain that the determined young man would be reading his famous letter at his command post the day after next.


On her way to the house for a quick shower, Lori stopped at the

42

Alamo. It was 4:30, and the traffic was already bad. Bob always stayed until 5, so she was sure he would be there. She wanted to bring him up to date on the remarkable progress the colonel had made. She knew Bob would be a basket case about the letter ceremony at this point with it only 2 days away, but Lori kept thinking about Travis' determination to walk once he was up—without coaxing from Marco. He didn't even know about the ceremony, but he was obviously intent on getting back to his post—even though he no longer had a command—as soon as humanly possible. She really did believe that her idea tossed out to Bob was likely to happen with Travis' sheer will in play.

The tiny employee lot was packed, and she headed to the pay lot near the Alamo. She pulled in next to an ancient, boxy van completely painted in a burnt orange and white cow design with the biggest horns she had ever seen affixed to the front. It was a rolling Bevo. The contraption had a Florida plate. She thought to herself—it was a step up from driving the Weiner Mobile because at least Bevo was pure beef, but she could not fathom why anyone would want to make such a spectacle of himself or herself driving the ridiculous thing. If you hung out around the Alamo long enough, you were pretty much guaranteed to see just about everything.

She stopped in at the gift shop quickly first, heading straight for the Travis "Victory or Death" mugs. This was the perfect gift for her new friend. Morena, the gift shop manager, headed toward her. Morena was a 67-year-old Latina whose parents had emigrated from Mexico, but she was as even-handed as she could be. Morena Alejandro would gladly sell anything to anyone who wanted it—on either side. She was a saleswoman extraordinaire. The elegant woman, who was still beautiful, pulled her thick, black hair back and wore it in an elaborate twist concoction at the back of her head. She had huge, expressive dark eyes and a ready smile, and she always wore lots of jewelry, big earrings and armfuls of bangle bracelets. Morena had always been particularly sweet to Lori, sensing the younger woman was having some issues trying to figure out her life.

Morena, her bright eyes shining, asked, "It's been a while since you have come to see me, Lori. What can I do for you today?" Lori liked Morena and popped her head in most days to say hi to the sales manager. She hadn't been there to do so since Travis was unearthed.

"Hi Morena. I'm so sorry—I haven't been here much. You will know why soon enough, I promise, but I have been about to go crazy with this job!"

43

"Volunteer work stirring cactus?" Morena laughed.

"Bob gave me a permanent job—just half-time right now, but he said it would become full-time. It's the answer to a prayer!"

Morena hugged her, the many gold bracelets clanging against each other as she did.

"I'm so happy for you, Lori. You live and breathe this stuff. You are Anglo, and yet you are always so respectful of everyone—and you really seem like a part of the 1830's when you are in your costume!"

"Stirring that cactus?"

"Yes, by all means! Is there something I can get you?"

"I want one of those 'Victory or Death' mugs," she said, pointing to the cups.

"Colonel Travis? I would have guessed you were more of a Davy Crockett girl," Morena teased her. "Travis was certainly brave, and he followed up with his actions what he said and wrote, but he seems a bit serious and stern for you. I think Ol' Davy would have been a hoot to know!"

"Probably true, but, you know, I admire all of them. Anyway, it's not for me, it's for a friend," she explained.

Morena took one of the cups and carefully checked it to be sure there were no cracks or chips. The things were expensive—$16.95, but they were big, sturdy mugs—a coffee drinker could put a lot of brew in one of these vessels. Best of all, if one was not too diligent about washing out his or her cup, the grounds didn't show since the mug was black inside as well as out. The cup featured one of the stock pictures of Travis, of whom, the story went, there were no true likenesses. The one chosen for this mug depicted a stylized, steely-visaged officer with fiery eyes. In big white letters were the words from his letters, "Victory or Death," with the word "DEATH" in larger print capitals than the rest and another quote from the defiant commander, "I shall never surrender or retreat!"

"Do you think young Mr. Travis took himself a bit too seriously?" Morena asked as she read aloud what was on the cup. "He sure looks grim! We got these in a couple months ago, but, honestly, I had never looked at it

44

very closely—too many other things to do."

Lori laughed. "Yes, I believe that is a strong possibility!"

She waved goodbye to Morena and headed to Bob's office downstairs. He was still there but was just getting ready to leave. Lori had the cup in her hand.

"Do you have a crush on this guy?" Bob asked when he saw it.

"It's not for me. It's for him. He seems to love coffee," she explained. "But, in answer to your question, I dunno—he is cute for a mutilated Alamo defender."

"I'm sure that's the standard most girls your age use in picking guys," Bob answered with a laugh. "How is our young colonel doing? I gather he was drinking coffee?"

"Yes. I didn't miss anything when I went home for that stretch, apparently. Maria said he never moved. After sitting there a while, I stood closely by him and talked to him softly, and he woke up. Dr. Gonzalez came in right after that, and we all talked. Gonzalez asked Buck—I mean the colonel . . . ."

"Buck?" Bob interrupted her.

"Uh, I asked what he was called by his family and friends, and he said that was his nickname—said I could call him that if I wanted," she explained.

"I had heard of his nickname, but you two are moving kind of fast, don't you think?" he queried with a smile.

"He just looks awfully young to be a colonel and Alamo commander and all that. I know he is, and that he's very serious about and proud of it, but I also believe it's crucial that we treat him as a human being, not JUST the survivor of the Alamo. And I think Buck is a great name! Buck Travis of Texas. It's perfect."

Bob was laughing at her, but he stopped after a moment. "I'm glad you stopped by, Lori, not just to tell me about Buck, but also because I've got some news. The governor is coming down from Austin tomorrow. He wants to meet the colonel. I've heard him speak of and quote from Travis

45

in his political speeches, so he's obviously an admirer. The governor will be back the next day for the letter ceremony."

Lori cringed a bit. "Uh, how is that going?" she asked reluctantly.

"It's still a problem. I can't find anyone short of the DRT—or you, but there's nothing I can do. I did call the DRT to alert them of the possibility. They're going to have lots of representatives here, anyway, and the lady I talked with said one of them would gladly do it if needed."

"I don't think it's needed," Lori said firmly.

"You don't?" Bob replied.

"Not only did he drink two cups of coffee and eat a breakfast of eggs, grits, biscuits, and bacon—feeding himself without help from me—a little shaky but doing it all himself, followed by a big fried chicken lunch, but the physical therapist had him sitting up on the side of the bed today. Shortly before I left, they got him up and, with an attendant on each side, slowly walked him across the room. They only intended for him to stand, but, on his own, he attempted the walk. He wasn't too steady, but he did it."

"Did you put the coat on him?" Bob laughed.

"Actually, yes. He seemed glad to see it. I told him I had to mend it, and that we weren't able to get all the bloodstains out, but the gentleman who was apparently so fastidious about his clothes when practicing law in the 1830's just seemed happy to have something of his own from his past, even if it is a bloody mess," she explained.

"Well, we've got the hat and sword in safekeeping here. And you have the rest of the clothes, such as they are, right? You know he was so obsessed with his appearance—or pleased at his commission as a lieutenant colonel of cavalry in the Texian forces—or both, that he ran out and ordered a fancy uniform. Unfortunately, it wasn't completed until after he was dead at the Alamo, so he was stuck with tying that military sash around his regular clothes when he commanded the fort."

She laughed. "I told him the hat and sword are at the Alamo. He is determined to get back here as soon as he can—told me he believes they will let him go if he can prove he can walk—that's why he's trying so hard. I bet he's dying to get his hands on that sword."

46

"To kill Mexicans?"

"I wouldn't put it past him. Anyway, I'll be at the hospital early in the morning—am going to sleep in my bed again tonight for a few hours at least. I'm going home now." Lori gathered her things.

"Well, as far as I know, the plan is for the governor to get to the hospital around 11:00 tomorrow morning for a very brief introduction, just so the two have met before the ceremony," Bob explained.

"Wait a minute. I thought you weren't planning on Travis being at the ceremony?" Lori asked, puzzled.

"I really didn't think so, but I was so unnerved when the governor's office called. They had heard somehow that it was him. I guess they have their special ways—and made the assumption that he would be there, maybe not to do the reading but just to be acknowledged. Sort of making it official. That makes sense, if Travis is strong enough—guess the hospital folks will figure that out. We can't hide him forever."

Lori gave a smug smile of victory. She knew that it was very likely that the crowd who would gather to hear the words of that famous letter would get a surprise they never could imagine. The governor seemed to think that Travis would be reading the letter. Lori was convinced it was likely, and Bob was skeptical but wishful. There was only one person they forgot to consult.

Very early the next morning, not long after 4:00, Lori showered quickly and washed her hair, taking a couple of minutes to dry it this time, and put on her jeans and lemon-yellow sweater, grabbed the last energy bar in the box, and headed for the hospital. Travis was asleep when she got there, but most normal people were at that time in the morning. She asked for a cup of coffee at the nurses' station and waited while someone got it for her. The stuff didn't really taste like coffee, but she didn't care. She sat in the darkened room while the colonel slept. The graveyard hours in a hospital for one who is semi-alert are the most unbearable, and Lori fidgeted in the uncomfortable chair, contorting herself in enough different positions that she actually wondered if she should take up yoga. She finally dozed. The shift change was at 7:00. Maria came on duty, coming in the room to announce that fact and check Travis' vitals again. Lori woke up. As Maria was wrapping up, she asked Lori if she had any idea what Travis would like to order for breakfast.

"He seems to have an affinity for Southern cooking—guess that makes sense since he's originally from South Carolina. He certainly liked the grits. I bet he would like something like pancakes if you have them as well? Whatever they bring, tell them to be sure to bring coffee. He seems to love it!"

The patient heard the voices and started to stir slightly.

"Pancakes?" he asked slowly.

"Buck, you've got darn good hearing," Lori laughed.

"I'm going to get fat if I keep eating but just lie here," he replied. "I've got to get up—got to get back to the Alamo."

He sat up, swung around slowly, and planted his feet on the floor. He was wearing anti-slip hospital socks and had not realized that until right now. His vision was coming in much better focus, and he turned his leg to look at the bottom of the strange sock.

Lori noticed. "They use those in hospitals now so that weak or frail people won't fall."

"Like me?"

"Like anyone in a hospital. I had my thyroid out several years ago. They put them on me—they look goofy, but it's just a precaution. You can ditch them as soon as you leave here," she added.

"Today maybe? I really do have to get back to the Alamo," he sounded hopeful. It still seemed strange to her that someone caught up in the battle and massacre was so eager to go back there.

"Uh, I don't know about that. Dr. Gonzalez might be able to give us some detail on that when he comes around," Lori explained.

She realized the colonel was staring intently at her.

"I couldn't really see you until now," he explained. He blurted out, "You're pretty!" Based on his eye movements, he was obviously also admiring the slim jeans and form-fitting sweater she was wearing.

48

Fortunately, he did not say whatever he was likely thinking about the change in fashion over the last 180-odd years. She thanked him demurely, but Lori was thinking to herself—this is February. Wonder what he will do when he sees what women wear in the summer!

One thing that she had been thinking about during the night, for the first time since it was now a possibility, was where Travis would go once he was released. He couldn't just hole up at the fort, although he seemed to think so. No one lived there now. And any relatives he had were something like cousins six times removed or great-great-great-great-grandchildren, the latter hard to imagine for a 26-year-old. He didn't know any of them. Lori's parents were medical providers, and they had a house with ample space. But she did not know how they would react if she suggested bringing him there. They did not even know he was alive. It was a dilemma—ask them first—and she couldn't yet tell them who he was until it was made public, or explore his reaction to the possibility, only to have it dashed if, for some reason, her family objected. But she really could not think of any other appropriate place for Travis to go. He was staring at her.

"Uh, Buck, I've got a question for you. I think it's very likely they will at least let you out to visit the Alamo before long. In fact, tomorrow is February 24." A melancholy look came over his face, but she kept talking. "There are several commemorative ceremonies they do every year at the Shrine—that's really what they call it now—and on February 24 they have someone read your letter written that day . . . ."

"To the People of Texas & all Americans in the world," he interrupted.

"Yeah. That one. It's still a big hit. When it got to east Texas, it was published in the newspapers and republished in all the eastern papers. Actually, by the time this phenomenon occurred, Santa Anna had already stormed the fort. But the text of your letter spurred such a feeling of patriotism that men from all over the United States flocked to Sam Houston and the Texian cause. They defeated Santa Anna, captured him, and made him sign over Texas at San Jacinto in April 1836—the battle only lasted 18 minutes. Your letter and the delay the Alamo stand caused in Santa Anna's movements are why Texas is free and now a great state in the United States today."

"Why didn't Houston execute him?" fiery eyed, Travis shot back.

"Houston had to let Santa Anna live in order to get him to sign Texas over."

49

Travis looked angry and surprised all in one. "I'd have let him sign Texas over, then executed him! I'm . . . I'm glad the letter served some purpose. I guess 'Victory or Death' didn't work out so well for us," he admitted sadly, lowering his head.

"Well, true, but your defiant spirit is inspiring, and in the end there was Victory, largely bought by you and your brave men—y'all just didn't get to see it, unfortunately."

She pulled out her bag. "That reminds me. I've got something for you! Americans have always been enterprising sorts, and there's now a gift shop at the Alamo selling items with themes related to the place. It raises money to keep up the portion of the compound that is still intact." She handed him the cup. "Admittedly, no one had any pictures of you, so this is a stylized guess by some artist. You do look determined in it, just like you do in person, although I don't think it's a very good likeness otherwise. But it has your famous words, 'Victory or Death' and 'I Shall Never Surrender or Retreat.' It's certainly YOU."

"Lori, thank you!" Buck replied with obvious pleasure. He held the cup close to his face and read the words emblazoned on it. "I really did mean those things when I said them—and I mean them now as well—can't believe someone actually used them on this. I will only drink coffee from this cup from now on. Makes me want some to think about it!"

"Well, you don't want what the nurses have at their station, I can tell you that—awful stuff that tastes like dishwater. I think the breakfast order will be here soon. There will be some with that, and we'll ask for more," Lori suggested.

She continued, "Anyway, what they normally do at this ceremony each year is have someone read your letter—sometimes dressed like you—then hand the letter to someone dressed like the courier, who is on his horse and rides out of the complex with the letter at the end. A few years ago, they had some extremely distant relative of yours who was a county sheriff read it. That year, they actually brought the real letter, which is kept under lock and key at the state archives in Austin, here, and people flocked in from everywhere to see it."

"Really? This much later?" he asked.

"Yeah. It was a big deal. There's really only one thing that could top the excitement that created, and that's what I want to ask you about. My

50

boss, Bob Gordon—he's," she started to say "in charge of" but quickly thought better of it, "responsible for planning these events at the Alamo, has been trying to find a reader. The sheriff is no longer in office, and he's not doing it. There's a reenactor who has done it several times before—people like me who dress up in your 1830's style clothes and give demonstrations about cooking of the time, how to fire period firearms, making brooms, military maneuvers, you name it. But he's apparently in another country right now."

"Hopefully not Mexico . . . ."

"I doubt it. But what would make far more sense than anything else would be to have you read it since you wrote it. We haven't told anyone you are alive. The newspapers"—she was careful not to mention television or social media—"and public know an Alamo defender was revived, but they do not know your condition or who you are. At some point we can't keep it secret any longer. Having you read your letter—if you are strong enough, would be the perfect way to handle the whole thing."

"I can't see it well enough to read it, but I don't need to. I know every word," he replied softly. "Yes, tell your Mr. Gordon I will do it. I will look a little rough if they keep this bandage around my head and with my clothes bloody and face messed up, but, if that will not scare off everyone, I would be proud to restate my letter. I still hold those views dearly."

"To change the topic, one more thing—I suspect you may be kept here a few more days, but they're eventually going to let you out . . . ."

He shot back quickly: "As soon as they do, I'm heading back to the Alamo," not thinking about how he planned to get there.

"I know," Lori acknowledged, "but you really can't live there. There's no garrison now. No one lives there. It opens for visitors every day, and there are people who work there in daytime hours—and some rangers who police the place at night."

"If there are rangers at night, surely there's a small room I can use as quarters?"

Lori shook her head negatively. "Not really. There's no food there or anyone to help you if you get weak," she explained.

"I'll be well soon—don't want anyone to help me. I'm used to taking

51

care of myself!" he said defiantly. "As to food, I can cook my own if I have to."

She didn't bother to try to explain that the corn and "beeves" he mentioned in the postscript to his letter to "the People of Texas & all Americans in the world" were no longer on the premises. It would be easy to end up in an argument with the legal mind of the Alamo if she weren't careful.

She took it easier, searching for words to get around the old mission. "OK, but, for the time-being, you are still not well. They may let you out, but they won't do it unless there is someone around to be sure you will be looked after—that's the way hospitals work these days. How would you feel about coming to live with my family, for a while, until you are stronger?" she ventured.

"Who are your people?" he asked, the classic Southern query of the 1800's.

"My parents would be perfect for this. My father is a major in the Texas National Guard—and a doctor to boot." She figured the military connection would appeal to him, and he did seem to show more interest in what she was saying after she announced her father's affiliation with the military. She went on: "My mom is a nurse—another plus. I have two younger siblings, a 15-year-old brother named Len and a 9-year-old sister, Vicky. My sister came home from school the other day and said that the teacher had shown a short movie about you in class."

"Movie? What is that?" Travis looked confused.

"Uh, I forgot you wouldn't know that one. It's basically a play, but now we have a way to make a copy of it and show it on a screen so the actors only have to perform once and you can watch the copy of it over and over if you want."

Buck had a very, very puzzled look on his face.

Avoiding the issue in the film about Travis' little son, she gave Vicky's opinion of the actor who played Travis. "She said the actor who played you was kind of cute."

"Well, if she sees the real me, she's not going to think so at all. I'll probably scare a 9-year-old to death," he replied, moving his hand to the

52

ruined right cheek. He had seen a glimpse of his wounds in the mirror when an attendant helped him into the bathroom and he discovered plumbing.

"Think about it seriously, Buck. Our house is all on one story—no stairs to deal with. My folks are both medical professionals, and we have plenty of room. If you are receptive to it, I'll ask them in the next day or two." She was holding off long enough for the public announcement as to the identity of the Alamo survivor to be made before asking.

"You don't think they would mind? I might not fit in too well, as I'm beginning to get the idea that there have been a lot of changes since 1836."

"I think you will be just fine," she replied, trying to block out thoughts of how he would react to cars, air conditioning—he might like that one in San Antonio, appliances, grocery stores, and all the rest.

"I still think my place is at the Alamo," he replied stubbornly.

The doctor knocked at the door, and Travis called for him to come in.

"Hello you two," Gonzalez greeted them. "So, Colonel, how is the vision today?"

"Still blurry enough that I don't think I could read, but I can see your face," Travis responded.

"Excellent. I don't think we're going to have to treat that. Soon, probably the day after tomorrow, we're thinking about unwrapping the bandages and taking a close look to see how you are healing. We may not need so much bandaging after that—will have to see when we check it. Meanwhile, I want to take a look at the other old wounds. We kind of left that until we could get you in better shape from the surgery, and I honestly think they're just scars at this point—look bad but no treatment needed."

There was a call coming in on Gonzalez' cell phone. He took it quickly, only saying "Great." He turned to the others: "The governor is on his way down the hall—will be here in just a minute."

"What?" Travis asked.

"He's a big fan of yours—came down from Austin just to meet you," the doctor explained. Travis looked confused—this was the second reference to someone coming from Austin—Lori had referenced it when

53

talking about the letter. To him, that was a person, not a place.

Not a minute later, there was a knock at the door. "Come in," Lori called.

Four men, obviously the governor's security detail, surrounded a man in a wheelchair. The governor rolled the chair up to the bedside, Gonzalez and Lori stepping aside for him. Travis stared.

The governor put out his hand, giving his biggest smile: "Colonel Travis, this is certainly the greatest honor of my life. You have always been my hero!" he practically beamed.

"Why, thank you sir!" Travis replied in a soft voice in his thick South Carolina accent. "I'm not sure what I have done that deserves that compliment. I was only doing my duty at the Alamo."

"Colonel—ONLY doing your duty at the Alamo? I know of no greater dedication and sacrifice in all of the history of this great state of Texas, indeed in the United States, than the defense of the Alamo. I cannot express to you the depth of my respect and admiration," the governor practically gushed, every bit of it sincere.

"Well, sir, I would do it again, horrible as it was, if I had to. Texas is worth everything to me," Travis responded.

"Son, you've certainly proven that. That's one thing I always liked about you. You made great statements, but you backed them up every time," the governor stated.

"Sir, we do make a fine pair, don't we?" Travis stared at the wheelchair.

"Yes," the governor laughed. "I'm not sure how much we could do at the Alamo if it happened again right now, but I would do anything I could to support you. Sad truth about my injury is I was not doing anything noble—just running down the street near my home when, in a freak accident, a tree fell on me—have been stuck in this chair ever since."

"I'm slowly getting up a little with folks holding on to me now. But since Santa Anna and his butchers carved up my face and the rest of me, I suppose folks will recoil when they see me for the rest of my life," Travis said sadly, the blue eyes almost filled with tears. The young colonel had been extremely vain about his appearance in his earlier life.

54

"Colonel, I'll admit that the scars are pretty bad—no point in trying to hide the fact—but stand proudly. They are scars born of a kind of valor that we sadly no longer see in this country. You are a hero among heroes. I cannot tell you how proud I will be to be at that ceremony with you tomorrow."

Lori thought, yes, that was it—the governor has been assuming Travis would read the letter all along—pretty much clinched it.

"Governor, I think the colonel probably needs to rest now," Gonzalez said in what was apparently a prearranged cue for the end of the meeting to conserve the patient's limited strength. Travis was looking very tired and white. The two men shook hands again, and the governor and his entourage hurried out into the hall.


It was the day of the ceremonial reading of the Travis letter, held every February 24, the anniversary of the day the Alamo commander penned the most stirring words in Texas—and maybe American—history and sent the missive toward the east for help by courier. The crowd was there and waiting for the program to begin. The governor was eager to start, Bob was pacing back and forth, and William Barret Travis had been lying in a small room off the gift shop trying to summon the strength to be pretty much carried to the ceremony until 5 minutes before. Elbert Jones and Jaime Valle, long-time Alamo Rangers, had carefully led him to where the dignitaries were gathering.

Earlier that morning, he had been shaved and dressed in his bloodstained clothing, and Lori had brushed his hair to the extent she could. But the swath of bandages around his head made that difficult, and one red lock stuck up above the bandage, and she couldn't do anything about it. The clothing was in even worse shape than her quick analysis earlier had determined. His boots were actually beginning to come apart, the ancient leather rotting. Lori had used super glue to try to hold them together through the ceremony as it was too late for anything else. A tear in the pants made itself known, and one sleeve seam in the old coat came apart. She had just this morning found out how bad it all was and patched the outfit back together barely in time for the brief ceremony, hoping it would make it through it without falling off of him. It was clear that someone was going to have to make a replica if Col. Travis was to continue to appear as himself at Alamo events in the future. After they got him dressed for the trip, the young man promptly fainted. This off and on

55

passing out was the result of damage to his brain, so, despite the fact that he was unconscious for the moment, he had been loaded into an ambulance and taken to the Alamo, Lori riding along in front.

The dignitaries were lined up in front of their assembled audience. There was no platform for the speakers. A platform would be better for spectators, but it did not work well for the governor or the colonel. It was difficult for spectators in the back to see, but the Alamo open space was so small that not that many people could crowd in anyway. A local choral group sang "The Yellow Rose of Texas" and "Texas, Our Texas," and a black Baptist minister gave an invocation. Someone from the DRT, who were bitter about being kicked out by the state after over 100 years of caring for the Alamo, sucked it up and made nice anyway in a brief speech because, after all, the Alamo was bigger than any intrastate feud over who should defend it.

Finally, Bob Gordon said a few words regarding the importance of the famous February 24th letter from Travis, newly penned up in the Alamo, the young lawyer desperately pleading his case for help from the outside world. The courier quietly sat on his horse just to the right of the dignitaries. The usual routine at this event was for someone dressed as Travis to read the letter, often from a seated position at a table, as if he had just finished drafting it. He would then hand it to the courier, who would take it and dramatically ride out of the complex. It would not work quite that way this time. Bob introduced the governor and sat down.

"Ladies and gentlemen, I cannot tell you how much this amazing document means to me, as a native Texan. It has for as long as I can remember. I first read the text in school so many years ago that I'd rather not say the number,"—there was slight laughter from the crowd—"but it still thrills me today. When I think of those men, surrounded by 20 times their number, the enemy waving a flag of no quarter and playing a tune that translates as 'slit throat,' knowing what would happen to them and still having the courage to do their duty, and, when the awful charge came, dying nobly and taking a large number of their enemy with them, my eyes well up with tears."

The governor said the words, but Travis' blurry eyes were tearing heavily, making it even harder to see anything. He wiped his sleeve across his face to clear them. The governor continued:

"As you know, we like to include our brave wounded warriors in any ceremonies here and around the state, where it is appropriate. We have a

56

young man here today who had brain surgery just 5 days ago. He was shot in the head in combat. His vision is messed up, although the doctors feel that is temporary, and it is improving, thank God, but he is going to recite the Travis letter since he cannot see it. There was a hush as the governor motioned to the two Alamo Rangers to gently lift Travis and guide him the short distance to the lectern. He would not know what a microphone was, and he couldn't see it clearly. Elbert quickly adjusted it up to accommodate his height. With the lectern in front of him, most of the crowd could not see too much of the bloodstained coat, and people who attended these things were used to seeing someone dressed up in 1830's garb doing the Travis routine. The messed-up face and bandaged head were explained by the governor's reference to wounded warriors. The crowd likely thought the young man was a victim of an IED in Afghanistan.

Supported by the sturdy arms of the rangers on each side of him, and in a surprisingly strong voice, in the Deep South drawl, the colonel repeated his famous words:

"Commandancy of the Alamo

"Bexar Fby. 24th 1836

"To the People of Texas & all Americans in the world—

"Fellow citizens & compatriots—I am besieged, by a thousand or more of the Mexicans under Santa Anna. I have sustained a continual Bombardment & cannonade for 24 hours & have not lost a man. The enemy has demanded a surrender at discretion, otherwise, the garrison are to be put to the sword, if the fort is taken. I have answered the demand with a cannon shot, & our flag still waves proudly from the walls. I shall never surrender or retreat. Then, I call on you in the name of Liberty, of patriotism & everything dear to the American character, to come to our aid, with all dispatch. The enemy is receiving reinforcements daily & will no doubt increase to three or four thousand in four or five days. If this call is neglected, I am determined to sustain myself as long as possible & die like a soldier who never forgets what is due to his own honor & that of his country.

"Victory or death.

57

"William Barret Travis

"Lt. Col. Comding.

"P.S. The Lord is on our side. When the enemy appeared in sight we had not three bushels of corn. We have since found in deserted houses 80 or 90 bushels & got into the walls 20 or 30 head of Beeves.

"Travis"

As he said his name in closing, he fainted. The two rangers gently and swiftly lifted him and got him in his chair. The dignitaries were all clapping, all but the governor standing, as were the spectators. Elbert had a bottle of water and was trying to get Travis to take some of it while Jaime discreetly held the colonel in place. When the applause finally died down, the governor took to the microphone again.

"I suppose all of you think that's incredible, right?" The cheering began again.

"Well, it is incredible, but not just because a wounded warrior was able to get through reciting the letter, although that alone would have been most praiseworthy. There's a good reason a man who just had brain surgery and cannot see to read was able to do that." He was about to let the cat out of the bag. "He knows that letter by heart. He wrote it. Ladies and gentlemen, in the most profound honor I have ever had—one I never could have dreamed of, I want to introduce to you truly the bravest man in the history of our state—and the most dedicated—Lt. Col. William Barret Travis."

The crowd went wild. Elbert had just gotten Travis to open his eyes, and the two rangers lifted the frail Alamo commander and got him back to the podium, where he stared at the blurry shapes of the crowd in front of him and wavered as the strong rangers supported him. Finally, sensing that Col. Travis was not well and that it would be merciful to let him say a word or two and sit down for good, they quieted down.

"Thank you, fellow Texians"—he used the old term familiar to his time and countrymen—"and fellow Americans. I'm feeling rather light-headed, but I want you to know that I meant everything in that letter, and, awful as the whole thing turned out, I would do it again if I had to. Please honor the memory of my brave men who fought that cruel and relentless foe. Keep their memories sacred. Again, I thank you. Victory or Death!"

Travis sank into Elbert's arms at this, as the crowd launched into another standing ovation. Someone handed the courier the letter, and he galloped off to the east for help for the beleaguered garrison.

The governor motioned to someone and wheeled himself to the microphone again. Whatever he was going to say was apparently off-script.

"Ladies and gentleman, as you may know, the Alamo, although owned by the state, has not had a military function in over 100 years. After the famous battle, it actually fell into serious disrepair and decay. U.S. forces, the Confederates, and then the United States again did treat it as a military base for some years, but not anytime recently. Now, the primary function of this place where so many gave their lives is as a shrine to the defenders"—no word from the governor regarding Mexican sacrifices—he was not shy about which side he favored. "But its military significance, all these years later, cannot be and should not be denied. Although we have a large building over at the base handling state national guard headquarters coordination and other duties, the Alamo should be represented among state military facilities as it is the genesis of all that has come since. As governor of the state, and with the approval of the General Land Office, who are responsible for the Alamo, I am recommissioning this fort as a state military complex, and, although the size of the Alamo and its other functions limit military tasks that can be performed here, it has long functioned as the stage for various military ceremonies and other related programs."

The governor turned to one of the aides, and the man quickly provided what appeared to be a clipboard with some official looking paper on it. Another aide handed the governor a pen, and he affixed his signature to the order, then read it to the assembled audience:

"On this day, February 24, 2017, under my authority as governor of the State of Texas, I officially recommission the fortress known as The Alamo as an integral part of the Texas state military system to be used as needed for the defense and protection of the state . . . ."

A few people in the audience were trying not to laugh at this last. The reference to "used as needed for the defense" that this conjured up was of the old defenders trying to hold out against a huge land force in the age of guided missiles. It was all kind of comical.

He continued, ". . . against any foes to freedom and our way of life. In pursuit of this order, I am appointing Col. William Barret Travis to the post commanding the fort, something at which he has some experience . . . ."

The crowd laughed, and Travis perked up slightly, trying to straighten up in his chair as Jaime still held him semi-upright.

". . . if the colonel agrees to serve." The governor finally ended his little speech to wild cheers from everyone.

"I guess y'all better try to get me up there again," Travis wearily directed his two attendants. Elbert and Jaime lifted him and pretty much dragged him to the microphone, again adjusting it up for his height.

Travis addressed the governor: "Sir, I thank you kindly for your words. I need not remind you that I was not entirely a success"—an understatement if there ever was one—"in keeping out the foe when I took this command the last time. But, if you truly desire my services in this capacity again, I will take it—for Texas!" He couldn't help but add his catchwords one more time, "Victory or Death!"

Everyone stood as Elbert and Jaime got the rapidly weakening Alamo commander back to his seat. He was out cold before they could get him in the chair, missing the last standing ovation on his behalf. The event wrapped up quickly with "God Bless America" and a benediction, and Travis was whisked back to the hospital, still unconscious. So much for military defense of the Alamo, at present, anyway.

# THE SHRINE

Major Clayton was at his medical conference. Elena Clayton was having her morning coffee when Lori came in—no surreptitious sneaking in to grab an energy bar this time. Although Lori really enjoyed sitting with Buck, and she made a point of spending time with him each day, the crisis was hopefully over, and she could resume more normal sleep habits at home. She poured some coffee and sat across from her mother.

"Mom, I've got a question for you."

"Lori, I've already gotten the paper."

She held the front section out toward her daughter. The headline read: "Colonel Travis back in command at the Alamo!"

"Yes, Mom, that's it," Lori admitted.

"I thought so," her mom said with a smile. "So you have been involved in navigating the young colonel's return to the land of the living?"

"Kind of. The whole thing was so weird. When the students started unearthing a body, I was like, oh how gross, just cover it back up. Quite frankly, I didn't dream it was a defender. The ironclad story has always been that they were all burned on Santa Anna's orders. I'll have to admit, curiosity began to set in as they uncovered more and more, and then found an intact hand. I knew at that point that there was something different about this. When they finished digging and got him out and turned him over, I just can't tell you how I felt. Poor thing—he looked awful—in fact, honestly, still kind of does. I checked his pulse while everyone else just sat there gawking. I'm the one who realized he was alive. He was a handsome young man—now he looks kind of freakish with those awful wounds. He's very confused."

"Lori, who wouldn't be in that situation? I can't imagine what things might be like 181 years from now," her mom interjected.

"They have him eating—he's got a great appetite. As you might expect from his actions in the Alamo saga, he's a very, very determined person.

61

He's trying to walk—his sole reason for living seems to be to get back to the Alamo. After all, he really has no other reason to live—everyone he knew is long dead. He had a little son from a failed marriage—that was a focus of the film Vicky saw in class. He hasn't said anything about that yet, but it's out there—another thing we'll have to deal with. Now that the governor has asked him to be in charge of the Alamo again, I'm sure he will work even harder to get back to his post as soon as possible."

Her mom laughed slightly and sipped on her coffee.

"You want a 'Victory or Death' mug for that?" Lori asked. "They've got plenty of them at the gift shop."

"No thanks, honey. I don't think that's quite me, but . . . ."

"I already got him one," Lori finished her mother's thought.

"Seriously, Mom, he's doing very well. Barring an unexpected setback, I think they may be releasing him in a few days—but there's nowhere for him to go. I've had a hard time trying to persuade him that he can't just park it at his command post and live in quarters at the Alamo. After so much of that in 1836, I don't think he understands why the Alamo is not set up for it now. I tried to tell him that his 'corn and beeves' as he put it in the letter are not there now. There's no source of food there—unless he wants to live on Alamo gift shop fudge. Actually, that sounds kind of good to me. I hope I wasn't being too presumptuous, but I've really been worried about this. I told him I would have to ask y'all, but I asked if he might like to come stay with us?" the pitch of her voice rose slightly and hesitantly at the end of the sentence.

Elena smiled. "I knew that was coming. It certainly took you long enough to get it out!"

"Well?"

"We've got plenty of room."

"He doesn't have any money, you know."

"I think we can handle it, although you did indicate the young colonel might eat us out of house and home?" Elena teased.

"Not really, but he is a young guy—you know how they eat—think about Len," Lori answered.

"True, but I don't think Mr. Travis will break the bank."

"What about Dad? What do you think he will say?" Lori asked.

"I'm not sure how he will take to being outranked in his own home, but I think I can speak for your dad. It will be fine, Lori." She patted her daughter's hand, then took another swig of the coffee.

Neither of them had seen Vicky standing in the doorway. She was staring, wide-eyed. She took a step forward, and Elena and Lori turned.

"Lori, you are kidding me, aren't you?" Vicky demanded.

Her mother held the paper out to her.

"Oh my gosh, it's true! It's like that crazy film. Only instead of someone from now going back to the Alamo, someone from the Alamo, and it's the same guy in the movie, is coming here?"

Lori nodded.

"But Vicky, there are a few things you need to keep in mind. First, the movie was just a movie. Second, in it, when the girl from now goes back in time . . . ."

Vicky cut her off: "Well the reverse is a whole lot better. I can't imagine anyone wanting to go to the Alamo!"

"That's part of it. In the movie, the modern kid who goes back in time knows about all the advances we've made. In the reverse, we've got all kinds of things that Col. Travis would not dream of," Lori continued evenly. "Although I'm sure he doesn't want another battle and massacre, obviously, the colonel would welcome being back with all the people he knew and loved. Remember the part about his little son? That child did grow up without a father, and, if I remember the story correctly, he did not have a very happy life. Colonel Travis will eventually ask about his son. He hasn't said anything yet—that's going to be a tough one to navigate. He doesn't understand most of what we take as second nature these days. You should have seen the look on his face the first time I moved the controls to make the hospital bed move. One other thing—I remember you called the guy who played him in the movie 'cute.' Well, this is the real guy, not the actor.

Trust me, he would be VERY cute except for the fact that Santa Anna ruined his face. The poor guy has a gunshot hole in his forehead, a long scar from a sword slash all the way down his cheek, and numerous wounds on the rest of his body. He's wearing his old uniform coat over a hospital gown. I had to sew it up after I had it cleaned. They couldn't get most of the bloodstains out. The thing came apart. In short, he looks absolutely weird."

"I guess we won't need to decorate for Halloween this year," Vicky noted caustically. "All we have to do is set Col. Travis in a rocking chair in front of the house. We won't have to buy any candy 'cause he will scare the kids off."

"That's awful, Vicky," Lori replied.

"I'm sorry—guess it is," Vicky apologized. "But you make him sound absolutely scary."

"No, really, he's not. The tailcoat over the hospital gown is weird and kind of amusing, and his scars are really bad, but, if you look closely at his face, he is kind of cute," Lori defended Buck.

"Lori's got a boyfriend," Vicky sang out.

Lori just stared at her. Elena smiled and took another sip of the coffee.


Lori walked into Buck's room—no one was there. She knew he wasn't likely—at least she didn't think so—to take matters into his own hands and try to walk to the Alamo. But there was nothing she could do but sit and wait until someone showed up. Not 5 minutes later, Marco and the colonel appeared in the doorway.

Marco announced, "He's making great progress—walked all the way to the end of the hall! Angie even let go of him for most of it, walking along just in case."

Travis had a look of grim determination on his face—sort of like the picture on the coffee mug, Lori thought. She praised his efforts. As the physical therapists were getting him back in bed, Dr. Gonzalez came in.

"We're going to run those tests I talked about now, if that's OK with you, Colonel?"

Travis nodded although he had no idea what Gonzalez was talking about. Another attendant came in and got the patient, just placed in bed by the departing Marco, up and helped him into a wheelchair.

Lori was in for another sit-and-wait session. She was dozing again, despite a more regular schedule, when they wheeled Buck back into the room.

Maria appeared, almost magically, it seemed. "We're going to take off these bandages now if you feel like it, sir?" she addressed Travis.

He nodded, and she began to unwrap the layers of gauze. She announced that Dr. Gonzalez would be back by shortly. Lori was staring intently as the bandages came off. The gunshot wound looked about the same as she had remembered when he had been unearthed, actually a little better since the blood had been cleaned off. But there was no way around it—the colonel had a very obvious hole in his head. Another knock at the door, and Gonzalez was back.

"Let's take a look and see how this is healing," he got right to the point. Maria moved out of the way.

After probing and staring, Gonzalez scribbled something on a notepad and declared that the wound was healing nicely. "In fact, I don't think he needs all those bandages. At this point, I think just something covering the wound will be sufficient. But, Colonel, be careful not to get it dirty or rub it, OK?"

Travis nodded his assent.

"You two—or whoever is going to make the decision—need to start making plans for where you are going to live, Colonel. In a couple days, I'm guessing you will be ready to go home, but I know, in your case, that's not as simple as it is for most people."

"I want to go back to my post at the Alamo," he started.

"Lori, tell me if I'm wrong, but I don't think the Alamo is set up with living quarters like it was during the siege?" the doctor observed.

Lori vigorously shook her head up and down. "I've been trying and trying to tell him that!"

"I know you have your old job back—read it in the paper this morning." He had a copy and showed the headline to Travis, who took it and, squinting, read a little of the story aloud. "But I think command of the Alamo, unless, we have another Mexican attack or some sort of other calamity requiring 24-hour-a-day presence, is now pretty much an 8 to 5 job."

Lori blurted out: "I asked my mom. She's fine with it. He's going to stay with us. My dad's a doctor, my mom's a nurse, and we've got extra room . . . . I work at the Alamo, so I can take my commanding officer to work every day."

Gonzalez laughed. "Sounds dispositive to me!"


Gonzalez decided he wanted to run a few more tests, and it was actually 3 days later before the colonel was finally ready to be released from the hospital. Still, only a 9-day stay for someone who had a musket ball removed from his brain was not bad.

The white-washed, subtly Spanish style Clayton home was a sprawling one-story affair originally built sometime in the 1950's for a doctor and his family of that generation. The place had been updated several times since and featured the latest in appliances and countertops per Elena's insistence. It was roomy with an open layout and easy to navigate with no stairs or other impediments. A couple of now-large cholla cacti that Lori had grown as a child from the tiny ones that were sold at the Alamo for a while were the main landscape feature in a yard that was mostly grass. Two pecan trees provided some shade in the huge backyard, far enough back from the pool that not too many of the messy leaves blew into it in the fall.

In preparation for Travis' stay, Lori and her family had been setting up the guest room for him and trying to think of anything he might need that was not already there. The room had a big television on the table in front of the bed. Lori got Len to help her move it to another room. She seriously doubted that Travis would have much interest in TV, even when he was introduced to it—and he might want the tabletop space. Fortunately, the bed was a comfortable queen size with the extra length needed for taller people. The simpler the better to decrease confusion at first was Lori's modus operandi. After all, they certainly did not have anything beyond the basics at the Alamo.

One thing that did pop into her mind—and sent her to see Morena again—was the fact that the colonel was a writer. Now who he would be writing to at this point, since all of his associates were dead, made her worry likely unnecessary, but maybe he wanted to start another racy journal. He had not as of yet been introduced to BIC pens and their cousins. Lori asked Morena if they had any quills and ink, figuring that was a Travis item the store might carry because of his fame for letter writing. Morena quickly produced a pretty cobalt blue inkwell, a quill pen, and ink, much to Lori's relief, as well as some sort of old-looking parchment paper that may have been similar to whatever they used in the 1830's and a blank book, meant for a journal or whatever the owner wished to write, featuring a picture of the Alamo church. She took the items home and placed them on the little desk in the room, clearing off all the clap-trap figurines and other junk that had accumulated over the years, putting it in a shoebox, and placing it overhead in the closet. She had also, on a whim, bought a Texas flag at the gift shop and, standing on the desk chair, hung it over one of the windows in the room. She knew that it did not really come into use until shortly after the Alamo's fall, but she could explain it quickly and was certain it would appeal.

One major problem for the young man was clothes. Although Lori was somewhat of a period clothing expert, she did not have a really good answer on this one. She had a pattern for a man's shirt—it could be lengthened for a nightshirt—that she had sewn for several of the reenactors. She stopped by the fabric store and got some cotton and rather hurriedly stitched a nightshirt for Buck, sewing any seam that could be accessed by sewing machine this time. He probably wouldn't notice, at least at first. She had also mended his one shirt. She would make another one or two like it when she had the time, and the drawers—would need more of those as well—and soon. Men's shirts of the period were totally different affairs in construction than modern shirts. They involved a t-shaped slit for the head and neck to go through, a number of gussets for neck and sleeves, and hand-sewn construction that was required because the close work was too tight to perform on a machine, the style predating sewing machines. Maybe, in not too long, he could be persuaded to convert to 21st Century fashions for times when he was not "on duty" commanding the fort. Considering that her time for sewing was limited, and one could not just go to Macy's and buy what he wore, she hoped so.

He would also have to be introduced to current notions of cleanliness—bathing frequently, deodorant, and the like. She wondered where she could find an old-time straight razor. She was sure the colonel would not want to grow a full beard, although they certainly were fashionable at present. He had seen and used the flush toilet at the hospital, a major improvement, no doubt, over the latrine where he had been found, and a strong attendant had gotten him seated in the shower for several thorough scrubbings. But he was not used to the current American standard of doing this every day. She kept thinking how smelly the 1800's must have been. Apparently, everyone just got used to it.. The fact was, they did not know any better.

Travis had not been out of the hospital since he was brought there unconscious except for the one brief foray to recite the letter. He had fainted when they took him, and he was out cold after accepting his appointment to command, so he had never seen a car, a freeway, or how little Bexar had grown into huge San Antonio. Lori would have to get him home in her little Cavalier. The more she thought about it, the more concerned she became. She did not want him to freak out and make her have an accident. Knowing she didn't have much time with the release set for the afternoon, she called Dr. Gonzalez—he had given her his cell—not long after 8 a.m.

"Hi Doctor! I've got a question—it's Lori. I'm calling from home," she announced.

"Everything OK with the preparations? We're getting close now," he responded.

"Yeah, but it dawned on me—he's never seen a car, much less been in one, except ambulances, and he was out every time he was in one of those. And when he thinks about San Antonio, he's thinking about a sleepy little town of around 2,000 people with a few dusty dirt roads. I'm a little concerned about his first foray out of the hospital being for me to get him home. Any chance I could take him for a short ride—actually, over to the Alamo is not far, so he could get the feel before I try the freeway with him?"

"I think that's a very wise idea, Lori. Are you coming back over?" the doctor asked.

"Yes, I was getting ready to come back right now."

"I'll have the necessary papers arranged. You will both have to sign a release—company policy—since he's still under the care of the hospital.

68

And I would recommend the back way—no interstates—for his first trip," the doctor advised.

"Will do. I'll be there shortly," she said.

When Gonzalez relayed the news to Travis that Lori was on her way to "take him somewhere"—the doctor did not commit where, he immediately jumped to the conclusion that she would take him to the Alamo. After the doctor left the room, the colonel, who was now able to walk slowly on his own, went to the little closet and retrieved his clothes, hung there by Lori the day before. By the time Lori got there, he was dressed in his shirt, cravat, vest, and pants. He could not manage the boots on his own.

"Looks to me as if the doctor told you what I've got in mind?" she asked at the sight.

With one-track-mind precision, he asked, "Are we going to the Alamo?"

She laughed. "Yes, Buck, we're going to the Alamo—but only for a very short visit this time. Do you want me to help you with those boots? I have a feeling this may be their last walk. I measured them and got with someone I know who does the period footwear—have some new ones just like them on order for you. Meanwhile, I made you a nightshirt. By the looks of the rest of your outfit, I think I'm going to have to reproduce it soon as well!"

He hung his head. "I'm sorry you have to do all of this for me, Lori. I should be able to get these things for myself."

"No, Buck, believe me, no one wears this stuff these days unless they are reenacting scenes from history. Anyone would have a hard time finding them. Fortunately, I really like historic clothing, so I know just where to go for fabric and how to make them!"

She helped him with the boots, difficult because he had to pull on them to get them on, but much pulling would take them apart. He stood and was putting on his coat as Maria entered with the forms.

"I think Dr. Gonzalez mentioned that both of you need to sign this for your little outing?" she asked. "Colonel, I need to check your stats one more time before letting you sign out."

69

Lori nodded. Travis looked puzzled as he wrapped his military sash around his waist.

She looked at him. "It's just another modern hospital requirement since they're responsible for you while you are in their care, and I'm responsible for you when I take you on our little visit. We have to sign out, so to speak."

She signed the form on the clipboard and pointed to a space for him to sign, handing him the newfangled pen. He had watched her sign with it, but he held it up and looked at it before he finally scrawled his signature on the page. A quick check of his blood pressure and temperature, and they were out the door.

As Lori led him out into the hall—he refused to sit in a wheelchair, most of the hospital workers stared. Many had worked with him, but they had not seen him dressed up in his colonel outfit. Lori was tall, had long legs, and had spent every day since Buck was unearthed running back and forth like crazy, so she had to consciously walk slowly for the sake of her still slightly unsteady companion. They were on the sixth floor, so they headed for the elevator. She explained to him just how big the building was, and he was looking around, staring at hallways that seemed to go in all directions, as they made their way through the maze. Lori tried to put a positive spin on everything.

"You can see how big this building is, Buck. It's eight stories high. We're on the sixth floor. There's a contraption called an elevator that takes you to whatever floor you want to go—don't have to do all those stairs."

He was still staring as she stopped in front of the "contraption." It opened, and a horde of people got out, most of them not even subtle about gawking at the man in the Alamo outfit. He did not seem to notice—or care. Fortunately, in Lori's view, no one else wanted to get on, so they had the elevator to themselves—until they hit the third floor. At that point it opened, and Travis jumped slightly, not expecting it. Two women, one black and one Hispanic, got on, each with several small children. The kids, seeing the costume, started squealing and asking their respective moms what Travis was. Of course, the moms didn't know.

Lori interjected: "Hi everybody. This is my friend Buck. He's from a long time ago—the 1800's. The hospital has been helping him get better. Do you like his outfit? He is very brave—he fought at the Alamo!"

70

One little girl clapped, and a couple of the boys asked Travis if fighting at the Alamo was hard. He told them briefly that it was. The elevator got to the ground floor. The kids waved and went their way with their moms, and Lori and Buck headed out the front door. People were coming and going, and most stared as the couple made their way past them.

As far as the eye could see, there were cars in the massive parking lot.

"Tell you what, Buck, why don't you sit here on this bench," Lori pointed to the right, "while I get the car," she directed.

"Car?" The colonel had apparently either assumed she had some horses tied up out front or they would hoof it.

"Oh yeah, I guess I didn't explain that. Let's both sit on the bench a minute. See all those things out there—they replaced the horse and buggy."

As if on cue, a red Volkswagen, the new style "bug," pulled in the swing drive at the front door right in front of them, and a woman got out. Buck was staring in amazement.

"They've got motors and run by themselves. We steer them. They have a brake for when you need to slow or stop. I've got to get mine. It's way over there," she pointed in the direction, "so it will take me a few minutes."

He still looked puzzled. "I don't really understand this at all, but I'm game if it will get me to the Alamo."

Lori headed for the car, leaving Buck to face more stares from the people hurrying into and out of the building. He would simply have to get used to that as long as he wore his Alamo clothes, and possibly even if he didn't because of the extent of the facial scars.

"Son, what happened to you?" an elderly man, wearing a cap indicating military service, asked as he hobbled up to Travis.

The man looked frail, and Travis instinctively scooted over and made room for him to sit down on the bench next to him.

"Alamo—Santa Anna," came the brief response.

"Alamo? Are you a reenactor? Did someone load real bullets at one of those reenactments?" the man asked.

71

"No. I mean Santa Anna did this to me. I fought at the Alamo," Travis said earnestly. "They dug me up and have been taking care of me here," he pointed backward toward the building. "But now my friend Lori is getting one of those—what did she call it—cars?—and is going to take me back to the Alamo where I belong," he explained.

The other man was not sure how to respond. He didn't know if his companion was a mental patient out for a bit of air or if there could be some truth to it. While he paused, a woman, heading at a fast clip for the hospital, stopped when she saw the sight.

"Hello! Are you the fellow they dug up at the Alamo? It's been all over the news."

Travis nodded. "Yes ma'am. I'm Col. Travis," he said rather quietly in his drawl.

The other man beamed. "Colonel Travis? Commander of the Texans at the Alamo? Really?"

"Yes sir. As you know, I'm sure, it did not come out so well for us," the colonel said regretfully.

The woman asked if she could take his picture, which confused him, but he assented. The man asked to shake his hand, telling him he had always been one of his heroes. At this point, Lori pulled up and got out of the car.

The woman had already gone in the building, happy with her picture of the Alamo commander, and Travis politely told the elderly man that he enjoyed meeting him and shook hands again. Lori guided Travis to the passenger seat of the car, shielding his head as he got in. The truth was this car was too small for his height. She buckled him in the seatbelt, telling him what it was for, then closed the door, which took two efforts since it really was not quite on right. She got in and buckled her belt, having a fight with her fractious door to get it closed, cranked up—the noise made him jump a bit, shifted into drive, and slowly started out of the lot. The windows were down because the air did not work, not too bad this day as it was cool.

Fortunately, it was a very short ride to the Alamo. Buck mostly stared at the other cars whizzing along, most faster than Lori as she was deliberately plodding at a much slower clip than her usual. They pulled in the tiny employee parking lot just as Bob was getting out of his car.

"Lori! Didn't expect to see you this morning after that last message about needing the time to get the house ready," he called.

"Hi Bob! I've got someone with me. Might need a little help," she replied.

She was already at the passenger side door, and Travis was trying to figure out how to unbuckle the seat belt. He was not successful, and she quickly freed him. He swung his legs to the ground and held onto the car door, pushing himself up while Lori held onto him, praying all the while that the door would not come off the car. Bob got there just as the colonel was standing on his own.

"Colonel Travis, sir, welcome back!" Bob made a poor attempt at a military salute although he had never served in the military.

The colonel gave a crisp salute in reply. "Thank you sir! I cannot honestly say I am happy to be here, given the awful memories, but I feel it is still my duty to protect and defend this post," the serious young man explained.

"Sir, with your permission, I would like to suggest that we take a moment so that I can show you what is left of the compound that you are familiar with?" Bob inquired.

"By all means," Travis responded.

He was fairly steady on his feet now, and he did look some better as the swath of bandages was gone, the red hair blowing in the wind on the breezy day. He still wore the patch of gauze over the forehead wound, but that was a major improvement over the bandages. It was 8:45, and the complex would open to the public in 15 minutes. That worked well, Lori thought—much better for Travis to have some time to get acquainted with the new Alamo boundaries before hordes of tourists descended on the place. The one positive, when the sightseers did arrive, would be that he would not stand out so terribly much as there were usually reenactors around dressed in 1836 garb, as she so often did—only not with all the blood stains. Bob was busy showing Travis locations with which he was already familiar, heading toward the church, when the colonel asked his host about the north wall, where the commander had personally directed the cannon during the battle and fell with the musket ball to his forehead. Although everything looked vastly different, Travis had his bearings and pointed north, indicating they should go there. They walked to the opposite end of the complex—the church was on the southeast end—and out into the plaza. Travis was so intent on the north wall that he paid no heed to the large white monument in the plaza. Bob pointed out a large building, which he said was a "federal" building, explaining, when the colonel asked, that United States business was conducted there. They crossed Houston Street and stood facing the southwest corner of the federal building, near a side entrance. Across the street to their left was the Hotel Indigo. The colonel proceeded to give them a tour of the north wall.

"Colonel, I know it all looks drastically different, but I'm guessing this is about where you were during the battle?" Bob asked.

Travis didn't answer. He had been calculating the distance, walking, not paying as much attention to the change in landscape as would have been expected. He pointed to the left of where Bob and Lori were standing toward the Indigo. They walked across the street, and he stood on the sidewalk at the side of the hotel.

"The northwest corner of the compound was near the back of this building," he pointed to the rear corner of the Hotel Indigo. "Fortin de Condelle—we had two cannon right here. Our men were perched on top of the rubble of what had been a corner room."

He then pointed back toward the federal building, leading the way back directly across Alamo Street toward the building, not bothering with going to the crosswalk, being totally unfamiliar with that concept. He stopped near the side entrance and stood on the spot, gazing at the buildings beyond. It was certainly different from the view he had in 1836. But William Barret Travis was not looking at the buildings. He was seeing land, land with thousands of enemy troops converging on him, yelling "Viva Santa Anna," *El Deguello* playing by the Mexican buglers, cannon firing under his direction, and musket balls flying. He was off in his world. Bob and Lori stared at his determined face, detached from the present. They could tell that, for this moment, it was March 6, 1836, for the Alamo commander. Finally, he came out of his reverie.

"About here and extending right inside this building was Fortin de Teran, where I personally commanded the cannon, and where . . . ." he trailed off. Finally, he began again, "This wall was crumbling, no matter how much we kept patching it, it was our weakest point. We heaped dirt outside and in the interior, but it wasn't enough to stop them." He looked down sadly.

74

Meanwhile, it was a busy weekday, and people were walking to and fro, many to work at the federal building. Most of them stared and went on. One or two gave a salute. A small group of curious onlookers stopped, standing behind Travis, Lori, and Bob at a respectful distance. Lori could see one of the men in the group watching turn to the couple next to him. She could hear him, too.

"That's Col. Travis—see the bloodstains on his coat? They dug him up the other day, and he read his famous letter at the ceremony!" He was not subtle about pointing, although it was obvious which one of the trio was Travis.

The colonel noticed them but did not go over to them. Desirous to not be overcome by emotion, he headed back toward the church, acknowledging the onlookers with a salute. Two of the men saluted back. Travis led the way, walking across Houston, this time at the crosswalk, solely because it led where he wanted to go. Fortunately, there was no oncoming traffic at the moment, as he also had no clue about traffic signals. He headed south down the opposite side of Alamo Plaza from the way they had come. Bob and Lori followed.

"Colonel, there's something I want you to see," Bob called to Travis.

The Colonel stopped and turned. Bob was pointing to the Cenotaph, a large monument to the defenders—the one the colonel had marched by on his way to the north wall without even a sideways glance.

"Do you recognize anyone on this statue?" Bob asked with a smile.

The young man stared a moment, then moved closer and saw his name above a figure that somewhat resembled him.

"That's me!" he exclaimed. "I guess someone did remember. It's a beautiful monument. I am honored—for myself and my command."

After staring in amazement at himself in stone as well as the other heroes of the battle, the colonel resumed his trek, Bob and Lori still in tow. Travis paused in front of a cheesy establishment advertising itself as "Tomb Rider 3D Adventure Ride and Arcade," where customers took pot shots at skeletons and other ghoulish figures. A man covered with tattoos who worked there was sweeping the sidewalk.

"Say, want a job posing as one of our targets?" the man asked as he took in the colonel's face and bloodstained clothes.

Travis had no idea what he was talking about, but he did understand the word "target" better than most people. "No thank you, I've already done that," he said quietly.

He turned to Lori and Bob.

"You know, my quarters were right about here. There were houses along the inside of the walls of the compound. I made my quarters in the Trevino House—should be about here."

He pointed at "Tomb Rider 3D" and the adjacent "Ripley's Haunted Adventure." Not far ahead was Ripley's wax museum.

As they reached the church, it was 9:00. The colonel did want to go in the chapel, but he did not tour it. He just stood inside, quietly, with his head bowed. Tourists were beginning to stream in slowly. A few stared, but most probably thought he was a reenactor.

"Colonel, I have a couple more of your things in my office—it's in the building with the gift shop, if you would care to get them?" Bob asked quietly. There were a few rules about the Shrine—no photography, men were to remove their hats, and voices were to be kept low, out of respect for the fallen Texians.

At the word "colonel," the tourists turned and stared.

"Sir, are you a colonel?" one boy stepped up to Travis and inquired.

"Yes, son, I am," the tall Texian responded softly.

The boy was staring up at him intently now. He was about 6, and Lori was noticing that Travis seemed particularly moved.

The child finally got the nerve to ask, "How come there's all that blood on your coat?"

Travis bent down toward him. "I'm really from the battle," he said quietly. "They found me and brought me back. I was very badly wounded," he pointed to his face. "But I will be fine now. I have been ordered by the governor to defend the Alamo again—that's my job," he gently explained.

76

The boy's mother stepped forward, a look of awe on her face. "Colonel Travis?"

"Yes ma'am," he said softly.

All of the people in the chapel stared.

"Sir, you are the greatest hero in Texas," the mother said. Most of the other people were nodding in agreement.

"Thank you for your gracious words, ma'am, but my men are the true heroes—please honor and remember them," he said quietly.

The colonel took leave of his admirers, following Bob and Lori out the door and to the building housing the gift shop.

"Bob, I want to introduce him to Morena," Lori said.

They went in the shop, where Morena, her bracelets clanging, was arranging a display. She stopped when she saw out of the corner of her eye that people were headed her direction. Before she even completely looked in their direction, she asked, "Is there something I can get you?" When she focused on them, her mouth formed an "O" in shock.

"Lori, this was your surprise? This is why you bought the mug . . . . Colonel Travis, it is such an honor !"

Lori had never seen her friend so stunned. Morena usually was not hesitant for words.

"Ma'am, I am pleased to make your acquaintance," the proper young gentleman responded with a slight bow. "I understand that you helped Miss Lori pick out that cup for me? I do appreciate your efforts."

"The colonel will be released formally from the hospital this afternoon. He's going to stay with my family for a while," Lori said, hoping Travis would not go into his desire to live at the Alamo. She continued, "Before we go, I want to show him the fudge, Morena!"

"Fudge? What is that?" the confused Texian asked.

"It's a delicious candy—really sugary but silky. Here at the gift shop, we have our own varieties of fudge," Morena explained. She walked with them to the corner where the fudge display was. There were numerous varieties, mostly chocolate.

"Do you like chocolate, Colonel?" Morena asked.

"I've heard of it but never had it," he responded, staring at the case.

A few of the varieties had been dubbed with names relating to the place. A smooth as silk chocolate that would cut evenly with a knife had been named for Bowie. Another with a mixture of nuts and raisins thrown into the chocolate so that it resembled trail mix was named for Davy Crockett. Disgustingly, in William Barret Travis' mind, as he hunched over to read the names in the case, there was one—probably some sort of vanilla, but he would have had no idea—dyed bright red and called "*El Deguello.*" Finally, there was an orange cream fudge, not quite the color of his hair, but named in honor of the redhead.

"I normally don't give away fudge, but this is a special occasion. A piece for each of you is on me," Morena declared. Bob declined, citing trying to lose weight. Lori and Buck stared at each other.

"Oh, come on, is there any question here?" Morena prompted.

"No ma'am," replied the colonel. "We'll have the one titled 'William B. Travis'!"

She cut their fudge, and they did not stand on ceremony as to eating it.

"We didn't have anything like this at the Alamo in 1836!" the fudge's namesake proclaimed. "In fact, we didn't have anything like this at any time I can remember in my life. Thank you ma'am. I will be seeing you as I am assigned to duty here as soon as I am well enough, thanks to the governor!"

Morena smiled warmly. "I read about that. You come by any time, Colonel. Your fudge will be waiting for you!"

He gave her a salute, and she saluted back, the bracelets jangling.

They headed downstairs, Lori holding onto Buck as this was his first attempt at stairs. He had already been on his feet much longer than Lori had intended.

Bob's small office was a pigsty. He was one of those people who apparently brought everything he did not want at home to the office to stash. That or he had so much junk, period, that there was not enough room for all of it at either location. A cheap vinyl ottoman in an unattractive sienna shade was to the right, just inside the door. It had four vinyl buttons on top at one time, but there were only three left now. Admittedly, the overhead lights were not the brightest, but Bob had managed to squeeze five table lamps, none of which matched and all of which looked like motel rejects after a renovation, into the small space. He had two houseplants in serious decline. There was a large safe in the room, with a pile of miscellaneous mess precariously perched on top of it. The little room had two "guest chairs," as office workers called them, and he offered them to Lori and Buck, who quickly took him up on it.

"Colonel, as I think Lori mentioned to you, we have your hat and sword here—found them with you," Bob started. "The hat was sort of crushed, and it's rather worse for wear, but we had someone in the reenactor group take a look at it and block it back into the original shape. The sword has some rust on it. We cleaned it but couldn't get it all off."

Bob opened his center desk drawer and seemed to take an interminable amount of time trying to find the safe key. He finally located it under what Lori, who had a clear view of the drawer from her seat, determined was a hodge-podge of junk that had no bearing on doing a job at the Alamo. Bob opened the safe and pulled out the hat and rusted sword. As he did, the colonel rose from his seat and took a step toward him. Bob handed over the things, and Travis stared down at them, then carefully put on the hat, aware of the bandage on his forehead.

"I guess the belt and scabbard are gone?" he inquired.

"Apparently so," Bob replied. "We did not find them. Someone in the Mexican army must have wanted a sword belt and scabbard and taken them off of you when you were buried."

Travis had a strange, distressed look on his face, probably from that word "buried," Lori thought.

"Buck, why don't you sit down," she urged. He was beginning to look rather pale. She knew she would have to get him back to the hospital and didn't want them reneging on the promise to release him because she had kept him out too long and taxed his very limited stamina.

"If you want a scabbard for that thing, we can get you one easily—and

79

a sword belt," she added.

The colonel perked up, although his face still looked wan. "Yes, Lori, that would be very helpful. An officer really needs a belt and scabbard for his sword in this business," he said seriously.

She tried not to laugh and didn't ask what he meant by "this business."

They headed back, Buck sleeping most of the way. At least she had accomplished her goal, familiarizing him with the car, modern roads, and large buildings. The road she had taken was nothing like the one she took to get home, but he got a taste of life in the big city. As she was leading the tired colonel into the room, Dr. Gonzalez appeared.

"Everything OK? I came by about an hour ago, and no one was here—kind of thought you would be back." The doctor didn't sound upset, just worried.

"Sorry, it just took longer than we thought once we got there. Buck wanted to see where the north wall was. It's at the federal building and over to the edge of the Hotel Indigo now. That part of the compound is no longer part of the Alamo complex. But it's where he commanded the cannon—and where he fell. We spent a little time at the chapel and stopped at the gift shop so he could meet my friend Morena, the manager. She gave us some fudge. He had never had it before—a delicious orange variety named for him because it is close to the color of his hair."

"That's a nice thought," Gonzalez interrupted. "Fudge and hair—I always like to think of those two things together!"

Both of them laughed, and Lori went on. "Bob turned over the hat and sword."

Gonzalez stared at the rusty weapon. The colonel was clutching it even as Lori was trying to help him swing into the bed. As soon as he was lying prone, he was out. She gently released the sword from his fingers and put it on the table, placing the planter hat on top of it.

"Sounds as if he's already had quite a day," Gonzalez observed.

Lori was worried. "You aren't thinking about keeping him, are you?"

"We'll check him out one more time before release, but, no, I think he can go home with you," the doctor tried not to laugh at her anxiousness. "I will caution you, though, Lori, the tendency toward fainting is not just because he's weak after surgery. It is a brain function issue—a minor one, but people who faint easily are at more risk, obviously. It's sort of like epilepsy, only without the seizures. Stressful situations will likely increase his tendency to pass out. There could be other anomalies like this that will surface. I don't think he is likely to ever be totally well, given what he has been through, but that does not mean he can't function relatively normally, at least for someone from the Alamo. You will have to watch him, though. And remember, that left arm and wrist were broken. If he starts doing more, that could be a problem. Most important, there will be psychological issues. I'm sure with your dad being a military doctor, you know about some of that with people who have been in combat—PTSD. You've got to remember that the colonel has been in what is probably the worst combat situation in the history of this country, and suffered mutilation and burial and coming back after 181 years. He has done remarkably well, so far, but there will be issues and problems. You will have to be gentle, patient, understanding—and tough to handle him. Do you think you are up to it?"

"Yes, doctor. I think I can. I certainly will try." A tear flowed down her cheek, and she quickly wiped it away. "I am sure nothing will come of it, and I haven't told anyone in my family—and certainly not Buck, but the truth is I think I love him."

Gonzalez smiled. "Lori, that's been obvious to me. Take care of your young colonel."

# THE LINE

The colonel, still fully clothed, lay on the bed sleeping until 3:00, when an administrative worker came in with the release papers. There was no insurance, as Lori made clear. Colonel Travis was a charity case, although the hospital would likely file a claim with the state and tie his injuries to his Republic of Texas military service at some point. The Texians declared independence while the defenders were stuck in the Alamo, although the defenders never knew that. To Lori's relief, they did not make a big deal of the bill when it was time to go. Dr. Gonzalez and Maria were in the room when Lori and Buck headed out. Lori thanked the doctor and nurse profusely for the kind attention and care they had given Buck, and he quietly thanked them as well, shaking hands with the doctor, and bowing slightly to Maria and taking her hand gently in an old fashioned gesture.

The roads were bigger, and the trip was longer—she took her usual route, the McAllister Freeway, north out of downtown, but there were no surprises on the way to the Clayton home. Lori had already solved what seemed to be a problem causing concern for Buck that certainly would not be for ordinary folks. She had called one of her contacts at the Texian Association while the colonel was sleeping that last day at the hospital. She kept a tape measure with her sewing kit and measured the sword and described it for a friend who specialized in period weapons, even taking a photo and shooting it via text. The sword had some numbers on it, which meant something to him but not to her. He thought it would be relatively easy to hunt up a reproduction scabbard and sword belt for the Alamo commander, especially since Lori said Col. Travis had said it was necessary for his job. After all, even though the colonel had not yet met any of them except Lori, he was de facto their commander.

Major Clayton had just gotten in an hour ago. Elena had, as she promised Lori, broached the idea of having Travis stay at their home in a phone conversation while the major was in Houston, and he was fine with the idea. He had hurried home on the last day of the conference, wanting to be there when Lori drove up with Travis. Len did not seem to care too much one way or the other, but his mom had urged him to stay home instead of going over to Andres' house to play guitar this one day. Vicky was about to die of excitement—the guy in the weird movie that had so touched her was coming to stay at her house!

82

Elena and Robert Clayton were having a drink in the backyard next to the pool when Lori drove up. Len was practicing on his guitar. Andres had been teaching him a little Spanish guitar technique. Len was hooked on the sound and working his hardest to emulate the musically talented Andres' performance, something he knew he would likely never achieve. Vicky was about to go crazy, pacing back and forth and staring out the window in the living room constantly. When she saw the car, she ran for the front door, slamming it on her way out. Len just shook his head and kept playing.

Lori was out of the car and moving to the passenger side as Vicky got to her. Vicky could see someone sitting inside, but she mostly saw a white hat. Travis was looking down, trying to figure out how to unlatch the seat belt. He had not gotten the hang of it yet.

Lori opened the door, and he looked up to see Vicky standing with her. He noted her height—looked as if she would end up tall, like her sister. Unlike Lori, Vicky had reddish hair and large green eyes. She had an oval face and a pointed chin. He figured she would be very pretty when grown.

"Hello, Colonel!" Vicky greeted him enthusiastically. "I'm Lori's sister. We saw a movie about you in school last week. You are a really brave guy!"

He looked a little startled but smiled, softly replying, "Thank you, ma'am! That's very kind of you. I am so pleased to meet Lori's sister—she has been an angel helping me make all these adjustments! And she has told me a little about you. I will be honored to get to know you."

Lori had the seatbelt unlatched and helped him get out of the car. Vicky looked up as he stood. The colonel was tall, and had a soft Southern voice like his stand-in in the movie. She thought he looked younger than the actor and would have been very good-looking had it not been for the sword slash. She tried not to stare too much, as she knew it was rude.

Once out of the car, he took the hat off with a flourish, and bowed toward her. She tried not to focus on the bandage on his forehead and the long scar on his cheek as he made his gallant gesture. Vicky giggled. This guy was great. A bit weird and old-fashioned, but his gallant deference made her feel like a princess on a pedestal without all the silly baggage associated with such a position..

Robert and Elena had heard Vicky slam the door, and they put down their drinks and came to meet the colonel. Len kept strumming on the guitar until Elena nudged him. He followed his parents out the front door.

Robert Clayton extended his hand to Travis, who shook it with more strength than Robert would have guessed the colonel had. Travis noted the major's appearance. Lori's height clearly came from her dad's side of the family. The major was tall and trim with the same blonde hair as his daughter, a little gray at the edges. He had the same blue eyes as Lori.

Elena welcomed him less formally. More gregarious than her military husband, Elena put her arms around the young man, telling him to consider himself a member of the family. He noted that Mrs. Clayton looked more like Vicky. She had the reddish hair, green eyes, and oval face with pointed chin, but, unlike all of the rest of the family, she was tiny—not much over 5 feet tall.

Elena got the same gallant bow that Vicky had received, and she smiled at the colonel's 1800's style.

Len finally moved from behind his parents. He looked just like his father, only younger—tall, blonde, and blue-eyed.

In a soft voice, Len greeted Travis. "Welcome Colonel, Lori has said so much about you. We're so glad to finally meet you." He couldn't resist following up with, "I really like music—all kinds. Maybe you could tell me something about songs of the 1830's?"

"You should have been in the fort when Congressman Crockett played his fiddle!" Travis replied with a smile. "With all that dreadful waiting for what we knew was impending doom, Crockett was the one person who could actually lift the gloom and make folks laugh or sing. Yes, I think I can recall some of the tunes he played."

Len, who had nothing against Travis but had been the least enthusiastic member of the family regarding the colonel's move to their house, solely because he just didn't care about the Alamo, looked at the man in a new light. The music of the 1830's—something new to explore. Colonel Travis might be fun after all.

Vicky practically dragged Buck into the house, anxious to show him his room. Travis followed obediently. The spacious, open house was enticing, and the Spanish style, both inside and out, lent a little continuity to what he was used to, although it was a major improvement over anything he had seen in old Bexar. The spacious room and large bed with lots of pillows were beckoning, and his eye caught the little desk with the quill, ink, and paper—something that pleased him. He was tired after the trip and sat down on the bed, placing the hat on the table next to the bed. Vicky immediately sat down next to him. Buck thought to himself—I seem to have attracted both of the Clayton girls. I never really thought about it much in the old days, but maybe I do attract women?

It was March 1. Lori was sitting at her computer trying to get a little work done, her purse and giant water cup stashed under the tiny counter in the cubbyhole. She could hear the phone ringing in Bob's office next door.

"The Mexican consul's office? You folks would like to schedule a meeting here?" she heard him say politely but with more than just a question mark in his voice. There was a pause, then Bob responded to something from the other end of the phone.

"Yes, yes, by all means. That would be wonderful! But I'm thinking it might be a bit difficult to get something together for the 3rd." He wanted to be very delicate as to how he put this. "You know we're commemorating the dead who fell on both sides in the battle on the anniversary on the 6th—maybe a couple weeks after that when the crowds are smaller and things aren't quite so crazy around here?" He hoped that would do it.

Lori tried to focus on her work as Bob worked out the details. Whoever from the consul's office was on the other end had apparently agreed to the suggested delay. She wondered if she could arrange a family vacation, including Buck, on fairly short notice.

"Lori, I expect you heard some of that?" Bob stepped in.

"Something about the Mexican consul's office folks wanting to meet with us here?" she asked. "I don't try to pry, but the proximity being what it is, I can't help . . . ." she trailed off.

"I know—no problem," Bob smiled. "They're going to send a couple officials for a visit on the 14th—something about possibly loaning an artifact from the Mexican National Museum. You know, we've tried various means of getting the New Orleans Grays flag for decades—to no avail. Santa Anna sent it to Mexico City quickly because of its value as propaganda showing the United States was meddling in the fight. No other flags are known to exist. There's a possibility the Mexicans destroyed them, and the debate over what flew over the fort is endless. We do know that Travis paid $5 for a flag and took it with him to the Alamo. That's likely the

85

banner they flew. The IMAX movie shows lots of different flags on the premises, but the fort flag is a sort of reverse of the Confederate Bonnie Blue flag—a pattern that far predates the Civil War in both Texas and West Florida. As depicted in the film, that was a white flag with one blue star with 'Liberty' above the star and Travis' slogan, 'Victory or Death,' below. It's similar to the Goliad flag. I can certainly see him having something like that made!"

Lori laughed. "You realize we can get an answer to what flags flew over the fort in a hurry?"

Bob nodded with a smile and continued. "Mexicans are still bitter about the Alamo. It's awkward for them. Santa Anna was so bad that Mexicans do not hail him as a hero. But, when push comes to shove, they naturally side with him against the defenders. They are rather insulted that we have managed to take their victory and turn it against them, glorifying the losing side."

"Well, it's not too hard, considering what Santa Anna did to the defenders. But I see your point. Lots of Mexican boys—who probably didn't want to be there—were killed by the sharpshooting of Davy and the gang," she said.

"I don't think the consul's office is holding it against us. And this is all very preliminary regarding the loan. I honestly expect, based on past history, that it likely won't come off. If they do loan the artifact—we don't know that it is the flag—that's just a guess since I know they've got it, it will be just that, a loan. I can assure you that Mexico will never give up their trophies from the Alamo, based on the way Texans have historically treated the whole event if nothing else. The Mexicans are extremely suspicious of Texan motives regarding the artifacts—with good reason. But I really wish this had come up last year."

"Believe me, I had the same thought," Lori said. "I wonder if we can keep him away from here that day."

Bob replied, "I doubt it. I'm going to try to keep it secret as long as I can, and right now, he's fixated on the 6th. The guy from the consul's office appeared to be a history buff—from a Mexican slant, of course, and acted as if he was looking forward to the meeting. He did mention Travis—had followed the story in the news. We really don't need another battle of the Alamo when the Mexican officials get here."

86

"Yeah," Lori agreed, "But remember who is technically in command around here!"

That wasn't the only issue Bob had to face that day. One of the folks at the Texian Association had come up with an idea and presented it to him—this one on very short notice. Knowing Lori's involvement with the Travis revival, the group had already been after her to bring the colonel to their meeting, which she agreed to do. The meeting was set for the evening of the 2nd, at which they planned a practice for the March 6 ceremony. The Texians were after one additional ceremony, and it had to be on March 5, the day before the battle.

Legend had it, and it was the premier legend associated with the siege, that on the 5th—some sources placed it on the 3rd or another date, Col. Travis, knowing that the situation was hopeless and they were doomed, gathered his ragged troops. He made an inspirational speech to them, telling them that there was no hope, no one else was coming to help them, and that he intended to stay and die at his post. He then pulled out his sword and drew a long line in the dirt in front of the assembled men. Re-sheathing the sword, he told them that no one would be thought a coward if he decided to climb over the wall and head out and take his chances. But he asked that anyone who was willing to stay and die with him cross the line. One Frenchman in the garrison took Travis up on the offer to leave and did sneak out. It was through a convoluted trail from his story that the myth developed. Everyone else crossed the line, including Bowie, who was so sick that he had to be carried across. There were few corroborations of the account, which had only surfaced many years after the fight. Of course, all of those who crossed Travis' line died.

Lori had been tasked by the association with confirming whether the story was true, which she promised she would do that afternoon when she went home. If the line was really drawn, the Texians wanted desperately to reenact the event the afternoon of the 5th. Bob had already committed that they could do the line ceremony if they got confirmation that it actually happened. Lori left work a little early, promising to ask as soon as she saw Buck so that she could get their answer for them.

Robert and Elena were at work, and the kids were in school. Buck had been very tired after his long day the day before, what with the Alamo visit and meeting the Claytons and getting settled in. He had still been asleep when Lori left for work early in the morning. When she got home, all was quiet. She didn't see him anywhere else, so she peeked in his room. He had gotten dressed but was lying on the bed asleep. Going in, she called to him, but he didn't respond. Slightly fearful, she touched his shoulder, shaking it slightly, and he awoke, staring at her.

"Looks like you are catching up!" she greeted him.

"Sorry—didn't mean to just lie here. I'm getting way too lazy—need to start going in to work," he apologized.

"Maybe so—if you feel like it, but it's fine for you to just rest. You have been through an awful lot," she said quietly. "To change the subject, Buck, I've got a question for you—coming out of your headquarters!"

"Oh?"

"Yeah. The Texian Association, the folks who dress up to look like y'all in 1836 and stage reenactments of life back then, want to do an additional ceremony—before the big one on the 6th that we'll practice for tomorrow night. But, as seems to be the case with so many Alamo stories, we don't know for sure whether the event even happened. This one has to do with the afternoon or evening of the day before—March 5, at least that's our best guess as to the time—"

"Asking the garrison to step across the line if they would stay with me and commit to fight to the end?"

"Well, I guess that's the answer," she said. "So it's true?"

"Yes ma'am, it's true. I knew no one else was coming at that point." He wiped away a tear running down his good cheek. "I felt I owed it to everyone to tell them. Honestly, had most of them wanted to bolt, they would not have gotten through. The noose was way too tight. But one or two might. One man, a Frenchman named Rose, took me up on it. Everyone else walked across my line."

"I'll tell them. The reenactment will be planned along with the March 6 ceremony at the meeting tomorrow night. I'll guarantee that you will be asked if you want to portray yourself at the event," she told him.

"Yes. It's my duty. At least no one's life will be hanging on it this time. I can't tell you how that felt, having those brave souls look me in the eye and walk across and stand next to me . . . ." He started sobbing.

It was all too painful for Lori to imagine. She figured the tearful reactions he displayed when faced with his past were enhanced by the brain injury. In his earlier life, the colonel would have made every effort to hide his emotions. Now they just came out. She hugged him.

"Good thing the scabbard came for your sword. Looks as if you are going to need it!"

Lori took her new boss to work with her the next morning. She was dressed in her dull rose 1836 dress. The plan was to stay all day, as the Texian meeting and practice would be held at 6:00 on the grounds. Colonel Travis wanted to tell Bob in person about the famous line and that the ceremony was on. He wore the sword to the office, as if that might be a necessary tool for the job as well as the ceremony. Before getting down to work, Buck, who had been very taken with Morena's fudge, insisted on going to the gift shop to see if Morena had more. He almost stumbled over Bella, who was winding around his feet. She was something else unexpected, although he had, of course, seen cats before and actually liked them. He reached down to pet her, as did Lori. Everyone who came by Bella, including the commander, was obliged to acknowledge her, the little queen of the place.

"Miss Morena, I have finally made it to my post!" exclaimed the colonel proudly, as he removed the hat and repeated the little bow that he gave to women.

"So glad to hear it, sir!" she gave him a salute.

"I'm guessing you are in search of something to eat?" she laughed. He was looking toward the back right corner of the large room where the fudge was.

"Yes, ma'am. I am."

"May I get you a piece. Lori?"

She nodded eagerly. "But I insist on paying for it this time. Buck—I mean Col. Travis—will be getting a paycheck at the end of the month, but for now it's on me."

Morena simply smiled.

There was precious little room for "office" space in the Alamo compound. Bob had wrestled with what to do for Travis in that regard. The church itself was not really a possibility as it was truly a shrine, and not even the commander should really impose on that sacred purpose. Plus, the small building was full up with displays, which would soon be removed as a restoration project was already starting. Even had that not been the case, it was so dark that no one could see to work there, although, Bob thought, that would have been the case with anything in the compound in 1836. The colonel would have burned lots of candles, if he had them.

The only other historic building dating from his time still extant was the long barracks, originally quarters for Catholic religious functionaries before the Alamo became a military installation. Travis' real quarters across the plaza, the Trevino house on the inside west wall, had been razed with the rest of the west wall. The wall was replaced by the row of post-Alamo buildings housing the tacky amusement businesses, including the wax museum where the colonel could see a depiction of himself if he ever chose to, something Bob could not imagine from the serious young man. The colonel's original location was not an option.

The upshot of all of this was that Bob had directed that a few of the displays in the long barracks be shifted around, leaving one small area on the end free as "headquarters" and partitioning it off from the displays. Following Lori's earlier action, Bob had acquired a quill pen, ink, and paper from Morena and placed them on a little writing desk in the room. The room was wired for electricity, so he found a desk lamp—not one of the many crowding his office—and placed it on the desk. He also placed a candlestick and candles at the colonel's disposal in case the commander chose to continue his old-fashioned habits. Ed, the maintenance man, when moving the desk into the room, had inquired if computer hookup was required for whoever would be occupying the office. All Bob could do was laugh.

The truth was that there was very little real work Travis could do. He had no troops to command. With his appointment by the governor, he would be involved in meetings, approvals, and the like regarding ceremonies to be held at the post, but Bob and other staff members ran the day-to-day "civilian" aspects of the work. And Travis would have been clueless as to what to do about any of that anyway. For the most part, he would likely roam around, in uniform, with the sword clanking against his thigh, conjuring up images of long ago and maybe answering questions of tourists, whether or not they figured out who he was. He would, by default, be the star of the show during Texas High Holy Days at the numerous Alamo ceremonies, most coming right at this time of year, the siege anniversary. Undoubtedly, there would be correspondence coming in for which a reply from the commander was the most appropriate response, and Bob would gladly "bump that upstairs" to his new boss. Although it would be in old-time script on old-time paper, using a quill pen, which was most appropriate if a bit quaint, this was Travis' greatest skill. His ability with words transcended time.

Lori had clued Bob in that the new boss was coming to work. He figured, based on the last foray and Travis' reaction to Morena's fudge, that they might be in the gift shop so headed upstairs from his office. Sure enough, the Texian leader was actually licking his fingers as Bob headed their way.

"Want me to show you your new office, sir?" Bob asked with a sloppy salute.

The colonel looked up, then saluted back with a grin. "This fudge surely is good!" he commented, turning to face Morena directly as he said it.

He tipped his hat and made another slight bow toward her, then followed Bob out the door, this time watching for friendly little Bella.

As Lori had already discovered in her decision to simplify the bedroom at home as much as possible, the colonel did not need much to make him happy. Bob's Spartan décor seemed to please Travis greatly.

"About the same as what I had before," he noted, looking around. "Although, of course, I was over there," he pointed in the direction of the wax museum, Haunted Adventure, and Tomb Rider. "Yes, it will do nicely. Thank you," he said to Bob in the soft drawl.

There was one extra wooden chair in the little room in addition to the wooden desk chair. The two men sat down to discuss exactly what Travis could or would do. Lori was very happy Bob had to navigate that one.

She went to her car and pulled out the skillet. The long-awaited cactus cooking demo was at hand. Morena came out to watch as Lori started a fire and began very carefully getting the spines out of her cactus, holding the pads down with one knife, while scraping the spines off with another, then cutting it in pieces. She threw a little bacon grease—calling it hog fat for effect—in the pan, then scraped her cactus pieces off the wooden board and into the crackling grease. All the while, she was explaining what kind of cactus it was—prickly pear, how people came to start eating it—it was originally a Native American food source, and what she was doing in the

91

preparation. It actually smelled kind of good, but that was because of the bacon grease.

A reenactor, dressed in an elaborate Mexican civilian costume, came up to her. He was a handsome, dark man just slightly overweight, with longish wavy black hair and bright, dancing brown eyes.

"Hey, Lori, what's the latest with Col. Travis? Did you ask him about the line in the sand?"

"Hi Raul! Actually, the new boss came to work with me today," she replied as she stirred her delicacy. "He confirmed it right away. All I had to do was tell him we were interested in doing an additional short ceremony on the afternoon of the 5th, and he immediately mentioned the line without any prompting. He also said he felt duty bound—you will discover when you meet him that just about everything is duty bound with Col. Travis," she laughed as she stirred, "to play himself in the reenactment."

"Fantastic! I'll tell everyone else. We may want to do a quick run-through on that one as well this evening. I would love to meet him."

"He's tied up with Bob now. I think they're going through the details of what exactly the colonel will do here," she explained.

"What will he do here?" Raul asked practically, raising his eyebrows.

"Well, we all know it's pretty much a made-up thing, except, quite honestly, for his participation in events and inspiration to all who come through here—and maybe he will write some more famous letters?" she shrugged as she continued stirring. She looked down. "It's about done."

"I don't mind if he writes letters, but I hope they don't carry the weight of his last batch," Raul responded.

"Yeah, I know what you mean. Want a piece of fried cactus?" She was taking the pieces out, one by one, and placing them in a big wooden bowl.

Raul eagerly reached for one. He shook his finger slightly. "Wow! Still hot, but, man, is that good!"

As he finished, he heard someone walking up behind him. He turned slightly.

"Finally got around to the cactus demo, I see, Lori! I would like a piece of that!" Bob laughed.

Raul was not looking at him, but at his companion. It was obviously the colonel—tall, young, redheaded, and in what the reenactors casually called a "Travis outfit." The young man had a hesitant, skeptical look on his torn-up face. Raul broke the ice.

"Sir—Colonel Travis, sir! It is such an honor to meet you. I'm Raul Cruz—I portray Juan Seguin in our reenactments," he practically gushed, hoping his fingers were not too greasy from the cactus as he held out his hand to the Alamo commander.

Travis gave a reserved smile in response and shook Raul's hand. He had looked the Mexican over quickly first, determining that he was not one of Santa Anna's men so, presumably, OK.

"A pleasure to meet you, sir, as well," he responded somewhat formally. Then he turned to Lori. "May I have a piece of that?"

Raul, Bob, and Lori all tried to suppress a laugh. Colonel Travis seemed to always be hungry, and he apparently would eat just about anything.

"What exactly do y'all demonstrate from my time, besides cooking?" Buck asked softly once Raul and Bob had gone on.

"Lots of things. The reenactors are so serious about trying to be authentic that they even have lists of acceptable activities. For women, there are the spinning, weaving, and sewing arts, washing clothes, rug beating, making soap, and making brooms. I like the period cooking best. The cactus is the most unusual item I do, but I make Texian cornbread . . . ."

"That sounds good!" Buck interrupted.

Lori laughed. "Well, there's that, and corn and cured meat. You can tell me for sure, but folks apparently didn't eat much fresh meat then—wasn't practical as there was no way to save it."

He nodded. "Yes, we actually had much more variety in food when I was growing up in South Carolina and Alabama. Didn't have too many chickens in Texas as it was too hard to keep the predators from getting them. I love chicken. We did go fishing in Texas."

"Men's demonstrations tend to involve making or fixing tools or weapons, firing weapons, molding musket balls, leather work, chopping and splitting wood, and—this one might suit you—making quill pens and demonstrating how to write with them!"

"Well, if anyone wants me to demonstrate how to write a letter," the somewhat incredulous young man responded, "I'll be glad to do that, but I just bought my quills from a store in San Felipe—didn't make them, although I could probably figure it out."

"At Christmastime, we lighten things up a bit—have period games for the children—a fun one is Devil Amongst the Tailors, Christmas carols, and I show folks how to make corn husk angels. Of course, there are the more 'fun' parts of 1836 life in general—the ones Congressman Crockett excelled at—storytelling and playing music!" she added. "Those are the ones I enjoy watching the most."

"He truly had a knack for that—the man single-handedly kept us somewhat sane when we were cooped up here. I can see how he got elected to Congress. I would vote for him!" Buck replied.

Lori smiled. She didn't want Buck to go too far into reminiscing about his sad other life, so she changed the subject slightly.

"One more thing about the demonstrations—I would really appreciate it if you would help me if something comes up where I need another person sometime?"

"Surely," he agreed, "I would be most honored."

"The so-called rules for all of this from the reenactors' association warn participants that they might get some strange questions from the public. When you are in character as someone from 1836—not exactly a problem for you, Buck, since you are a character from 1836, there are some difficult queries the public may ask you."

"Such as?"

"Your favorite food, which has to be something they ate in 1836—should be an easy one for you. What do you like most and least about your new home in Texas? Can you read and write?—again, that one will be easy. What social conventions do you like to break and what do you do in your free time?"

"I might need to be a little careful on that one," Buck interrupted with a little frown. "Some of my free time was spent more judiciously than other."

"Well, and here's another one that could be related to that—'What types of sickness have you had since you've been in Texas?'"

"Same thing there—I hope they don't ask me those!"

It was just after 5:30, closing time at the Alamo, and the Texian Association members were almost all assembled for their meeting. Lori had taken Buck to the River Walk to find something to eat for dinner before the meeting. She had been thinking about Mexican, but he spotted the Republic of Texas Restaurant—not hard to do with their colorful umbrellas and Texian theme—and would not be dissuaded. Although the colonel was a good fit for this establishment, he continued to turn heads as usual. But people there seemed to assume they were both just reenactors, especially since she was "dressed up" as well. The food was delicious, and Lori was grateful to see Buck's one-track mind result in something pleasant.

Raul and the rest of the "troops," as well as their ladies, were lounging on the grounds in back of the facility when Lori and Buck strolled up. Most of the reenactors were sitting on the ground, talking in groups. When the couple approached, everyone stood, the men automatically coming forward and standing in some semblance of a military formation. They all, in unison, saluted, then gave three "Huzzahs" for their heroic leader.

The colonel seemed very comfortable with all of this, and gave a salute in return, standing and facing his "men." Lori, standing slightly off to the side, wondered if he was going to go ahead and draw the line with his sword right now, but he did not. He did introduce himself:

"Ladies and gentlemen, thank you for honoring me so. As I am sure you know from the news reports, I am William Barret Travis, and the governor of Texas has graciously returned me to my post in command of the Alamo. I take my responsibility very seriously, and I will make every effort to discharge my duty to the best of my ability for the honor of Texas and the country. I continue to believe that the brave sacrifice of my garrison in 1836, horrific though it was, was a necessity to buy time for those to our east to rally in the face of Santa Anna. Although I hope it never comes to that, I would personally make that sacrifice again, for Texas, if the situation requiring it arose. I look forward to our effort, in the meantime, to educate

95

today's citizenry as to the events in which I partook so long ago. Victory or Death!"

Wild cheers erupted from the reenactors. The colonel made a slight bow, then resumed his ramrod straight posture, gazing out at his troops for a moment. He finally ordered them to break ranks. Lori noted that he clearly was a commander, knowing exactly what to do. Good thing the Texian Association worked so hard at authenticity and hopefully met some of his expectations!

The meeting was not a very formal affair, and that part of the gathering lasted no more than 10 minutes. There was an acknowledgment of Texas Independence Day. Someone moved for Col. Travis to be made an automatic member, waiving dues, application forms, and other requirements, which was immediately seconded and voted on, unanimously "for," of course. At that point, Raul, who was vice president of the group, the president being the reenactor who was out of the country when Bob was searching for someone to read the letter, made the announcement that they would be doing the line in the dirt ceremony at 3:00 on the 5th—just 3 days away. He had worked out the details with Bob earlier that afternoon. As to exactly how it would be played out, he started to give instructions, then stopped abruptly and turned to Travis.

""Sir, you are, obviously, the only person here who was present at the original. Would you mind giving us directions?"

The colonel stepped forward and gave another salute, and the men saluted in return. Lori was thinking she was glad she was not in the military. She noted how different the modern reenactors likely were from the real defenders. Most were overweight, some even obese, a situation she was quite sure would not have been the case in the food-deprived Alamo. One man looked old enough that he might have been there in 1836, a tall, extremely thin, bent old man with a face as wrinkled as a prune.

"Men, I will call you up in single-file formation, every man to line up facing me, with about 12 feet separating us. That marker noting the event is a little too close to the church. I will stand approximately where I stood in 1836. I will make a few remarks about our situation and my intent to stay and fight, and let those who want to leave do so with honor. At that point, I will step forward slightly, walk to one end of the line, unsheathe my sword, and draw a line with it across the dirt. I will then ask everyone who is willing to stay and fight with me to cross that line. Historically, there was one gentleman who did not; everyone else did. Of course, I see far fewer participants this go-around than in the original, so it makes little difference to me if one man wants to decline to cross."

"Sir, with your permission," Raul asked, "I believe we would all like to cross the line and stand with you on the 5th."

"Permission granted," the colonel replied with a slight smile creeping through his serious mien. "Now, let's run through it one time."

Everything went like clockwork. Travis provided a noble-sounding extemporaneous speech that was likely his original, Lori thought. He lived and breathed those last few days of his life, and, the way he recalled his famous letter when he was so weak he couldn't stand, she was pretty sure that the words he pronounced at this practice had been heard before, long ago. That would be settled on the 5th when he spoke at the ceremony—she would listen carefully to see if he repeated today's version.

When the colonel was through drawing his line across the grass at the back of the complex with his sword, and everyone had come across to join him to die for Texas, they had to move on to the finale. Lori felt much more trepidation about this than the line ceremony. The fact was, although the solemn ceremony on the 6th was, for years, the province of the dying Texians, it now was a two-sided affair. Mexican reenactors had their own organization, made up of partisans as fervent for their side—or at least close to it—as the Texians were for theirs. The modern routine had El Presidente and a handful of his thousands of troops come in, sometimes with the Generalissimo on horseback, and sometimes a few others mounted as well. They played *El Deguello* as they came in and formed in front of the church. Then the Texian defenders marched in, no horses, and with someone with a sword, dressed as Travis, directing them. They stood in formation, guns at the ready. Then, each side would fire a volley. While the troops were coming in, someone, often a Hispanic woman to make sure there was some sort of representation for the female half of the population in our multicultural country, made a speech telling of the sad events of that day in 1836 in as neutral a manner as possible. Then followed the most lengthy part of the event, descendants of the long-dead defenders laying wreaths, all featuring yellow roses, and some the names or, if there was one, pictures of the related defenders. The Travis relatives, Texans and a few all the way from Alabama, a number of them with that same red hair as the colonel, normally appeared in force with a large wreath, as befitted the fact that their ancestor was the commanding officer. They had been clued in by Bob that there was no need to bring a wreath this year, but they were anxious to meet the young man who propelled their family to fame so long ago. A very few Mexican families brought wreaths to honor their loved ones. Finally after the families and numerous DRT chapters and other groups laid all the wreaths in the crowded little grassy area, the troops filed out, first the Texians, then the Mexicans. That was it, short and sweet. Called "Dawn at the Alamo," the goal was to be through right as the sun was rising above the old chapel.

Lori cringed as Raul got up to explain what they were going to do. Fortunately, he did not say much. There was no need to run through the entire routine—so he thought—because all the Texian Association members knew it. He did hurriedly run through the basics, and there was mention of the Mexicans but no detail as to which Mexicans, and certainly no reference to Santa Anna or *El Deguello*. Consequently, they did not really practice most of the ceremony, especially since the aforementioned Mexicans were not there. There was a quick march in alignment to the position where they would stand at the event, the colonel at the side of the line with his sword, but that was it.

It was late when they finished all of this, and the Texian reenactors were all dying to do something other than die in the Alamo—they wanted to meet and talk with their leader. Poor Buck was getting very worn out, and he had to sit down to keep from falling over. Finally, after Lori thought everyone there had extracted at least one handshake from their commander, she got him up and out of there and back home where he promptly fell on the bed, asleep, still dressed. She was pleased that everyone had met Buck, and she was sure the line drawing ceremony would be wonderful—but March 6 not so much. Of course, the original hadn't been too great, but she was concerned about what Buck might do if he saw Santa Anna or heard *El Deguello*. She had witnessed his initial caution with folks like Dr. Gonzalez and Raul, Mexican but clearly not the hated enemy.

After that very full day of work and event practice on the 2nd, Lori and Buck took off and slept late on the 3rd. She had to wake him up that morning. He was still in the same position he fell into when he landed on the bed the evening before, obviously exhausted. She shook his shoulder slightly.

"What?" he mumbled, still pretty much asleep.

"Buck, you've been sleeping for 12 hours!" She shook him again slightly.

He rubbed his eyes. "Sorry, I was just so tired," he apologized.

"That's OK. You needed the sleep. I've got some coffee brewed. Want some?"

"Yes, maybe that would help," he said with a yawn.

He followed her into the kitchen and stood while she got his "Victory or Death" mug and a cup for herself from the cupboard. The guy seemed to appreciate coffee more than anything else in the world. He looked so serene—not a look one normally saw from William Barret Travis—with his coffee in hand. They were enjoying the brew when a noise came from down the hall.

"Vicky, what are you doing here?" Lori asked in surprise.

"Boy, Lori, you really have been out of touch—teacher planning day. I'm here all day," she responded. She turned up the friendliness. "Hi Colonel! How are you doing this morning?"

"Sleepy," he responded.

"I love that cool cup," she told him. "Lori picked the perfect one for you!"

Although she was only nine, Vicky pretty much did whatever struck her fancy since her parents were gone to work much of the time when she was home. She got a mug and helped herself to the coffee. After all, if Col. Travis liked it, it was good enough for her.

"Vicky, is there anything to eat around here?" Lori asked.

Her little sister was right. She really was out of touch as to the routine goings on of the family lately.

"Yeah. We've got some cinnamon buns in the breadbox. Mom got them at the store yesterday," she responded, getting up to get them. She opened the box and plopped it in the middle of the table, no standing on ceremony with plates and other accoutrements. Buck didn't care. He reached for one immediately, Lori not far behind. There were nine when they started, none when they finished.

"Buck, you know some of the pieces of your outfit aren't going to last too much longer. I'm thinking I need to take you with me to a fabric store and get something so I can start making replicas," Lori advised the colonel, who was downing his last gulp of coffee, ready to pour another cup.

He wasn't sure what a fabric store was, other than the obvious from the name, but he nodded. Travis liked nice clothes, but he had always just paid other people to produce them, not worried about the details, although his diary made clear that he had, personally, bought fabric in his prior life.

Lori continued, "I think we should use this day off to shop for fabric so I can get started making some of these pieces before something tears up or falls off of you during one of these ceremonies—depending on the details, that could be awfully embarrassing!"

He nodded again, not incredibly interested in the idea of picking out fabric, poured the coffee, and inhaled it before taking another swig of it. Vicky quickly volunteered that she would like to go with them. Lori couldn't say no very well, although she knew her little sister had never displayed the slightest interest in Lori's historic clothing hobby. The child had a crush on Col. Travis.

By 11:00, the colonel had drained most of a pot of Joe, and they were ready for their next adventure. There were still a few chain fabric stores, although one of the largest chains had closed all of their locations and gone bankrupt lately. Sewing had made a nosedive in popularity. Folks who needed costumes for their historic impressions were an exception to this general rule, and there were a few unique shops scattered around the country specializing in historically appropriate fabrics and notions for reenactor clothing. Fortunately, and obviously fueled by the fact that the Alamo was in town, San Antonio had one of these establishments. It was a small store, out of the way, and much of their business was actually mail order from people around the country looking for something that met picky historic specifications for an impression of whatever or whoever they were trying to represent. That's where they were headed. The lady who owned the place, Cathy Johnson, knew Lori well and had even met Vicky when she tagged along once before, but Cathy gave that same stunned "deer in the headlights" look that Lori had seen numerous times from people when she first gazed on the colonel.

"You've got to be kidding!" were the first words out of her mouth as she continued to stare.

"Cathy, this is my friend Col. Travis—of Alamo fame," Lori introduced the colonel, who, as usual, made his little bow and extended his hand to the shell-shocked proprietress.

100

Cathy stammered something about a great honor, and the colonel gently thanked her, then Lori got down to business.

"Cathy, we need your help. As you can see, the colonel could use some new clothes. What he is wearing is what he wore at the fight—was buried in these," she started, noting that Buck looked down as she said it. "While we will want to preserve his Alamo uniform, it is coming apart—I have already had to mend pieces several times. I need equivalent fabrics for the coat, vest, and pants to what he has on now."

Still a little bit in awe, Cathy gathered her wits and pointed them to a back corner of the store. "We have the reenactor fabrics over here."

Lori recalled that, but the truth was that she had mostly made ladies' items, which were forward and to the left of the wools.

"Colonel, I don't mean to be presumptuous, but would you mind if I felt the fabrics in your clothes? It will make it easier for me to find appropriate pieces of the correct weights," Cathy inquired.

"No, not at all," he replied quietly. He stood straight and stiff as she felt the rather thick wool of his coat and the slightly lighter weight wool of his pantaloons, and then asked, "What is your vest made of?"

He unbuttoned the double-breasted coat and revealed a pale golden yellow silk waistcoat with a slight pattern to it, like the coat, badly bloodstained.

Cathy wisely and calmly ignored the stains. "Hmm? Yellow. Do you want yellow again?" she asked him.

"I thought it went well with the blue coat," he answered. "What do you have that would do?"

Lori was thinking to herself—yes, it's as he recorded in his diary—he is sort of particular about clothes—for a guy.

They walked to the next row of bolts, lighter-weight fabrics than the wools, many of them heavier silks similar to his vest.

"Well, there is one light golden yellow—actually, not quite the same but very similar to what you have on. What do you think?" Cathy inquired.

101

He examined it, looking at the bolt, then glancing at his vest, then at the bolt again. "Yes, yes. I think that would do quite well," he responded.

They headed back to the wools and found the pieces for the coat and pants. Lori had all of the measurements and relayed the fabric amount requirements to Cathy for cutting. She picked up some flannel for more drawers and linen for a couple of shirts for Buck as well. She would obtain buttons for the coat from one of the sutlers—there was at least one that specialized in Texian and Republic of Texas goods. Vicky fidgeted and stared at the colonel while Lori worked with Cathy. Finally, she motioned to him to follow her. They went out front while Lori wrapped up her mission.

"Colonel, I have a question for you," Vicky began.

"Yes?" he inquired.

"In this movie about you, a girl from our time goes to a library and is reading a book for a report she has to do at school. She opens the book, and the last half of it is missing—empty pages. Anyway, as she starts reading, she is transported to the Alamo . . . ."

"That's no place for a young girl to go, believe me!" he exclaimed.

"Yeah, I know," Vicky answered. "But, in the story, she did. As she read more, pages of the book, which was a biography of YOU, filled up. Finally, near the end, she was back at the Alamo again and was reading an old letter left on a desk. It was from you to a friend, asking him to take care of your little son. You came in and said it was private and for her not to read it . . . ."

Vicky was so into her story that she did not realize how pale Travis had turned. He suddenly dropped like a rock, just missing her when he fell.

"Lori! Lori!" she screamed for her sister, who had just paid and was getting ready to head out the door. Lori ran as she saw Buck on the ground. Cathy followed her in horror.

"Oh, my God, what happened, Vicky?" Lori cried, dropping the bags of fabric and stooping to lift Buck's head slightly.

"I don't know, he just dropped. I was telling him about his movie," she explained. The child, who was not usually afraid of anything, looked scared to death. "I hope I didn't somehow kill him?"

"Huh? What do you mean?" Lori asked.

"I mentioned the part in the movie about his son . . . . I wanted him to tell me about that."

"Oh, Vicky, you didn't!" Lori cried.

Vicky looked terrified. Lori turned her attention to Buck. She looked him over carefully. There was no apparent damage that she could see. She turned back to Vicky.

"Did you see if he hit his head?"

"No, he just kind of crumpled—don't think he hit his head—at least not with impact," she responded.

"He's subject to frequent fainting—one of the results of the brain injury," Lori explained to her little sister. "He faints quite a bit, but, if you brought up the topic of his little son, I'm sure that did it. You said yourself that the movie showed that he really did love his child," Lori explained.

She was somewhat exasperated that Vicky had done this, although she could see why the child would want to explore it. The movie had obviously really made an impression on her.

Lori was sitting on the pavement with Buck's head in her lap, stroking his hair. He finally started to awaken, turning his head slightly, then looked up into her face. His eyes were full of tears. They came streaming down his face, and he shook slightly. Lori held him close.

"It's OK Buck, really, it's OK. Vicky didn't mean to hurt you," she said gently.

Finally, after what seemed like forever, he felt well enough to stand with Lori's help. She got him back in the car and home as quickly as possible. She put him to bed, where he promptly was out. Lori sat quietly by the bedside. Vicky was there, too. She touched the sleeping man's hair.

"He's got such pretty hair. He's not going to die like in the movie, is he?" she said in a whisper.

Lori hugged her. "No, honey, he's weak, but he won't have another Alamo. He won't die. But you need to be sensitive to other people about things that could hurt them. I know you are curious about his son, since it was a focus of the movie, but think from his perspective before you say anything. Just because—what was it you said he said in the movie—something about lots of things being worth living for but few worth dying for but freedom was one of those?"

Vicky nodded, a tear rolling down her face.

"Well, he did not want to die. He was young and smart and had lots to live for and had a little boy. He also had a fiancée who made him very happy. His child and girlfriend are all long dead in the distant past. Think how you would feel . . . ."

"I'd rather not—it's too . . . too sad," Vicky said slowly.

"Right. Think how sad it was for him when you mentioned his little boy—the child grew up without his dad," Lori said quietly.

"But, like in the movie, he knew he was doing it—he knew he would not see his son again," Vicky pleaded.

"Yes, that's true. But it was something he felt he had to do so that freedom might prevail, for his son and all the generations who came after—like us. He made a very great sacrifice, Vicky, and he has given everything he had and all he loved. Fact is, the poor guy really pretty much fixates on his duty to the Alamo. It is our duty to this brave young man to give him some reason for living beyond his past, which no one can retrieve, and functioning as the commander of the Alamo, which is a constant reminder of the horror of that place. He's only 26."

"That's what the librarian kept saying in the movie," Vicky interjected.

"Well, he was right. But Buck is with us now, and he's still only 26. We need to find reasons for him to want to live now."

"Do you suppose he would let me call him Buck?" Vicky ventured hesitantly.

"Ask him. That's what I did. But right now, let's let him rest. I wouldn't bring up his son again—he will do it in time, when he's ready. When he does, we need to be ready to support him. By the way, the little boy's name was Charles Edward Travis," Lori told her sister.

Vicky brushed her hand across the pretty red hair, then she bent over and kissed him on the forehead.

The colonel stayed home on Saturday, as did Lori. He was still drained from the day before. She had originally planned to go in to work, but she had called Bob on Friday afternoon with a brief report as to Travis' reaction when Vicky mentioned his son. Considering that Sunday was the line ceremony and with March 6 looming, Lori determined that she needed to keep her charge calm and rested as much as possible for the events ahead. He awoke at 8, dressed himself, made a quick entry in his diary, and ventured out into the quiet house. Everyone seemed to be sleeping, but, mercifully, someone had put the coffee on. He had no clue what to do with the bizarre-looking machine that produced the brew, but it had stopped making noise, the indicator that the coffee was ready. He had seen where Lori kept his mug, and he retrieved it and poured a cup of Joe. He fought tears as he thought about young Charles. He could still picture his child's sad face when he hugged him for the last time, leaving the boy in the care of his friend David Ayers. Of course, he did not know what happened to Charles after that. He had tried desperately to shove it to the back of his mind, as he did Rebecca Cummings, the special sweetheart who laughed and loved and made him forget all those earlier one-night stands that he had dutifully recorded, scribbled in Spanish, in his journal. Once he had become close to Rebecca and they exchanged engagement gifts, a ring from her to him and a brooch from him to her, the fooling around slowed considerably, but not completely, although their relationship was apparently not one that waited for marriage. Young William Barret Travis was growing up, although still subject to occasional lapses, duly recorded for posterity. Now, all these eons later, all of that was dim history—except to him. He wiped away one more tear, then turned his full attention to his coffee. He was staring at the "Victory or Death" cup when he heard a noise. He looked up and saw Vicky. She noticed as a strange look passed fleetingly across his face.

"Colonel? Are you feeling OK today?" she asked hesitantly.

"Yes, I am—got some rest. How about you?" he replied kindly, knowing the child had not meant to hurt him. Children were one of the colonel's weaknesses. He obviously liked them, and the diary and other accounts were replete with mention of his buying candy or a book for a child of some friend or acquaintance.

Vicky nodded. She got a mug and helped herself to a cup of coffee.

"I'm fine," she said, looking at him earnestly. "I would never hurt you deliberately," she continued. "I like you very much."

"That's sweet, Vicky. And I know you wouldn't hurt me. I like you very much, too," he said softly.

"One more thing," she asked, her green eyes round, "I'm not into formality when I can help it. Could I call you Buck like Lori does?" She almost looked fearful of what his answer might be.

"Surely! The way you put that reminds me of when Lori did it! I'll give you what I said to her—Buck it is!"

She giggled and ran to him, putting her arms around him, then returned to her place, and they both sipped their coffee in the silent house.

A half an hour later, the place came to life. The rest of the family arose, some showering, while Elena, who was ahead of the pack, came in for her own cup of brew, then started working in the kitchen.

"Eggs and grits OK?" she called to Buck.

"Yes, ma'am!" he replied. "Anything I can do to help?"

"I've got to ask, as commanding officer, did you do anything to help in the kitchen at the Alamo?"

"No, not really," came the sober response.

"That's what I suspected. No offense, colonel, but I want to be sure breakfast is edible! Quite frankly, I don't have a high opinion of what you folks likely ate back then—kind of got the idea that good food meant it hadn't spoiled and wasn't too tough to eat. And I certainly would have to question what the commander might turn out!"

He laughed. "I see your point. I could set the table. I know how to do that!"

"All right, then. Plates on the shelf above where we keep the mugs—I see you already found that. We mix and match around here. As long as everyone has a plate, a cup, and utensils, we're good!"

"And the utensils?"

106

She pointed to a drawer directly underneath the cabinet where the plates and mugs were. "It's kind of hard to miss, the way I have it set up!"

He laughed, counted in his head the number of people, and very neatly set the table while Elena scurried around. She always cooked bacon ahead, allowing her to simply pull it out of the freezer and pop it in the microwave to warm up. Buck stood far enough out of the line of fire as to not get in her way, but he watched her intently. All the machinery she was using was amazing to him. But bacon still smelled just like it did in 1836. The rest of the family was now there, everyone assembled. Lori and Vicky helped dish out the grits, eggs, and fried apples, while Buck took a knife worthy of Jim Bowie and cut apart a pan of biscuits and placed them in a basket. Robert and Len, sipping coffee, watched the finely-oiled process with delight. Who knew that the commander of the Alamo could do something beyond give orders, write a great letter, wave a sword around, kill Mexicans, and die bravely for his country?

Buck had thought the egg meal at the hospital was good. He really did not know what good was until he tasted Elena's version. He thought he had died—again—and this time gone to heaven. Just sitting around a table with a family who indicated he was welcome made him feel a slight hope that there was some purpose in all of this beyond just the need to mount another stoic defense of the Alamo. The young man, who, with his Baptist background, could be religious at times but more often flaunted religious teachings, was having one of the former moments right now. He said a quick prayer to a God he thought might be up there somewhere, giving thanks for something beyond blood and killing in the Alamo.

It was March 5, time—this afternoon at 3:00—to draw the line. In anticipation of that fact, both Lori and Buck headed in to work. They got there right at 9:00. Bob was getting out of his car as they pulled in. Buck went straight to his quarters—he hated to hint to Morena about fudge every time he showed up at the place. Lori headed to her little cubbyhole. Bob settled in at the sty. Among Lori's other duties was checking the mailbox each day. Having been off the previous day, she headed out to check for yesterday's mail, followed by the meowing Bella, who wanted something to eat besides fresh rat. Lori opened the box, pulled out several pieces of mail, and started sorting through the letters. There was nothing that looked exciting, although there was one envelope in a child's scrawl addressed simply to "The Alamo." She handed the cache over to Bob, who sorted through it quickly. The child's letter caught his eye, too, and he ripped the

107

envelope open as Lori was heading back to her station.

"Hey, Lori, you've got to see this one," he called to her as he was reading. "Although the envelope was addressed to the Alamo, the letter is to the colonel. I'll have to walk over to his office with it."

It was written in very poor, unsteady writing on pink paper with red hearts that looked for all the world like something someone bought at the after-Valentine's sale. The letter itself was something else:

> "Dear Col. Travis,
>
> > "You don't know me. My name is Marcie. I am 9, and I live in Dallas. My mom told me that they found you at the Alamo and that you fought there a long time ago. I hear you are very brave. She said you were shot in the head and had been in the hospital. I hope you are OK. I am in a wheelchair. I was hit by a car right before Christmas, so I know what it is like to not feel good.
> >
> > "We saw a movie about you in school. It was very sad. I cried. You had a little boy in it but had to leave him to go die at the Alamo. I am glad you are back and hope you are OK and not too sad.
> >
> > "Love,
> >
> > "Marcie Adams"

"Oh no, poor child!" Lori exclaimed. "But, Bob, we can't give this to Buck to answer."

"Why not? It's addressed to him, and last time I looked, it's a federal offense to take someone else's mail."

Lori explained the scene with Vicky at the fabric shop.

"You said something briefly about that when you called the other day, but I didn't know the details," Bob said. "Well, what do we do?"

Lori glanced up at what she thought was a passing shadow. Buck was standing there. He had heard the whole thing.

108

"It's all right, Lori. Really, it is," he said quietly. "I've got to come to terms with it. Could I see what she says?"

He reached a hand out toward her, and she handed him the letter. As Travis read the injured child's words, he started tearing up, looking rather strained, not as if he were going to go into a faint, but just at the thought that a little girl was caught in such a terrible situation.

"That movie must really be popular in the schools," Lori observed.

"I will admit I would like to see how they are portraying me," Buck responded. "I will answer this child, and try to comfort her. I can't really imagine that something from me will make her feel any better, but I'll do what I can. I suspect it took her quite some effort to write this," he noted with keen perception.

He looked up, staring at them with what could only be described as anguish. In a voice so soft it was hard to hear him, he asked, "Do y'all know what happened to Charlie?"

Lori had read a little about Buck's son, but she did not know the details. Bob, well-versed on all the Alamo lore, did.

"Colonel, have a seat, son," he said kindly. Buck sat down and stared at Bob.

"Your little boy ended up going to live with his mom, who was raising Susan Isabella—I think you knew that?"

Travis nodded slowly, his eyes downcast. He felt for the daughter he never knew, too, although there was all that mystery in the history books about whether or not he thought that child was his. Either for that reason, or because she was a girl, in an age where men put more stock in their male children, the little daughter was not quite the same as his son. To his credit, he had, in his will, left his possessions to be divided between the children.

"Your ex-wife and her second husband died of a fever, and I believe Charlie went to live with his grandparents for a time. Anyway, he grew up and became an officer in the United States Army, but there was some issue, and he was cashiered."

Travis looked up—he was mortified but told Bob to go on.

109

"Charlie ended up practicing law in Texas. I read something that indicated he did pretty well as an attorney. He never married—died young and was living with his sister at that time."

"Poor, poor Charlie. I hope somehow, someone was able to convey to him why I had to do it," Travis sighed. He put his head in his hands and wept. Lori walked over to him, holding him by the shoulders.

"It's OK, Buck. Really, it is. It sounds like your kids looked out for each other. I try to do that for Vicky—and she does for me. It will be OK, really, really. Look up at me."

He lifted his head, and she wiped some of the tears from his face. He leaned against her for what seemed an eternity before getting up slowly and heading to his office.


It was mid-afternoon in no time. At 2:30, the Alamo's defenders had congregated, not anywhere near the 180+ the fort was supposed to have but enough to make a good showing. The plan for this event had come in so late that not much publicity surrounded it. Lori had posted something on the Alamo website, but that was it. The Texians were milling around in front of the church, talking with each other, their ladies in groups in their long dresses, doing the same. Chains guarded the patch of grass in front of the church, as it was the location of a mission cemetery. Most everything else in front of the old chapel was paved. The only other patch of grass, forward and on the south end of the chapel, would have to do, as the word had come down from on high that the cemetery was off limits, even for the commander. Colonel Travis, sword buckled on, walked from his office out to the front of the church. He gave instructions to Raul to form the men, and Raul ordered them to stand in line facing their commander. Travis looked stern and serious, as would befit the situation on these men's last full day of life had this been the real thing in 1836. The colonel stood straight as an arrow, sword at his side, and repeated what Lori was sure were the words he had said on that day long ago:

"My brave comrades, I feel I must tell you the truth of our situation. I have held out hope that some of our compatriots would come to our aid, but, alas, I fear that is not the case. Had they come, they should have been here by now. That said, we face a force of 20 times the number we have. The Mexicans have received their reinforcements and have tightened their stranglehold on the Alamo. It will not be long now—a day or two at the

110

most, I am quite sure, before they attack in force. We cannot hold them, and we must consider that the reality is that we will soon be in eternity. We have three choices. We can surrender, and dishonor our cause of freedom and liberty. We can attempt to escape—I will not run from the enemy. The reality is that either of those options, in addition to being dishonorable, will likely not save any who attempt them. I, for one, have determined to stand and fight here as long as I have breath in my body, to take as many of the hated enemy with me, and sell my life as dearly as I can. This I will do even if you leave me alone. However, I know that many of you have wives and families. If there is anyone here who wishes to go over the wall and try to escape, it will not be held against him. That said, I will be eternally grateful to any of you who stand with me in this last fight that is coming."

After some of the tears she had dealt with in one-on-ones delving into Buck's sad past, Lori noticed that he was awfully steady and his voice strong and clear at this somber and depressing event, his speech being about as tragic as anything could be. Travis pulled his sword from the scabbard and walked to one end of the line of men, gathered several deep, unlike the original in 1836 and even the practice for this ceremony, a last minute adjustment made because there was not enough unpaved ground for the men to spread out in a single line. He placed the point of the sword in the grass and drew a relatively straight line along the front of the gathered garrison. When he was finished, he returned the sword to the scabbard and walked to the center of the line again.

"Whoever will stay and fight, come cross this line and stand with me!"

There was a pause, and a few of the men looked at each other, then slowly they started across the line, one or two at a time, turning and standing with their leader. In this version, unlike the original, where Moses Rose declined to die with everyone else, they all crossed the line. Travis pulled out the sword, raised it above his head, and dramatically shouted his signature line, "Victory or Death!"

Pretty much all tourists at the site that afternoon stood at attention watching the solemn reenactment. Whispers went through the crowd—the man giving the orders and making the speech is not a reenactor—he is Col. Travis. The crowd was almost reverential in their quiet observance, obviously in respect for the Alamo's commander.

At the conclusion, many of the spectators remained, chatting quietly with the reenactors, hoping to at least meet the colonel. He shook many hands, quietly acknowledging kind words about his speech and his valor and leadership. It was getting close to 5:00 by the time everyone dispersed.

"Buck, we need to get home and get some sleep if you're really serious about being here at 3:30 in the morning!" Lori called.

"They kind of got the jump on us before—got to our sentries before they could alert us. I intend to be up earlier this time!" came the response.

Lori shook her head. Was he in 1836? She really didn't know.

# ARMAGEDDON

One additional problem with the Battle of the Alamo besides the gore, massacre, mutilation, and cremation, was that the fight was VERY early in the morning, as Buck's concern had indicated. Needless to say, this little issue paled in comparison to all of that blood and destruction, but it was tough on the reenactors who were dedicated enough to get up in the middle of the night and put on all the antique clothing and equipment to go downtown and playact the gruesome events. It would have been a lot easier had the fight been in broad daylight a-la John Wayne. The commander of the Alamo had been chomping at the bit to get there ahead of everyone else, nearly driving Lori crazy talking about it the night before. Consequently, as the Clayton household slept, Lori donned her dull rose frontier dress, secured all of the blonde hair loosely, and went to Buck's room, knocking softly on the door so as not to awaken everyone else. She had put on a pot of coffee on the way. The room had no alarm clock—something else she figured she would unglue him. He didn't hear her, so she crept in, shaking him by the shoulder as usual. He started to say something, and she put her hand over his mouth. "Buck, shh! Everyone's sleeping. Get dressed quietly, and we'll head on over there."

Without a word, he followed her orders. The new boots had come. The old ones had completely come apart, to the point that, when asked, Bob declined even to use them for one of the museum cases at the Alamo, although the relics would be preserved for posterity. Travis was now strong enough to pull boots on by himself. The gauze pad on his forehead had finally been retired, so his face looked as good as it was going to get unless Lori was able to work a miracle with concealer, which she had not yet tried, or a plastic surgeon got involved. Quite frankly, Lori could not really imagine Buck consenting to surgery, despite his tendency toward vanity. He was still in his old, bloody clothes. There had been no time for anything else, and, quite frankly, as long as they stayed on him, they were certainly the most appropriate attire for this particular ceremony. They sat in the nook drinking coffee, "Victory or Death," before heading out. The Claytons, although they were already deeply attached to Buck, especially Vicky, declined the opportunity to get up in the middle of the night to see him fight it out with Santa Anna. The streets were deserted as Lori drove the Cavalier to the Shrine. It was so early that no one was there. She almost stumbled over Bella, on her nightly patrol, while heading to the building housing the gift shop and offices and unlocking the door. She had some paperwork to do and had found virtually no time to do anything at work lately, so she settled in to get a little of it out of the way, while Buck stood outside, on the lookout for enemy forces.

There was a chill wind blowing at 4:00 a.m. as the small Mexican force approached the Alamo on horseback, in the dim moonlight, with only the street and security lights providing any illumination. Vincente Montoya had been doing this for years. He enjoyed dabbling in military history, and he could trace not just one, but three ancestors who had served in Santa Anna's army at the Alamo. One of those had been killed attempting to climb a scaling ladder to the top of the fortress' north wall. Vincente was one of those people who always got there early for appointments. He liked to be sure everything was in place—that all i's were dotted and t's crossed ahead of time. His day job was running his Nissan dealership. When he was not fighting old battles, he was tinkering with cars—always had. He was a handsome man of 57, his dark hair just beginning to show a few tinges of gray at the sideburns and temples. Anyone looking at him would have guessed he was 10 years younger. He had an easy manner and friendly smile. For Vincente, generally, the key to life was not taking things too seriously. It was a trait that endeared him to most people he met, although, if push really came to shove, the gloves would sometimes come off—but only in an extreme situation.

Vincente, in the beyond-gaudy uniform and ridiculous feathered headgear of El Presidente, was followed by Enrique Losa, his best friend, portraying a colonel, as well as Luis Estrada and Tomas Rosales. Bringing up the rear of the mounted column were Vincente's son Andres with his bugle and his best friend Ciro Vigil, the horsemen followed by a score of infantrymen. Andres and Ciro were only 15, new recruits to the reenacting habit. Andres was a serious, studious young man. He loved music more than anything in the world—it spoke to him. He was tall with dark, wavy hair and blessed with long eyelashes that a girl would kill for. Ciro, a stockier boy, slightly shorter than his friend, was actually showing some interest in history and warfare, but Andres was only looking for an opportunity to play the most famous and inspiring tune associated with the Battle of the Alamo, *El Deguello*. He would proudly proclaim the Mexican assault and victory in song.

The ceremony would not start until 5:30, and there were only two or three onlookers there, one who looked like he had been drinking and been there all night despite a clearly posted sign on the grounds that proclaimed "Alcoholic Beverages Prohibited." None of the Texian reenactors had left

114

their comfortable beds to "die" in the Alamo quite yet, so the Mexicans had the place to themselves—no defenders there to do any defending.

While Vincente provided the usual directions to his troops, who had all done this before—except for the two boys—and did not need their Generalissimo's instructions, Andres put his bugle to his lips. He wanted his performance to be perfect, and he was a bit nervous about playing in front of a crowd, particularly in light of the fact that, although the music made him proud, he knew some Anglos saw it very differently. If they could only understand that he was not really a Mexican soldier and that his intent was not to rub in the faces of devotees of the slain defenders that the real El Presidente had decreed that the Texians would all die and this music was the reminder of that promise. This was for the honor of Mexico, whose land the Anglos had stolen. Santa Anna had been harsher in his punishment of the intruders than perhaps, at least according to modern standards, was appropriate. But they did need to be taught a lesson—and they had lost the battle. That was the one thing that not only galled Andres but even more so his father and his father's friends. When Vincente was young, the Mexican troops were not welcome at the March 6 commemoration. They were viewed as evil killers who destroyed brave Americans and patriots. In today's more enlightened, if not totally realistic, world, the Mexicans had participated in the event for a number of years, although the Texas Trinity and their adherents were always the heroes of the story. Vincente had expressed his frustration off and on at being tired of hearing about Crockett, Bowie, and Travis. He admitted that he wished Santa Anna had just packed them off to Mexico as prisoners of war and put them out on display in Mexico City toiling on public works projects to work off their sentences for treason and rebellion instead of killing, mutilating, and burning them and thus making martyrs of them for posterity.

The sad, eerie notes of the old Moorish bugle call rang through the crisp, cold air as Andres began his practice.

"I demand that you cease immediately! You cannot play that on this sacred ground!"

Someone was shouting and running toward Andres and the rest of the Mexican troops, but it was too dark to see him. The man repeated the demand, coming closer at a rapid clip, white pants becoming visible in the darkness. Finally, he was close enough that they could see him, still coming and waving a sword dramatically over his head, and still shouting at Andres to stop the music. He was wearing a Texian "uniform," such as it was, made up of the aforementioned white pants, a blue tailcoat, red officer's sash, and

115

planter hat, and swinging the sword wildly toward the horsemen. When he reached them, slightly out of breath, he stopped just short of Vincente and pointed the sword at his throat.

"Obviously, you are not really Santa Anna, but you must be some sort of deranged scum to emulate him. A fine thing—a sycophant masquerading as a sadistic and vicious murderer veiled as a pompous ass! I am ordering you to get out of here NOW!"

Vincente tried to suppress a smile, putting on a stern, no-nonsense El Presidente expression. "You are ordering ME to get out of here?" Again he tried not to laugh.

The swordsman was getting more agitated. He shouted his demand again, loud enough that he likely awakened anyone in the vicinity who might have been attempting to sleep. For effect, he swung the sword in Vincente's face.

Vincente was mad at this point. "Look, you fool, we won this battle, and we're getting a little tired of the hero worship and theatrics some of you display every year. The part about a Trinity of Bowie, Crockett, and Travis actually is religious sacrilege for those of us who are sincere Catholics . . . ."

The angry Texian swung the sword again, very close to El Presidente's nose. "I don't know about any Trinity involving Bowie—cannot really imagine Bowie in the Holy Trinity, but the point of this ceremony is to honor the Alamo garrison slaughtered and mutilated by your vicious and inhuman army of killers," he shot back. "Now get out of here on your own now, or I will make you get out!"

"You are going to make me leave?" Vincente could not help a slight chuckle. He studied his adversary's face. There was a long gash on the right side, running all the way down his cheek, as if made by a sword. Maybe he had accidentally stabbed himself in a rage during some prior scene.

"Look what you did to me! Look at me! I am an example of what you did to all of us!" the man shouted. He took off the hat, revealing an ugly scar from a gunshot to his forehead. Vincente noticed blood stains on the side of the blue coat. The man was shaking with rage and had gone white, looking as if he would faint at any minute.

"Son, I didn't do anything to you. I don't know you—have never seen you before. You obviously have gotten into a fight with something, and it

116

got the better of you, but it wasn't me. You need to take some sort of anger management course or see a counselor . . . ."

The Texian shot back, "Santa Anna did this to me! I was shot in the head, but the sword and bayonet wounds—I've been told—likely came later. Your men . . . your men mutilated everyone . . . ."

He stopped, finally going silent for a minute. Vincente just stared.

"Santa Anna did this to you? The real Santa Anna?" he asked incredulously.

"Yes!" came the response, in a tone that sounded as if the speaker was spitting nails. "You must have heard about it. They were digging around the complex and found me. Wish they had not. Now I'm here, and I still have to deal with you people!"

Vincente was still staring when the Anglo swung the sword again. Vincente ducked to miss it, and his El Presidente hat fell to the ground. The other man moved quickly to the back of Vincente's horse, jabbing the rear of the animal as hard as he could with the sword. Vincente careened off toward the rear of the building, shouting and trying desperately to stay on the fleeing horse. He could hear the Texian shouting something at him about revenge as he unceremoniously headed away.

As soon as the Generalissimo was out of the way, the Texian turned his attention to the other Mexicans. He walked past the line of horsemen, seemingly with no fear or acknowledgment, and stopped at Andres and Ciro, waving the sword once in front of Andres' face and continuing his tirade.

"Don't you EVER play that again around here, do you hear me boy?" the man shouted. Andres was shaking. Before he could answer, the sword came down, knocking the bugle from his hands. It fell to the hard ground, dented and damaged. Andres was wide-eyed with trepidation, but Ciro, watching from slightly further away from the sword's threat, looked angry.

"Now get out of here, all of you, NOW!" came the repeated command.

Andres took off on his horse, no thought of retrieving his instrument ever entering his mind. Ciro followed him, but first he turned and glared at the infuriated Texian. Except for Enrique, the other men calmly turned their horses, and with some attempt at dignity, slowly headed out of the

117

Alamo complex, the foot soldiers behind them, in good order. Loud calls from Vincente were now coming from somewhere in back of the building, and his frightened mount had run back to the front of the church and out into the plaza. Enrique sprinted into the gloom and toward Vincente, who was trying to extricate himself from a large prickly pear cactus. Enrique helped him up gingerly, and Vincente started attempting to pull some of the barbs from his clothing with his gloved hands. He quickly directed Enrique to head back to the front and try to catch the perpetrator, then get help for himself.

Enrique ran toward the front of the chapel, sweating in his hot uniform despite the cold breeze. When he was in earshot of Elbert and Jaime, he shouted:

"There's some kook in a defender getup waving a sword around and yelling something. I can't make out most of it, but he called Vincente a sadistic murderer masquerading as a pompous ass—got that much. Then he plunged the sword into Vincente's horse's rear, and it took off, throwing Vincente headlong into that big cactus at the back of the building."

Enrique had to stop to catch his breath. A small crowd was forming as he continued:

"The crazy guy then swung the sword at Vincente's son as he was starting *El Deguello* and knocked the bugle to the ground and dented it. He was yelling something about that tune was never to be played at this sacred spot. The rest of us scattered as he was threatening and still waving the sword—seemed pretty adept with it. I've got to check on Vincente. Don't know where the nutcase went, but he was standing over there," Enrique pointed in the direction, "with his arms crossed, a look of satisfaction on his face, when I got out of there."

The onlookers were staring, but the sword-waving maniac was nowhere in sight. Elbert tried not to laugh. The situation was actually dangerous, and he didn't want anyone to get hurt, but it was no surprise. Someone, probably Bob, should have clued in Vincente and the other Mexican reenactors about Travis before they gathered for the predawn ceremony.

"Jaime, take a look around. If you see him, try to calm him down and get him away from people, especially Hispanics. And, if you can dislodge that sword without a threat to yourself, by all means, do it!" Elbert ordered the younger ranger.

118

"So, Elbert, what is this all about?" Enrique inquired, still breathing hard. The two headed for the cactus as they talked. Vincente could be heard in the distance, swearing and making declarations that he would kill the swordsman when he found him.

"That's Col. Travis," the ranger explained with a shrug. Elbert, a tall, large black man with wide shoulders, was at a loss to explain the Southern gentleman who commanded the Alamo.

"Colonel Travis? You mean THE Col. Travis? I heard they had found a defender body at the dig and it had a pulse, but I figured anyone in that condition would still be in the hospital."

"He actually made his first brief visit here back on the 24th, 5 days after he underwent brain surgery. They dragged him out here from his hospital bed and propped him up standing between Jamie and me to read—actually recite—his famous letter. He got through it, then promptly passed out, and they sent him back to the hospital. But first, the governor recommissioned the Alamo as a military post and put the colonel back in charge. Lori Clayton brings her new boss to work when he's well enough to come."

"Oh, no! Brain surgery. That might explain some of it," Enrique responded as they walked.

They were at Vincente, sitting in front of the enormous cactus and still shouting obscenities and threats to the defenders, or at least this one, worthy of the real Santa Anna.

"Brain surgery? Who had brain surgery?" Vincente stopped railing long enough to ask.

"Colonel Travis."

"Huh?"

"El Presidente, I'm afraid Col. Travis won the second battle of the Alamo," Elbert explained. "The guy with the sword is the real Travis. He's the defender they dug up."

"Well, the stories about him being crazed from drinking mercury for his venereal disease must be true, that and maybe a touch more lunacy after experiencing the siege and battle. He may be a so-called hero, but he sure knows how to throw a conniption fit, and he's dangerous. You need to find a way to corral him before someone gets hurt," Vincente advised.

Bob Gordon could tell when he drove up that something had happened. Jaime had returned quickly to his post in front of the chapel after a quick check of the premises found no swordsman. There were more people coming now, mostly trying to position their blankets and get a good seat for the little ceremony. Most were clueless as the swordplay was over before they got there, but everyone was talking about it. Bob hurried to Elbert and Jaime, who were trying to answer questions from a disturbed Anglo mother, who had brought her children and was concerned for their safety if someone started swinging an edged weapon around. Jaime was left with the overwrought mom while Elbert moved to a quieter spot to tell Bob what had transpired.

"I'll have to apologize to Vincente. There's no good explanation—and no excuse, but there's nothing we can do with the famed commander of the Alamo except maybe take away his sword for the good of all, including the colonel. He's going to provoke someone into killing him, even if he doesn't hurt someone else. Meanwhile, I'm assuming we've got no Mexican army representation? I can't remember how they used to do it before we included both sides. And I don't know how I'm going to explain it. These days, half the people who come to this are Hispanic. We'll probably get a discrimination complaint. I'll see if I can get Vincente on his cell," Bob glanced at his watch, trying to turn it so he could see in the gloom. "Not much time left, and, uh, where is Travis?"

Elbert shrugged. "Don't have any idea. Jaime and I looked around for him immediately after the incident, but we didn't see him."

"Well, so we've got no shows for the entire winning side and the leader of the losers. Honestly! I wish we didn't have to do this," the frustrated Bob replied.

It was 5:15 when Bob finally thought to look in the colonel's office. Sure enough, he was sitting there at his little desk, a candle the only illumination in the dark, small room.

"Colonel, I understand you chased off the Mexican army?" Bob asked.

Travis was still mad. "How dare they show their faces on this day?" he yelled.

120

"Uh, well, you've got to admit, they did on the original," was all Bob could think of to say.

That did not help the situation with the infuriated Alamo commander. Lori, who had missed the whole thing, had finally finished her tasks and appeared behind Bob.

Bob continued in a firm tone. "We've got 15 minutes to come up with a plan. The spectators are here, your troops are ready to be lined up, Colonel, and the Mexican forces are nowhere to be seen . . . ."

"As it should be," Travis interrupted.

"OK, yes, well, you certainly took care of that little detail," Bob remarked. "But the reality is that we've got a program to put on, and the usual routine will not work since you just single-handedly took out the Mexican army," Bob explained evenly, hoping Travis would calm down enough to participate in what was left of the ceremony.

"All I know to do is make an announcement, I'll do it at the start, that unforeseen circumstances caused the participants representing Mexico to not be able to attend. And, whether you like it or not," he turned with a stern look at the colonel, "we may very well have to have a second, all-Mexican ceremony after the Texian one . . . ."

"I will run them out of here again!" Travis interrupted with a threat.

Bob didn't pursue it. He had to concentrate on getting Travis to calm down and stand with his men. "We will do the Texian lineup as usual. There will be a speech by Morena. I'll clue her in so she can make some adjustments if she has to—will have to ad lib that. Your men will fire their volleys. We will introduce you, Colonel. Then folks will lay the wreaths, someone will play bagpipes, the troops will file out, and that will be it. Now let's get on over there!" Bob said forcefully.

He surprised Lori, who didn't know he had it in him, but someone had to take control if they were going to get through this. Travis was still mad, but he followed Bob to where the crowd was waiting, then headed for his little Texian garrison.

Travis was giving directions to Raul regarding putting his men in line. Bob was whispering to Morena, dressed as a Mexican lady, with a grayish purple shawl over her head, going over the speech. It did mention

121

something about the Mexican forces coming in, what would have been Vincente's cue to move forward. She would abbreviate that a bit. Fortunately, most of it would still work. Bob finally got Vincente on his cell phone 5 minutes before the program was to start.

"I'm so sorry," he started. "I really didn't dream . . . ."

"That's OK, Bob. I guess it's kind of funny if you can step back from it—would make a great scene in a comedy movie about the Alamo."

"A comedy movie about the Alamo? Not a very funny subject," Bob responded.

"Well, there was 'Viva Max,'" Vincente reminded him.

"Yeah, I had almost forgotten about that one—an oldie. Anyway, we owe you one. The colonel is here about to line up his troops—guess he's pretty confident they won't get killed this time. Boy was he mad—still is."

"He's something else. Some toxic combination of red hair, drinking mercury, and not having such a great time the last time he was here on March 6," Vincente laughed. "You do need to watch him because with that fiery temper—and the sword—he could really hurt someone," Vincente advised.

"Yeah, I know. We hadn't seen anything quite like this out of him at the hospital, letter ceremony, or line in the sand."

"Santa Anna wasn't at those events," Vincente reminded him. "If they had to dig up a defender, too bad it wasn't Crockett instead of Travis. I think his personality was a lot more easy going! Anyway, if it's all the same with you, we'll do a little Mexican Army commemoration after the colonel and his men have cleared out."

"Sure thing. Again, I do apologize for this. I know what you mean about Crockett—only thing we would have had to worry about there is the PETA folks coming after us. I've got to get out there and render a little apology to the crowd. See you later, El Presidente!"

Bob nervously straightened his tie. Although the classic story of the Alamo remained engrained in most Texans—a small, brave garrison of Texas heroes fighting for freedom was trapped and finally overwhelmed and slaughtered by brutal and cruel dictator Santa Anna, the fact was that

122

Hispanics did not quite see it that way. And there were more Hispanics than Anglos in San Antonio these days—actually pretty much always had been. The Alamo administration had been very careful over the last few years to not tread too heavily on anyone's sensibilities. Although the governor had thrown a wrench into this officially, the reality was that Col. Travis was off in his little 1836 world, worrying about a military situation that no longer existed and hopefully would not again unless his actions precipitated something from the Hispanic community. Bob continued to direct ceremonies and other events at the fort. Travis' early arrival and Vincente's early practice for the battle anniversary had caught Bob off guard. His failure to warn Travis specifically that Mexicans would attend was deliberate. He figured it was better to not risk provoking Travis ahead of time. The colonel had a reputation for a fiery temper in his earlier life, and what Santa Anna did to him and his men would, Bob had suspected, likely make for a really bad reaction on the part of the Alamo commander if faced with El Presidente again. Unfortunately, his hunch was certainly correct. On the other hand, he had to admit he had really dropped the ball by not warning Vincente of the colonel's suspected predispositions, although, he maybe should have but did not know that Travis would react so strongly.

Bob stepped to the microphone and looked out at the crowd, more what appeared to be Hispanic faces than Anglo based on a quick glance. He cleared his throat.

"Welcome everyone. As those of you who have been here before on March 6 can attest, we have the 'Dawn at the Alamo' program to commemorate the lives of the men who gave their lives in battle on both sides."

Bob was sweating. He prayed that the colonel was busy forming his troops and did not hear the last part of the sentence, as he was not anxious to be on the point end of that sword. He glanced over slightly. Travis was giving directions to the Texians. So far, so good.

He continued. "Due to an unforeseen circumstance, the Mexican Army participants could not be with us now, but they will make up for it with a second event at 7:00." He paused and took another nervous glance at the troops. "I hope you will all attend that as well. Now I will turn things over to Morena Alejandro, who runs our gift shop. Come and see her and pick up a coonskin cap or some of our incredible fudge today!" Bob put in a plug for the financial end of the operation.

Morena came forward, a solemn look on her face, the purple-gray

123

shawl draped around her head. The bracelets jangled slightly as she put her speech on the lectern. She began in her clear, melodious voice:

"A blood-red flag was flying from San Fernando church in downtown Bexar. It was the middle of the night when General Santa Anna ordered his army to make the attack. By 5:30 in the morning, on Sunday, March 6, 1836, they were at the approaches of the crumbling fortress called the Alamo. The exhausted Texians, kept awake for 12 nights by cannon fire and the playing of *El Deguello*, a bugle call signifying no quarter, did not hear the Mexicans coming. Santa Anna's men dispatched the sentries quickly and were upon the fort by the time the defenders were awakening and their commander, Col. Travis, was aroused from his bed."

At this point in her speech, Col. Travis, who had actually been awake for hours, formed his men and they started a slow march, with the notable lack of precision one would expect from American volunteers. They halted at their designated position in front of the church, lining up with the colonel to their side, his sword unsheathed. Colonel Travis, in 1836 and at present, always looked a little overdressed in his lawyer clothes compared to his troops. They were in worn, grimy garments, some buckskin with fringe, almost all in varying shades of brown. There were several raccoons perched on soldiers' heads—the Tennessee boys. The soldiers stood in formation as Morena went on:

"The outnumbered Texians were able to repel the first two charges of the Mexicans, but, on the third attempt, Santa Anna's forces were too much for them. At the north wall, Col. Travis fell early in the fight with a musket ball in his brain, his last words reportedly "Never surrender." His men fought on without him. Davy Crockett, the famed frontiersman, assumed a leadership position in his sector, fighting off the onslaught of enemy troops, even swinging his rifle at the oncoming Mexicans, before he was cut down." She followed the traditional script, not getting into the controversy of whether Crockett might have survived and been executed after the battle. "And Jim Bowie, deathly ill in bed, rose with his last effort and emptied his pistols into charging Mexican soldiers, then grabbed his famous knife, before they killed him with their bayonets. It only took the Mexicans about an hour to overrun the fort and kill all the defenders. Not long after that, General Santa Anna entered the compound, where he gazed on a ghastly scene. All of his enemies were dead, but the Texians had taken hundreds of Mexican soldiers with them. A few noncombatants were allowed to leave the ruined fortress, and Santa Anna ordered his dead to be buried and the enemy garrison to be burned on funeral pyres. That was the sad end of the famed Battle of the Alamo."

That was Travis' cue, and he ordered his men to present arms, then to fire three volleys into the air. The men then stood at attention while Bob made another announcement.

"Those of you who have been here before will recall that the Travis family usually comes forward first with a wreath honoring their relative, the Alamo's commander, Col. William Barret Travis. They have come to pay tribute to the battle today, but I gave them a call about a week ago and told them there was no need to bring a wreath this time. If there is anyone who is not yet aware of it, we found the colonel buried in the compound at the archaeological dig on February 19. Although badly injured—the find did confirm the Mexican ball to the brain, as well as numerous other wounds, he was alive." Bob pointed in the direction of the line of Texian defenders. "Ladies and gentlemen, the officer commanding our Texian reenactors today is Col. Travis."

All of the Anglos and most of the Hispanics cheered wildly. The colonel took off his hat, which revealed the head wound, and bowed to them. The sun was now just beginning to come up over the old church. Travis put on the hat and walked over to the podium as his relatives came forward to meet him. There were a couple minutes of handshakes and hugs as the family met the ancestor who made their name famous. Bob motioned to Travis, who seemed to have calmed down since the incident with Vincente, and asked if he would like to say a few words.

Never hesitant, the Texian commander stood at the lectern, Bob adjusting the microphone up for him. His appearance in front of the crowd resulted in another standing ovation as the rest of the Travis clan headed back to their position.

"Thank you, everyone, for being here today to honor the memory of my brave men—men who, despite the fact that they knew it would be their last fight, nevertheless gave it every ounce of courage and determination to fend off the brutal and evil"—no one could accuse William Barret Travis of mincing words—"foe and selling their lives as dearly as possible. They will never be forgotten as long as there is an Alamo. God Bless Texas and the United States. Victory or Death!" He tipped the hat and bowed slightly, then headed back to his little army.

At this point, Bob, back at the podium, began the roll call, announcing the various defender families and patriotic groups, one by one, as they placed wreaths on the grass near the church. Not surprisingly, the King of the Wild Frontier got the largest floral arrangement.

125

Finally, when all of that was over, a bagpiper in a kilt played "Amazing Grace." Everyone stood. Men, except the Texian soldiers and their leader, removed their hats, and many people in the audience put their hands over their hearts. Colonel Travis gave the command, and the Texians filed out in order.

Vincente had carefully adjusted his huge general's headdress to be sure it sat squarely on his head, then turned his horse into the plaza. He still had not gotten over the confrontation with Travis. The man disrupted and ruined the entire ceremony and instantly created more of a split between Hispanics and Anglos than there had been since the colonel actually faced Santa Anna all those years ago. Of course, Travis was sincere in his beliefs, even if wrong, but the time warp had already spelled trouble once, and Vincente had the uneasy feeling it was far from over. Andres had been left shaken. Someone had loaned him another bugle, but he had tried to beg off the whole thing after the confrontation. Despite urging from Ciro and his father, Andres did not want to have anything to do with the Alamo. Vincente had insisted, however, trying to not let Travis' ranting shake his son's pride in his heritage. So, with the borrowed bugle at the ready, Andres, with Ciro, followed the other riders. They sat on their horses in formation in front of the old church. At a signal from his father, Andres put the bugle to his lips and began *El Deguello*.

From the left, seemingly out of nowhere, came the Alamo commander, running toward the horsemen, waving his sword.

"Oh, no, you've got to be kidding," Tomas said, to no one in particular.

Enrique whispered something to El Presidente.

"I told you before, get out of here NOW. You are not to tread on this sacred spot of ground!" Travis shouted at Vincente.

"Colonel, I've had about enough of you. You disrupted the traditional ceremony we do to respect both sides in this battle this morning. Heaven knows what you did at your little one-sided presentation as none of us were there, but we are damned sure going to honor our men. And we're going to do it right now. I would suggest that YOU get out of here, as I will guarantee you will not be happy to hear what I intend to say. Now get out of my way, or I will force the issue."

126

His words did not move Travis. He swung the sword toward Vincente, uttered a threat to El Presidente, then yelled, "You don't scare me!"

"OK, that's enough. I've had it," Vincente said. "We'll have to redo the entrance and start again, but we need to clear this up first."

With that, he dismounted, handing the ridiculous hat to Tomas. Vincente summoned Enrique and Luis, and they dismounted as well. Without saying another word, all three headed toward Travis, who stood his ground. As they got within range, the colonel took a broad swipe at them, but he missed, and Luis grabbed the weapon and threw it as far away from the Alamo commander as he could. Enrique, who was the largest and strongest of the three, grabbed the Texian and held him.

"Get a rope or tie or something," Vincente said.

"Will this work?" Ciro called. He produced a strap for a backpack, dismounted, and walked over, handing it to Luis.

They tied Travis' arms securely behind him and pushed him to a sitting position. Vincente addressed him.

"Colonel, I warned you before that you would not enjoy this ceremony. I strongly suggested that you stay away for the sake of your somewhat unsettled mental state if nothing else. But you seem bound and determined to wreak havoc on anything that does not suit your outdated and, quite honestly, insane views. OK, then, you are here now, and you can watch Santa Anna come in and conquer your precious Alamo. Normally, we do not get into personalities, as we try to conduct the joint ceremony with respect for the men of both sides, but you destroyed that this morning. As a result, you are going to have to sit through some harsh words about your compatriots—and yourself in particular. The only thing you will like about this is the fact that we will not kill you this time. Do you know who I feel sorry for in all of this? I'll tell you—the Alamo defenders, not because they all died but because they were cooped up in this place for 13 days with no way to get away from you!"

A fair-sized crowd had formed to watch General Santa Anna's grand entrance despite the chaos of the morning that threw any plans and scheduling for spectators for the day's events totally out of sorts. The Texians were the heroes, but Santa Anna and his guys had much more spectacular trappings, and kids loved the horses. The attendees were almost exclusively Hispanic, the word having spread of the split caused by the

127

Texian leader. Some people were pointing and laughing at Travis, tied up and sitting on the ground. But the colonel was quiet, at least for the moment, as Vincente directed his "troops" to head out, then turn and make a proper grand entrance with Andres hesitantly sounding *El Deguello*. As the formation came in, Travis stared in disbelief, uncontrollable tears streaming down his face at the horrific memories this exhibition entailed and his inability to stop it. Finally, he bowed his head so that he did not have to see it, but that did not shut out the sound.

Vincente addressed the crowd in Spanish, as would be appropriate for General Santa Anna. Poor Travis had taught himself a rudimentary version of the language when he came to Mexican Texas. He learned enough that he was able to actually navigate Espanol for his law practice, which was rather impressive, and so that he could use the language to write discreet details of his romantic encounters in his now-famous diary. As a result, the Alamo commander not only had to listen to Vincente and his men, but he understood everything they were saying.

Vincente, in character, defended his decision to storm the fort despite the high casualties that would entail instead of just starving out its occupants. As Santa Anna, he noted a government decree "requiring" the summary dispatch of all insurgents fighting against Mexico. He praised the bravery and efficiency of his soldados in annihilating the hated foe. As he wrapped up, still operating in 1836, he stated coldly:

"So now, I suspect Senor Travis and his companions are in Hell, where the enemy chief is no doubt answering for his many sins."

Travis shouted, "Who died and made you God?" As El Presidente, Vincente ignored him.

After Montoya finished his in-character long-winded salute to his soldados and their courage in scaling the walls, taking the fort, and dispatching all of the enemy troops, he turned his attention to the dead Texians. This part of the speech was not so much Santa Anna speaking but a Mexican take on the myth of the Alamo. Anglos who were present, and the number could be counted on one hand, would not have understood him unless they spoke the language, but it translated to:

"We have sometimes been disparaged for our rough treatment of the enemy who fell into our hands. War is harsh. In fact, I believe it was General Sherman, in the United States' Civil War, who said 'War is Hell.' Looking back on it now, from a purely public relations standpoint, it would have been better to send the few survivors back to Mexico City as prisoners. What everyone forgets about this battle and so-called massacre is that the Texians were fighting fiercely, and, I will admit, very bravely. Almost all of them died in battle, as would be the case in any battle of this type. Only a handful survived, and yes, they were executed. As to the criticism regarding mutilation of the bodies, again, it was a public relations disaster, but dead men do not care if another sword thrust is made in their bodies. The cremation was a necessity for health reasons. We ran out of room to bury our own soldados. We certainly would not have been able to handle burial of the Texians as well. Remember, these were not ordinary soldiers. They were a ragtag band of misfit criminals bent on taking Mexican territory. The simple fact is they all got exactly what they deserved.

"Over the years, we have heard it said by some old-time Anglos that the three major leaders of the Texian side constitute a sort of 'Texas Trinity.' Why? Just because they died, ostensibly for Texas? The very idea of these men being compared to the Holy Father, the Lord Jesus Christ, and the Holy Spirit is blasphemous at best. James Bowie was a land speculator wanted for his crimes throughout the then-southwest of the United States. He was a slave trader and alcoholic whose excessive drinking rankled the so-called commanding officer, Travis. Davy Crockett, the 'King of the Wild Frontier,' was the best of the three. Although he was not a control freak like Bowie and Travis, he was called colonel as an honorary, furthering the confusion as to who was in control at the Alamo, three arguable commanders for 180-some men. That right there shows incredible stupidity and disorganization. To Crockett's credit, despite a failed career in politics and just about everything else he did, he was likeable and got along with people.

"The real problem, for the Texian defenders and for us Mexicans, came from the ostensible top. The Alamo commander, Travis, was crazy as a cut snake. He was too young and inexperienced to be in command of anything, and his character traits were damning in and of themselves. The young man showed his impulsive and impatient nature at the very beginning of the conflict, when the Mexican forces were willing to talk. Travis' response was to fire the biggest cannon in the place. It is, admittedly, given the track record of the Mexican army, unlikely that they would have let the Texians walk free, and it is a certainty that the leaders would have been executed. But Travis killed any hope his men might have when he fired that shot. All of those 'Victory or Death' letters and the possible line in the sand point to a young man with a crazed death wish. That may have been fine for him if that is really the way he wanted to go out from this earth, although it shows some serious imbalance in his thinking processes. But he was a commander responsible for his troops, and he doomed them and took them

129

with him to whatever kind of purgatory dead rebels go to. Some students of the battle focus on Travis' diary where he's very up-front about the fact that his sex life was of major importance to him. He carefully reported sexual adventures and kept score of each one. Not surprisingly, he ended up with a severe case of venereal disease, unnamed but probably syphilis, and dosed himself by drinking mercury. That was the only so-called cure at the time, but the mercury did destroy the minds of those who kept gulping it over time, and there is serious question as to the sanity of the Alamo's commander by March 6, 1836."

Vincente made the mistake of pausing briefly, not looking at Travis, whom he had pretty much forgotten in his desire to defend the Mexican side against the persistent criticisms that were repeated over and over. He looked out into the crowd, pausing for emphasis.

"You vicious, degenerate low-life—I promise, on my honor, you will regret those words! You will pay dearly for every one of them!" Travis shouted toward him.

Vincente turned in his direction. He realized he probably should not have gone so far publicly in his critique, but he really had not been thinking about Travis when he digressed into the failings of the Alamo's greatest heroes. He had intended to make the point that the Trinity was not so holy, that they were mere men like anyone else. He had so wanted this ceremony to be about honoring the Mexican soldados, including his ancestors, and not the ongoing controversy as to who was right and who was wrong at the Alamo. But with William Barret Travis alive, that was simply not possible. Vincente looked to the crowd, who were staring with a look that clearly said this was not part of the program script.

"Like I said, there was a serious question about the sanity of the Alamo's commander by March 6, 1836. Everyone likely has seen the news reports by now regarding the defender they found at the archaeological dig. This is Col. Travis," he pointed to the infuriated Texian. Vincente then addressed Travis in English:

"Look, son, you've got to get over this fixation about killing every Mexican in Texas. San Antonio has far more Mexican-Americans—and most of them are citizens, than Anglos today—as it did in your day. Look at the crowd who have come here to watch this simple ceremony with quiet respect." He gestured toward the people watching the show. "If you are going to survive, you're going to have to learn to get along with them. As to this desire to go out in a blaze of glory, you've already done it in spectacular style once. You will never be able to top that, and normal folks have no desire in that direction at all. You need to get your head on straight before someone gets seriously hurt."

Someone in the crowd shouted "Viva Mexico! Viva Santa Anna!" Others took it up, and Travis, with a glazed look in his eyes, just stared.

Vincente issued orders for his little troop to line up, all except Ciro, whom he ordered to free the colonel. While Ciro worked to untie the knots in his strap, Travis fidgeted and tried to strike the teen. As the strap came free, Ciro backed quickly away from Travis, then ran for his horse. Travis grabbed the sword and ran after him. Vincente motioned Enrique, and the two dismounted. They ran to where Ciro was trying to mount and fend off the sword-wielding colonel. They pulled Travis off of Ciro from the back and yanked the sword from him, and the teen quickly jumped on his horse.

"Obviously, my warnings have not been getting through. I regret that you have forced me to take more drastic action," Vincente angrily threatened Travis.

"So does it truly end like last time? Is the all-powerful El Presidente going to dispatch the one remaining Alamo defender?" the colonel asked sarcastically, not seeming at all scared at the prospect, but angry and cold.

"No, Colonel. I wish they had never found you because, as the original Santa Anna said, you are a troublemaker. But I'm not going to kill you. However, there are some lessons you are going to have to learn to live in today's society. In fact, I suspect some of them would have helped you do better in your day. Enrique, Tomas—tie him to that post, facing it."

"I don't think Ciro's strap is long enough for this," Tomas observed.

Enrique eyed the colonel's sash and called for Ciro to dismount and hurry to them. He did, and with Enrique and Tomas holding Travis tightly, Ciro untied the sash and tied Travis to the post with it. Vincente dismounted and gave his hat to Ciro. It was getting awfully warm for the whole costume at this point. He walked over to where Travis was tied. Vincente pulled up the tails to Travis' coat and secured them above where he was tied at the waist.

"Colonel, I think the only way to get your attention is to humiliate you. You act like a temperamental child, so I'm forced to treat you like one."

131

As General Santa Anna, Vincente had a riding crop, and he started to apply it Travis' rear end in hard, even strokes. Travis was determined not to cry out. At five, Vincente stopped.

"Untie him, and let him down," he ordered.

The audience had mostly stayed, knowing that this whole event, from the time Santa Anna's troops had first ridden in, was not anything like the usual March 6 routine. Vincente could see that everyone was staring. All he could think of to say to them was:

"In the 1830's, the style coat gentlemen of means wore was called a tailcoat, likely because it had two tails down the back. But, as you just witnessed, it covered the wearer's tail, which we just tanned. No killings at the end of this Alamo battle, but we did beat the enemy."

Some of the people in the crowd picked up the cry of "Viva Mexico! Viva Santa Anna!" again. Folks were laughing as Travis sank to the ground in embarrassment. He lay face down as Vincente mounted his horse and rode out at the head of his troops. Ciro was laughing as he passed Travis. Andres was horrified at the whole thing, determined that he would not have anything to do with any of this Alamo playacting from now on. A few crowd members walked up to where Travis lay, staring, but no one spoke to him or touched him. Some folks milled around to talk with the soldados for a few minutes. Soon, they were all gone.

Andres had loaded their horses in the trailer hitched to the back of the truck, which was parked at the end of the plaza on permit for the event. Vincente had just thrown his huge hat in the truck bed and shed the general's tunic when he realized he had dropped his keys somewhere. Andres was distressed, wanting more than anything to get away from the Alamo, but he went back to the mission to help his father try to find the keys. After all, they weren't going anywhere without them. Travis was still lying where they left him, but Vincente was more concerned about the keys. The horses had kicked up some dirt and dust, which made the search a bit harder. Andres finally located the keys in some grass next to the pathway.

"Come on, Dad, let's go. I'm sick of this place," he said, heading toward the truck.

"Just a minute—he's still lying there. I want to check on him," Vincente told his son. Andres sighed.

Vincente walked over to where Travis lay, very still. A few people had gathered around, staring, but that was all they did. He bent over and touched the man—he was warm, still among the living.

"Vincente! I'm so sorry about your program. I mean . . . the way it all went. But he really doesn't realize what he's doing . . . ."

It was Lori, waving at Vincente and running toward him. The Claytons and the Montoyas had been friends for years. She stopped when she saw Travis on the ground.

"Oh my gosh. Is he dead?" she cried, running to the prostrate form.

"No, I don't think so. I'm going to turn him over," Vincente answered.

With a little help from Lori, he got Travis on his back. He had fainted, but Lori's check of his pulse revealed it was strong and normal.

"Andres, get one of those Cokes out of the cooler!" Vincente called to his son.

The boy ran toward the truck, wishing he could stay there, but he was back quickly with a cold Mexican Coke. Most people who had tried Mexican Cokes liked them better than the American version because the Mexicans used real sugar instead of corn syrup in the formula. The Mexican Cokes were more expensive than domestic, but they were worth it for anyone not on a budget.

"I've got to ask," Lori looked at Vincente with a smile, "Are you going to give the Texian commander of the Alamo a Mexican Coke?"

"I want him to come to, and it's the only thing I've got. He won't know what it is, and besides, maybe it will make him somehow less belligerent towards us!" he laughed. Travis moved slightly. "Now hold his head up, and I'll try to get some of it down him. Last thing I want after all of this is for the *Express-News* tomorrow morning to run a headline to the effect of 'Santa Anna impersonator chokes Col. Travis with Coke.' I wish I had a bottled Coke. This can is hard to maneuver."

"What happened?" Lori asked. She had seen some of the program, knew Vincente was unhappy about separate Texian and Mexican ceremonies and that Travis had made some threats earlier, but she had not seen the end of it.

"He just would not stop shouting, interrupting, and waving that damn sword in my face. We tied him up, and I warned him he was going to have to listen to some harsh words about himself, as my goal was to show that there is a Mexican point of view in this event. I critiqued the Alamo leaders, and I was, in retrospect, too hard on Travis, especially with him sitting there. I called him crazy and went into the mercury treatment thing—shouldn't have gone that far. When I asked Ciro to untie him at the end, Travis grabbed the sword and chased him. At that point, I was hot, tired, and had simply had enough of the Alamo commander. We tied him to a post, and I used General Santa Anna's riding crop on the colonel's rear. We rode on out, but I had dropped my keys—came back to look for them, and he was still there, lying very still. Although a part of me wished he were dead so we wouldn't have to deal with him anymore, my conscience got the better of me, and I checked."

Some of the Coke was running down the lapel of the ruined coat as Vincente tried to get it in Travis' mouth. Vincente glanced down at the colonel's coat.

"Don't worry about that. I'll clean it off later," Lori volunteered. "With all those blood stains that the cleaners couldn't get out, it looks awful, anyway."

"Yeah. Honestly, before anyone even gets a taste of his difficult personality, I think he turns them off with his appearance. Between the gunshot hole and scar on his face and the remains of his uniform, he looks like a Halloween Alamo zombie, quite frankly."

Lori tried to stifle a laugh, saying softly, "He doesn't have any other clothes—he doesn't own anything . . . ."

Vincente cut her off: ". . . except that damn sword."

She nodded with a grin and continued, "I think he might be kind of cute if we could get him in some jeans and a t-shirt and maybe let me try dulling the scars with some of my concealer."

"Honestly—of course, I'm not a woman—'cute' is not a word I would ever think of applying to William Barret Travis. But maybe we could improve his appearance, if not his personality. What about one of those 'Victory or Death' black t-shirts they're selling at the gift shop?—certainly would suit him!" Vincente replied.

"I can figure out the t-shirt, but I'm at a loss as to fitting men's jeans," Lori shook her head.

"I'll tell you what. Let's make a date next weekend, now that all this battle stuff is behind us, and take Col. Travis to get some new threads," Vincente offered.

"Wait a minute? Santa Anna taking Travis to buy clothes? Oh, that's just too precious!" she laughed. "If you really mean it, I think some other impression than constant 'commander of the Alamo' might help soften him a bit."

"Anything is worth a try. Look, I think he's beginning to come to—his eyelids fluttered a bit," Vincente turned his attention to Travis. "Mexican Coke—it works every time."

"Ssshhh! He may hear you," Lori laughed.

"I want him to hear me—a better headline: 'Colonel Travis revived by Mexican Coke!'"

"Honestly, Vincente, you are sooooo crazy!" Lori grinned.

"What's . . . what's going on? Where am I?" the confused colonel looked up to see Lori and someone who looked like his Santa Anna nemesis but not in the goofy hat and coat.

"Battle's over for this year, Colonel. I believe there's a brief commemoration ceremony tonight, but I think you've had enough Alamo. I know I have," Vincente sighed.

Vincente made a point of not mentioning the specifics of the closing "Dusk at the Alamo" ceremony, where Raul would reprise the role he had played for years portraying Juan Seguin, the Tejano captain who buried the ashes a year after the fight. He gave Seguin's eulogy pronounced in 1837, usually standing next to a huge wreath with a picture of Travis in the center and small South Carolina, Alabama, Texas, and Texian two-star tricolor flags sticking out of it. The wreath would hopefully not be present this year, but Vincente did not want to find out nor for the colonel to, either.

Travis sat up slowly, and Vincente handed him the can. "What is this?"

"Uh, it's what we call a soft drink—don't think they had them in your

135

day. No alcohol—just a sweetened drink," Vincente explained without saying where it was from.

"Are you the fellow who was playing Santa Anna?" Travis squinted in the sun to see Vincente more clearly.

"Yes, yes I am. My real name is Vincente Montoya," Vincente explained.

"Why are you helping me?" the colonel replied in a suspicious tone.

"Because, Travis, I don't have anything against you. Santa Anna did, and I was portraying Santa Anna in a program. As Santa Anna, I hated you, but I don't even really know you," Vincente responded.

"So why all the accusations and humiliating me in front of a crowd by whipping my butt?" the colonel demanded.

"Because I have a hard time getting your attention any other way. I know you are a lawyer, and maybe that's why, but you talk way too much. You need to sometimes listen to what other people have to say."

Vincente could tell that the colonel was not particularly pleased at that, but he did not shoot back a response, instead draining the last bit of the cold Coke.

"Now, one more thing. How would the two of you like to come, as my guests, to Ramale's tonight? They are having a roasted jalapeno eating contest at 7:00," Vincente offered.

"You are on, General. I'll show you what a Texian can do!" came the quick response. Lori and Vincente just stared at each other.

What Vincente did not tell Travis, but Lori knew from many visits to the restaurant, often with members of Vincente's family, was that the owners, Diego and Maria Ramale, were first generation Americans who were intensely proud of their Mexican heritage. Maria had traced her family tree and had numerous great-great-great-somethings who had fought against the Texians in the revolution. Fortunately, the couple was welcoming to all guests and did not refight the Battle of the Alamo or any of the other conflicts with the Anglos who flocked to the place simply because the food was delicious and the hosts gracious. But Col. Travis, in his uniform, might be pushing the edge of the envelope.

136

Lori and Buck headed home after the three battles of the Alamo on the 6th. The pre-dawn Montoya practice would have been enough, and for Buck, the Anglo-limited honoring of his soldiers and himself was by far the best, with Vincente's Santa Anna routine certainly coming in last as not the nightmare of the 1836 original, but the worst thing short of it. Both Lori and Buck dropped on their beds when they reached the house around 10:00 in the morning. The curious Claytons didn't get to ask them about the day's events until the two woke up in the late afternoon. Lori had almost forgotten about Vincente's invitation, and Buck's acceptance of what to him sounded like a challenge, whether it was truly that or just Vincente stating the fact that it was monthly pepper night.

When Lori walked onto the patio, where the rest of the family had congregated, she was inundated by questions. Buck, who had not bothered to comb his hair, came out shortly after, the red hair sticking out rather wildly. Vicky was actually laughing at him, pointing at it, until, embarrassed, he tried to smooth it down with his hands. Lori was about finished with the day's wrap-up when he appeared.

"Well, anyway, after the Mexican ceremony didn't go so well, Vincente graciously invited us to dinner tonight at Ramale's as his guests. Considering what Buck did to him earlier, I think it's awfully nice . . . ."

"Hold on a minute, Lori, what about what he did to me?" Buck interrupted.

"You gotta admit, Buck, you started it. And I'll give you a tip—maybe folks in the 1830's went around waving swords at people—I expect a much higher percentage of the population wore swords then—but it's kind of intimidating . . . ."

"He's supposed to be Santa Anna—he shouldn't be worried about a sword . . . ."

"Buck, anyone, likely including Santa Anna, doesn't want his nose cut off by a sword. Now this is going nowhere fast. Do you want to go to Ramale's?" she asked, tiring of the war.

"Yes, it sounds fun," he said, using a word that did not sound like something folks in the 1830's would have said, but which he used with delight in his diary. The young lawyer was always in search of and gratified when he had "fun."

137

Robert turned to Elena. "I'm getting hungry just thinking about Ramale's. How about you, honey?"

"Sounds good to me," his wife replied.

"I want to go—want to see Buck beat the Mexicans in the jalapeno contest," Vicky announced.

Lori rolled her eyes.

Len was already going. Andres had invited him, completely apart from the Lori and Buck invitation. The Montoyas had planned to pick him up, but Elena called Rosalia, Andres' mom, to tell her that the Claytons had all decided to go to Ramale's, so Len would just meet Andres there.

Ramale's cantina was a hole in the wall. Had they ever had a fire, likely only whoever was sitting at the front table would have made it out alive. It was long and dark and had multicolored Christmas lights strung on the walls for lighting. That was their only bow to the stereotypical Mexican decorating scheme—no piñatas, Dia de los Muertos in general or La Catrina in particular, cactus, sombreros, or the rest. The place was about as stripped down as a restaurant could be and still serve people. Pieces of Fiesta Ware and other pottery styles, a piece of this here and that there, all mixed up, were used to serve their adoring public. In wall corners, large bunches of dried chili peppers hung from strings. Although the dining "room" so to speak was not much more than a long hall, painted a sort of hideous guacamole green, the place did open out at the front entrance. That was where the pepper-eating contests were held. On jalapeno nights, once a month, several square tables were put together, formed in a bigger square with a hole in the center—on the order of a square doughnut. Anyone who wanted to try their luck at the contest pulled up a chair. Needless to say, this attracted mostly males. Friends and relatives of the contestants stood around, behind the square, urging on their favorites. Ramale's was within walking distance of the Alamo, although not on the River Walk.

The Claytons and Buck loaded up in Robert and Elena's SUV and headed for the jalapeno showdown. Vincente and Rosalia were already there as well as their oldest daughter, Juana—Vicky's teacher, their third daughter, Margarita, and Andres. The Montoyas had come in Vincente's truck with Juana, Margarita, and Andres sitting in the bed. They were just getting out when the Claytons drove up. The families had known each other forever, but, aside from Vincente and Andres, the Montoyas had not met Buck. Used to their exalted status in Mexican reenactor circles as the family of El

138

Presidente, seeing the Texian defender outfit was a jolt, despite the fact that Vincente had clued them in ahead as to exactly who Buck was and that he could get overly excited about the Battle of the Alamo. Vicky ran to Juana and hugged her as soon as she got out of the car, blurting out:

"Look Juana, it's Col. Travis—the man in the movie you showed us! But now that we've gotten to know him, we call him Buck!"

Juana laughed at her enthusiasm and moved forward to shake hands with the colonel, who doffed his hat and gave his little bow to the young woman. He repeated the performance upon being introduced to Rosalia and Margarita. Although it was quaint, it was rather elegant and sort of sweet. They all moved into the little restaurant. The place always smelled of some kind of incense—seemed like the same odor as in church, giving it a slightly foggy atmosphere.

"Well, so it's time to—" Vincente turned to the colonel, "Shall I say it? Draw the line!" he announced.

Travis couldn't help a smile at that one.

"So who wants to try their luck with the roasted jalapenos? Colonel, I think everyone else knows, but the way this works is, if you want to participate, you grab a chair. They bring out heaping plates of roasted jalapenos. They don't count by how fast you eat them but by how many you eat. There are X number on a plate, I forget how many, but they have them counted. Of course, you can't crawl along and finish the next evening, but, like I said, it's based on numbers."

"I'll just watch," Lori said quickly. Although she thought eating contests could be amusing entertainment, she never liked the idea of doing that to herself. Not surprisingly, the other women begged off with her, as did Andres.

"I'm getting too old for this kind of thing," Robert said, stepping back with the spectators as well.

"I'll give it a go," Len said, sitting down.

That left El Presidente and Col. Travis facing each other, standing.

"Well, why not? We've already done it three times today," Buck said. "This is likely going to be fun."

139

The two men sat down. People were continuing to stream into the restaurant, all staring at Travis as they came in. Most headed past the square table arrangement, but now and then someone plopped down to wait for a plate of peppers. Vincente and Buck had just received theirs when Enrique Losa came in with a lady. He was still wearing his uniform from this morning's event. Buck had his back to Enrique when the latter walked in the door, and the chair on Buck's right was empty. Vincente was to Buck's left, and Len was across the way. As Enrique walked up to the empty chair, Len's eyes got huge, and he choked on the pepper juice, having a coughing fit. Vincente ran to his aid, but he was fine. As Travis turned and saw the Mexican uniform, he jolted.

"Relax, Colonel, it's Enrique Losa from this morning, remember? War's over. Unlike you, I suspect, I didn't intend to wear this getup tonight—was running late, had all-day commitments, and never got a chance to change. This is my wife, Ana. Ana, this is Col. William Barret Travis of Alamo fame—no kidding. We refought the battle several times this morning, if I remember correctly?" He turned to Travis, who was chewing peppers but nodded, and continued, "But that war's over right now. We're in a fight over peppers."

"Nice to meet you, Colonel," Ana greeted him.

Buck just waved at her, trying to smile a bit, but his mouth was full of peppers. Folks in the restaurant were really staring now, as the two men next to each other in the opposing uniforms from the battle downed pepper after pepper. Len, unsure why he had ever gotten into this to begin with, quit after one plate, admitted defeat, and got up and moved over to where Andres was standing. Lori and Vicky were enthusiastically urging on Buck, while Juana and her mom did the same for Vincente. Juana's sister, Margarita, was quieter. Ana just watched Enrique, not making a sound. After another round of plates for the contestants, most bowed out. Only El Presidente, the colonel, and Enrique kept going. Unlike the other women, but probably making much more sense, Ana began urging Enrique not to overeat. Finally, either her persistence got to him, or he really had enough. Among uniformed military personnel, the colonel had won the day. But he was still in a brutal competition with El Presidente, albeit in civilian clothes. Another round of plates was called for. Montoya, at 57, was disadvantaged by age, but he was an ethnic Mexican with pepper juice in his veins. The Anglo colonel was not well, but he had the advantage of being 26 and very thin—he had more room to pack food. Both of them, after all the Alamo fighting of the morning, were determined, for the honor of their causes, to win victory. Lori kept thinking about Buck's slogan. If this kept up much

140

longer, someone would get victory, but it was very possible that someone would suffer death in her view. They were both obviously slowing down as they neared cleaning the plates on round three. As the server prepared to bring another round of plates, Vincente waved them off.

"I give up. Colonel, you can have it. Right now, I don't want to see another pepper!"

Pepper juice running down his chin, the red-haired Alamo defender grinned in victory. As he got up from the table, he promptly fell over, Vincente catching him as he went down.

The colonel revived quickly, and everyone moved to a series of regular tables at the back, shoved together by the servers for their large party. Buck and Vincente were content with the house salsa and chips while everyone else ordered real meals. The Ramales normally presented a small Mexican flag stick pin to the winner of the pepper contest before that person left the restaurant, but Vincente clued them in that it was probably best to leave off that tradition this night as the young man who won was Col. Travis.

GENESIS

The San Antonio River runs through the town of the same name. In the 1700's, the Spaniards constructed a series of connected ditches and dams around San Antonio de Bexar between the town and the five missions around it. This water control network allowed for drinking water and irrigation in areas where otherwise there would be none. The system included seven acequias, or gravity-flow ditches, as well as the dams and an aqueduct. The network was extensive and elaborate. By the 1900's, much of this had been abandoned. However, a small portion of the system that ran through and around the Alamo had since been reconstructed and placed in operation at the old mission. The ditch was around 4 feet deep and was home to giant goldfish, or koi. In a sad incident some 30 years ago, the then Alamo cat—the mission had a history of cat mascots—had been found drowned in the acequia. It was not absolutely clear what had attracted her to the ditch and caused her unfortunate demise, although a pesky raccoon, possibly trying to evade being made into a hat, was one possible culprit.

The fish were an attraction in the park-like setting in back of the old church. For people who liked nature and verdant gardens more than blood and gore, it was a favorite part of the complex. Young parents brought their children here to walk around. Sometimes, on weekends, the reenactors would set up displays of 1800's life beyond the acequia. This is where Lori did her cactus frying demos. Children would stand and point at the fish swimming in the acequia, run through the grass among the old trees, and stare at the funny clothes of those in 1836 costumes or, sometimes, folks representing periods long before, when the Alamo had served as a Spanish mission for converting the local Natives.

Lori was setting up for a cactus demo on what was turning into a broiling hot day. The sun was beating down, and the bodice of her 1836 dress was wet with perspiration. She wiped sweat from her brow, not wanting it to drip into her skillet, although that probably would not have fazed a lady of Alamo days. Strange clothes were not solely the province of the reenactors. She observed a frizzy-haired woman walking by wearing an old forest-green T-shirt that proudly proclaimed that she was the "Squirrel Whisperer," the image complete with a fairly realistic picture of two tree rats looking as if they were smooching. Probably an old hippie who had too much cannabis that morning. The shirt looked as if maybe it had been in

142

the woods too long, as did its owner. Buck strolled up as the Squirrel Whisperer came by. He made a face, and Lori caught it. He was becoming more aware of the 21st Century and the fact that it could be as weird as the 19th.

"I know you will probably give me the same answer your mother did when I asked her if I could help with breakfast, but is there anything I can do?" he asked.

"Yeah. You want to get the spines off?" She handed him a cloth sack that looked like an original container from 1836, full of cactus pads.

Another woman walked by and looked in their direction. She had what appeared to be her teen daughter with her. The mom had cropped hair, the top half—to about her ears, was whitish, and the bottom half was a rich purple. It matched some huge purple earrings dangling from her ears and her purple t-shirt and Capri pants. The daughter had a neon shade of the same, so bright it looked as if it would glow in the dark. Buck was taking in the sight.

He turned to Lori and asked, "How come people stare at me?"

She looked up and caught a glimpse of the women, screwed up her face, and replied, "Good question! Of course, I've actually heard that purple hair is in now. Unfortunately, tailcoats aren't."

Lori had several knives and other implements on an ancient and worn little table that had one poorly repaired broken leg and gave every indication of having been there during the battle. He calmly picked out two of the knives, using the longer one to spear a pad and pull it out of the sack.

"If the knife isn't long enough, you can always use your sword!" she laughed.

He was so intent on what he was doing that he didn't answer her, just smiled slightly. Holding the cactus pad down with one knife, he cut off the outside edge or rim with the other knife, which was sharper. That eliminated a lot of spines. He then softly scraped the pad with the knife, knocking off the spines. He repeated the process until he had disarmed all the pads.

She glanced at his handiwork. "Have you done this before?"

He didn't answer, just asked, "Do you want me to cut them in smaller pieces? I'm done with all the spines."

"Yes, please! They're not going to be needing me for this from now on. And I'm sure it would have a higher entertainment factor for folks to watch the head man do it!"

But she did take over and do the frying in "hog fat." The colonel was corralling the spines with his knife, finally shoving all of them off one end of the table into Lori's sack. A large number of tourists were standing around, and more were heading their way as the smell of the bacon, more than the cactus, was attracting them.

Suddenly, a woman cried in anguish, "Necesito ayuda!"

Buck dropped the knife and ran toward the direction of the cry. A Hispanic woman was shouting hysterically and pointing to the acequia. When he got there, he saw a little girl, no older than 3, in the ditch, flailing in fear. He threw his hat on the ground and climbed down into the acequia. The child was panicked, crying and waving her arms in an attempt to stay afloat.

"Ven a mi! Ven a mi!" he said softly to her, reaching toward the child.

She was terrified, and the strange clothing of the man probably did not help, but she reached out her tiny arms toward him, and he pulled her up and out of the water. Carrying her back to the point where her frenzied mom was standing above, wailing, he lifted her up and into the hands of a strong man at the edge of the acequia. Then, with a hand from Jaime, who had heard the cries and come running, Buck climbed out of the ditch, the wool clothes sopping wet.

The mother was holding and caressing her daughter, who was crying and shaking slightly. Buck quietly asked her if the child was all right, and she nodded, tears streaming down her face. "Gracias, gracias," she said, looking up at the tall Anglo in the funny and drenched clothes. He gave the child a hug and headed back to Lori, receiving a spontaneous ovation from the bystanders who had witnessed the event.

"So the hero of the Alamo is not just brave in battle but also saves little children! Here, Buck, I saved some cactus for you!" Lori pushed the tin plate in front of him.

It was the Saturday after the battle. The previous evening, Vincente had called Lori to be sure they were still on go for the shopping trip. She had, in what little spare time there was, mostly evenings, started work on the reproduction 1836 clothes. She started with the vest, or waistcoat as it would have been called in Buck's day, knowing that would be the easiest, if the least important piece. She would do the pants next, as Buck's were wearing out. A second tear had to be mended after the acequia incident. Pants were the most critical piece of his costume, certainly. But he really did need the option of something less complex than his uniform, and 21st Century styles were way less complex. And they were available en masse at stores.

Lori's plan was for Vincente to pick up Buck and herself, then head for the Rivercenter Mall, which was on the other side of the Menger Hotel from the Alamo, in other words right there. They had a Macy's, which was Lori's first guess for where to shop. If the search for jeans proved successful, their next stop would be to see Morena and get Buck a "Victory or Death" shirt. Lori was glad to not be in the hot reenactor dress today. For some reason, unlike the situation at Ramale's and certainly at the Alamo, where it seemed pseudo-normal, she was a little weirded out by the fact that Buck intended to walk into Macy's in his colonel outfit. It was obvious that he was oblivious to the possibility that folks might see this as really strange. He didn't have any choice about it, anyway, but this was all the more reason to get him some normal clothes for the places where "Alamo commander" just didn't quite fit. She had not told him that there was one place in the mall where it did fit quite well. The IMAX theater showed a documentary film about the battle, which, as she recalled, featured Travis, not Crockett, unlike most Alamo movies. She toyed with whether to suggest that they go. She had seen it several times, once with the Montoyas, so she knew Vincente had seen it. Vincente had, after the viewing, pronounced it a little too slanted toward Travis & Co., which it likely was from a modern perspective. But Buck had expressed interest in the little film Vicky described, although he would not understand the concept of what a movie was until he actually saw one. Maybe this should be that opportunity.

Vincente blew the truck horn to let them know he was there. The old truck, which Vincente drove most of the time despite having a car dealership and a small fleet of new personal vehicles, only had one bench seat. All three of them squeezed in, Lori in the middle.

145

"OK, Lori, I don't usually hang out at the mall. Where are we going?" Vincente asked.

"I thought Rivercenter, maybe? They've got Macy's," she answered.

"At least I know how to get there. Rivercenter it is."

Vincente found a place in the parking lot. Lori was getting even more nervous at the prospect of getting out and strolling into the mall with the Alamo commander, with his messed up face and the blood on his coat. As much as she cared about Buck, she had to steel herself to be seen out with him in a situation like this where everyone was guaranteed to stare.

Sure enough, as they got out of the truck, a family was getting out of a car parked one space over in the row right behind them. The children and mom in the family were staring, and one boy, she guessed around 12, went beyond just pointing and gawking.

"Look, Mom, it's an Alamo guy!" They had obviously toured the mission at some point.

Buck, unfazed by this, tipped his hat to the lady and her kids. The boy saluted, and Buck returned the salute. The dad, who had been doing something in the car, got out and hit the lock button on the key.

"Parking must be at a premium around the Alamo today. The reenactors can't even get a spot," he noted.

The stares continued as they headed into Macy's. Had there been any items for which she needed to shop, she would have begged off the jeans hunting expedition and gone her way. But Lori did very little shopping, and there was nothing she needed, so she tagged along to the men's department.

There was only one clerk in sight, and he was on a phone call, turned the other direction at the little sales counter as they walked up. Fortunately, they were early enough that the store was pretty much empty. The shoppers had not quite gotten there in force yet. When the clerk got off the phone and turned, he started.

"May I help . . . ." He seemed unable to finish his sentence.

Vincente calmly jumped in. "Yes, this young gentleman is looking for some clothing that is a little more up-to-date than what he is wearing . . . ."

The wide-eyed clerk found his words, interrupting Vincente. "Just about anything would be more up-to-date."

Buck just stood there, having assumed his "colonel" position, ramrod straight.

"What are you looking for and what size do you normally wear?" the clerk turned to Travis.

"I really don't know," the colonel responded in his Southern drawl. "I'm really from the Alamo—from 1836 . . . ."

"Col. Travis! Sir! I read about you—thought it might be from the uniform." The clerk held out his hand eagerly, and Travis shook it.

"I did keep up with the latest trends in clothing before . . . before the fight," Buck looked down for a moment. "But I have no clue about sizing or options today."

Lori suggested the jeans, and the clerk took a tape measure and, shoving the bulky sash up a bit and, snaking the tape measure under the colonel's coat, measured Travis' waist, then inseam and the length of his leg. He headed over to a circular rack and hunted up a couple of pairs of pants that he thought might fit the Alamo commander.

"Sir, we have a dressing room over there," he pointed. "Right behind that fake potted plant."

Travis looked confused, not knowing what he was talking about.

"Come on, Colonel, I'll go with you to show you the ropes. And jeans are a tight fit—getting them on is a little different from some trousers," Vincente explained, leading the way.

"Can't be too much harder to get on than pantaloons," Buck replied.

The clerk stared after him, while Lori shook her head and smiled.

This mission was a success, and Vincente thought to pick up some modern underwear and socks as well, and some sneakers for the clueless Travis, so the hard part of setting about remaking Buck into a semblance of a modern man—in appearance, anyway, was done.

147

"One more thing before we head over to the Alamo," Lori asked. "Buck, there's an IMAX movie that they only play here about the fight. It's very brief. You are a major character in it, of course. Do you want to see it?

"A what?"

"Remember Vicky's description of the movie she saw at school—that we have a way to keep a copy of a play basically? Well, this is another one of those, only it's a special type on a huge screen," she tried to explain, to no avail. It was one of those things that had to be experienced, and trying to convey that to someone from the 1800's was impossible.

"Do I get killed in it?"

"Yeah, unfortunately, I think so, since it's the story of the Alamo. But, if you want to see a short movie to see what they are, this is a good opportunity. Do you want to see it?" she reiterated.

"I guess so," he said with a little hesitation in his voice.

Vincente didn't really want to see it again, as he did get tired of the old story about Buck and his friends fighting off the Mexican hordes. And he seriously questioned if this was a good idea on Lori's part, considering the finale. But he didn't say anything, just made an excuse about an errand he had to run at the other end of the mall and said that he would be waiting out front for them when it was over.

The film showed constantly, on the hour, starting up again shortly after each 48-minute showing ended. Since it was early in the day and this film had been around for eons so most people had seen it one or more times, they had no wait. That did not stop the ticket taker from stopping dead in her tracks when Lori and Buck walked up.

"Huh?" was all she could say at first, her mouth open.

"I've been told that I'm in this thing," Buck told her.

"Yeah, I guess so," she recovered her senses enough to reply. "I heard about an Alamo guy being found. Guess you're the one?" He nodded, and she continued, "Sure you want to see this? It's not going to turn out too well for you, you know."

"Believe me, I'm aware of that," he responded. "I've already come back

148

once. Maybe I'll have to do it again!"

She stared after them as they headed toward the theater. The cavernous space was eerie. The screen was enormous, the intent being to make the audience feel like they were in whatever program was being shown. In this particular case, that idea had questionable merit for viewers in general and Buck in particular. Fortunately, Lori saw only a handful of people waiting for the start of the show. The place was nearly empty. Not knowing how Buck would react when the Mexicans broke through on their third charge—at least that's the way she thought she remembered it happening, she was not anxious for many witnesses. At least it would be brief.

It had been years since Lori last saw it. It featured a rather grubby Alamo with rather grubby defenders, and a good-looking redhead who bore some passing resemblance to the real thing playing the lead. The Texian rebels raised a white flag with a blue star with "Liberty" above and "Victory or Death!" below emblazoned on it. Buck pointed at the banner, whispering to Lori proudly that it was "his flag," another mystery solved.

The story of the brave little band went on. Travis drew his line, then waved his sword and shouted "Victory or Death!" and gave his cat's eye ring to little Angelina Dickinson, and ended up finally standing at the north wall directing the cannon fire and waving his sword until shot in the forehead. Lori glanced at Buck, who, even in the dim light, she could tell was rather pale. The film featured one variation on the account where Travis, fading fast from the forehead wound, ended up, from a sitting position, summoning the strength to dispatch a Mexican officer with his sword, as the Mexican attempted to finish off the dying colonel. As his sword sank into the enemy soldier on screen, the real Buck weakly murmured, "Never surrender." Lori felt something heavy on her shoulder. It was Buck's head. He had fainted. Fortunately, he missed Santa Anna's survey of the dead littering the place and his request to see and rather lengthy viewing of the Alamo commander's corpse, including pushing the colonel's blood-covered sword out of Travis' dead hand with his boot. As the film was ending, she shook Buck to try to revive him.

"Buck, are you OK?" she whispered.

He was slowly coming to. "What happened?"

"You mean to you now or in the film?"

He looked dazed. "I'm confused. Where am I?"

149

"We're in the theater. The film just got over. You passed out when that Mexican officer plunged his sword toward you and you skewered him with yours just before you expired on the screen. I can see why. You are lucky you passed out. It didn't get any better after that. Let's get out of here if you think you can walk."

She led the weak and dizzy Buck out of the theater, past the ticket taker, who was not surprised, and to a wooden bench right outside. Vincente was waiting.

"How did the battle go, Colonel? Did you turn the tide this time?" he asked.

"Shh, Vincente. He passed out toward the end." Lori threw a look that said "shut up" to him.

Buck was coming back to the present and realized he did not just see someone coming at him with a sword and his final life's effort in killing the Mexican. He turned to Lori. "You said you can watch that over and over? I think I'll pass on that."

"One of the best ideas you have ever had, Colonel," Vincente replied. He was anxious to close the book on "Alamo, Price of Freedom" and get out of the mall. "I wish I could think of somewhere else to go first, but I guess we're headed back to the Alamo to look at those shirts Morena has?" he asked.

Buck looked pale. For the first time since they had known him, the Alamo commander's countenance gave the distinct impression that he did not want to go to his post.

"How about we get ice cream at the Menger first?" Lori suggested. "That mango is incredible—a bit pricy, but it has a wow factor!"

Vincente, looking at the drawn face of the colonel, agreed. Heading toward the mall exit, they passed the Battle for Texas Museum, where a grinning, faux Davy Crockett was hawking tickets. Buck, still not recovered from the film, never even noticed, much to Lori's and Vincente's relief. Davy paused to stare at his commanding officer, gave a quick salute, then returned to his ticket sales.

They sat in the elegant Colonial Room, savoring the expensive ice cream. All of the servers were Hispanic. They stared but went about their duties as usual. The ice cream seemed to revive the colonel, who had never tasted anything like it before. He seemed to enjoy it immensely. Some color had returned to his face by the time they finished. Vincente paid for the treat, then they walked over to the Alamo.

Morena was busy with a customer as they walked in. On Saturdays, the place was always packed with tourists, pretty much standing room only. She saw them in the distance, gave a big wave, then went back to her customer. Buck stared in the direction of the fudge, as usual.

"You just had ice cream, Buck," Lori noted as she watched him crane his neck toward the back right corner of the store.

"I know . . . but it's awfully good," came the response.

"Well, our mission right now is to get you a 21$^{st}$ Century shirt with your 19$^{th}$ Century battle cry emblazoned on it—follow me!" Lori directed.

Sure enough, in amongst a variety of shirts featuring Ol' Davy swinging a rifle and with a dead raccoon on his noggin and Jim Bowie cutting up Mexican soldiers with his vicious knife as the enemy closed in around him, was one for Travis, a bit more refined, as befitted the commander. No pictures of the colonel drawing his line—which would actually not have been bad, or, worse, getting shot in the head. Simply a black shirt with the Victory or Death logo above a picture of the Alamo and the year 1836 below.

"Turn around, Buck," she ordered. "I'm sure you're going to wear a large, but I want to hold the shirt up against your back!" He followed her command.

Some of the customers had noticed the tall young man in the defender outfit and had ceased their efforts to spend money at the shop long enough to stare in curiosity.

"Say, are you the one they dug up?" one man called from across the way, unfortunately, in Lori's view, causing more patrons to focus in their direction.

Travis nodded in assent as the man came toward him. "Which one are you?" the fellow continued.

The colonel had experienced enough of this kind of thing at this point

151

that he understood the routine. "Well, you don't see a coon on my head, do you, or a really large knife in my belt?"

The shopper, who didn't seem particularly well-versed on the history of the Alamo, shook his head in disappointment. "So you ain't Ol' Davy, King of the Wild Frontier, are you?"

"Most definitely not," came the reply.

"And who's that other fella?" the man persisted.

He seemed to be ignoring the possibility that it could be someone other than one of the Alamo's Big Three, and it was obvious he had not read—or at least retained if he did—the story of the defender's revival. A homely looking woman, apparently his wife or girlfriend, whispered in his ear.

The man continued, "Sorry, I saw the film over at the theater, but I had a hard time keeping everyone straight. Bowie is the guy with the knife, right?"

Travis nodded. "Yes, Bowie is the guy with the knife," he repeated the man's detailed analysis.

"So you must be the other one—the leader—Travis?"

The colonel smiled slightly, trying desperately not to be rude and laugh outright at the man. "Yes, I'm Col. Travis."

Another bystander asked, "So Colonel, what are you doing buying a 'Victory or Death' shirt?"

"Well, after all, I did come up with the phrase," came the reply.

At that point, Lori tapped him on the shoulder. "The large will do just fine—it's preshrunk, too."

"Huh?" he looked at her.

"Don't worry about it. Believe me, this is fine. Let's go over there," she pointed toward the fudge.

"Yes ma'am!" Buck replied. Vincente rolled his eyes.

Lori was headed to the back of the complex with her sack, a Texian cornbread cooking demo being in the offing, when a middle-aged woman with stylish blonde hair and better-than-usual clothes for a tourist hailed her.

"Ma'am, do you work here?" the woman asked in a slightly annoyed tone. Her accent clearly indicated she was a Texas native.

"Yes, I do! I dress up for demos, but I also do some office work. Is there something I can do to help you?"

The woman had reached Lori and stopped, stating tersely, "I've got a complaint!"

"May I help you?" Lori asked again, hesitantly.

"No, I need to see a manager," the visitor replied firmly.

"Sounds like maybe you need to talk with Mr. Gordon," Lori replied. "Come with me."

She led the tourist to the gift shop and down the stairs to Bob's sty. He was at his desk, just finishing up a call. He hung up and stood.

"Bob, this lady has a concern and asked to talk with a manager," Lori said.

Bob motioned for the woman to sit down, and Lori headed out as fast as she could.

"Bob Gordon, ma'am. What can I do for you?" Bob queried.

"There's one of your reenactors that you need to do something about. I don't know if they are employees or not, although the girl who just left said she does reenacting and is employed here. Anyway, this guy is a disgrace. He should not be representing the Alamo—will turn off all the visitors, quite frankly."

Bob was alarmed. "Has someone done something . . . inappropriate?"

153

he queried in a worried tone.

"No, he hasn't done anything at all. He seems to just sit there on a bench over near that huge cannon," she pointed the way. "I'm guessing he must be a wounded warrior. I know the feds have some requirements about not discriminating, but this guy looks so awful that he's going to have a repelling effect on people—especially kids. His face is badly disfigured, and he's actually got what looks like bloodstains on his reenactor clothes—I don't get that. Maybe he needs to do something less public. I teach at a private school in Fort Worth—was down here for a conference and thought I'd come by as it's been years since I've been to the Alamo. I was thinking of arranging a field trip for my class, but I'm not sure I would want them to see this man if he happened to be here. It's that disturbing. He just does not represent what the Alamo is all about!"

Bob burst out laughing. He couldn't help it. The teacher went from being mildly annoyed to looking downright angry. She started to get up.

"Well, if that's the way you folks respond to a citizen's concern about keeping the Alamo as a reverent shrine to the defenders, I don't think I'll be back at all, with or without my students!" She turned to go.

"Ma'am, please, sit down," Bob said in a firm tone.

The teacher, startled, turned back and reluctantly sat down, still annoyed.

"Yes, I totally agree with you that the major 'mission,' if you will, here is reverence for the men who died in the battle. You know, in the films they show gallant Col. Travis drawing a line with his sword, jovial Davy Crockett with his raccoon on his head and playing a fiddle or telling tall tales, and fierce, tough Jim Bowie with his menacing knife. The sad fact is that, although we like to remember them that way, that's not what they looked like after Santa Anna got through with them."

The woman was staring at Bob as if he had gone daft.

He continued. "What was left of the brave defenders as the Mexicans started hauling the corpses out for disposal had nothing remotely of the gallant, jovial, or tough to it. Travis, Crockett, Bowie, and the others were, quite frankly, just shot-up, bludgeoned dead carcasses drenched in blood in the end . . . ."

154

She started to rise again. "I don't need to hear this disrespectful . . . ."

"Sit down and hear me out, please. It's gruesome, yes, but that's what makes their stand so remarkable—what makes these men so remarkable. They knew that was coming, although they may not have actually visualized the horror of the aftermath, and yet they persevered. The fellow you saw is the one we found at the dig here—don't know if you saw that in the news?"

She nodded slightly. "Saw something but figured the guy died or was in a hospital . . . ."

"No, he works here—in fact, the governor put him back in charge of the place. I guess, technically, maybe you should have been referred to him for your complaint!"

"Back in charge of the place? Is that what you said?" she asked.

"Yes, that's what I said, and he does sometimes like to sit near his big cannon. It's the one he fired at the Mexicans when they showed up with their red flag. He was a good-looking young man and rather vain about his appearance in his earlier life, and he's extremely conscious of what Santa Anna did to him."

"Colonel Travis?" the woman asked meekly.

"Yes, ma'am," Bob said softly with a little smile.

She hung her head. "Well, I guess even a teacher never stops learning," she smiled. "Forgive me, but I think I need to go—there's someone else from whom I need to ask to forgiveness," she smiled.


Bob Gordon woke up a bundle of nerves on March 14. The two mid-level reps from the Mexican consulate were scheduled to show up for the meeting regarding the possibility of a loan of something, they still not had said what, from the Mexican National Museum, at 10:00. The fact that mid-level folks were being sent made it clear that this was simply a fact-finding mission. The question was what did they want? Bob was sure it would go nowhere, but he still wanted to be gracious and put on a good face for his guests. They may very well have had ancestors at the battle for all he knew. Fortunately, they would not be dressed in Mexican military uniforms, antique or current, as they were civilian functionaries. But they were employees of the Mexican government.

There had been no way to hide their coming from Travis, who had bitterly denounced the meeting, demanding that it be canceled. Bob tried to reason with him, explaining that, although chances were very slim, it might lead toward being able to have something the Mexicans had from the battle return on loan to the Alamo. The colonel didn't care. He was adamant that no Mexican government officials would set foot on the grounds of his post. He had turned and stomped out when Bob said it was set and there was nothing he could do to change it. Bob hoped Travis would stay in his office, brooding about Santa Anna or whatever he did when he got into these 1836 snits. But, with past experience in mind, he sought ought Elbert, warning him that he might want to alert all of the rangers to be vigilant. He didn't want any more battles on the order of the experience on the 6th.

Promptly, at 10:00, a couple of men wearing suits walked in the gate. They had parked in the nearby pay lot. One of them asked a bystander to direct him to the gift shop, Bob having told the consulate that his office was below the store. The woman pointed in the direction and went on. Bob had no intention of having his guests try to find their way down to the pigsty—in fact, he had no intention of taking them to see the sty. He was standing a little in front of the building, awaiting their arrival, and it was fairly obvious from their dress that the two men heading his direction were not tourists. The visitors seemed slightly disoriented. Mexican government officials did not usually come to the Alamo these days.

Bob gave a wave and started to walk toward them. When he got close, he extended his hand and introduced himself. The two men, Raul Perez and Roberto Tomas, shook hands and gave their names. Bob figured that his best ice-breaker might be to start out with a little tour of the place and talk while they walked.

The Mexicans were very friendly but understandably reserved about what possibilities were out there regarding the loan. Bob did learn that the artifact in question was a flag that supposedly flew over the fort when it was taken—it almost had to be the New Orleans Grays flag. That was the most useful piece of information he was able to glean from the conversation. After a tour of the church, he led them over to Morena's shop and introduced them to the famous fudge. The two men somewhat added balance to Travis' choice by asking for the *El Deguello* dyed-red vanilla fudge. Good thing the colonel didn't see that, Bob thought to himself.

They walked out of the building, Perez, who spoke clearer English than

Tomas, commenting about the delicious fudge, when Bob heard rapid footsteps. He glanced up just as Travis, sword in hand, reached them. He had his arm raised, the sword pointing to the sky.

"I demand that you leave this post immediately! No Mexicans are allowed in this fort!" he yelled.

Perez and Tomas looked at each other, then at Bob.

"Colonel, put the sword down now!" Bob shouted.

It was no use as he should have known. Travis swung the weapon at the two visitors, who parted to the sides as it came down between them. Jaime had heard the yelling and was running toward them, reaching the colonel before he could strike another blow. Jaime wrested the sword from Travis' hand and threw it as far as he could, the weapon landing under a pecan tree. Travis was no match for Jaime's bulky strength. The ranger had the colonel's arms pinned behind his back in no time.

"Sorry, sir," Jaime apologized to the man who was technically in command. "You can't just murder any Mexican who comes in the gate."

Travis struggled to free himself, to no avail. "Murder? Murder?" he shouted. "What do you think they did to us!"

Perez was trying not to laugh, and Tomas looked slightly annoyed. Bob was embarrassed. Perez, who kept up with current events, took the lead in the awkward situation, turning to the angry colonel, who had uttered another threat to the Mexican officials after Jaime contained him.

"Colonel Travis, I assume? Sir, your bravery in defense of the Alamo is legendary. Your defiant personality is, too!"

Travis let loose with the most vulgar response he could think of—in Spanish: "Besame el culo!"

Perez burst out laughing. It was infectious, and soon Tomas and Jaime were chuckling as well. Bob did not speak Spanish and was clueless.

Jaime pushed the Alamo commander ahead of him, away from Bob and his companions, Travis fruitlessly squirming to free himself from Jaime's grasp and still yelling. Bob apologized profusely for Travis' outburst, ending simply with saying, "We don't know how to control him."

157

"I had heard that Col. Travis had returned to the land of the living," Perez told the others. "He's still fighting the battle after all these years. That poor young man is not quite right. You might call him a bit disturbed," he said with a smile. "We will dismiss the incident—and the colonel—as entertainment," he laughed.

The next morning, Lori and Buck drove into town as usual. She had been off the day before but had dropped him off at his command post before heading off to do errands and then trying to get some work done on sewing his clothes. He had seemed agitated when she picked him up but hadn't said anything. This morning, he was just quiet. When they got there, Buck headed for his office to scratch out something with his quill. Lori hurried to her cubbyhole. Fortunately, it was not a dress-up day. As she stuffed her purse below her feet, Bob called her.

"Lori, got a minute?" he asked. As she turned in to his office, Bob queried, "Did the colonel say anything to you about yesterday?"

"No. In the evening, he seemed kind of in a snit about something, really quiet and brooding. I didn't ask."

"The two guys from the Mexican consulate came over for our talk. I really didn't have a good place to sit down with them with things being so cramped here and some of the renovations going on, and I certainly didn't want to bring them down here . . . ."

She giggled. "Wise decision."

"Anyway, I figured this was casual enough that we could just walk around the grounds while we talked. I got a bit more uptight when they showed up dressed in dark suits—was concerned that they thought I might not be showing proper respect without a formal meeting. Fortunately, they were very nice. One guy, a Mr. Perez, who spoke better English than his companion, was particularly gracious. Not many Mexican officials visit the Alamo. It's a sore point with them. They see us as having turned their victory into a moral victory for Anglos—that Texas Trinity thing."

She nodded, and he continued.

"I took them over to the gift shop to meet Morena and her fudge. That seems to be an ice breaker for just about anybody. She gave them free samples, and they picked the *El Deguello*. I was relieved that you-know-who did not see that."

Lori was laughing at this point.

"Well, that may seem funny, but it got deadly serious after that."

"What do you mean?"

"We had just left the gift shop, when he showed up, running toward us, waving the sword and ordering the Mexicans out of his fort."

"Oh no."

"You should have seen the stunned looks on their faces. Worse yet, he followed through and swung the sword at them. The two split, one to the right, one to the left, and the sword came right down between them. Fortunately, Jaime had heard the commotion and got there in time to grab Travis before he could take another swipe at them. Jaime made the mistake of telling the colonel he should not try to murder every Mexican he saw, and Travis, in a rage, shouted back something about the Mexicans murdering 'us'—his command. It was awful. Fortunately, Mr. Perez and his companion handled it very well. Perez did actually address Travis, telling him something about his bravery being legendary but also his personality!"

Lori was laughing again, although she knew something serious was eventually going to come out of one of these confrontations if they continued.

"Anyway, after Jaime led Travis away, Perez noted that the colonel seemed to be a disturbed young man, but they would chalk him up as Alamo entertainment. I hope that is true, but I doubt Travis will ever see the one remaining flag that flew over his fort," Bob said sadly.

"So what do we do?" Lori queried.

"I don't know. You know the rapidly changing demographics are making it worse for Buck. Hispanic folks tend to have a way different take on the Alamo and always have. But there's also a big shift in viewpoints among scholars and historians to where it's not just a black and white issue of brave, outnumbered defenders against a massive army lead by a megalomaniac anymore. William Barret Travis is suffering another defeat, this one to his personality. And he caused a lot of it himself. Did you ever

159

read Long's history of the battle?—it's been out for years now but has a much more updated view than the older histories," Bob asked.

She shook her head. "Uh, no. Actually, I never tried to read all of the Alamo scholarship around. I read some of the books years ago. One was *13 Days to Glory*—way back, but I'm more into the clothes, cooking, life on the frontier kind of thing," Lori began.

"Yeah, I know. Well, Long created a firestorm among traditionalists when the book came out. The academics who debate all this stuff are often proclaimed pacifists. They certainly tend toward a liberal bent, but they still like a good fight, just with the pen, not the sword. Although they don't use bullets, sometimes the words can cause tremendous damage. The direction in publications has been going more and more that way since, busting the myth of the Texas Trinity as it were. Travis comes in for particularly scathing treatment. Honestly, the fact is the writer didn't have to do much to create the image of a self-absorbed, fanatically cause-oriented, impetuous young dandy with a death wish, who, though basically smart and very good with words, comes off as disliked by his men, addicted to sex, mentally impaired from the mercury treatments, vainglorious, and something of a fool."

"Buck?"

"Yes, Buck. I'm not saying I think all of that is true, but there are elements of it that have some credence. All you have to do is look. The fact is that Travis handed them the ammunition they are using on him."

Lori had a puzzled look on her face.

Bob continued, "The source Long and the others since have used for this unflattering portrayal is Buck himself—the diary. He didn't know it at the time, but he was quite effective in destroying himself given that someone who came along after he was dead could use his words in a way to form an impression of him. The result is that modern scholarship is destroying the colonel as effectively as Santa Anna did, only, in this case, it's not physical."

"That's awful," she said softly.

"Well, all you have to do is quote him and put a damning spin on his words—piece of cake."

160

"Poor Buck."

"Long was particularly cruel. He ferreted out every little thing that Travis mentioned and ridiculed it—left no stone unturned. There was an old story about a woman who murdered her husband in the neck of the woods Travis was from in South Carolina. Tied to the story was a reference to the place as 'Pandemonium'—home of devils or chaos. Long made a point of noting this was appropriate for the colonel's birthplace, insinuating something about him clearly, when the story was about someone else. He made fun of the fact that Buck noted his use of lavender and bergamot."

"I can guess why he did that," Lori shot back. "They didn't have deodorant back then ."

"True, but most people did not commit to paper their use of it in detail—and that was in town. Buck was dealing with rough and ready frontiersmen in the Alamo—they did not use lavender. They likely laughed their heads off at the cocky young fop outside of his presence, possibly in his presence."

"He doesn't seem that cocky to me," Lori interjected.

"I think the Alamo knocked a little of that out of him. But he was in his earlier life. Now, he's not the handsome rake with a bevy of belles that he was then. He's famous, which is something he wanted desperately, but he had to give up a lot of other things to get there. It is clear from the evidence that the men of the garrison did not warm to him the way they did to a much tougher customer—Bowie, who would wrestle and drink until the cows came home. That's what the Alamo garrison needed in a leader, not a high-brow young lawyer with fancy clothes and crazed notions of freedom and liberty who gave them long-winded speeches and spent most of his time in his quarters writing all those letters. Long ridiculed Travis' law practice, noting a case where the issue was a stolen chamber pot."

Lori could not suppress another laugh.

"I think that's unfair," Bob continued his analysis. "Fact is that frontier lawyers took what cases came to them, just as attorneys do now."

Lori was still laughing.

"I don't think anyone would sue over a chamber pot—or let's update to a toilet—now," she suggested.

"Maybe not, but attorneys do take what they can get a fee from. Long's critique even included the fact that Travis meticulously wrote down what he paid for everything, how much he lost at card games, or the amount he spent on candy to give kids. Sadly, Long did not note that Travis was consistently kind to children—had a weakness for them."

"Well, that last is just being sweet—he does like children. That's obvious from the way he treats Vicky, his reaction to the letter from the child in the wheelchair, and the fact that he jumped in the acequia to save that little girl—and she was Hispanic," Lori defended Buck.

"Long treated the figures in the diary as evidence of another obsession. He really did emphasize the long list of negative traits and said nothing positive about him except acknowledging the writing skills. An oft-copied review of the Long book called Travis, as described by the author, a 'syphilic satyr' and a 'buffoon'—doesn't get much worse than that. Like I said earlier, even more revisionist accounts have come out since. And they're all piling on, making the story bigger and worse until they've created a Travis no one would like and most would despise. I get the distinct feeling—and this is in the old accounts, too, but I've seen it in action as well, that the colonel does not fancy being laughed at. A guy who goes around wearing an Alamo costume and waving a sword is already at a risk of that. Once the revisionist historians get through with him, he will probably wish Santa Anna had burned him."

Lori wiped away a tear. It was no longer funny. "How can I protect him from this?" she asked.

"Sad thing is you can't. Colonel Travis is going to have to learn to blend in a little better in the 21st Century, appearance-wise and with his views, or this trend may destroy what Santa Anna could not."


The two of them stood in front of the little plot of ground, straight and serious, almost like the farm couple in *American Gothic*, although much younger and better looking. A small crowd of tourists had formed around Lori and Buck. It was 9:30—early in the Alamo visitor hours, but not so hot as to be unbearable for the task at hand. They had commandeered a small plot of land in the garden area in back of the buildings for their vegetable growing demos.

Lori welcomed the spectators with a smile. "Good morning, everyone!

162

We're going to show y'all how to plant vegetables properly in frontier Texas. I am Lori Clayton. I've been a volunteer here at the Alamo for a couple of years."

"And I'm William Barret Travis. I've been here at the Alamo a little longer than Lori—181 years. They dug me up in February," Buck explained to laughter. He launched right into the demo: "Now there are several ways to prepare the soil. You can dig a hole for each seed with a trowel, or you can make one continuous furrow and drop the seeds in at intervals. Either way, you don't want it too deep. I'm going to make long furrows, and for that you need something sharp to cut into the soil. I realize y'all may have to find something else, but I'm going to use my sword." He held it out so they could see it.

"Gives that drawing a line in the dirt thing a whole new meaning," Lori added to more laughter.

"I think we should line the okra plants up over here, the peppers over here," he explained to her, pointing directions for each.

"You're the military man. Wherever you think everything should go is fine with me, Colonel," she replied with a laugh and a salute. "While he's setting up the troop configuration he wants for seed placement, I'm going to tell you about some of the seeds we like to plant in our little garden."

She reached into an old cloth sack and pulled out some antique-looking seed packets from an heirloom seed company. It was the most authentic thing she could find, though, truth be told, the early settlers saved seeds from last year's crops and didn't put them in packets. A family came up to the side, quietly watching. Travis stood and used the point of the sword to make shallow furrows for the seeds. He proceeded to draw eight perfectly even lines in formation for his troops—four for the peppers to the left, and four for the okra to the right.

Lori glanced at him and called out, "You aren't going to yell 'Victory or Death' are you?"

"No, but why don't we see who can plant faster?" he challenged her. "You take the okra, and I'll take the peppers."

"Winner gets what?" she laughed.

"I don't know—I guess the 'Victory,'" he replied.

"I don't much like that if I don't win," she retorted. Everyone was laughing. It was the most entertaining demo at the fort since Crockett and Bowie's last performance.

More people came up to watch the demonstration.

"That sword comes in handy for drawing all kinds of lines, doesn't it, Colonel?" a man who had just walked up called.

Travis turned, smiled slightly, and tipped his hat, then returned to the work at hand.

Lori continued, "Okra is great for hot climates—like San Antonio, and it's a staple of Southern dishes, so we've got some okra seeds. You will recognize them as the little pink spheres that you see in an okra pod. They're just dried now." She held a handful out and showed them to the audience. "The most popular items to grow in these parts are peppers—all kinds. The seeds are very light-weight and relatively flat. They absolutely thrive in the hot weather—as long as we don't get too much rain."

A rather fat woman, bulging in her clingy pink t-shirt featuring, of all things, Hello Kitty—Lori didn't think they made the items, which mostly appealed to young children, in those sizes—called out in a country voice that placed her from somewhere around Alabama: "Y'all aren't going to have a crop that you can actually eat in 13 days—no point in bothering!"

Lori and Buck turned to each other and smiled. He didn't bother to face the woman and give dignity to the comment by responding.

"You, sir," Travis pointed to a tall, large man in a blue shirt. "Yell 'Go' and we'll start."

Lori and Buck were each positioned on their knees at the far end of the garden patch. The man gave the command, and the two frantically started dropping their seeds and covering them up. Although Lori had been doing this alone for a couple years, he was obviously ahead of her. Of course, he wasn't wearing a cumbersome dress. When they were about halfway through, she glanced hurriedly his way.

"I thought you're a lawyer?" she asked, putting another seed in a hole.

"I am, but I grew up on a farm," he replied, still ahead of her and adeptly dropping the seeds and covering them.

164

Finally, he dropped his last pepper seed in a hole, covered it, and jumped to his feet, yelling "Victory or Death!" and giving his little bow to the crowd.

"Shut up, Buck!" Lori responded as she covered her last seed. "You don't look like Victory—your white pants aren't white anymore."

Buck suffered another tear to the ancient pants, this time at the knee, while he was on the ground planting pepper seeds. Both of them were dirty. Why anyone in the grungy 1830's chose to wear white pants was unfathomable to Lori. All of the 1836 clothes would have to be washed. But the crowd loved it, giving them an ovation for a job well and entertainingly done.

The newly planted seeds needed water. Buck instinctively went over to the old well, quickly realizing when he got there that it was no longer in service. At that point, he tied ropes to the handles of a wooden bucket, weighted it, and lowered it into the acequia, a couple of children standing at the edge admiring the goldfish moving out of his way. The water was gently poured on the new seeds. He had to make numerous trips to get them all watered.

"How come you don't just use a hose? The Alamo has running water. I just washed my hands in the bathroom," a child who looked to be about 8, asked.

"Well, we didn't in 1836," Buck replied, carrying the last of the bucketfuls to the hopeful future crop.

The crowd was dispersing, and the sun was high overhead, beating down on Lori and Buck in their 1836 regalia.

"Let's go inside the church—it's dark and cool in there," Lori suggested.

Buck had only been back inside the old chapel twice since 1836. Both were very quick walks in the main sanctuary. He had not "toured" the exhibits in that hallowed ground. In fact, the subject had not come up. As they entered the dark little church, they had to adjust their eyesight slightly. Badly needed restoration of the inside of the chapel was already starting, and the artifacts on display there were slated to be moved out to some other location very soon. The place was full of tourists milling around, as usual. There had been exhibits in the main sanctuary, showcasing old pre-1836 documents tracing the mission history of San Antonio de Valero, but they had been removed the previous month. The exhibits that drew the tourists, however, were not those relating to mission life in a language most Anglos could not read as well as being difficult because of the quaint penmanship of so long ago. The rooms off to the left of the main sanctuary held glass cases with pathetic few mementos of the battle—personal belongings of the defenders. Buck had not ventured here.

"How come everyone seems to always head that way?" Buck asked Lori as they were standing in the cool darkness.

"To see Davy Crockett's vest and one of his rifles," she responded flatly. "We can go if you like?"

"I . . . I don't know," he wavered.

"Well, we certainly don't have to." She didn't want to push it.

"I guess maybe I'll poke put my head in the doorway," he said, still hesitant, but she followed behind him.

The tourists were thronging around Davy's rifle, especially the men, pointing at it and sometimes raising their voices in excitement beyond what was appropriate in the Shrine until nudged and cajoled to quiet it down by their female companions. One of Davy's elaborate embroidered buckskin vests—not something that would be remotely stylish today and actually was not in the 1830's, was on display. As the card noted, it was not the one he wore in the fight. Once in the tiny room with the herd, one had to pretty much commit to stand there until they slowly moved along.

Lori suddenly thought of a reason for backing out, glancing back toward the sanctuary. It was virtually impossible to swim against the tide without making a huge scene, and she was already there and with a guy in a bloodstained 1836 costume. She wished she had thought to come up with a convincing excuse for never entering here—Morena's fudge, anything but the slow forward motion of the throng. Finally, the large number of men discussing the caliber projectiles Davy used and how far off he could hit a man began to inch forward so that another group of like-minded males could have that same conversation. The sick feeling in Lori's stomach was getting stronger. They moved ahead to the next case. Lori tried to stand in front of Buck, although she had seen all of this before. But he was enough taller that he had a clear view over her shoulder. All of a sudden, he fell, the scabbard clanking on the stone floor as he hit.

166

"Buck!" Lori screamed, certainly breaking the rules about quiet in the Shrine. She ducked to the ground, pulling him up and holding his head, afraid that he might have hit it on the hard flagstone. The tourists moved back slightly, giving them a little room. A few of them continued on to the next case, around the corner, but most just stood there staring. Someone alerted Jaime that there was a medical incident. The ranger came running.

"Lori, what's wrong?" he asked when he saw them. "Colonel, are you OK?"

"I realized when we got to the Crockett exhibit that we shouldn't have come in here, but there were so many people coming in that it was too awkward to try to get past them to get out. I think he saw it—went down like a rock," she looked up at Jaime.

Jaime checked Travis' pulse and felt his forehead. "I think he just passed out. Give it a couple minutes. I'm going to get some water—will be back in a sec," he said.

The tourists were all staring.

"Buck, wake up. I'm sorry. This was an awful idea. I shouldn't have brought you in here," Lori said softly, still cradling his head and brushing the red hair with her hand.

"Pardon me, lady, but what's going on?" one woman with a northeastern accent finally asked.

"Did you read in the news about the Alamo defender who was revived?" Lori asked.

The woman gave a puzzled look, but several of the other people nodded affirmatively.

"We found him during an archaeological dig. The defenders were supposedly all burned by Santa Anna, but we found this one thrown face down in the latrine. See the gunshot wound?" she pointed to the obvious hole in his forehead. "The other wounds were the mutilation by Mexican soldiers—they did that to the defenders' bodies after they killed everyone. We did DNA. This is Col. Travis. The ring in the case was given to him by his fiancée. It's the one he tied on a string for the only little Anglo girl in the fort, Angelina Dickinson. He put it around her neck the night before the attack, knowing he would no longer need it. I shouldn't have let him see it."

Jaime was back with some water, and the two of them got Buck to take a little of it. He moved his head slightly, then opened his eyes. Rules or no rules regarding noise in the Shrine, the tourists cheered the Alamo's hero.

Lori was still feeling guilty about letting Buck see the ring. She wanted to do something special for him, and she hadn't been able to get the "Victory or Death" flag out of her mind. Late that night, after everyone was asleep, she went through her voluminous array of fabric remnants, uncovering just what she wanted—a nice piece of high-quality, silky white cotton. She would hand-draw the single star and stencil the letters, then paint them in blue fabric paint to make Buck's flag. She would spend a little time late each evening as she had a chance to recreate the banner that flew over the Alamo.

"Sir! Can you tell me about Davy Crockett?" Travis looked down to see a small boy, around 7, staring up at him and pulling lightly on his sash.

The colonel motioned the child out of the crowded pathway. "Let's sit over here," he guided the boy underneath one of the pecan trees where it was cooler in the shade. "So what is your interest in Congressman Crockett?"

"I think his coonskin cap is really cool!" the child answered enthusiastically. "And I know he supposedly killed lots of bears, wrestled alligators, and went down fighting, swinging his rifle at the Mexicans," the boy continued. "Saw his story on the Disney channel on TV."

This last was Greek to Travis, but he got the general idea where the child was coming from.

The boy looked at him squarely, "Sir, did you know him?"

"Well, yes, I did," Buck replied. "He was a fine, fine man. I'll have to say he was one of the few people I've ever known who was able to draw all kinds of different folks together. He liked people, and they liked him."

"Did he really wear a coonskin cap and buckskin coat and carry a gun called Old Betsy?" the boy continued.

"Some of the time," came the answer. "But he told me those caps are kind of hot unless the weather is really cold, and they can get stinky!"

The child wrinkled his nose. A more serious look came across his small face. "Tell me, why did they kill him?" the boy asked sadly.

"The Mexican general, Santa Anna, was a cruel and heartless foe. He didn't like it that the defenders were fighting for freedom—American style. A man like Congressman Crockett had a hard time even being cooped up in the Alamo for the time of the siege. He certainly wasn't going to let some crazed dictator tell him how to live his life and take away his freedom to choose what he wanted to do and when. The Mexican culture, at least then, did not include freedom. Crockett and all of us knew the value of being free to make your own decisions. Honestly, a life without that is not much of a life. And that sacred right was worth everything, even life itself, to preserve. That's still true today. That's why Crockett and all of the defenders fought so hard and were willing to make the supreme sacrifice."

"He's my hero," the boy replied.

"An excellent choice. I am sure Congressman Crockett would be proud and honored. When you think of the congressman, think of his bravery and love of liberty. But also think about the first thing I told you about him—how he related to other people. If you can master that skill, and I'll have to admit that I am not so good at it, it will help you immensely in dealing with all the things you have to handle in life. I kind of envied him when I saw the ease with which he got along with others. I realized that's a rare gift."

The child looked at him seriously. "Sir. My name is Will. Thank you for telling me about Congressman Crockett," he used the title Buck had repeated several times. "I'd like to shake your hand!"

Will put out his small hand, and Buck took it.

"Sir, thank you for being brave and fighting for freedom," Will said.

His mother was calling him, and Will turned and ran toward her, turning back a couple of times and waving to Travis, who waved back, a sad look on his face as he remembered Charlie.

169

Lori and Buck pulled in as usual and headed their separate directions. It was an icy, windy day, late for that kind of thing but still March. She had paperwork to do and was glad she did not have to dress up and cook something over a fire—although the fire didn't sound bad. Travis walked over to his unheated, dank, and dark little office. It would have seemed primitive to Lori or anyone else, but the uncomfortable quarters were the norm of the colonel's life up until the last few weeks, and he thought nothing of it. He lit a candle and started work scratching out responses to letters with his quill. He enjoyed the quiet—was not, at heart, a people person. He had a tendency to be reserved, although there was a streak of the party animal in him, as reflected in the reports of his forays with the ladies and his great enjoyment of dances so very long ago. One source, and for once it was not his diary, told of Bowie handing Travis a letter warning him of the Mexican army's approach toward Bexar and the fact that Santa Anna was in command of their forces. This was during a fandango put on by the officers to celebrate Crockett's arrival in town. The party lasted until 7 the next morning. As the story went, Travis basically told the knife-fighter that he was dancing with the prettiest girl in San Antone at the moment and to let him be. Bowie set him straight in a hurry, warning the young colonel that the news was important enough that he needed to read it. Travis had grown up a bit since those last days of his old existence, not because the young man wanted to, but simply because he had lived a disaster that would have been incomprehensible to him before the siege began. It moved him toward his serious side even further. Although Lori could make him laugh now and then, all in all, Buck was a sad creature from a sad time, feeling that he had been plucked out of his life and dropped into something he truly did not understand.

He huddled in the cold, trying to concentrate on the correspondence before him. After a while, he heard voices. He got up from his desk and went to the door, cracking it slightly. There were not as many visitors this day—it was Thursday—as the Alamo got on weekends, and the weather likely curtailed intentions of some would-be tourists as well. But there was a group standing not far from his door, a middle-aged man with gray hair and beard and spectacles, haranguing a group of much younger people, all of them bundled up against the wind. Buck stood quietly, trying to hear some of what the man was saying. The audience was listening to the lecturer with rapt attention, no one dreaming that they were being eavesdropped on by someone in the long barracks. He finally was able to pick up a question from one young man in the group.

"So what was wrong with these guys as a rule?"

The man leading the conversation, a somewhat angry-sounding speaker with a clear, excellent voice, explained his take on it.

"Well, it's not so much what was wrong with the Alamo defenders as compared to people today. The problem is that they've all been put on a pedestal, all that Texas Trinity talk. And as is the case with all of us now, there are some more noble folks and some who, quite frankly, deserve to go to Hell."

The kids laughed.

"Professor, who do you think deserves to go to Hell?" someone asked.

"Although I suspect more of that rough crowd ended up there than in Heaven, it's kind of hard to know for sure. We don't know a whole lot about the rank and file—don't even have a for-sure number of men who were there and only partial names for a few who definitely were. But of the top names I would pack off to the Devil right away, I would have to say Col. Travis."

"Just for being in command?" a female student asked.

"No, for being in command and making an absolute jackass out of himself. He had been doing it for years, so his actions at the fort were just a continuation of his rather juvenile behavior. He didn't cotton to anyone telling him what to do, but he was inflexible and difficult when in charge."

The young people laughed. The professor continued, "Travis is an interesting character. He was bright but very young and immature. When he ran to Texas to get away from everything else he screwed up, he got involved with the revolutionary faction. He lied on his papers to get into Mexican Texas, saying he wasn't married. And he came in after Mexico put a ban on any more immigrants, making him a type who is in the news constantly today—an illegal alien. Makes you wonder what Travis would have done had the Mexicans built a wall!"

Another collective laugh ensued from the group

171

"Travis was contumacious, contentious, quick-tempered, impulsive, and intense. And, although it is assumed that most people want to be liked somewhat by their peers, it was definitely not first on his list. He came off as priggish to many people and was somewhat of a joke to some, a loose cannon and troublemaker to many others. He was an overly ambitious, promiscuous, degenerate young dandy who put perfume in his hair and read voraciously. I will give him credit for being literate. Most folks on the Texas frontier could not read. Travis read every romantic novel he could get his hands on, and his reading helped hone his one true skill. He was an excellent, albeit dramatic, writer, turning out propaganda for his cause, including those famous Victory or Death letters. His propaganda worked, but it was too late to save him.

"The problem with Travis, or at least the fatal one—this guy was one big problem—was his skewed view of reality. This noble idea of dying for the cause. He was a Southerner, and you saw lots of this same thing in the next generation in the South in the Civil War. He believed it in his inner core, but he also attributed it to the other 180-odd folks who likely did not really share his vision of going out in a blaze of glory. To his credit, the hotheaded young twit's follow-through was superb. After a life of one total failure after another, he went out in one incredibly dramatic last life's disaster. The idiot deserved it—and he got what he wanted, but the tragedy is that he took everyone else with him."

"Dr. Jones, was he any worse than any of the others? The way you describe them, they're all some kind of scum who failed in the U.S. and were running from something," one of the young women asked.

"I don't know that it's fair to say that about all of them, but many were running from something. As to Travis being worse, actually, yes, I think so. He was the leader, so he had a lot more responsibility. I think an argument could be made that his rash actions, like going off half-cocked firing that big cannon when the Mexicans might have been willing to make a deal at the beginning of the siege and then bragging about it in his famous letter, got everyone killed.

"Travis was a real firebrand. He worked at open rebellion for 4 years after he got to Texas. He's sometimes called the Voice of the Texas Revolution. He was constantly drumming up business for insurrection and was involved in numerous altercations with the authorities before he ended up at the Alamo. One of them involved a prank letter he sent to the local Mexican garrison commander where he was living at the time, Anahuac, in an effort to get the commander to release some runaway slaves who

172

belonged to Travis' legal clients. Travis, only 22 at the time, found himself imprisoned in a brick kiln, tied to the ground, for his efforts. A couple of fictional accounts insinuate that the officer of the guard abused Travis and another attorney who was being held. Travis did have it in for the officer, but I've found no corroboration as to the claims in those accounts. Other Texians eventually showed up in force to demand his release, and the post commander threatened to kill Travis immediately if any action were forthcoming. Travis heard this, and from his position staked to the ground, yelled for his would-be rescuers to not mind him but come ahead! They didn't, and he was eventually released instead of being sent to Mexico proper for trial.

"Three years later, we find our hero commandeering a ship and forcing a small Mexican contingent to surrender to him. He gave them 15 minutes to capitulate and threatened to 'put every man to the sword' if they did not. The Mexicans surrendered, interesting in light of what eventually happened to him. He ticked off a large proportion of the Anglos with this stunt. They thought he went too far. The Mexican authorities made the mistake of putting a price on his head. Travis vamoosed, and the local Anglos were angered by the call for his arrest and came around to his side for the most part. Travis stopped running when things calmed down. He refused to apologize for his actions and really seemed to have no clue that many law-abiding citizens were turned off by his foolhardy escapades. He was on the fringe of polite society, accepted on the surface because of his growing prominence as a successful attorney and, to some degree, because of his status as a War Party leader, but society matrons and other stalwarts talked about him behind his back.

"He knew Santa Anna had his number from these past brushes with the authorities, but he didn't give a flip. He was a dramatic young fool who didn't know what he was doing—or maybe was too crazy to care. Although technically married, the story goes that he was convinced that his wife was fooling around with another man, and there's some question as to whether Travis killed the guy. The colonel was a notorious womanizer, and he recorded all of that, keeping score, in his diary. He picked up a bad case of venereal disease and recorded that, too, as well as his purchases of the only treatment available back then, drinking mercury, that made you go crazy if you did very much of it."

The students all laughed at the mention of the mercury and its results.

"What's so bad about his sex life?" one male student asked. "Everyone does that these days, although most people don't take notes or keep score."

173

There were a few laughs, and two of the students turned with a critical stare. Truth be told, many young Americans today would not likely see anything too outrageous in the colonel's sexual escapades. But there was one aspect of it for which he would be condemned.

One young woman asked, "Sounds like he didn't respect women at all?"

"No," the instructor responded, "I doubt he thought of women as anything more than objects for his pleasure. He was a self-absorbed 'Southern gentleman,' with a death wish to go out in dramatic fashion."

"Guess he accomplished that," one of the students noted.

"Those old Southerners had some peculiar ideas about what they called 'honor.' In addition to his condescending attitude toward the native Mexican population and total lack of respect for women, he also, as would be expected of his class and type, owned slaves. He had no compunction about whipping them. He whipped one older man for getting drunk and recorded the act in his journal, and he actually brought a slave into the Alamo as his personal servant."

"You're kidding, right?" the same young woman who asked about Travis' lack of respect for women asked.

"No, but this was one of the few times in history when being a slave was a good deal. The young servant, Joe, was with Travis on the firing line and saw him fall, then, having more than met his obligation to his master, high-tailed it to relative safety in the church. Although the Mexicans dispatched all of the defenders, they let Joe live, figuring he was held in captivity and not an active participant in the insurrection. Joe is the major credible source as to what happened to Travis. History is rarely that fair. You all know they found Travis' body at the dig and revived him?"

A few of the students nodded affirmatively.

"He wasn't quite right before. I hear that he's really just a shell now—have not seen him. Now that he's back, it's a serious problem. There have been numerous news reports about him causing disruption whenever anyone he even perceives as Mexican shows up at the Alamo. He waves a sword and threatens them in most of the accounts. Someone will eventually get hurt if this is allowed to continue. If someone, Hispanic or otherwise, humiliates him enough, he might just do away with himself. It may sound

174

callous, but, in my opinion, that would be the best answer. He clearly is just a symbol at this point. His soul, if he ever had one, was dead and buried in 1836. He's just a facade acting out a historical drama. And Travis was shallow in his real life in the 1830's. He was an abject failure in everything he did. He was born in South Carolina. Lots of crazies are from there. They tried to start a Civil War for 30 years and finally succeeded, or, should I say, seceded."

Again, laughter from his audience.

"But the family moved to Alabama. When he was a very young attorney there, his mentor, who passed for a prominent legal mind in frontier Alabama, if there was such a thing," Jones said disdainfully, drawing another laugh from his students, "was charged by a client with collecting debts due from Travis. The young man was drowning in debt trying to pay to keep slaves and the standard of living he thought a gentleman of means and his family should aspire to have. The older attorney made a fool of Travis in front of a packed courtroom full of guffawing spectators. The jury held against him, and he knew a warrant for his arrest would be forthcoming shortly. Travis reacted by immediately fleeing west out of the Heart of Dixie as fast as he could, never looking back, leaving his pregnant wife and young son behind. So he is very sensitive to embarrassment. If someone can force him to make a big enough fool of himself in public—and he has a talent for that, he may kill himself—problem solved. Too bad Santa Anna didn't burn the redheaded crazy with the rest of the garrison. Then we wouldn't have to be dealing with him running around wielding that rusty sword and yelling 'Victory or Death.'"

"Does he really do that? Here at the Alamo? That would be so funny to see," a dark-haired female student laughed.

"But Dr. Jones, do you really want him dead? Isn't that going beyond just the historical analysis?" one young man inquired insightfully.

"Well, maybe I should rephrase that," Jones responded. "It's not that I want anyone dead. But Travis is already really dead—he has no purpose, no reason to be here. Honestly, if the man does have any soul at all, it would be merciful for his sake for him to go and be with his compatriots, as he would call them in the quaint language of the day."

"Kind of sad," someone else added.

"Yes, it is. He did have a talent for writing. But all in all, he did far

175

more damage than he did good. In my humble opinion, his actions only helped to get all those people killed."

As Buck moved his hand forward to shut the door, everything went black.

"What was that?" the young man who had asked the professor about wanting Travis dead asked. "Did y'all hear something?"

"Yeah, sounded like something fell," a young woman responded.

The group slowly moved apart, each member looking around.

"Over there—that door is slightly cracked. Wonder if it came from there?" the young man pointed.

The whole contingent slowly moved that way, the student who noticed the door taking the lead. The others huddled together, several feet behind him, while he stuck his head in the door, at first not seeing anything in the dark. Then he gazed downward.

"There's someone on the floor! Must have fallen.," the young man said.

He tried to open the door, but Travis was blocking it. The student slowly inched it open, pushing the unconscious man slightly ahead of him, just enough that he could squeeze in and pull Travis out of the way. As he did and the door came free, the rest of the crowd hesitantly followed.

"Oh no!" Jones exclaimed as his eyes adjusted to the virtually nonexistent light of the little candle. He paused and stared downward, then continued in a condescending tone, "Class, this is the brave commander of the Alamo, Col. Travis."

They stared at the figure on the floor. He had the red hair Jones had mentioned and the 1836 clothes. His eyes were closed and his pallor white.

"Look at those scars. His face is ruined," one student pointed.

"I wouldn't want to live looking like . . . ." a young woman added, not quite finishing her thought.

The young man who opened the door knelt down and checked the colonel. "I think he just fainted," came the analysis.

176

They all stood staring while the student held Travis' head. Finally, the colonel started to come to, making a faint sound and then shifting his head slightly.

The student called to him, "Colonel, can you hear me? Are you all right?"

Travis opened his eyes and was met with the sight of the entire group standing around him, staring down at him. His eyes rested on the professor.

Travis said weakly, "You want me dead?"

"No, son. I said you basically already are dead," Jones responded coldly.

Travis closed his eyes. Some of the students, feeling uncomfortable, moved toward the door. A few stayed, continuing to stare.

One female student finally headed for the door, saying "I'm going to the building across the way. . . .to see if there's anyone who knows him."

A few minutes later, she was back with a frantic Lori, who ran to Buck. Staring at the sight of the pretty young woman at the fallen man's side, Jones shook his head.

"There's one thing I've got to ask you, Travis. How do you do it? Most men would kill for your ability to attract women," Jones queried. "It was one thing in the 1830's, but with your face carved up and the silly costume, I don't see how you are still managing it!"

The students laughed, Lori glared at Jones, and poor Buck just tried to focus. A few more minutes went by. The student who had been holding Travis' head turned the colonel over to Lori and stood up. He and the student who got Lori and Jones were the only members of the group still there.

Directing his remarks to Lori, Jones said, "That young man is a sad case. He would be better off dead. I assume the falling is tied to his brain injury? It would be merciful if he would simply not get up sometime after one of these falls."

Lori looked at him in angry horror and Buck stared in shock, but Jones had already turned and headed for the door. The two remaining students gave her sympathetic looks but headed out after the professor.

Lori got Buck up and in his chair. He looked dazed at first, then just stared downward, not acknowledging her presence.

"Buck! Look at me," she begged, turning his chin up toward her. "Are you OK?"

He finally looked at her, and she saw the anguish in his eyes, but he said only, "Yes, Lori, I'll be fine. Don't worry."

The words had no meaning behind them, but all she could do was go along. He would not say anything more. Whatever had happened, he seemed determined to keep it to himself. She had learned not to pry. Once he seemed more his old self, albeit in a melancholy mood, she left him to find Bob.

"Someone named Jones—apparently a college professor, with his class," she finished her description.

"Oh, I bet that's Lyle Jones. He's coming back tomorrow for a book signing," Bob recalled. "He teaches at UTSA, in the history department, of course. He's got a great mind and he's mined all the Alamo sources for his books. But he's a college professor. What can I say?—revisionist to the core! But he does know his stuff."

"Bob, we've got to cancel his book signing," Lori interrupted.

Bob looked stunned at her suggestion. "Lori, I can't do that on such short notice. Lyle is a well-known writer, very distinguished among scholars. And he will bring folks here who might not normally come to visit the . . . ."

She cut him off. "Yeah, he'll bring in the people who want this place to just be a mission. I'm not knocking the mission years, but there are four more missions without a famous battle around this town. Most people who come here come because of the battle . . . ."

"True, but there's a move on to change all of that—not to eliminate acknowledging the battle, but to explore more fully the other aspects of this wonderful old place. Most of those other aspects are, if not warm and fuzzy, at least less grisly than March 6, 1836," Bob came back.

"You don't really fall for all of this, do you?" Lori asked.

178

"Well, honestly, no—at least not completely. You know that, Lori. But there are plenty of folks out there with that view. And there are even more, as I already warned you the other day, who are trying to turn the tide on the battle story so that it's not just the good Americans with their Trinity versus the evil Mexicans. Lyle Jones is one of those people. Truth is, I read his new book. He blasts Santa Anna and his guys, too. Santa Anna is easy to crucify, believe me. But it rubs the wrong way when someone does that to longstanding American heroes, even though common sense says they had their faults, just like everyone else . . . ."

Lori interrupted, "But Bob, I'm not talking about the Texas Trinity in the abstract—you know that. I'm talking about poor Buck. He's here now. That professor and his ilk are treating him like he's not human, just a relic of an old battle, and bringing up every sin the poor guy ever committed. Although I'll admit that Buck should never have been so diligent about writing down every single one of them for posterity."

"Lyle does go too far. He not only states the old facts, ferreted out of every crevice in archives holdings in the most remote places, but he's one of those historians who attaches modern standards to people from a couple of centuries ago. That's not fair, but a lot of historians take that tack. In the colonel's case, he is particularly cruel. I think Travis fared worse in the book, relatively, than any other major player. If he had been burned with the others, it would still be unfair, but it would not matter as much. We'll just have to try to keep the colonel away from Lyle. I would consider canceling or postponing or something if it weren't tomorrow, but that's just too short notice."

"I understand, Bob, but I'm really worried," Lori said.

On the way home that evening, Buck was silent. He just stared ahead. Lori tried a few times to start a light conversation, to no avail. When they reached the house, he begged off on dinner, something the usually ravenous young man would never do. He went in his room, closed the door, opened his journal and added a brief entry, then collapsed on the bed, exhausted.

Buck was up ahead of the others the next morning. He was hungry, especially after missing dinner, but that was his stomach. His head and heart didn't care. But he did want some coffee desperately. Fortunately, Elena or someone had set the fancy machine to brew the stuff automatically as usual. It was making a noise indicating the procedure was in gear when he

179

came in the kitchen. He reached for his "Victory or Death" mug just as the sound subsided. He poured a cup and sat down on the bench in the nook, hoping he could have some time to himself before anyone woke up.

No such luck. He heard footsteps coming no sooner than he had taken his first sip of the aromatic brew.

"Vicky! What are you doing up so early?" he asked as he saw her.

"Hi Buck! I just wanted some coffee." As usual, she headed over to the cupboard and pulled out a mug, then poured a cup of Joe.

"You feeling OK today? I know you weren't yesterday," Vicky asked, a look of genuine concern on her small face.

"Yes, Vicky, I promise, I'm fine," he reassured her.

"Good! You're a little different, Buck, but you're a really special guy," she said. "I really, really like you—even better than the version of you in the movie!"

"I've got to see this movie," he laughed. "You're wonderful, too. I know I can always get the straight truth from you, Vicky—that's something very special you only get from a genuine friend."

She slid closer to him on the long cushioned seat. "I'm so glad you came back, Buck. I hope you stay with us forever."

He looked down at her with a slightly sad, sweet smile.


Lori was so nervous that she was having a hard time focusing on her driving in the morning traffic. Buck was with her, but he was still in a taciturn mood. He had been a little more communicative at breakfast, with everyone there. Vicky had been particularly solicitous of him, and he seemed to respond with gratitude for her affection. But now he was just silent. She tried to get him to talk a few times, then gave up and concentrated on getting the car to the parking lot safely. Once there, she parted ways with Buck, who wished her a good day and gave her a little kiss, then headed to his dark little office.

The book-signing event was at 2:30 in the afternoon, right at the height of the tourist influx, as was surely intended. But Lori knew that the professor would be setting up shop in the plaza at the edge of the Alamo grounds considerably before that time. Technically, as she understood it, Jones did not even have to get permission from the Alamo as his table would be on the city-owned part of the premises, for which he had a permit. But Jones, according to Bob, had apparently asked just the same, maybe to make a good impression. Lori headed downstairs, stuffing her purse and big cup in the cubbyhole, and started on her paperwork—fortunately, not much of that today. She would make a point of checking the mailbox around 2:00 so she could eye Jones' setup. Lori was in hopes that Buck had way more paperwork to do than she had—anything to keep him busy. At least writing with that quill was slower than her email responses on the computer.

Lyle Jones, his wife, Mary, and three of his students, all of whom had been at his walk-around lecture at the old mission the day before, showed up right at 2:00. A few minutes later, Lori sauntered out toward the mailbox. She glanced in their direction but did not stare or go close. They had quite a few copies of the new book. Rows of books had been placed on the ground on some plastic. There was a nice stack on the professor's little table, ready for him to write whatever the purchaser wanted an author to write, as he sold each one. Since Jones was positioned at the entrance, many of the tourists, unless they were so eager to see Davy's rifle that they couldn't wait, stopped to flip through a copy of the book. This had already started as Mary straightened the row of books and made sure there were several pens available for her husband. Two of the students were counting inventory in the back of the Jones' van, which had been authorized to pull in the plaza for purposes of unloading. The third one, a young man, was standing and talking with the professor, who was seated behind the table. Lori glanced over toward the long barracks. Buck's door was completely closed. She headed back to the pigsty to give Bob the mail.

"Dr. Jones, what is your overall take on the Alamo situation?" a man was asking the author.

"It's been hashed and rehashed to the point where sometimes it seems all that's left is mush," Jones replied, raising a laugh from the bystanders, "But I wanted to take a close look at the personalities involved. Think, those of you who work, about your offices, your co-workers, for a minute—how many jerks, screwballs, goof-offs, sycophants, Gestapo types, you name it, you deal with, albeit on a minor scale, each day? Well, it's the same with the Alamo. No one wants to admit it, at least regarding the Americans involved. It's fine for us Anglos to do it to Santa Anna. He's an

181

easy as well as inviting target. The Texians' end was truly tragic, gruesome and inhumane, no doubt about it, on Santa Anna's part. But these rebels were a zany bunch of rough, difficult characters who engaged in all kinds of illicit and immoral behavior—honestly, just like folks we all know today. I've gotten some flak from the traditionalists who want Saints Davy, Jim, and William to remain in heaven, but the fact is at least two of these guys, and maybe all three, are prime candidates for the other place. I'm just asking folks to be a little bit realistic about human beings, even if they are brave heroes. They're still human, and that means a myriad of faults, some funny, some tragic. I have probed their characters in depth, and I've come up with some conclusions that are hard to deny. In the case of the Alamo commander, Travis, he basically handed me the list himself. He kept an incredibly detailed diary where he laid out a list of sins that would curl your hair . . . ."

"I'm going to do a lot more than curl your hair if you don't apologize immediately for the garbage you just uttered as well as that revolting discourse yesterday!" The colonel, sword in hand, was standing with the tip pointed toward Jones' face.

The professor sighed. "Colonel Travis, I had hoped you were going to just expire and join Bowie in Hell when you keeled over yesterday, but I see I was too optimistic." Jones turned from the man he had been talking with to face Travis directly.

"Let me set you straight! I did not, nor do I now, have a death wish. There is an enormous difference between wanting to throw one's life away for the sake of fame or remembrance and being willing to give that life in the last extremity for the sake of liberty and freedom, without which life, for me, has no value. I demand an apology now, or you WILL regret it!" Travis shouted.

"Or what, Colonel? Are you going to challenge me to a duel?" Jones asked in a surprisingly calm tone with the sword in his face.

"Only gentlemen are asked for satisfaction. You, sir, are not a gentleman," came the angry response.

Jones was trying not to laugh, even with the very real threat of the sword in front of him. Travis was so mad that he seemed oblivious to Jones' reaction. The professor pointed toward the chapel.

"Colonel, why don't you head on back to the church. You can either refight the battle there if you wish, or, I might suggest that you consult God—if you know who that is—in the sanctuary and ask Him to help you get your head on straight. Now please go, for whichever purpose appeals more to you, and let these good people converse with me about my book."

Travis lunged across the table with the sword, nicking Jones in his upper arm. The professor looked down in horror, although little damage was actually done. The colonel fell head first, over the table, his rear end across it, the sword flying somewhere toward the Jones' van. His old pants split, and stunned onlookers were beginning to laugh. Jones was staring at his arm, looking for a gushing fountain of blood which would never come. The nick barely broke the skin slightly. Finally, when the professor's examination determined that he was in no danger of bleeding to death, he turned his attention to the colonel, who was still lying over the table. He gave Travis one swat on the rear, then lifted him enough to shove him off the table onto the ground. Travis lay motionless. The collective look of the book signing fans was shock.

"What the Hell was that all about?" someone finally asked.

"Ladies and gentlemen, remember what I was just saying about the Americans at the Alamo? That they were a crazy bunch? This gentleman who just slashed me with his sword is the Alamo commander, Col. William Barret Travis, a brave man, true hero, great writer, and absolutely insane."

"Do you think maybe we ought to check on him?" someone in the crowd asked.

"No. You can't kill him. He's like a vampire—keeps coming back," Jones replied.

Several people in the crowd stared at Travis, who was on his side, his face up.

"Looks like a zombie with that face," a teen boy said.

"Yeah, he just goes as himself for Halloween. The Alamo would be smart to do a Halloween Night with Col. Travis as the premier attraction. They could sell tickets and bring in some revenue," the teen's female companion added.

A trio of young adults approached Jones' little table, two men and a woman. One man was in a national guard uniform, the other in a t-shirt, jeans, and cowboy boots and hat, and their female companion was wearing a t-shirt and jeans. The young man in uniform stared at Jones, glanced at his watch, then resumed his look at the professor.

"What's this all about?" he inquired of Jones.

"Just everyday routine at the Alamo now that Col. Travis is back among the living," the professor replied with a shrug. "He manages to make a scene doing something crazy every day. He just stabbed me in the arm with his sword." Jones was holding his arm for effect.

"Colonel Travis? The Col. Travis?" the fellow with the hat asked.

"Yeah, right down there," Jones pointed to the ground on the other side of his little table, where the unconscious man lay.

"How did that happen?" the young woman asked. "And you really mean Col. Travis of Alamo fame, not an impersonator?"

"Didn't you see it on the news? It's been all over the place. They found him at the archaeological dig at the Alamo latrine, face down, an appropriate place for the colonel, I might add," Jones couldn't help interjecting. "If you missed the initial report, he crops up regularly in the news when he pulls some kind of crazy stunt waving his sword at people—such as today, where he took offense at my book because the portrait I painted of him is not exactly complimentary and took a swipe at me with that rusty old thing—got me. I hope I don't get blood poisoning!" Jones was still holding his arm as he said it.

The young woman knelt by Buck's side, brushing the hair out of his face.

"He faints all the time—one of the results of the head injury. Insanity is the other, although he already was subject to some of that when he was at the Alamo way back," the professor explained.

The young woman looked up in anger, and her two companions had looks on their faces that indicated they were less than pleased as the professor dug a deeper and deeper hole for himself.

"Sir, maybe you would be happier if you would just high-tail it to south of the border?" the man in uniform asked Jones. "Colonel Travis is a hero among heroes—Texans should honor him for his incredible sacrifice and

184

devotion to our state. I don't want to hear any more of your badmouthing him. You hear?" He took a step toward Jones.

The other young man was now kneeling on Travis' other side, but the colonel was still out. The cowboy looked up at Jones. "Are you sure it's just fainting?"

"Yeah, regardless of what I think of him, which is not much, I can assure you, it's just fainting—a result of his wound. He will come around shortly and be, if not just fine, at least conscious," Jones explained.

"Like I said, this man deserves our respect and honor, not degrading insults from an ivory tower intellectual who is clueless about military sacrifice," the man in uniform lectured the professor. "I salute Col. Travis, and I can't say how pleased I am that he has this second opportunity at life. If he is not totally well, I think that is certainly understandable given the horrific battle and wounds he endured. He needs help and support, not animosity and hatred."

He followed his words with a salute directed at the unconscious Travis. The trio glared at Jones, and the military man took another look at his watch.

"Unfortunately, we have to go as I have to get back to the base, but I'm telling you, sir, you should revere and honor this brave man and his incredible sacrifice, not degrade and insult him. Your treatment of him reflects on you, not the colonel, and the reflection is not good."

The trio, angry looks directed at Jones by all, reluctantly left the unconscious man. As they did, some of the other tourists who had witnessed the encounter cheered them.

Buck was beginning to come to. Mary Jones got a bottle of water from her van. While everyone else was chatting about the scene Travis made, Jones' book, and the trio who stood up for the colonel, she discreetly got Travis to drink a little something. He thanked her quietly, then put his head back down. Finally, after a long time and once he felt less lightheaded, he limped off, away from the crowds.

185

# DESPAIR

Lori found the hat on top of the sword, obviously placed there by the Joneses or someone who had been to the book signing. The Joneses, the books, the tourists—everything and everyone—were gone, as it was closing time. Buck was gone, too. She got Bob, and they looked everywhere—no sign. Lori knew that it was not like Buck to leave his hat, and especially his sword. She fantasized for a minute that Mexican government officials had spirited him away to try him in Mexico City for his crimes against their government, but she knew that wasn't the case. At her urging, Bob called Lyle Jones on his cell. Lori didn't want to talk with him, but she wondered if he might know something. Jones was in the waiting room at a walk-in clinic, having thought more about the rusty old sword and the possibility of blood poisoning or tetanus.

"No, Bob, honestly, he made a major scene, then came across the table with that sword. Got me with it—my arm is still a little sore, then fell across the table, ass up, and his pants split, so he made a total fool of himself. I had predicted to my students, yesterday, that he had a propensity for that kind of thing and with that high-strung Old South sensitivity he has, he would probably be so humiliated and mortified that he would kill himself. I suspect he's slunk off to do that some way if you really can't find him. I know it seems sad, but he's a very, very unhappy person. I really do believe it will be merciful—the best thing for everyone."

The phone was on speaker, and Lori was horrified.

"Dr. Jones, I'm Lori. I came to get Col. Travis yesterday when you were there. You can't really mean you hope he dies?"

"Like I said yesterday, ma'am, I don't want to actually wish anyone would die. But I do think young Mr. Travis is extremely disturbed, that it's not going to improve, that he wants to be with his comrades from 1836, and that he will find a way to make that happen. You have to admit that it will be more peaceful for everyone when he does. If he did not pick up that sword, which obviously means a lot to him, and y'all can't find him, I think he may have done away with himself."

It was getting dark, and most everyone had gone home. The Alamo

186

rangers had assisted Bob and Lori with their search of the grounds. Elbert notified the city cops, and they sent a cadre of officers out to look around, but they failed to find anything either. Bob finally insisted that Lori get in her car. The two left, the last two cars in the lot. Lori's tears made it hard to see the freeway, and she almost pulled into a car in the next lane, finally slowing down and staying in the right lane as she could not stop crying. She had left one cryptic phone message for her family to the effect that a comprehensive search of the grounds revealed nothing. As Lori dragged in the door, her face wet with tears—and alone, the Claytons knew something was terribly wrong.

Vicky, her green eyes huge, asked in a trembling voice, "Lori, where is he, where is Buck?"

"I . . . I don't . . . know," she stammered.

Elena took control, steadying her tall daughter and steering her to a chair. "Lori, honey, what happened?"

Lori repeated what she knew of the book signing incident, as it had been relayed by Jones to Bob, and that she found Buck's hat and sword and the search for him turned up no clues.

"I know you don't feel like it, honey, but we've kept dinner warm—thought it would be nice for all . . .would be nice to eat together tonight," Elena said. "We need to be strong to think strong about how to help poor Buck."

Lori wasn't hungry, but she let her mom guide her to the table. Everyone ate in silence, Vicky as well as Lori crying.

After the meal, while Elena continued to try to lift Lori's spirits, and feeling a bit like the girl in the movie shown at school, Vicky headed for Buck's room. His journal was sitting on the little desk. She sat down and opened it, turning to the end of the written material. Buck's last entry read:

"30 March 2017. A chill, uncomfortable day. Spent it working in my office until I heard voices outside—a professor and his students. The professor was lecturing them about ME—cruel, unfair words. Everything went dark. Next I knew, I was on the floor, all of them staring at me. More cruel words. I do not understand or fit within this world. If it were not for Lori, I would wish to end this unnatural existence."

187

Vicky closed the little book, hesitant to tell Lori or her mom what she had done.

The coffee was ready, as always, when Lori awoke at 5:30. There was no point in going back to bed, although the Alamo didn't open until 9:00. She had finally slept, drifting off out of sheer exhaustion. It had been a brief respite from the tears, but now they were back in force. She attempted to wipe them away, trying to keep them out of her coffee, which she was drinking from the "Victory or Death" mug.

Elena came in, calling softly, "Lori? Honey?"

"Mom, I'm OK, really," she lied.

Elena poured a cup of coffee. "You're not fine, Lori, I know. But we'll find him. We're going with you today. He can't have gone too far. It's not like he can drive. We'll find him," she tried to soothe her daughter.

"But Mom, I'm afraid . . . ."

"Afraid, of what, honey?"

"What . . . what . . . if he's . . already dead?" she finally got the words out.

"Let's don't think about that, Lori. I don't think he is. Let's think about finding him and getting him back here safe where we can take care of him, OK?"

Lori nodded, but she did not feel at all confident of what her mother was saying. Vicky had appeared, unnoticed and eager for some coffee. On hearing Lori's words, she exited quickly, returning shortly with Buck's book, open to the "30 March" entry. The truth was that it gave no clue as to where he might be, only that he was teetering on the edge of despair.

The police had put out an APB but had received no tips. It was hard to imagine someone dressed the way Buck was being able to blend in and not be noticed. The Claytons did accompany Lori to the fort, but they were no more successful than anyone else who had conducted a search. The police continued to scour the area, to no avail.

After 2 days of no sign, it reached a point where there was no choice left but to be on the lookout but go back to some semblance of normal routine. Every couple of hours, on break, Lori would walk around the compound, poking her head in the long barracks and elsewhere, looking under and behind displays, and in some of the lush shrubbery made possible by the acequia on the grounds, all to no avail. She would sadly return to her cubbyhole. Bob was especially solicitous of her, even walking upstairs and talking Morena out of a piece of fudge for her in an attempt to make her feel better. But everything at the Alamo reminded her of Buck—especially the fudge. Although she hugged Bob for his thoughtful act, the tears were streaming again, even though Bob had deliberately chosen the Crockett chocolate and nuts, not the Travis orange.

Lori had been working full days lately to make up for half-time work she had missed earlier when caring for Buck. She didn't mind keeping busy, although she was finding herself wishing it was somewhere other than the Alamo. At lunch, she took her paper sack with a piece of cheddar cheese and a pear and sat on a bench in front of the shed housing the drink machines. Nearby was a fence, behind which were the small graves of Ruby, the Alamo cat who had drowned in the acequia years ago, and famous C.C.—for Clara Carmack—who had lived to be around 19 and was an institution at the old mission before her death in 2014. Offices, including one for the Alamo Rangers, were behind the fence as well. As Lori sat in silence, the current feline mascot, pretty long-haired calico Bella, came up to her. The cat, who sometimes hung out in the offices, tended to roam this area frequently.

"You just want my cheese, don't you?" Lori asked the cat, hoping no one could hear her and think she had flipped out.

Bella rubbed back and forth against her legs, then looked up at Lori with her luminous eyes.

"OK, you win," she said, taking one more look around to be sure there was no human to hear her. She broke a nice little chunk off her lunch and put it on the ground for Bella, who went for it immediately.

Meanwhile, Bob was on the phone with Lyle Jones. Jones had either had a religious experience or he was not quite as inflexible in his analysis as he had given every indication of being.

"Hey, Bob, I guess there's been no news on the colonel's whereabouts?" Lyle inquired.

189

"No. He's just vanished into thin air. You would think someone in that getup would be easy to spot."

"That's for sure," Lyle responded, trying to suppress a little laugh. "I do have one more idea, if you don't mind me coming over?" he said, raising his voice slightly in question at the end.

Bob was stunned. "Lyle, let me get this straight—is this about trying to find Travis? Or maybe just his body so we can close the book on him for good this time?"

"Well, of course, we don't know, whichever. I still say he's got some major emotional and/or mental issues, but I—I'll have to confess, with a lot of help from Mary, I have revised my view slightly. I still think he's unhinged and that my historical analysis, based largely on what Travis himself wrote, is spot on. But I am not so sure about what I said about him not having a soul and not really being here now—still don't think he wants to be. But I may have been wrong in not viewing him as a regular human being."

Bob knew this was a big concession for the serious-minded professor who prided himself on his conclusions based on facts. "Well, I wouldn't say Travis is a regular human being, but he is human. He has thoughts and feelings just like the rest of us . . . ."

Jones stopped him. "Yeah, but, unfortunately, it seems like his thoughts and feelings usually end up manifesting themselves in waving that rusty old sword around. Anyway, if it's all the same with you, I'd like to come over around 2:00."

Bob seriously doubted that Lyle could crack the case when the police and everyone on the Alamo premises had been unable to do so, but it wouldn't hurt for the professor to come by. What had made him change his mind as to the value of a search—or, more importantly, the possible value of Travis—was a mystery. It almost had to be Mary Jones, as Lyle had hinted. Bob wondered what she could have said that would persuade the professor.

Lyle pulled up 5 minutes before 2:00, heading downstairs to the sty. They closed the door so that Lori would not hear, although she, at the moment, was giving a demo out back.

"So what's on your mind, professor?" Bob asked, offering Lyle a seat.

190

"I'm thinking—alive or dead—that he's probably somewhere around the north wall," Lyle said. "After all, that's where he expired the first time."

"I took a cursory walk around the federal building and the Hotel Indigo, and I saw the police nosing around there once," Bob replied. "With his mindset, that does make sense, and it certainly hasn't been the focus of the search since I think everyone sort of assumed he would stay on the current Alamo premises. I guess we could take another walk in that direction if you want?"

"Yeah. I'd like to do that—just to satisfy my curiosity. I don't think he could get in the federal building once it closed—would assume that's around 5:30. He was lying at the side of my table for the remainder of the book signing, and I believe he was still there when we began packing up. Let's see, with the signing going on for a couple hours, it was probably close to 5:00 before he left. I wasn't paying any attention."

The two men headed north, crossing Houston and walking to the left of the face of the Garcia federal building. Bob paused. He remembered the little Alamo compound tour with Travis on the commander's first return to his post since 1836—how the colonel had pointed out the spot where he had directed the cannon in the battle. They glanced around the side entrance not far from the front corner, then walked down the sidewalk along the side of the building heading north on N. Alamo Street. Almost at the intersection with Travis Street, near the back corner of the building, was a service entrance. Signs announced "Clearance 12' ft. 6 in.'" and "Caution vehicles exiting." The two men looked into the gloom. No one seemed to be around, so they cautiously started to walk in. A guard seemingly appeared out of nowhere, halting them and demanding to know what they were doing poking around. Bob and Lyle quickly identified themselves and explained that they were looking for Travis, and the guard, who, like everyone else in town knew that the colonel was missing, let them go but not in the building.

"Well, if he's in there somewhere, I guess they'll find him when his corpse starts to decompose," Lyle said with a shrug. "But, if that entrance closes with the rest of the building, and I'm sure it does, I really don't think he's in there."

"The northwest corner of the compound was at the back of the side of the Hotel Indigo, right over there," Bob pointed across N. Alamo Street.

"Let's head over there. At least I don't see any armed guards," Lyle

191

replied with a smile.

They crossed N. Alamo at Travis and walked down the sidewalk parallel to the one they had just traversed on the other side of the street, coming to the parking lot and an alley in back of the hotel. There were three bright blue dumpsters on the far side of the parking lot, against a brick wall.

Lyle gestured toward the dumpsters. "Let's check them out."

One couple had exited the hotel and were just getting in their car as the two men stopped in front of the dumpsters. They gave quizzical looks but mercifully got in their Mercedes coupe and left. Bob and Lyle walked around the dumpsters, bending down, looking.

"What's that?" Lyle pointed.

Bob stared. There was a tip of something, bright red, at the very back of the far side of the second dumpster. "Military sash?"

Lyle walked to the back of the closest dumpster and bent down.

"It's him. He's on his side—looks to be in sort of a fetal position—but I can see the white pants and blue coat clearly," Lyle pointed.

Lyle was in better physical condition than the overweight Bob. He squeezed between the back of the first dumpster and the brick wall, through the narrow space in back of the center dumpster, reaching the still form, and knelt down to check for a pulse. He looked up at Bob, who had, with difficulty, followed him, crouching in the extremely tight spot.

"He's still alive, but the pulse is kind of weak—and his breathing seems to be rather shallow. I guess we've got to get him out of here," Lyle ventured.

"Now that we know, you sure you don't want to just leave him another few days to take care of the problem?" Bob asked in jest.

"For one thing, from a purely legal standpoint, I think we're in trouble if we do, and, quite frankly, I made up my mind that I would try to help if it came to that before I came over here."

Bob raised his eyebrows, then bent forward awkwardly. "So does one of us take his shoulders and the other his feet?"

"Yeah . . . say, what's this?" Lyle noticed a piece of paper lying on the ground.

"Probably a suicide note if your theory is right," Bob replied.

"Could be that or a piece of trash from the dumpster. Can't make it out in this light," Lyle responded, putting the paper in his coat pocket. "Yeah, let's get him out where we can see more."

Lyle gingerly stepped over the still form to reach the head and took the unconscious man's shoulders as that was the heavier and more important load. Bob struggled with the colonel's feet, having to back out of the tight space. As they got Buck out and on the ground, a few hotel guests, office workers, and other passers-by had noticed and were beginning to congregate out of curiosity. Travis was deathly white, and his skin felt cold and clammy.

"Is there anything on the paper?" Bob asked.

Lyle took it out of his pocket and read:

> "I am hopeful that by the time anyone finds me, I will be wherever my compatriots of 1836 are. Although I truly appreciate the efforts of all who worked to give me a second chance at life, I fear that too much time has gone by for that to be effectual. I do not understand your new world, and I feel more comfortable with my own. I feel my duty is to remain with my valiant command, wherever they may now be. That said, I truly regret having to bid farewell to Lori and Vicky and all of those who have been so kind to me. If I am able to think and feel and remember, wherever I am going, I will cherish their love and kindness. If, per chance, I am still among the living when you find me, I would ask that you do me the kindness of letting me go to meet those whom I understand and whom I hope understand me.

> "Victory or Death

> "William Barret Travis"

Lyle noted, "Looks like there's a faint circle drawn around the word 'Death' in his slogan. I'm afraid my guess was right. He truly does want to go."

Bob was fumbling for his cell phone. "I'm going to call Lori—get her over here so that she can say goodbye," he said shakily. "This is awful."

"Lori," he tried to sound calm, when he got her, "If you have a moment, could you come over to the north wall . . . ?"

"North wall? You mean of the original compound?" Lori asked, perplexed. Then it set in. "North wall? Never mind. I get you. Right now!"

She ran as fast as she could, not even looking at the traffic on Houston Street as she dashed across. One car was coming up fast but slowed in time to miss her. She saw a crowd of people on the far side in back of the Hotel Indigo and rushed across N. Alamo. She paid the onlookers no heed, barging through them to where Buck lay motionless, Bob and Lyle kneeling next to him. She sat on the ground beside him, pulling his head and shoulders onto her lap and stroking the red hair and kissing his ruined face.

"Buck, please, Buck, open your eyes! I love you," she cried, oblivious to the fact that she was making a scene in front of a growing crowd of strangers.

One of those strangers, stepping up to Bob, asked if they shouldn't call an ambulance.

"I don't know—he left a note specifically asking that we not," he told the man.

Lyle handed Lori the note. She took it with her free hand. "What's this?"

"He wrote instructions to whoever found him—was trying to go to his world of 1836," Lyle said as gently as he could.

Lori lashed out at him. "You caused this. You said all those hateful, horrible things about him . . . ."

The professor looked down. "I did go too far. I'm sorry. That's why I called Bob and asked if it was OK if I came over to help him search. But read the colonel's letter—he mentions you—he is obviously very fond of you and someone named Vicky."

"That's my little sister. Yes, he loves kids—is so sweet to them. You didn't mention that in your book—just that he was crazy for listing the

194

amount he paid for candy that he gave children!" Lori looked up at Lyle.

"Lori, read his letter, please," Lyle responded gently, no intention of battling out whether Travis was a good guy or bad at this point.

Lori read the sad little note. "So you think we should honor his wishes and let him sign off?" she looked up at Lyle and Bob.

"No, not at all," Lyle said, much to her surprise. "I just thought you should have the major say in it after all Bob tells me you've done for the colonel."

"Then, for heaven's sake, someone call an ambulance right NOW," Lori shouted through her tears.

"Hold on, Buck, hold on, help is coming," she called softly, still stroking his hair.

Five minutes later, the sirens were blaring, and Buck was strapped on the gurney and loaded into the back of the van in no time. Lori ran for her car. Bob and Lyle headed for theirs.


Lori had calmed down considerably. She was sitting by the still-unconscious Buck. The emergency room staff had hooked him up to fluids. Two days without water were part of the problem. The doctor on duty pronounced that he thought Buck would be fine, but that it was good they had found him when they did. Another day or two might have been a different story. Not surprisingly, the hospital wanted to keep the fluids flowing and monitor him overnight, so Lori set in for the old familiar routine. Once Bob and Lyle were gone and the latest round of checking Buck's vitals was done, Lori called home. She got Vicky.

"Can I talk with him?" she pleaded.

"He's still out, but he's doing well," Lori told her sister.

"All right then. I'm going to tell Mom, and we'll be right over. I want to sit with him, too!"

Of course, Vicky also told Juana, who told her dad. Vincente and Rosalia called Elena, who was on her way to the hospital, and said they would be over in an hour. When Elena and Vicky got there, Buck had awakened. Lori had instructed Vicky to bring something current for her to change into as well as Buck's new clothes. The hospital staff had put a hospital gown on him, and Lori would have to repair his Alamo pants before he could be seen in public in them again. When Vicky clued her in that the Montoyas were on the way, Lori got the nurse to remove the needle just long enough to get Buck into his modern clothes. When the Montoyas got there, they saw a transformed young man, thoroughly up-to-date in his jeans and t-shirt. Although everyone was wise enough not to say Buck looked better as a modern man, they did say how good he looked, hoping to discourage the defender costume except when he was at the Alamo playing commander.

Lori's phone rang. It was Bob.

"How's the colonel doing?" he asked.

"He's awake—you should see him. Actually, I think there's something he wants to tell you," Lori said.

"Put him on the phone . . . ."

"I dunno . . . Uh, wait a minute, let me see . . . ."

Bob heard her call: "Buck, do you want to talk to Bob on the phone?"

He looked slightly unnerved.

"There's nothing to it, honestly. It won't bite you—really tame compared to fighting off an enemy army. Do you want to try it? If so, put it up to your ear," she directed.

He slowly took the strange looking rectangular object, placing it against his ear as Lori directed.

"Now say 'Hello' into it."

"Hello?" he said rather hesitantly.

"Hi Colonel! How are you doing?" Bob asked.

"Just fine, sir. I wanted to tell you . . . Thank you for looking for me . . . I don't think I really want to die . . . just get kind of mixed up sometimes

196

when . . . ." He didn't seem to want to finish.

"That's OK, son. We were really worried. I guess you know how much Lori cares about you—poor girl was about to go crazy! She was driving me crazy."

Lori made a face toward the phone.

Bob continued, "And I was very concerned, too. And Professor Jones had some second thoughts—called me and came over and asked about searching at the north wall. Honestly, the professor is more responsible than anyone else for finding you, although I'm pretty sure he's still going to say he's justified in putting all the stuff from your diary in his book."

Once Bob was off the phone, Buck turned to the Claytons.

"I didn't want to hurt Lori or Vicky or anyone I love," Buck said sadly. "I'm so sorry I did."

At that both Lori and Vicky moved in as for an attack, one on each side, closing in on him and holding him and hugging him. He stuck his arm out with the phone, hoping someone would relieve him of it. Vincente did.

Once all of the company had gone, Lori reached in her large purse and pulled out a paper bag.

"Buck, I made something for you. I hope you will like it," she said softly.

He took the bag and pulled out something soft and folded. There was his flag—the flag that flew over his fort—his Alamo.

With tears in his eyes, he reached forward to Lori, and they embraced, as he whispered softly, "It's beautiful! I love you, Lori. I love you."


Bob looked up. Lori was in the doorway with a tall, rather large woman standing next to her.

"This is Mrs. Alice Bensen," Lori introduced the woman. "She's from Alabama, and—she'll have to fill in the details for you, as I got kind of confused when she explained the relationship to me," she turned and

**197**

smiled at the woman, who smiled back, "but she's kin to Col. Travis and would like to meet him."

Bob stood and walked to them, extending his hand to the Alabama lady.

"Welcome to the Alamo," he greeted the newcomer, who seemed slightly nervous about her mission. "I'm Bob Gordon, I'm an administrator here. The actual boss, as you might have heard, is the colonel. The governor put him in charge of the fort."

Mrs. Bensen gave a little laugh. She was a bit intimidating because of her size, and middle-aged with red hair about the same shade as Travis' hair, but her demeanor seemed mild and gentle.

"I don't want to disturb him. Fact is, it's been so many years that I'm not sure what a distant relationship means—if anything—at this point. I don't want to intrude on his life here, but I would like to meet him! The family has an old portrait of him that we all revere, and we put it out on display every March 6 and have a little get-together, just to remember what he did," she explained in a Deep South drawl.

"I am so glad you took the time to come by. Follow me, and I'll introduce you to the colonel," Bob offered. "You will see soon enough that the two of you definitely have one feature in common!"

"The hair, right?" she laughed softly again. "Yes, truth be told, most of the Travis clan have the red hair. It must be dominant in our family!"

They walked across to the long barracks, where Bob knocked on Travis' closed door.

"Come in," the colonel called out.

As he opened the door, Bob warned Mrs. Bensen quietly, "It's really dark in here. He does things the way they were done in 1836—one little candle for illumination!"

Buck had gotten up and was heading to the door as it opened.

"Colonel, I would like to introduce you to someone. Do you notice anything about this lady that jumps out at you?" Bob asked.

198

"We have the same hair," he replied immediately. "Are you kin?"

"Yes, Colonel, I think I have it figured out that you are my uncle five-times removed," she gave the quiet little laugh again. It seemed strange since Buck was clearly young enough to be the woman's son. "I'm Alice Bensen from Alabama. I'm descended from your little brother Mark, who was just a child when you left for Texas," she explained. "I am so honored to actually meet you and so pleased that you have an opportunity to—," she paused to try to find the right words, "continue your young life."

He gave her a sweet, sad smile. Buck only had the one extra uncomfortable wooden chair in his office, so he asked Mrs. Bensen if she would like a personally guided tour of the Alamo complex, to which the Alabama woman responded with delight. To her credit, Mrs. Bensen showed no overt reaction to Buck's scars as they stepped out into the sunlight and the mutilation became much clearer.

"I like your uniform—very dashing," she complimented him.

"Thank you, ma'am," he responded with his little bow and a look of surprised delight. "I'm going to be honest with you. I think that's the first time—since I've been back—that anyone has said anything complimentary about my dress. Most folks either laugh or say they think 1830's styles are weird," he replied with a true look of happiness on his face.

"Well, you look every inch the brave military man!" Mrs. Bensen replied.

Buck beamed.

Bob told Mrs. Bensen how pleased he was to meet her, then left Buck and Lori with the Alabama lady to give her a tour of the place. Buck would give her all the details on the current complex, but first he wanted to go to the furthest point—and the one of most importance to him—to show his kin, the north wall. With the colonel leading the way, the trio crossed Houston carefully, jaywalking at the point of the main entrance to the Garcia building, traffic as likely stopping because of the colonel's distinctive outfit as because it was clear someone wanted to cross the busy street. He explained in detail how the wall was configured with the hill of dirt piled up against it, and that the location was really inside the current building, slightly beyond the general public access area in the lobby. They went in and admired the murals on the walls, quickly picking out the Alamo figures, and Travis pointing to himself. They then headed out and to the side entrance to the building, as close as they could get outside to the spot where Buck had commanded the cannon.

He looked in Mrs. Bensen's eyes, a sad little look, and said softly, "This is approximately where I fell."

She could see the emotion in his face, and instinctively she moved toward him and put her arms around him.

"It's OK, Colonel, it is," she comforted him.

He wiped away a quick tear, wanting to keep his military bearing as he had obviously impressed his distant kin.

"Thank you," he said simply. "If it suits you, please call me Buck—you know, the family dubbed me that, and it stuck through the rest of my life."

"And I'm Alice—please!" she responded.

Lori stood behind them, watching silently. She had been worried that some of Buck's family might try to use his fame in some way, but Alice Bensen clearly was not that type. Although the relationship was distant in years and Mrs. Bensen lived far away, it was good to see Buck with some kind of actual tie to another human being, and a thoughtful, kind one at that.

After Travis finished the depressing part of the tour involving his earlier demise, he lightened things up a bit with his explanation of the rest of the compound, not focusing just on the gory battle. Little Bella came sauntering by and walked right in front of them.

"Oh, what a lovely cat! I just love cats—have three," Alice declared as she reached down and picked up the mascot. Bella made nice to her and purred.

"We have a history of cat mascots," Lori explained. "Sadly, there was a poor kitty who showed up during the battle—probably was actually trying to get away from all of that. But the Mexican troops, saying it was an 'American cat,' dispatched it as well as the American people."

Alice wrinkled her brow. "That's awful! Poor little thing. Well, this one is absolutely adorable." She held the kitty closely, and Bella sucked up to the cat lady, turning the purring machine on super-loud. She finally squirmed, and Alice gently bent down and released the cat, who sauntered on down the path as if nothing had just happened.

It was getting late in the day, and Alice said something about having to meet her husband.

"You have got to come with me first!" Buck said, his eyes bright.

Lori knew exactly what he had in mind. Sure enough, he headed for the gift shop and Morena, Lori and Alice in tow.

"Well, Colonel, I was wondering if you would come by today!" Morena greeted him.

"I've got someone I want you to meet!" the young man replied, obviously pleased that, for the first time since he had been in the present, he could introduce someone. "This is my—what did you say, Alice?—five-times removed great-niece, Alice Bensen," Buck gestured toward Alice. "And Alice, this is my good friend Morena Alejandro. She runs this wonderful shop!"

Morena shook hands with Alice. "So pleased to meet you. It is wonderful that the two of you found each other. Family, even over many years, is special," Morena said. "Fact is, if you are around the colonel very much, you will pretty quickly perceive that there is a reason why he calls the shop wonderful!"

Lori was laughing, and Morena looked as if she were about to.

"Come with me." She led the trio to the corner and the fudge. "They apparently didn't have fudge in the 1830's," she explained. "But our young colonel has become addicted to the stuff!"

Alice stared at the varieties. "I can see why! They all look wonderful!"

Buck pulled some bills from his pants pocket. It felt good to have some spending money and be able to pay for things now that he was receiving the salary for his commander job.

"Morena, we would all like some fudge," he announced. "Alice, pick any one you want—except, you can have it if you wish, but that red one," he pointed, "is named for the no quarter bugle call the Mexicans used on us when they stormed the fort—I avoid it," he advised.

201

Alice laughed. "Well, I see there is another one that suits me much better, and I suspect I'm not the only one?" she laughed.

Morena cut a box of the Travis orange fudge into three large pieces, bid the trio goodbye, and they were out the door. As Alice parted from Buck, she gave him a big hug, and he hugged back, tears glistening in his eyes as he thought of those even further distant days with his family so very long ago. Alice had the Alamo address, but she wrote down hers and handed him a small piece of paper containing it.

"I hope you don't mind getting letters written with an old-fashioned quill?" he asked.

"No, Buck, I don't care what you use to write—just write me, OK? After all, writing is your greatest talent. You take care, hear?"

One more hug and she turned to go, turning back once to wave as Buck and Lori stood.


"Hey Buck, want to see the movie we saw in school?" Vicky called as Lori and Buck walked into the house from work. "Juana let me borrow the DVD," she added enthusiastically.

Lori headed to the kitchen, not wanting to see any more Alamo films. Vicky was holding a small, clear box, thin and square, with something flat and circular visible inside. Buck stared at it. Vicky noticed his confusion.

"Oh, that's just the DVD disk," she explained, an explanation that did not erase the perplexed look from Buck's face. "You can go see a movie like y'all did at the mall . . . ."

"No thanks," he cut her off. "I don't ever want to see that again."

Vicky would not be dissuaded.

"Well, this is a lot more efficient. You just pop the disk in the slot and turn on the TV," she explained.

Buck had seen members of the family, especially Len, turn on the strange screen and sit, staring at it while it depicted a play, same as at IMAX, but he did not have the slightest inclination to watch it. But that wasn't the real problem for Buck.

"Really don't want to see myself die again," he admitted.

Vicky persisted. "This one is way better—you don't actually die in it, and it's even shorter than the one you saw," she continued her argument. "Please, Buck. This was my introduction to you—even before I knew you. Do it for me?" she asked.

Buck stared at the pleading green eyes.

"All right, Vicky, for you I'll watch it," he surrendered for once.

The little movie, meant for school kids, was hokey in the extreme as to the old librarian and his decrepit post. Even Buck realized that and laughed at the character and cobwebbed building that looked like a Halloween prop or a crypt in a silent film. When the film's heroine, not far from Vicky's age, ended up at the Alamo, Buck's interest increased. He silently watched the story unfold and the book of his life fill with pages, and Vicky caught him wiping a tear or two at the mention of young Charles being left as the colonel finally went out the door to impending doom. Vicky moved closer on the couch and put her arm around him.

"It's OK, Buck, it really is," she said softly.

As he wiped one last tear, he turned to her.

"Remembering is so hard," he started. "But I like this one much better than the other one. I was proud to draw my line, and I'm flattered that whoever wrote the story thought of me as someone who would rescue a child from danger—although she shouldn't have been in the Alamo! And the gentleman who portrayed me honored me with his performance."

"But you did rescue a child—that kid who fell in the acequia. Lori told me all about it. That was another reason I wanted you to see this," she added. "Yeah, I think the guy who played you did a great job. And he is kind of cute—but not as good looking as you are."

Buck's hand moved instinctively to the ruined right side of his face.

"No, Buck, honestly, the scars don't obfuscate it—you are a very good looking guy. I know Lori thinks so!"

Buck smiled his sweet smile, hugging Vicky. "Thanks Vicky. I'm glad I saw this one. It's much better than the one at the theater."

Lyle Jones had thought of a new approach for handling the controversy between the traditionalists and the revisionists—and to possibly sell more books, but, more importantly, to set out the issues and hopefully resolve them with the one living defender. He proposed to Bob the idea of a sort of panel discussion set up on the Alamo grounds where Jones and Travis could discuss their views, the public could watch, and Alamo scholars and interested persons could ask the two men for their opinions on anything Alamo. Jones knew there was some risk in this as the reality was that, though he was a leading scholar on the subject and had the resume, speaking skills, and scholarly articles to back up his views, he was still at an extreme disadvantage compared to someone who lived through the siege and the start of the battle. And, although he was an antique one, Travis was a lawyer, as well as a military commander. It would be a fascinating match-up.

"Uh, Lyle, did you approach the colonel about this?" were the first words out of Bob's mouth when he heard Lyle's proposition.

"Not yet—I wanted to run it by you first. My guess is that he would take it as a challenge—sort of like that duel I didn't have to fight because I'm not a gentleman. I think we're hopefully beyond the swordplay at this point, but I am sure he would like to present his version. And much of it, given he was really there, will be invaluable because in all these 180-plus years, no one has heard anything from a live defender. Honestly, I'd be very interested in what he has to say."

"Ask him. I've got the sword in my office for safekeeping right now. I don't think there's any risk!" Bob laughed.

The so-called panel was a very informal affair compared to what Lyle Jones was used to in academic circles. Those events were usually at scholarly conferences held in some choice location such as Boston or Washington, D.C. This one was a matter of setting out a beige folding cafeteria table and a couple of matching metal chairs in the grass on the grounds in back of the Alamo church. Anyone who wanted to attend could do so free of charge, but he or she would have to stand or sit in the grass. It was a no-frills academic event. Where this was definitely roughing it for Jones, it was not for Buck. For one thing, this was his turf. After all, not only had he commanded during the famous fight, but he was in command

204

now. And there were no air-conditioned conference rooms with acoustical systems in the Alamo in 1836.

Lori was still working on his reproduction clothes. She had finally finished the vest and was beginning on the pants—arguably too late, but she had little time for sewing these days. She had patched up the split in his originals shortly after the book-signing incident, but it had not been possible to do a neat job with the frayed fabric. Fortunately, the tails of the coat pretty much covered it. He continued to wear the old costume to work every day. Alice Bensen's characterization of the colonel's uniform as "dashing" had only encouraged him, as if he needed that. Lori had hoped he would just wear the jeans and Victory or Death shirt to this second round with Jones since it was such a casual affair, but Buck insisted on playing his commander of the Alamo role for this one—no real surprise. Bob still had the sword and scabbard in his safe and was hoping Buck was so busy thinking about the panel discussion that he would not miss them.

Buck was not used to speaking into a microphone. When he had done it to recite his letter he was going in and out of consciousness, and it was so dark he probably didn't even see it at the "Dawn" ceremony. The truth was someone just adjusted it to his height and hoped for the best as he totally ignored it. Bob showed it to him this time, telling him that it would amplify his voice and to speak into it when answering a question or otherwise talking.

There were a few die-hard Alamo junkies there for this event, but the truth was that it was pretty much the usual weekend tourists roaming through. Some would stop and listen to a little of the discussion, then amble on toward the koi in the acequia, spot Bella and head in her direction for a pet or two, or proceed to the drink machines and short Alamo film at the very back of the complex.

Bob emceed the event, introducing the two participants. The approach was simple. Each man was allowed to give a brief analysis of the participants in the Alamo battle and what precipitated the whole thing for starters. Jones repeated his line that the defenders had been held up as saints when they were very clearly sinners. Travis didn't deny it—he couldn't with the diary out there, as well as Jim Bowie's reputation. But his take was that their sins did not really matter. They were patriotic Americans fighting and willing to die for Texas and freedom. He got some cheers from the audience for that. As to what precipitated the whole thing, Jones argued vehemently that the Americans took Mexican land under Mexican rules, then tried to usurp those rules and establish an American-style system, with

205

little respect for Mexican law or customs. He described the whole thing as basically a land grab. The attorney for the defense, on the other hand, stated that the Americans were invited, even encouraged or lured in with promises of cheap land, in a desolate area that Mexico wanted populated. They were promised freedom to live the way they wanted under the Mexican Constitution of 1824, then the Chameleon of the West consolidated power and pulled the constitution out from under them. The fact was that there was some truth to both positions, as is usually the case in politics. One young man in the audience pointed this out, Jones and Travis let it go, and they moved on.

The last debate segment was the tough one, a serious and detailed discussion of whether the defenders were saints or sinners. Lyle Jones had thought long and hard whether to repeat his signature comment regarding the Trinity, and he decided, in the words of Davy Crockett, to "go ahead."

"Those of you who have heard me speak before have already heard this, but I really believe it is true. There is a cult of hero worship built up around the Alamo defenders because of the awful conditions they endured for 13 days waiting for what they knew was certain death, and then the horror of that death, mutilation, and cremation when it finally came. There's no denying that Santa Anna, even if he was right on principle of whether the defenders were a legally constituted army or 'land pirates,' as he called them, was ruthless and sadistic in killing the few who survived the battle, mutilation of the bodies, and how he disposed of them. But the flip side of the story is what I like to call the veneration of Saints Davy, Jim, and William . . . ."

There was no sword this time, but Buck couldn't resist interrupting: "I do rather like that last one!"

The audience broke out in laughter. Even Jones couldn't help laughing, and it was a lot better than the other possible alternative—sword in his face.

Jones went into specifics about the failings of the three leaders and the confusion having three prominent men directing such a small force created. He tried to be gentle in his words when discussing Travis, with the man sitting next to him, but he did not hold back from mentioning the rashness of the young colonel in firing that cannon. As evidence, Jones read from a self-serving letter written by El Presidente himself, when the general was an old man, in which Santa Anna pinned the blame for the massacre on Travis:

"I will add that, that conflict of arms was bloody, because

206

the chief Travis, who commanded the forces of the Alamo, would not enter into any capitulation, and his responses were insulting, which made it imperative to assault the fort before it could be reinforced by Samuel Houston who was marching to its succor with respectable forces. The obstinacy of Travis and his soldiers was the cause of the death of the whole of them, for not one would surrender. The struggle lasted more than two hours, and until the ramparts were resolutely scaled by Mexican soldiers."

Travis had finally realized that he might stand a better chance against the professor if he took what the other man said calmly, not sword or temper first. So, despite the fact that Jones had actually quoted from the Evil One himself, the colonel listened. But he came roaring back in his verbal response, stating that it was clear from the get-go that Santa Anna had no intention of letting anyone go if he took the fort. He noted that he had been told of Col. Fannin's surrender of the Fort Defiance garrison and execution of his command. He argued that it was clear that surrender would not have gotten the men in the Alamo any mercy. The idea that it was Travis' fault that a man commanding a huge army chose to slaughter the entire little band of Alamo defenders was preposterous.

He continued, "Although, personally, this idea is not too appealing to me for what should be obvious reasons, Santa Anna could always have proposed terms whereby he would kill me but let the others live. With his history and the proposed surrender at discretion, it was clear to us that his choice was to kill everyone."

He went on to note that there was a long history of Santa Anna's murdering of prisoners, including during a similar revolt in the state of Zacatecas in 1835. During the Texas Revolution, El Presidente cited the trumped-up Tornel Decree stating that Mexican forces capturing insurgents were required to execute them. Of course, as dictator, Santa Anna could have dropped or waived the decree had he really wanted to do so. He announced up front with his blood-red flag and music signifying "slit throat" what the intent was. Travis' firing the cannon in defiance made no difference as to the dictator's intent, although the colonel did admit that he knew that Santa Anna particularly had it in for him and considered him a "troublemaker." As to whether anyone surrendered or the claim by El Presidente that the fight took over 2 hours, Travis could not speak, as he had been shot down long before then.

Jones and Travis got through this tense conversation without the colonel, even sans sword, taking a swing at the professor or any other violence. A few academic types, members of the Texian Association, Vincente Montoya, and members of the public inquired regarding uniforms, arms, and what folks in the Alamo ate. When Bella came strolling along almost on cue, someone asked if the old story that Lori had intimated to Alice Bensen really was true that the Mexicans, in their frenzy of bloodlust as they were bayoneting anything that moved at the end of the massacre, spotted a cat and killed it, saying it was "un gato Americano."

The colonel and the professor stood and shook hands, and people came up singly and in groups to ask them questions and thank them for their program. Bella headed away as the people moved in.

THE DEFENSE OF THE ALAMO

Lori ran to Bob's office. "I've got someone from a Chihuahua, Mexico—not the little dogs, military academy on the phone. He wants to talk with, as he put it, 'whoever is in charge,'" she said.

"Transfer him to me," Bob instructed.

A few minutes later, he stepped into Lori's cubicle.

"You're probably curious about that one?" he asked.

She nodded.

"It's a boys' school, equivalent to high school—all cadets. They want to visit the Alamo. The guy didn't speak the best English, but he said that their victory is one of the high points in Mexican military history, and he wants the kids to see where it happened. They plan to come in on a school bus, driving up through the desert . . . ."

"Oh, no, you've got to be kidding!" Lori moaned. "Won't they be wearing some kind of cadet uniforms most likely?"

"I didn't ask, but usually military school students do," he replied.

"That's not going to work—trust me," Lori shook her head in disbelief. "I can just envision it now. About the time they get off the bus, or certainly if they are ordered to stand in formation or something, I'll guarantee someone's going to get hurt. They'll see more than just the site—there will be another battle of the Alamo!"

"I can try to convince him to play tour guide and show them around the compound. He does speak a little Spanish. I don't," Bob replied.

"Oh, come on. How long do you think that would last? And he might take you out just for mentioning it," Lori warned.

Bob looked slightly disconcerted. "So any ideas about how to handle it?"

"He still hasn't asked about his sword?" Lori queried.

"Not yet, but I expect it any day," came the answer.

"Let's pray he doesn't before they come. By the way, did you set a date?" Lori raised her eyebrows.

"Yeah. Next Monday."

Ignoring Lori's advice, Bob convinced himself that it would not hurt to ask. He knocked on the closed door of the colonel's dark little office.

"Come in," Travis called.

"Got a question for you, sir," Bob asked. Travis motioned to the spare chair, and Bob sat down.

"We have a group of high school kids coming in by bus. They're driving—from Mexico."

Travis cut him off. "I don't want to have anything to do with Mexicans, even if they are children."

"I know, but hear me out. They're not young children—will be in their teens as I understand it. They want to see the Alamo . . . ."

"Probably so that they can gloat over their victory," Travis interrupted.

Bob knew the colonel was probably right on that one, but he tried to downplay it. He would have to be crafty to persuade the difficult Alamo commander to assist rather than thwart his plan.

"They're just kids. I suspect they are proud of being Mexican just as we're proud of being American, but you've got to remember—this is just a quick visit for them. You are the premier expert on the Battle of the Alamo. You could be quite persuasive in skewing whatever viewpoints they might have toward our direction if you choose to do so. You are a lawyer, and I've heard you speak as well as read your written words. You do possess the powers of persuasion, Colonel, should you choose to use them."

Travis made a face. "But Mexicans—the enemy? You want ME to show them the place where they did this to me," he pointed at his face, "and killed everyone I was fighting with?" He shook his head. "I think that

210

is asking too much."

"Well, think about it. But they're coming in on Monday. They might get a much better perspective of the American side if you came at them with a convincing argument as to the brutality of Santa Anna, while showing some finesse, instead of charging them with . . . ." Bob stopped as he realized he had made a fatal error.

"That reminds me," Travis asked, "Do you know where my sword might be?"

Bob had no choice but to explain that he had locked the weapon in the safe when the colonel went missing. They walked to Bob's office, and he hesitantly searched his middle desk drawer for the key and retrieved the sword, handing it over in fear and trepidation to the eager defender of the Alamo.

After Travis had gone back to his quarters to draft something with his quill or walked toward the north wall to think about his demise—or whatever he did with himself when Lori wasn't involving him in a demo to keep him out of trouble, Bob stepped into Lori's little workspace.

"Got a minute?" he asked. There was no one else around.

"I saw him heading upstairs with the sword," Lori noted, not even looking up. "Wonder what it will be next time?"

"Well, like I said, the Mexican high school cadets will be here Monday. The superintendent of the school said he thought they would be in on the school bus around 1:00 in the afternoon. You know Leslie and I are heading to the islands tomorrow."

Leslie was Bob's significant other—a guy. Bob was gay, but he kept it strictly under wraps. Lori was the only person who knew, the result of a fluke phone call coming in one day. Everyone at the mission just assumed that Leslie was a woman, and Bob was determined to keep it that way, now more than ever. He could not imagine what Col. Travis, with his reputation as a ladies' man and stuck in 1836, would think—or worse, do—if he ever found out.

"Our plane is going to get in Monday morning around 9:00. I should be back in plenty of time to meet the superintendent and his charges. But, if we're delayed for any reason, would you feel comfortable meeting them and

211

showing them around?" he asked.

"Sure, I'll be glad to—except there's just that one issue," she hesitated.

"I don't know any more to do about the colonel than you do, Lori. In fact, you have way more influence over him than I do. If you can think of any errand to send him on . . . ."

"The guy is dressed up funny and can't drive—where can I send him?"

Bob shrugged. "I don't know. What about posting him at the north wall and then making sure the cadets stay at the south wall where Davy was?" Bob laughed.

"Well, y'all enjoy your vacation. You've earned it. I'll do something with Buck, even if I have to hog-tie him," Lori replied.

"That might be more entertaining than a vacation!" Bob rejoined.

It was Monday morning around 8:30 when Lori and Buck got to the fort. The archaeological site was still mapped out and barricaded, but the students had not been digging for the last week. Maybe spring break or exams intervened. Although she noticed their absence, Lori paid little attention to that kind of thing. She went her way, stopping to pet Bella, popping her head in to see Morena, and then heading downstairs. The colonel headed to the long barracks. Lori had let the ever-present paperwork get behind as she had a number of demos, including a reprise of the cactus dinner as well as the okra and pepper event with Buck, lately, so she was trying to catch up. She was attempting to fill out a complex online invoice form when she heard someone running down the stairs. It was Elbert.

"Emergency group meeting!" he called.

"What?"

"I dunno. Jaime said he heard and to pass it on to all staff. Bob's on vacation, isn't he?" Elbert asked.

"Yeah, he is," Lori responded. "What now?"

212

She followed Elbert up the stairs. Tom Rosser and Melia Bravo, teens who worked as volunteers under Morena in the gift shop, were headed toward the front of the church, the apparent gathering point. Several other shop employees and other staff were in a small group ahead. Elbert and Lori followed, all heading toward the front of the complex.

"Wonder where Morena is?" Lori asked aloud.

Tom heard her. "The colonel said she could stay and, as he put it, 'man the gift shop and guard the fudge,'" he shouted.

"What?" Lori asked.

"Colonel Travis has called some kind of meeting out front of the chapel," he replied.

At that point they were there. Jaime, a half-smile on his face, was standing in front of the church, on patrol duty. Buck was standing there, too, with the sword buckled on, holding a rather rickety pole he had procured from somewhere, and on it was Lori's rendition of the "Victory or Death" flag. Lori was seriously concerned that he was going to order all the employees into formation and draw a line. He looked very determined and a bit "off"—maybe in 1836 again. Everyone stood there in little groups of two or three, staring at each other, bemused.

"Thank you for coming on such short notice," the colonel began. "You may or may not have heard that there is to be what has been described as a 'visit' by Mexican military cadets today. I understand they are supposed to arrive at 1:00—at least, thank God, that will be in broad daylight!"

Yep, Lori thought. It's 1836 again—no pre-dawn attack this time.

"I understand that Mr. Gordon has taken a few days respite, and, as the governor of Texas has appointed me to command the Alamo again, after all these years, it is my duty to see that the aforementioned . . . ."

Aforementioned—there was an 1836 word, Lori thought to herself.

". . . .military incursion by Mexican forces must be deterred at all cost."

All cost—Lori noted—let's all die for the cause.

"I realize that none of you are military personnel, but this is an emergency, and we must make what limited preparation is possible to meet the foe," he went on, deadly serious. Tom and Melia were trying desperately not to laugh.

"Ed, Elbert, Jaime, and Tom—I want y'all to shift those barricades," he pointed to the dig site, "forward in front of the church. We have got to block the entrance. If we do not have enough material to form a solid wall, we can bring some of the furniture from the offices to fill in," he continued.

Melia was rolling her eyes. Tom elbowed her, afraid that the colonel would see her. She whispered under her breath, "He's nuts!"

Travis continued, pointing at various items he wanted "redirected," in other words, moved.

Tom calmed himself enough to say with a semi-straight face, "We don't have any weapons, sir."

Lori almost lost it. Melia did. The colonel turned toward her with a fierce look. "This is serious. We must meet the enemy here, and this time, we must prevail!"

"But sir, again, I ask, with what?" Tom's eyes were dancing.

"I don't suppose any of the cannon are still functional?" Travis asked in earnest.

Elbert shook his head in the negative. Thank God, Lori thought.

Travis continued, "I have my sword. Ladies, while the gentlemen are placing the fortifications, I want y'all to search for anything we can use to arm ourselves—kitchen knives, boards, ANYTHING that might deter these so-called cadets," he commanded. "And, if nothing else, we have honor."

"I beg your pardon, Colonel, but honor isn't going to stop an enemy force—not that I think these kids are really a threat," Elbert started to explain.

The colonel cut him off. "These are Mexican nationals, sir. They are heading toward the Alamo as we speak. It is imperative that we have a warm reception ready for them when they arrive! You are all dismissed."

214

Lori, Tom, and Melia hurried toward the back of the church, where they dissolved in laughter.

"I could get one of those kid's Davy coonskin caps and that popgun we sell. Think the colonel would go for that?" Tom asked.

Travis' first concern was to get his "Victory or Death" flag standing upright, which was accomplished with the help of Jaime and Tom. With the flag flying, and to his credit in this military emergency, the commanding officer pitched in and helped the men in his extremely small "garrison" prepare for defense. But with all of the barricade material from the dig "redirected," and a few other barriers, including some fencing, there still was not enough to cover the entire front before the church. As Travis had intimated, the next step was to start hauling office furniture up from below the gift shop to extend the defense line. Bob had a fair-sized desk, and it was eyed quickly by the commanding officer. He ordered all of the junk dumped on the floor and drawers removed so that the heavy piece of furniture could be gotten up the stairs. Desk chairs, three smaller desks, a couple of cabinets, a credenza, and three tables were dragged up the stairs and added to lengthen the line. The offices at the back of the compound were raided for further fortifications. Finally, although it was not high enough to prevent an enemy firing at the defenders from hitting them, the colonel had a solid pile of miscellaneous obstacles barricading the old church. He stood looking toward the plaza, as if expecting to see Santa Anna approach at any moment. Tourists were coming up as usual, taking pictures, pointing, and staring at the line of desks and chairs, orange barricades, and tables, with the colonel standing right behind it. Most people, after a few minutes of watching this, headed for the River Walk. It was obvious no one was getting in the Alamo today.

It was 12:30 when Bob finally got there. As he got out of the car and walked across the compound to within sight of the church facade, he stopped cold. He just stared at the huge pile of junk—until he recognized his desk. Travis was not in sight. Bob seriously thought about getting back in the car and heading somewhere, anywhere, other than here. The Mexican cadet bus would be here any time now. What would they think? Bob watched as the tourists continued walking up, staring, stunned, pulling out their cell phones, and heading to the River Walk. A few bystanders, curious enough to wait, stood around to see the show. It was too late to try to undo any of this. As Bob stood there, he caught sight out of the corner of his eye of a large group, all in gray/blue clothing—the cadets. He squeezed through the fortifications, walking onto the plaza. The bus had paused on Crockett Street by the Menger Hotel, and the students were disembarking. They were wearing simple uniforms in a dull cadet blue, with white cross straps over their chests. They marched in formation the short distance to the church. A middle-aged man, in the same uniform but with epaulets, halted them while he gazed in shock toward the Alamo.

At the same moment, Travis, with the Alamo employees in line behind him, marched up to the barricade, and with sword drawn, ordered all of the employees in position manning the defenses. All of them were holding some sort of "weapon"—a knife, a board, or one of the fake rifles sold at the shop. Tom and Melia were still laughing.

Armed with a rolling pin from the kitchen, she whispered, "Oh, God, I hope no one gets my picture doing this. I'll never live it down!"

The military school superintendent was still staring. Bob finally walked out to meet him in front of the barricade.

"Major Amaya?" he asked hesitantly.

"Si," the man responded.

"I'm Bob Gordon, I'm on the . . . I hate to admit this right now . . . administrative staff here," he told Amaya, trying desperately not to laugh. Bob put out his hand, and Amaya shook it.

"I am curious, Mr. Gordon, is this an impromptu demonstration of the battle?" Amaya asked with a grin.

"Did you hear about Col. Travis, the Alamo commander, by any chance?" Bob asked reluctantly.

"Si, that made the news all over Mexico. While General Santa Anna is not our favorite son in Mexico generally, Col. Travis has quite a reputation of his own—and not a good one. We took notice that the colonel is, shall we say, 'back.' The man in the defender outfit, I assume?"

Bob laughed. "Yes. He's a character. Really not such a bad guy on the whole, but he . . . and I apologize for this but there's nothing I can do to change him . . . still hates Mexicans today. And he goes off into 1836—I suspect, in his mind, he's there right now."

"He was shot in the forehead in the battle, if I am not mistaken?" Amaya replied. "Perhaps, he is not quite all here?"

216

Bob nodded. "I think Travis may have been a bit off when he tangled with your folks the first time. I'm sure the wound didn't help."

Amaya laughed. The cadets had pulled out cell phones and were taking pictures and video, and pointing at the colonel and laughing. Bob and Amaya were out of earshot of Travis, but they were staring at him, and he was looking back, grim and determined, sword at the ready.

"Men," he shouted—apparently including the women in that as well, "If they make a move toward us, be ready to use your weapons as best you can!"

Melia turned her head and put it on Tom's shoulder, holding her rolling pin in front of her.

"Straighten up, soldier!" the colonel ordered.

She righted herself, but she was still laughing. It was impossible not to.

"No offense, Major, but, in our lingo, we would call this a 'Mexican standoff,'" Bob told his guest.

Amaya smiled. He was being very gracious about all of this, Bob thought to himself.

"So, Mr. Gordon, do you want us to charge them, surrender, or continue this 'Mexican standoff'? Your preference," Amaya offered.

Bob shrugged. "Wish I knew what Travis has in mind. The cannon in the Alamo don't work . . . ."

Amaya laughed again. "Well, I'm glad to hear THAT."

"I think if you charge them, the employees will just let you through. I'm sure they're about to die laughing—which is better than dying defending, which is apparently what Travis is thinking about."

"I much prefer the former," Amaya agreed.

"But Travis will probably take a swing or two at someone with that sword if past performances are any indication. I don't want anyone to get hurt. I guess you could try demanding his surrender?" Bob asked with raised eyebrows and a smile.

217

Amaya walked forward, almost to the defenders' line, knowing—or at least hoping—that Travis did not have a real gun somewhere.

"Sir, we demand that you surrender the Alamo to our forces. We outnumber you, and your defenses are too weak to withstand us," he addressed Travis.

"Never! Come and take it!" the colonel shouted, echoing the famous slogan from the Gonzales cannon incident.

Amaya walked back to Bob. "He's crazy, but he's dead serious," Amaya said. "He's got a strange look in his eyes—sort of like a death wish."

"Yeah. He does that sometimes. So he won't surrender. Honestly, no surprise there—that 'I shall never surrender or retreat' statement from his famous letter. I kind of doubt you folks feel like surrendering to him, considering you have driven all the way up here . . . ?"

"I don't mind, really, if it will get the colonel to move the barricades and stop the war," Amaya said. "Defusing him will be a victory."

"Yeah, you know his slogan, and God knows, we've heard it enough around here lately, is 'Victory or Death'—and he means it," Bob said.

Amaya noted what had been said many times in response, "That didn't work out so well, last time, did it?"

Regardless, the good-natured major approached Travis again.

"All right, Colonel, you win. I will surrender my forces if that is agreeable to you, and, as I understand to be the case, you Americans do not follow the no-quarter policy that our General Santa Anna employs?" Amaya was playing it perfectly.

"That is correct, sir. Americans do not murder their prisoners, unlike your leader. If you surrender your arms . . . ."

"Colonel, you may look if you wish, but we are not carrying any arms," Amaya broke in.

"Very well, sir, in that case, I accept your surrender. You may line your troops up and we will make an opening in the fortifications so that you may march in to make the formal surrender to our forces!"

218

Amaya got his cadets in line as Travis ordered Elbert, Ed, Jaime, and Tom to dismantle enough of the defense wall that an entry could be made.

Amaya solemnly marched his students through the hole and onto the Alamo grounds in front of the church. He halted his line, and turned and faced and saluted Travis, who saluted in return.

"Sir, I surrender my force to your care and protection. I request that we be treated honorably as befits the agreement we have made," the major said seriously.

"It is done, sir. I see that your men have no weapons," the colonel responded. "You may dismiss them. We will parole all, and they may return to their homes."

The upshot of all of this was that the cadets were now on the grounds, free to roam around and tour the old mission, until whenever Travis devised some sort of paroles that they could take home as wonderful souvenirs of their trip to Texas.


Lori was on the tail end of finishing the reproduction pants. It was a good thing, since her last attempt to mend the originals had not held due to the fraying of the ancient fabric. It had not mattered this time, as the coat tails adequately covered the colonel's rear, even if his troops did not, in the military crisis with the Mexican cadets. The reproduction pants had been a complicated project, as the construction was very different from anything seen today. Much of the clothing covering the upper half of the body, such as men's coats and ladies' bodices, was constructed differently in the 1800's, but much of that involved seam placement, especially regarding armholes. The 1830's pants were a whole different matter. Not only did they far predate zippers, but they also predated flys, that not having come into vogue until closer to the Civil War. The front closure on these things was a convoluted "fall" involving two wing pieces that met and buttoned in the middle with a flap that pulled up over them and buttoned at the top. The center back top had a gusset piece sewn between the back ends of the waistband, which formed a "V", and eyelets with a pull-through string provided some attempt at waistband fit, the rest being left up to buttons added for attachment of suspenders, or "braces," as they called them back then. The pants were easier than the coat would be, but more alien. For now, until Lori could get time to sew the buttons and buttonholes on the front panel—and have Buck try them on again so she could mark them for

219

hemming, he would be stuck in the present, apparel-wise, anyway.

As Lori and Buck drove to work, she was trying not to laugh at the thought of yesterday's little skirmish. Buck had sunk into quietude again, as he tended to do after these flare-ups. Elena had been at the nook with coffee in hand when the two showed up that morning. She had the newspaper, but she did not show it to them. That had to wait until they got to work.

Lori was standing in the door of Bob's office, staring at the mess. He had the paper, too, and he was not hesitant. The headline read: "MEXICAN 'ARMY' SURRENDERS TO TRAVIS!" with a half-page picture panning the view of the chapel, fortifications in place with the "defenders" at the ready and the colonel standing stiffly, with the sword held high, Lori's flag fluttering in the breeze behind him. Bob held the paper out to Lori. She burst out laughing. Meanwhile, Bob was standing amidst piles of his precious junk, thrown helter-skelter by the "troops" following the colonel's orders to impress the desk for military purposes.

"It was funny until I got here this morning and realized I had to put all this stuff up," Bob sighed.

"Maybe it's an opportunity to throw some of it out?" Lori hesitantly suggested.

"Yeah, you are probably right, but he sure turned this place upside down. Where is he today, anyway?"

"Went to his dark little headquarters, as usual. We probably won't hear much out of him today for a couple of reasons. First, he usually shuts up for a while after these things, and second, his pants didn't make it through the fight intact, so he has to dress like a modern guy until I get the reproduction finished."

"Lori, I'd like to make a suggestion," Bob replied. "Hold off as long as you can on the uniform. I do think that makes him worse."

Later that day, when she retrieved the mail, there was a package addressed to "The Alamo." Lori handed it to Bob, noting, "I hope it isn't an explosive!"

He seemed unconcerned and, reaching into his pocket for a little knife, cut the tape and opened the box. Inside was a rather worn stuffed animal

220

Chihuahua from the old Taco Bell advertisements featuring the dog and the "Yo quiero, Taco Bell" catchphrase. There was also a note:

> "To whomever is REALLY in charge of the Alamo: Please give this to Col. Travis with my compliments!"

Luisa Montoya was reading the paper as well. Vincente's 63-year-old cousin had devoted her life not to family or making money but to furthering Hispanic rights. Luisa was passionate about human rights. Her father had been an alcoholic, and she had a tough time growing up. But she was smart, earning a scholarship to UT, where she majored in political science. She was below average height, with a stocky frame, dark hair peppered with gray, and piercing dark eyes. Luisa was a formidable adversary, but she battled for her cause with a sense of humor as well as finely honed political and strategic skills. She avoided all of the silly hoopla about a long-ago battle to the extent possible, and she made a point of not setting foot in the Shrine of Texas Liberty. But she could laugh at it—and did when she saw this morning's *Express-News*. She called to Angelo Ramirez, her one assistant at her little nonprofit, La Voz. Angelo, at 26, was the same age as the crazy colonel—at least in modern years.

Angelo, a tall, slight, studious-looking young man with glasses, appeared in the doorway. "You bellowed?" he asked, obviously not intimidated by his boss.

Luisa laughed. "Yes. You've got to see this." She handed him the paper.

Angelo stared for a few minutes, then read some of the text aloud:

> "Apparently, the Battle of the Alamo is not over. Colonel Travis, who has returned to the fort, if not the present, ordered Alamo staff to place impediments in front of the old church yesterday out of concern about a Mexican invasion by high school students from Chihuahua. Fortunately for all involved, there was no bloodshed this time, the commandant of the high school cadets gracefully 'surrendering' to the famous Alamo commander."

"It's funny, and you have to give the school superintendent credit for his action so that he basically won the day in the end—although I have a

221

feeling the colonel never figured that out. And it did prevent another altercation involving Travis using his sword on someone, but it has gotten out of hand. No one at the Alamo wants to, or maybe can, what with the governor's appointment of the crazy fool to his old post as commander, stop him from these antics. But it's gotten to the point where we need to think about putting some pressure on the authorities to put an end to it," Luisa said.

"But what can we do since the governor appointed Travis to command, so to speak? If I remember right, he even recommissioned the mission as a military base!" Angelo smiled and shook his head slightly.

"We know this governor is not going to remove Travis after putting him there. It's just a token so they can pay him something and honor a hero, but they're being irresponsible letting him cause one dangerous situation after another with that sword. I think a rally at the front of the church may be our only option. But for it to have any teeth, it's going to have to be a big one. To put it in perspective, kind of like when Santa Anna's army showed up in 1836. That will get the attention of the public in a peaceful manner, make clear that the Alamo's current purpose is not to precipitate more fighting, and, if Travis acts out, which he undoubtedly will, make him look like even more of a fool . . . ."

"He already did that yesterday," Angelo noted.

"True, and that's good. No one got hurt, the Mexicans took peaceful and reasonable action, and everyone in town is laughing at the colonel's little stunt. But it was a small affair between the school kids and Alamo staff members impressed for 'duty.' We need a huge showing of citizen concern to get the attention of someone who can put a stop to this. Too bad they ever dug him up . . . ."

"Yeah—too bad Santa Anna didn't burn him with the others," Angelo intervened.

"Well, anyway, I think with a large enough army, so to speak, we can defeat Travis again at the Alamo, and make sure we wrap it up so that it never has to be done again!" Luisa added.

"Uh, you don't intend to kill and burn him?" Angelo asked hesitantly. Luisa could get fiery in her dedication to her cause.

She laughed. "No, that's where I differ from Santa Anna. Had I been

El Presidente, I would have sent him in chains to Mexico City to toil on a rock pile or whatever convicts did back then."

"You intend to ship him off to Mexico for trial?" Angelo queried.

"No, not that, either. I just want to put a stop to the sword waving and other silly-seeming but actually dangerous fake military situations he creates. I personally think he needs to be institutionalized, but certainly some kind of corralling. We'll see."


Vicky thought it was funny when she saw the paper, but she did not laugh at Buck, unlike just about everyone else. When he got home with Lori, he was still very quiet. It was time to get his mind on something other than yesterday's military action. Elena had an end-of-day meeting at the office, as seemed to happen about once a week, so Vicky had been tasked with coming up with something for dinner. Her plan was to prepare nothing. She made an executive decision—it was time to go out for barbeque! Len had disappeared to Andres' house as usual to work on his Spanish guitar, an obsession with him lately that was almost as bad, if not as dangerous, as Buck's obsession with guarding the fort. It was fortuitous that Buck had to wear his jeans, as he would fit in way better at the restaurant than in the old uniform. Maybe, if they were lucky, no one would know who he was. She figured that was just what he needed—a situation where he did not have to defend the Alamo for once. When her parents got home, she clued in her mom, who approved heartily, pleased that her little girl was as astute as she was and certainly had made an adult decision—as well as having gotten out of cooking a meal.

They piled in the SUV and headed to Wingo's Texas Bar & BBQ, which had the disadvantage of being 15 miles west of town but well worth the mileage. It was Buck's first trip outside the city proper. Although barbeque was pretty much the state official food and had been forever, the civilized version was much improved over slaughtering and hacking into pieces for sticking over a fire one of the "beeves" referenced in the postscript to the February 24, 1836, letter.

Tall Buck was sitting between the two Clayton girls in the back seat, as each of them wanted the honor of sitting next to him. Lori had ordered him to face her on the drive over and was trying to use her concealer on the scars, putting a little on, rubbing it in with a finger, then feathering the outer edges with a tissue.

"On his forehead, let's just comb his hair down," Vicky suggested.

Elena turned to look. Poor Buck looked like a trapped animal, but he kept his mouth shut and let the girls work at improving his looks. It seemed that only incidents involving the Alamo riled him. Vicky handed Lori a comb, and she pushed the red hair sweeping to the side across his hairline down and more in his face.

"Great idea, Vicky! I think that makes a major difference—and actually, Buck, it's a much more modern hairstyle for a guy, anyway!" Lori exclaimed.

He just stared at her with a half-smile on his face.

By the time they got to Wingo's, the sword slash on his cheek was somewhat less obvious, and the gunshot wound was largely obscured by his hair. Between that and the t-shirt and jeans, he decidedly did not look like an Alamo defender.

Wingo's was rustic in the extreme. The place was originally a rambling 1800's farmhouse, not as old as the Shrine but certainly aged. There was one enormous old oak tree that looked as if it had seen better days hovering over the place. The house may never have been painted—certainly was not now. How come it had never burned down over the years was anyone's guess. There was a fence set some yards to the back of the structure, and inside the dusty enclosure were several hogs and to the right a smaller enclosure containing a flock of chickens. Beyond the enclosures was a field in which cattle were grazing. Apparently, Wingo's served their meat fresh. The parking lot was dirt—no paving. But it was jammed full. That was the advantage of having no landscaping—it didn't get in the way of extra customers pulling in and cost absolutely nothing to maintain. The aroma coming from the old building was heavenly.

The inside of the place was just as unadorned as the outside. Servers wearing jeans and t-shirts, the shirts advertising Wingo's and featuring a steer horn logo, hustled to keep their numerous customers happy. Tables varied in size and shape, all rough wooden affairs, as were the chairs. There was a large open area in what had probably been the parlor in some earlier life before the rooms were opened up, where bands sometimes played and line dances were held. At present, there was no action in the parlor, but it was early yet. The Claytons stood patiently, next to the busy bar, waiting to get a seat. It was always that way at Wingo's.

By the time they were finally led to a table, a band had shown up and was setting up for the evening. The menus were so old they were falling apart. That either meant they did not go up on prices as often as most restaurants did or the number of patrons was so great that menus just tore up faster than they did most places. Regardless of which it was, the owners apparently saw no need to replace them. Buck didn't care that the menu was falling apart. He was not used to reading menus, but he certainly enjoyed reading the descriptions of the various platters. Everything the restaurant offered appealed to him, but he finally followed the lead of Lori, who ordered a standard rib platter and onion rings.

The band had set up and was playing Country & Western, the only thing that ever played at Wingo's. The music had some familiar threads here and there, although it was basically alien to Travis, but he was paying little attention as he was totally focused on the food. To his delight, both Lori and Vicky had more than they could eat in the sumptuous platters, and each gave Buck a rib and a few rings. As he was putting a ring in his mouth, a young couple came up, the woman in a white halter dress, a foolish choice for eating barbeque.

"Hi Lori, long time no see!" the woman hailed her. Lori licked her fingers, hoping there was nothing sticky on them, wiped her hands on her napkin, and got up and hugged her, then shook hands with the guy, whom the woman introduced as Van. Robert made a half-hearted rise from the other end of the table, then quickly resumed eating. The Alamo's Southern gentleman rose, gave a slight bow, and stood next to Lori, extending his hand as Lori told them he was her very good friend, Buck. She deliberately left off the last name, although she didn't think it would be obvious tied to his nickname. The couple went on after a moment of chit chat, and Buck eagerly resumed eating.

They were just about finished and the band was in high gear when Lori saw Vincente and Rosalia come in out of the corner of her eye. She had no way to signal them that the goal was for Buck to remain incognito. It didn't take Vincente long to spot the Clayton party, and he headed their direction, Rosalia in tow. Fortunately, the music was so loud and the crowd so noisy that maybe anything Vincente said might not be heard.

Robert and Buck rose as the Montoyas got to them, and Elena got up and hugged Rosalia.

Vincente, staring at the new and improved Travis, determined to encourage the look.

"Son, I can't tell you how much better you look," he started.

So far, so good, Lori thought. Vincente had a rather booming voice, and it carried.

"I can't tell you how much better you look in that than you do in your Alamo uniform!"

The patrons at the two tables immediately behind them turned and stared, one woman whispering something to another, who then asked someone else what she had just heard—as if to get a confirmation.

"So is one of you a reenactor?" a man at the nearest table asked Lori.

"Uh, why yes, I do period food preparation and other demos at the Alamo," Lori replied quickly.

"I thought someone said something about an Alamo uniform," the man persisted.

Vincente turned to him. "Why don't you know? This is Col. Travis of Alamo fame—he's updated his look a little bit for forays outside the fort!"

Lori was dreading some sort of reaction, particularly after the newspaper coverage of the little mini-siege. The man who had asked the question about the uniform banged his cup on the table, shouting for quiet. Lori was mortified. Finally, the band stopped playing, and most of the patrons quieted down.

"Ladies and gentlemen!" the man announced. "We are graced with and honored tonight by the presence of a man who towers in Texas history. Of course, in Texas, that says a lot. You might not recognize him because he's not in uniform this evening, but this gentleman is Col. William Barret Travis!" He pointed out the colonel for anyone who might not be able to figure it out.

The crowd went wild, everyone standing and hooting and hollering and clapping. Buck made his little bow. Apparently, he was a lot more popular at some institutions than at others. Meanwhile, the band was playing again, this time the country tune "Price of Freedom" in honor of the distinguished man gracing the barbeque joint with his presence this night,. It sounded like things were getting ready for a line dance. Both Lori and Vicky headed for the open area that served as a dance floor, as did a number of other patrons.

226

The older crowd mostly watched the show. It may have been Texas line dancing, but it was newer than Buck. He watched, with an eye on Lori and Vicky, but he pretty quickly determined the moves were not for him.

Vincente's phone rang, and he excused himself and walked outside where it was quieter. It was cousin Luisa.

"Well, I know you wouldn't call me if you didn't have something in the works," Vincente laughed.

"Actually, cousin, I do! It's totally peaceful—no one can get hurt, but we're finally going to march on the Alamo!" she said.

Vincente was thinking to himself that maybe San Antonio was getting too nutty for him. "March on the Alamo? You mean like Santa Anna?"

"No cannon or rifles. We're soldiers of peace . . . ."

Vincente rolled his eyes. Fortunately, Luisa couldn't see him. "What's the point, to just say we don't like the Alamo, to have it torn down, to refocus the purpose?" he asked.

"We know they'll never tear it down, although I walked by it yesterday. Didn't go in—have a thing about that place. It does look rather worse for wear. The state will probably up taxes so they can fix it. I would resent that when there are so many needy causes."

Vincente was just nodding and trying to think about something else, but he had to respond to her off and on. "So how many people and when?" he asked.

"However many show up. We're recruiting every which way we can. As to when, I'm afraid I can't tell you . . . ." she said.

"Can't tell me? Like what if I wanted to come?" he interrupted.

"You've never shown any interest in La Voz before—seem to be content with dressing up like Santa Anna every year and playing into their hands," she said, accusingly but with a sweetness in her voice that told him she was not really angry at him. "We are not saying when it is going to be until the last minute as we start, as we don't want to be stopped by the authorities."

227

"Uh, well, I thought I told you about my Santa Anna impression. It was awful this year. Colonel Travis is back from the dead, and he manhandled Santa Anna's troops and the entire program, single-handedly."

"Yeah, you did say something about that. Well, he's an issue, too. That will be a part of the rally," she said.

"You can't just knock him off, you know. It's illegal. Besides, we had a rough introduction, but he's not that bad for the crazed commander of the Alamo," he laughed.

"Well, whatever, but he is an issue. I have no intention of hurting him, but he does need to learn to shut up and that things have changed since he ran the place in 1836!"

"That's true, but I have not been able to change him. Too bad you're not here, though!"

"Why? Where are you?"

"Wingo's," Vincente replied.

"Anglo reactionaries," she said with a trace of true anger in her voice.

"Maybe so, but they have the best BBQ in these parts," he laughed. "But what I wanted to tell you is that the restaurant is graced with the presence of the great Texas hero tonight."

"Travis? I told you they are reactionaries!" she shot back

"Well, I wish I had taken a photo on the phone of the colonel. He's wearing jeans and a t-shirt—admittedly with his 'Victory or Death' slogan on it. But he looks like a regular guy!"

"I'm glad to know he shows a little flexibility. That uniform is goofy. But it's not the clothes that make the man. Underneath the t-shirt and jeans, he's still the same colonel—will fight to defend the Alamo against anyone Hispanic."

"Yeah, Luisa, you are probably right on that one."

"Buck, back before we found you, I promised my mom that I would paint the sunroom. I really need to go ahead and get it done," Lori announced. "Do you want to help?"

"I've noticed all the colors on the walls in your world, but, you know, we didn't paint anything when I was growing up in South Carolina. The house was just unpainted wood. Same when we moved to Alabama, except for a short while . . . a little house I lived in when . . . when I was married. Of course, in Texas in those days, you were doing well just to have a wooden shack over your head, even in the towns. But if there's anything I can do where I won't just get in your way, I'll be glad to help," he offered.

"OK. First thing is I'm going to the old rag pail where we throw worn out clothes we want to tear up and use for rags. I'll find you something out of that to put on long enough to get this job done."

"I could wear my old pants . . . ."

"The seat is still out on those things, Buck. I want you to look decent, even if ratty," she said, leading him to a large garbage can in the garage. She fished through it until she found some old clothes of her dad's which, she was sure, would hang on the thin colonel, but at least he wouldn't get paint all over the t-shirt and jeans. She was going to have to get Buck some more clothes. She threw the clothes to him and ordered him to change—a nice feeling, calling after him, "Those clothes are so holey that folks will really think you are part of the Trinity," then got out her grubby old clothes she saved for these projects.

When they were dressed down appropriately, she asked, "Can you shift all the furniture on this end of the room to the other end? We'll do this end, then move everything down here to do the other half." He started moving things while she found all the needed supplies in the garage.

He was pleased with himself for quickly getting the area cleared and had a self-satisfied look on his face. Lori walked in the door.

He asked, "What color are you going to paint it?"

229

"My favorite shade—it's called Yellow Rose. Actually, you might be interested in the story. After the fight at the Alamo, Santa Anna headed east, and Houston whipped him at San Jacinto—think I told you that."

He nodded.

"Well, the story goes that there was this lady named Emily Morgan who was mostly white but had a little Negro blood. She . . . how shall I say it . . . distracted Santa Anna for a while, and that helped Houston win the battle."

"Wish she had been in Bexar," he shot back.

"Yeah, I guess so. Anyway, and I'm sure you're familiar with this term, she was called the Yellow Rose of Texas, the yellow part being because she was of mixed blood. She's a famous heroine. That big hotel near the Alamo is named for her. Remember all the yellow roses on the wreaths at the March 6 ceremony? Yellow roses are a Texas symbol, and it's my favorite flower."

"Sounds like the perfect color for the room. I'm honored to have a part in this," he replied, giving his little bow to her.

"We better get to it, or we're not going to get finished until everyone gets home, and it gets much harder with other people getting in the way, trust me," she advised. "I'll show you what to do, but I'd like you to do the high parts since you're taller, and I'll do the low parts. The roller is handy for long expanses of wall, like over there," she pointed, "But most of this wall with all the windows is going to have to be painted the old-fashioned way—with a brush."

She showed him how to place the drop cloths and warned him not to accidentally step in the roller pan. As he approached every task, Buck was quiet and serious as he painted, making sure he missed nothing. Three hours later, they both had paint in their hair and on the old clothes and their skin, but they were finished. The room was a gorgeous pale lemon yellow.

"You know, Lori, thinking about the gorgeous flower, you are my Yellow Rose," he said, pulling her toward him and giving her a quick kiss.

"Buck, you have paint all over your cheek. I think you just got it on me!" she laughed. "But that was the sweetest thing you have ever said!"

Once they got cleaned up, Lori told him, "I want you to try on the pants I made for you. I still have to do those buttons and buttonholes—need to place those and figure the right length for the hem. I think I can finish them up this evening. Dave Eaton said he's doing a Davy Crockett performance at the Alamo tomorrow. He said Mitch Stevens, who portrays Bowie at some of these events, said he would try to come."

"I'm assuming based on what you just said that there's also a Travis stand-in?"

"Well, yes, actually, if you want to know, there was before the real thing showed up—a guy named John Williams. But he's switched to doing Bonham or anyone they need to do courier runs—he likes to be on a horse. I don't know how much you remember from the letter-reading ceremony, but he's the one who took your letter out of the fort. He is from South Carolina—talks like you! Anyway, I'm sure folks would enjoy it if all of you appeared together."

"You know, it gives me a really sad feeling . . . ."

"I do know, Buck. I started not to tell you. But fact is, if I didn't have your pants done and we go in to work tomorrow and crowds start flocking to a guy in buckskins with a raccoon on top of his head and another guy with a really large knife in 1830's costume and no Travis, only there's the real Travis in modern clothes . . . I think you get the picture."

"Sometimes being commander of the Alamo is a burden," he said softly, but with a little smile.

"Honestly, Buck, I would think that being commander of the Alamo would always be a burden!"


Dave Eaton, at 55, was only a few years older than Congressman Crockett. He had the same sallow complexion and longish dark straight hair. He also had the advantage of being from Tennessee and talked with a mountain twang. Dressed in a buckskin jacket that looked as if it had been around since 1836 and with the raccoon nestled on his head and a long rifle in his hand, he made a fairly convincing, if not exactly Fess Parker style, Davy Crockett. The children certainly knew who he was. Davy was far and away the most famous and popular of the Alamo defenders. Eaton, as Davy, was sitting on the ground with a throng of children sitting in a semicircle around him. He was regaling them with tall tales, as one would expect. One little girl asked to pet his hat, and Davy obligingly leaned forward so that she could stroke the deceased raccoon. The Crockett impersonator, taking his cue from Disney, was always careful to stick to the homespun yarns that made the congressman so popular all over America and in the sad little Alamo when his stories were the only bright spot amidst the forthcoming doom. He did not want to traumatize the children with what really happened to Davy and everyone else. He kept it light, and he kept it fun. Finally, he pulled out his fiddle and played tunes of the era. He was on "Long, Long Ago" when Col. Travis strolled up, wearing his sword, with a pretty lady in a dull rose print dress on his arm.

The congressman was near the end of his tune, and he finished it up quickly, then stood and removed the cap and bowed slightly to Lori. She liked all this bowing to women that men did in the 1830's.

"Congressman Crockett, I see you are working on a legion of future voters!" Travis greeted him heartily, holding out his hand.

Eaton had seen Travis at recent events and met him once, but never when Eaton was Davy.

"Colonel, pleased to see you. You are looking fine this beautiful day. And your lovely lady," he nodded to Lori, who gave a little nod back. "Do either of you have any requests?"

"How about 'The Irish Jaunting Car?'" Lori asked. She had researched that one. The tune was later used in the famous Southern Civil War song, "The Bonnie Blue Flag." She particularly favored the bouncy old air.

Congressman Crockett immediately set to playing the lively tune, which jumped and jolted about as much as a ride in a jaunting car, Lori, channeling her Civil War ancestor of the same name, singing the pre-Civil War version. Travis and the children clapped to the tune. The tourists had all noticed at this point and were heading for the reenactors to watch the show. There was one more person heading their way too, and he carried an Arkansas toothpick.

"And Colonel, is there anything that you would particularly like to hear?" Crockett asked as the jaunting car finally halted.

"Sir, do you know 'Rosin the Beau'?" Travis asked politely in his drawl.

Crockett immediately started in on the rollicking drinking ballad. It was apparently a Travis favorite despite the colonel's reputation as a teetotaler. He sang along with it—something it would have been hard for Lori to imagine from the rather stern and serious commander in the old fortress. But he had a good voice.

The new arrival came up to Lori's free side, tipping his hat to her. Travis sang on, oblivious. The newcomer, a strong-looking man of above-middle height with strawberry blonde hair, was wearing a dark hat somewhat on the order of Travis' headgear, but the brim was not quite as broad. He had on a brown jacket, an olive silk vest, brown trousers, and high boots.

"It seems our young colonel is enjoying himself today, Miss Lori. It would benefit us all if he would learn to relax more," the man said. "Of course, it's hard not to enjoy oneself in the company of the congressman!"

Lori laughed. Mitch was fully into his Bowie impersonation. She just hoped he didn't get roaring drunk or pick a fight with the uptight Travis as was famously really the case. When Rosin the Beau had finally gone to Hell, Travis turned and saw the knife before he even saw Mitch.

"Colonel Bowie, surely you must have a request?" he asked.

Bowie gave a slim smile. "Well, actually, Col .Travis, considering that 'Rosin the Beau' covers my two favorite subjects—drinking and Hell—I like to drink and I have always hoped that you would go to Hell, I am afraid you beat me to it. I think I will have to be satisfied with that!"

The Alamo "defenders" in the crowd laughed, including their leader. Crockett played another favorite of the times, "Home Sweet Home," then wrapped up with the popular new American anthem of the day, "America," to the tune of "God Save the King." The tourists insisted that the members of the Trinity pose for pictures, then Lori ordered the three leaders to follow her, marching them to the gift shop and Morena. All the shoppers stopped and stared as the heroes of the Alamo entered with the pretty Texian lady in the lead. Morena laughed as Lori led them to the fudge counter. Melia was working the fudge. After the rolling pin incident, she had decided to surrender to the fact that work at the Alamo just involved one weird surprise after another. So having the three top guys come to her counter together was just another day at work.

Lori reached in her dress pocket and retrieved some bills. We'll have one of the Bowie, one of the Crockett, and two of the Travis!" she said. Melia gave her a knowing look, screwed her face up slightly, and got the fudge.

When it was all over and Buck and Lori were walking across the plaza, he told her, "You know, they are both really good—honestly, it was almost like going back—being with the men again . . . ." he forced himself to stop.

"I know, Buck. Even I could feel it."

High noon on this April day was already indicative of the fact that it was promising to be a scorcher. Lori was sweating in her faded old frontier dress, standing in front of the patch of peppers and okra she had planted with Buck. Each day, except when it rained, he had faithfully watered the plants with buckets of water from the acequia, ignoring the suggestion of using a hose made by the little boy on planting day. Now the over-half-grown plants were thriving, and some of them carried blooms that would, hopefully, give way to the vegetables that were these plants' purpose. A number of the plants actually had produce hanging on them. But there were also weeds. So, although it was not the stuff of legend, Lori and Buck had decided to perform an impromptu weeding session, not so much intended as a demo but to keep their vegetables from being subsumed by the interlopers. She was getting tired of waiting when she saw the usually prompt Buck, in his old uniform, wearing the original pants with a patch over the seat, neatly sewn by Lori for this grubby demonstration, strolling at a rapid gait toward her.

"Sorry, spilled ink all over my desk—had to clean it up!" he said.

That was one Lori never had to worry about.

A few people stopped and stared as they knew Lori and Buck were up to something with the vegetables. Lori was holding some 19th Century weeding tools, and she handed one to the colonel.

"Want to see who can weed the fastest—you know, 'Victory or Death'?" he looked at her.

"NO! Not after last time," she replied firmly.

"Just thought it would make it more fun," he grinned.

234

"Maybe I'm a spoil-sport, but I don't think being out-weeded by a man who is going to jump up and shout 'Victory or Death' would be a lot of fun," she replied.

Lori set into her work, as did Buck. As with the planting, he was more adept at digging out the weeds, moving much faster than she did. They were perspiring heavily in the hot sun, having made the mistake of deciding to do this exercise in the afternoon. Buck finished first, but he had enough sense to not jump up and declare victory this time, instead moving next to Lori and helping her with the rest of her last row.

"We need to start harvesting—especially the okra. It's much better when the pods are young and tender. You can't chew them once they get so big," he told her, staring at the plants.

Lori had her trusty broken-down table set up, and her big wooden bowl on it. She grabbed the bowl, and the two of them went down the rows of okra first, then the peppers, picking the vegetables that were ready, far more peppers than okra pods.

"I've had okra and tomatoes—wonder what okra and peppers would taste like?" Lori pondered the thought.

"I love okra, but it could use a little spicing up—want to throw everything we've got in the bowl in a pot and put it over the fire?" Buck asked, staring at the produce.

Lori was thinking to herself that it was pretty hot to start a fire and make things even more uncomfortable, but fact was the old pioneers had to do that, so she did. Spectators were crowding around now to see what the reenactor couple were going to do next. She got the fire going, and Buck went to the acequia with his bucket to get some water. Lori threw the vegetables and enough water to cook them, as well as a little salt and pepper, into her big black pot. Before long, the okra had cooked to a less bright shade of green, and the water had a slightly gooey texture from the release of the mucilage in the pods. The peppers took on a slightly different hue, as well, indicating they were also ready. Several of the other reenactors had shown up, and Lori set out some tin cups and wooden bowls. Bowie, Crockett, and Seguin stood around, uncertain looks on their countenances. This early in the season, the batch was small. Seguin refused to try it. Bowie and Crockett were not as crazy about the okra as some of Lori's other concoctions—especially since there was no "hog fat" to enhance the flavor. But South Carolinian Buck loved it, practically wolfing it down.

235

"Like I said, I've always loved okra—but those peppers add a little touch to it that makes it absolutely heavenly!" he said blissfully.

"Hey, Lori! Long time no see!" a friendly voice called.

Lori looked up from the boiling concoction in her pot. This time it was a sort of Texian stew. Most of the tourists had trickled off, there being a demo by Crockett and Bowie down the way.

"Anthony! What are you doing at the Alamo?" Lori laughed. "I didn't recall you particularly enjoying Ms. Watson's 11th grade history class!"

The young man who had hailed her reached Lori and her steaming pot of vegetables and pork. Anthony Robbins was tall and thin with chocolate skin and curly black hair.

"Smells good. What is it?" he asked hesitantly, aware that pioneer food was often not to the tastes of modern Americans.

"I decided to try boiling some cactus pads with potatoes, turnips, peppers, and carrots—and a few ham pieces and the ever-present hog fat that makes it palatable," she replied.

Anthony made a face, twisting his mouth to the side. "I think I'll pass."

"You're in luck—the reenactor rules forbid us from letting anyone other than our fellow reenactors or the Alamo staff taste our gourmet meals," she laughed.

"Well, that's kind of what I wanted to talk to you about," Anthony replied.

Lori's eyebrows arched with curiosity.

Anthony continued, "I'm not exactly sure why, but I thought it might be fun to try out reenacting. Only thing is, since I'm black and I don't think there were a lot, if any, black folks at the Alamo, I gather I wouldn't fit in too well."

Lori was still laughing. "Based on what I remember of your struggles with Ms. Watson, I can't imagine you getting into history!"

236

"There's a lot of difference between listening to that woman's whiny voice and memorizing dates as opposed to dressing up in 1830's clothes and maybe getting to fire period weapons. And I figure it's kind of like a play when you're in character. I always liked school plays," he explained.

"Well, true. That woman got on my nerves, too, and I love history," Lori agreed. "Actually, what about doing an impression of a Mexican soldier? That might seem more natural?" she asked delicately.

"I thought about that," Anthony responded. "But, and I'm not sure why since, the way I recall it, a lot of the defenders were Southern slaveholders, I just would rather be a Texian!"

"Uh, well, there was one black Texian at the Alamo who became semi-famous," she replied.

"Sounds perfect if no one is already doing an impression of him!" Anthony said enthusiastically.

"No, uh, I don't think anyone's ever actually thought about portraying him. I've got to admit there is some not-exactly-blatant-racism in this hobby—just simply not thinking about everybody—you know what I mean," she said earnestly.

"Would anyone have a problem if I looked into this guy's life and, if I decide I like him, maybe depict him at some of the First Saturday events?" came the response. "By the way, what's his name and backstory?"

"Normally, I'd say it's fine, but there is one little problem," she replied candidly. "The guy's name is Joe—there's actually a biography and a novel out there about him. He was in the fight but was allowed to live since Mexico didn't have slavery. When Santa Anna let him go and he got back to what passed for Texian civilization, he told his tale. His story was crucial to providing information as to what happened to the slain defenders as he was the only guy left alive in the fortress."

"Wow! A bona-fide hero! I'm liking this better all the time!" Anthony was getting his hopes up.

"Yeah, but . . . like I said, there's one little problem," Lori replied. "Joe was a slave . . . ."

He shrugged. "No big deal—that's par for the course back then. I can

237

suck up to the white folks if I have to!" Anthony brushed her off with a grin.

"Normally, yeah, I would agree, but he was the slave of the Alamo commander . . . ."

"Even better! That puts Joe in the know as to the decision-making that went into the Texian actions!"

"Yeah, that's true," Lori said, reaching her long wooden spoon to the bottom of her pot to stir its contents. "By any chance, did you see the news about an Alamo defender being found at the dig here?" she asked.

"I remember something about that, but the guy was shot in the head and mutilated if I remember right. I figure he either died or is a vegetable in some medical facility."

"Nope. He's working here, dressed in his bloodstained clothes and not at all hesitant about waving his rusty old sword at anyone he considers the foe," she laughed.

"Sounds like the head wound had an effect? That could be dangerous," he replied.

"Poor thing—he really does try, and I really care a lot for him—was there when they dug him up and have gotten very close as I've helped him navigate the last 181 years. But it's a struggle for him—and sometimes for those he comes in contact with as well. But the problem for you would be that he's Col. Travis—the commander. I don't think the colonel has a complete grasp of modern America's take on slavery . . . ."

"I get it," Anthony replied, but he was persistent. "Well, do you know where I could get a copy of Joe's bio and maybe, if I like him, get some 1836 duds and join the party? Maybe we could just not tell the colonel who I'm supposed to be and hope he's too busy trying to figure out how to whip the Mexicans?"

Lori laughed again. "Yeah. Actually, my friend Raul has a copy of the bio. It's fairly new, and he was talking about it last week. I'm sure he'll lend it. I think he has the novel, too—it puts more of a human face on Joe. I read both and actually enjoyed the novel more. I'll introduce you as soon as I'm through with this stew—almost done now. I suspect Raul will be by shortly, as the reenactors have truly amazing noses for figuring out when

238

the frontier fare is ready for consumption!"

Anthony looked at the steaming pot and made a face. "I guess I'll have to eat that stuff!"

Ten minutes later, men in 1830's garb were heading for Lori's huge pot. Raul was in the vanguard, Crockett and Bowie, finished with their weapons demo, right behind him. And heading from his office in the long barracks was the head man.

As they reached Lori, she was dishing out the steaming vegetables and ham in her tin cups and wooden bowls—whatever vessels she could find. The reenactors were trying to act enthusiastic, although the looks on many faces indicated something else. The one true defender was not too picky about her concoction, having eaten far worse in his day, and he eagerly accepted a bowl and started eating. Only when he had finished did he notice the young black man in his modern clothes, staring at all the 1836 folks with their bowls and tin cups, and talking with Raul, who was nodding and smiling. Anthony, who had noticed the bloodstains on the coat before he saw the colonel's face clearly, determined to keep his focus on Raul. Buck was still hungry, and he asked Lori for another bowl of her special recipe.

Luisa smiled. She had massaged every network she had available, including Anglo student groups and black churches as well as the myriad of Hispanic organizations, political, Catholic, neighborhood, and otherwise. The fruits of her effort were slowly, quietly, moving en masse to the old mission, coming from every direction to surround the fortress, just as Santa Anna did in 1836. But there were two differences. Luisa's army did not come—most of them anyway—armed with weapons, and she was apparently a better recruiter than El Presidente—her army was at least 10,000 in number. They did not chant or sing, they just moved steadily and stealthily, slowly forward toward their goal. The lead elements were at the Alamo Plaza, and she was right behind them, with Angelo at her side.

Ed was on the chapel roof cleaning up debris. He was used to various programs and rallies at the Alamo. It was a magnet for that kind of thing. But, when he heard a low, muffled noise, he walked to the edge of the roof and looked out. There was a sea of people converging on the place from all different directions—rather disconcerting. I guess that's how the old defenders felt, he thought. He realized that, although this was not that dire a situation, hopefully, no one on the staff seemed aware. The throng was

239

silent, no words, no chants, no music. He called Elbert, then placed a quick call to Bob. Travis was in Bob's office, the two talking about an upcoming national guard ceremony.

"Really?" Bob said. "We'll be right there."

"What is it?" the colonel asked.

"Don't know. Ed is on the roof cleaning up. He said there's a large, silent group of people heading toward the church from different directions. He walked around the roof perimeter."

The colonel went into 1836 mode immediately. "We need to determine what the enemy is planning this time. The church didn't have a roof when I was here before, but we had gun emplacements up there and could look out. How do you get up there now?" Travis asked, urgency in his voice.

"You have to climb a ladder. Come on, I'll show you," Bob replied.

As the protesters reached the church, Luisa noted the usual hubbub of tourists one would expect at the attraction. She signaled her lieutenants, and quietly they moved forward. These three were armed, not with the intention of causing harm to anyone, but to add weight to their instructions to the tourists and employees milling around the Alamo. At Luisa's signal, Carlos, Juan, and Julian fanned out. Angelo was behind them, observing. There were a few squeals or screams. No one attempted to fight. They all moved back away from the three men, corralling themselves nicely at the rear of the property, just as Luisa had hoped would happen. Carlos returned, the other two keeping watch on the sightseers and staff.

"We've moved the tourists to the back of the compound, behind the buildings," Angelo reported after conversing with Carlos.

"Good. I don't want anyone to get hurt in this. There are usually several rangers roaming around this place if I remember right," she added. "Did you see anyone with a gun?"

"There were two, but Carlos, Juan, and Julian disarmed them quickly. It was such a surprise for the locals—apparently no one tipped their hand."

"Where's Col. Travis? If he's dressed in uniform, he should be easy to spot." Luisa asked.

"That's what's strange. There were only two rangers and no one who looked like Travis. There were a couple of people in costume, a blonde girl and a Tejano defender. I suppose that's what he was supposed to be. We put them with the tourists in back, but no colonel."

"That's weird. He would be guarding his post unless he's sick. Maybe he didn't get up from one of those falls," Luisa replied. "Well, for now, I guess we'll just go on with our speakers and see what transpires. When he's done," she said pointing at the current speaker, "I'm going to say a few words."

An elderly Anglo speaker who looked like a holdover from the hippie era with his long gray hair in braids and wire-rimmed shades, wearing a faded t-shirt with a peace symbol on it, was at the podium. He was shouting into the microphone.

"Even if you don't give a flip for human rights, as is clearly the case with our new President," the speaker said with unbounded sarcasm, "a wall will do no good. If you don't believe me, ask Col. Travis—the Mexicans will come right over it!"

There was an eruption of laughter and cheering from the crowd. The man who was speaking finished up quickly, and Luisa stepped to the microphone.

"Gracias! To all of you who have taken time away from your busy day to be here, I am so appreciative. Not just for Latinos and Latinas," she added, noting a number of Anglo faces, mostly young people—probably college students—and black people in the crowd, "but for everyone who wants fair treatment and a fair interpretation of the history of this place. As you know, the Alamo has always been rather a sore point for many Mexican-Americans, and it certainly has been for me. This is my first trip here in over 20 years, although I live in San Antonio," she said. "While I will admit that the Davy Crockett frontiersman image is entertaining for children, the stock story of the Alamo goes way beyond Davy's skill with wrestling bears and alligators."

The crowd laughed.

"Hispanic children can relate to that as much as Anglos. But, as we know, it's much deeper than that—the old Trinity thing, the veneration for the massacred, mutilated heroes who were burned instead of given a Christian burial, Travis' noble words about freedom and liberty, and on and

241

on. While I think everyone can agree that Santa Anna really fouled up and hurt his own reputation with his treatment of the defeated enemy, everything up to that point is not that simple—there are two sides. You definitely can make an argument that some of the brave defenders were illegal immigrants and that the whole thing was an Anglo land grab."

A cheer spontaneously erupted from the throng.

"And these brave heroes—and they were brave, don't get me wrong—brave to the point of being foolhardy . . . ."

Again more laughter.

"Were not such heroes after all. You have heard it time and again, but Bowie should have been in prison. Crockett, while entertaining and popular with people, was a semi-literate incompetent bumpkin in politics. Travis was a colossal failure who ran away from that failure by heading to Texas. He definitely was an illegal immigrant. Funny how it's OK for him but not for people today. His diary tells you everything you need to know about him, including numerous raunchy comments he wrote about his sex life. The way he got around, half the people in Texas may be related to him. The Don Juan of the Alamo had a hard time keeping his pants on, and he kept score. One gets the feeling he had a list of every woman in frontier Texas and was checking them off as he bedded each one . . . ."

"Madame, YOU did not make the list—you are surely the most unattractive female I have ever laid eyes on!" came a voice from somewhere, without benefit of a microphone but shouted loudly.

Luisa stopped talking and looked around. Angelo did, too. Finally, his gaze fixed.

"There're some people on top of the roof," he pointed upward. Luisa shielded her eyes from the bright sun and squinted to see them.

Sure enough, there were a couple of men dressed like rangers, two others in civilian clothes, and one, obviously the source of the comment, in "uniform" and with a sword in his left hand.

Luisa motioned to Carlos and pointed toward the roof. "What do you think?"

"Tranquilizer bullet—will take him out but not kill him. I can hit him

242

from here. Actually it will be easier than if he had stayed on the ground. They'll have to carry him down from the roof."

"You're sure a tranquilizer bullet will knock him out but not hurt him?" Luisa asked.

"It's a very light dose. As long as I don't hit him around his heart, it should be OK. And I can't see his face that well from here. Didn't you say he has head wounds? I wouldn't want to hit him in the head. Honestly, that's not good, anyway—could blind him."

"Do you think you can get him without hitting him in the head or around the heart?" Luisa asked.

"I can't guarantee it if he moves right as I sight him, but I'll certainly try."

"Last thing I want is to kill him. He's crazy, but he doesn't deserve that. And it would make the conflict with the Anglos even worse, not to mention the legal implications," Luisa stated.

Meanwhile, another speaker had taken to the microphone, and he turned, looking up at Travis. "Colonel, it's a lost cause. We demand you surrender and come down from the roof now!"

"Vete a la mierda! I will die before I surrender," Travis yelled, waving the sword dramatically in front of him. "Victory or Death!"

Carlos was a very patient man. He held the gun, sighted on Travis, for what seemed an eternity. The colonel mostly stood still, the sword in the air in front of him, but he would move a little now and then. Finally, he waved the weapon to the side, then over his head, and Carlos pressed the trigger.

A few seconds later, Travis' head bowed, the hat sliding off, and he fell, the sword falling from his hand. Carlos was sure his victim would crumple when the bullet hit him, but he miscalculated badly. The colonel fell forward, off the roof of the church.

The crowd stood transfixed in horror. These people were not Travis fans, but the sheer awfulness of it left them stunned. The colonel lay face down in front of the church, absolutely still.

Luisa did something she never in all her life would have thought she

243

would do—she ran to Col. Travis. She didn't touch him or try to lift him—there were probably broken bones. But she knelt by his side, saying over and over, "Colonel, I am so sorry!"

Angelo knelt by her, trying to comfort her. "You didn't know, Luisa," he said.

"I should never have encouraged Carlos to shoot a tranquilizer dart at him up there on that roof. I was so tired of all the defender stuff, and then he wouldn't just shut up and be reasonable and come down," she said, crying. "Did someone call an ambulance?"

"Yes, I did," Angelo said softly. "Really, you didn't know. He may be OK. If he's not, I think he really did want to be in 1836," he continued.

"He might have wanted to be in 1836, but, if he's dead, that's not where he's going," she said sadly.

When there was something that sounded like a possible shot, gasps of horror, and the speaker stopped speaking, the crowd stood silent, staring. Those at the back of the throng could not really see what was going on. Finally, Luisa got up and went to the microphone.

"Everyone, we have had a serious accident. I know I was not too kind in my appraisal of Col. Travis today, but he was on the roof of the church with some other people. He fell from the roof," she stated the obvious, deliberately not mentioning Carlos, although most people heard his gun, "and is lying on the ground in front of the church—not moving. An ambulance is on the way. Please pray to Our Lord Jesus and the Blessed Mother Mary for the colonel. He is not evil—he is just a very confused young man from another time. He needs all of our prayers now. In view of everything, this is the end of the rally. You may all go home. God be with you."

The siren screamed as she left the microphone. She quietly directed Angelo to tell the men holding the tourists corralled to keep them where they were until they could get Travis off to the hospital. The ambulance was there as she got back to Travis. The paramedics asked what happened.

"He was shot with a tranquilizer dart—was standing on the roof of the church and fell to the ground. We were afraid to try to move him—didn't know what might be broken—he has not moved."

244

"A tranquilizer dart?" one of the attendants asked.

"Yeah. It's a long story," Luisa answered.

"That's quite a fall. If he hasn't moved at all, that's not good," the man looked to the top of the church.

The two paramedics supported Travis' body, paying particular attention to his head, and very carefully turned him over. His eyes were closed, and he was very pale. One man checked his pulse.

"He's alive—it's very faint," he told Luisa. "We're going to rush him over there and see if there's anything they can do—probably internal injuries. And they'll have to do X-rays. His neck may be broken from that kind of fall."

They got the unconscious man on the stretcher and into the ambulance and were off quickly.

Luisa turned to Angelo. Tell Juan and Julian to let everyone go home. I wouldn't spread the story—just say there was an accident, and we cut the rally a little short."

Lori had been standing with Raul in his Tejano outfit, as well as Morena, Tom, and Melia. She was hot and tired of standing there, and she was dying to get out of her frontier dress. She was scheduled to cook cactus today, but the time for that had come and gone. None of the staff or tourists knew much about what had caused them to be forced to the back of the property by armed men, but they heard enough to know that it was some kind of rally. Bits and pieces of the speeches came through. They were relieved to finally be allowed to go home. Lori had not seen Buck all afternoon. She assumed he must have been in his little office. The door was closed, and she knocked, but there was no answer. She cracked the door—no one there. Common sense told her that if the rally was Hispanic, and the men with the guns definitely were, Buck would be defending his post. She walked around the front of the church—nothing there.

"Lori, Lori!" It was Jaime.

She turned. "What's the matter. Is everything OK?"

"I guess you were in back with everyone else, right?"

245

"Yeah, why? And have you seen Buck?" she asked.

"We were on top of the roof—Elbert, Bob, Ed, the colonel, and I. There was a huge pro-Hispanic rally—thousands of people. There were a lot of speeches, and one woman made some remarks about Travis. He said something derogatory back, and the next rally speaker ordered him to surrender. The colonel told him to go to Hell in Spanish."

"That sounds like Buck," she laughed.

"Well, it's not funny. Some guy associated with the woman—she was apparently heading up the rally, fired a tranquilizer dart at Travis. He fell forward, off the roof. They've taken him to the hospital . . . ."

Lori screamed.

Jaime held her. "Let me take you there, OK?"

She nodded slightly through her tears. He clued in Elbert, and they were on their way.

"Patient fell off the roof of the Alamo church," the paramedic explained as they brought in Buck.

"What?" a tall, broad-shouldered male nurse asked.

"There was an enormous anti-establishment rally at the Alamo. Actually, all law enforcement and emergency personnel were notified once it got going, but they apparently didn't get a permit—just sort of showed up and took over . . . ."

"Kind of like the old battle?"

"Yeah, only this was fast. They didn't wait around 13 days, didn't even seem like 13 minutes before they got there. They controlled the visitors and staff on premises and blocked off access. It was well-planned. Fortunately, they were peaceful. There were a few people on the church roof. Someone in the crowd shot a tranquilizer bullet at this guy, and he fell from the roof."

"Ugh. Been a while since I've been over there, but that would be quite a fall," the nurse said as he hooked up equipment to check Travis. "Does he have anyone with him?"

"No, not that I saw," the paramedic responded. "I've got to get back on duty."

"Say, one more thing—do you have a name?"

"Yeah. The woman in charge of the rally told me he's Col. Travis—REALLY. I remember they dug him up a couple of months ago."

"OK—that may make it even more complicated." The nurse stared at Buck. "He fits the description." The other man was already hurrying out of the building.

Jaime dropped Lori off, then headed back to his post. By the time she saw Buck, the uniform had been replaced by a hospital gown. He was white as a sheet, eyes closed, absolutely still. The hospital bed was set flat, no one wanting to move or bend anything until the tests showed any possible breaks or other damage. About the time she sat down, someone came in to wheel Buck out for tests. Lori felt like she was in the movie "Groundhog Day." She was sitting there in her frontier dress, waiting to see if Buck would live or die. She wondered if his life would ever be normal enough that these incidents would not be so routine. She could not imagine what Travis and the other men were doing on the roof of the church to begin with, although she was sure it was his idea and that he was reconnoitering the enemy or something like that. But for someone to shoot a tranquilizer dart at a target standing on the edge of a roof was crazy, unless the intent was to kill him. Well, it didn't matter now. She knew she would have to call home and that Vicky would drag everyone to the hospital. But, with Buck unconscious and no test results yet, she saw no need for everyone to come and sit. She was actually dozing after the stress-filled day when they wheeled Buck back in the room.

"The doctor said he will look at the X-rays right away—will be in shortly to tell you what he found out," the nurse said.

She thanked him and promptly nodded off again.

"Lori? Lori?"

She woke up with a start. Must have been dreaming. She looked around, then realized Buck's face was turned toward her. He was looking at her.

"Buck! Did you call me?" she asked, moving toward him and brushing

247

his hair with her hand.

"Yes, Lori—what happened?" he asked weakly.

"Well, Buck, you outdid yourself in Alamo adventures this time—you fell off the top of the church with thousands of people watching. But it wasn't your fault . . . ."

His eyes were wide with alarm. "I don't remember . . . ."

She was so tempted to say, "You mean YOU don't remember the Alamo?" but she realized he wouldn't get the meaning at all. Instead, she continued, "A man with the protesters shot you with a tranquilizer bullet, and you fell off the roof," she said.

"He shot me with what?" Buck asked.

"It's something they have now where you can shoot someone with a projectile that doesn't hurt them but makes them unconscious. They were trying to get you to stop yelling 'Victory or Death' or whatever you were saying up there and waving your sword around. But they didn't count on you falling forward. They've run some tests to see what injuries you have. Obviously, you did not break your neck, or you couldn't be looking at me the way you are. Can you feel your arms and legs?"

"Yes. Only thing that hurts is my left wrist—kind of throbbing, and left shoulder is kind of sore."

"They should have the results very soon. And you could have other issues, like internal bleeding, after a fall like that, but I am so glad you didn't break your neck." She moved toward him and placed her head next to his.

The door opened, and a very young doctor came in. He smiled at the sight of Lori in her 1836 dress.

"I'm Dr. Davis," the man introduced himself.

"Lori Clayton—I work at the Alamo," Lori responded. "If the nurse hasn't already told you, my friend here is Col. Travis, who also is associated with the Alamo," Lori motioned toward Buck, and the doctor smiled.

"Colonel, I am honored to meet you and greatly relieved that you are awake," Davis shook hands with Travis. "I have some very good news.

Doesn't look as if you broke anything. You've got a sprain in your shoulder and a rather bad one in your left wrist, but all in all, you came out remarkably well. For what it's worth, looks as if you broke that left wrist and the arm at some time in the past per the X-rays. They healed a bit off, but I assume it hasn't caused you any trouble. As to your current situation, I think the fact that you were unconscious, and thus relaxed, helped with the fall. I want you to rest here for another hour. Then I think we can wrap up that wrist and shoulder and get you a prescription for those sprains and let you go home," Davis said, then as an afterthought, added with a grin, "I understand there was a huge rally at the Alamo today, and that you went up on the roof to check for enemy movements?—might be better to try to avoid that in the future if you can. In uniform, I suspect you make an inviting target!"

There was a firm knock at the door. Luisa took a deep breath. After Travis was taken away by the ambulance, she headed to the police station to explain what had happened, leaving with the possibility of criminal charges pending, the extent of those charges depending on whether the colonel lived or died. The colonel's fall forward was an accident, but the tranquilizer bullet clearly was not. She then headed for San Fernando Cathedral. Now, having just come from confession, she felt she had to do this.

Travis called, "Come in."

"Colonel, you are awake!" she said as she saw him staring in her direction.

"Ma'am, I have not changed my mind—you still are not on my list," he said firmly.

She burst out laughing. "I think I can live with that loss, Colonel. But, honestly, despite the fact that I don't think we will ever see eye to eye—maybe we are not meant to, I cannot tell you how relieved I am to see you awake and responsive—even though your responses are a little peculiar!"

Travis wanted to stay rigid and aloof with this woman who conjured up thousands of Mexicans and led them to the Alamo. He saw her as a female Santa Anna, but he did appreciate the humanity and courage she showed in coming to see him.

"Thank you," he said quietly.

249

# THE DIARY

Lori was not a serious student of the 1836 battle and the men who fought it. She knew a lot about it just because she was into history and worked at the Alamo, but she did not pour over books analyzing the military leaders and events of 1836 in Texas. That said, she had heard enough about Buck's famous diary, and Bob had told her that the colonel's entries only spanned a little less than a year—not lengthy, that she determined to read it for herself. Bob loaned his copy to her, with the caveat that Buck might not be thrilled if he discovered her with it. She placed the little book deep within her enormous purse so there would be no chance of Buck seeing it stick out the top of the bag.

Since they lived and worked at the same place, Lori's options for reading the colonel's most private thoughts were limited to very late at night in her room. Consequently, the little book was slow going. Travis' entries were abbreviated, although extremely detailed, particularly as to amounts of money spent for purchases, gambling, and sex—where he specified to the penny. The editor added copious footnotes explaining the details of who and what were mentioned by the author. Travis made reference to another book—an autobiography that apparently did not survive the Runaway Scrape. San Felipe, where he lived and practiced law, and other towns were burned by Houston's forces as frantic settlers fled eastward from Santa Anna's army sweeping toward them after annihilating Travis and his command. In his surviving diary, he noted on "12 September" of 1833 that he "wrote a short memorandum of the principal events of my life up to 1832 in my Common Place Book," such books being an archaic method of collecting jottings and memorable tidbits employed long ago by persons with a literary bent. The autobiography would cover up to age 22 or 23. Most people do not write the stories of their lives at that tender age. Whatever his motives, that book was apparently long gone. For whatever reasons, the young man who read any book he could get his hands on in frontier Texas seemed to be most comfortable when he was writing things down.

Lori was glad the diary only spanned from August 30, 1833-June 26, 1834, in a way. Although she would have loved, had they existed, to read entries for each day of his short life, she did not have the time. However, she found herself eagerly awaiting the dark quiet when everyone finally went to bed and she could get a little time with Buck as he was in the 1830's before she would fall asleep, her face on his open book. She hurried through most of his jottings regarding his legal career as Lori did not know much about what attorneys did day to day. She did note that punishments could be tough as the defendant in one of the cases he mentioned was sentenced to 15 lashes for some misdeed. She was more interested when he said he bought turnip seeds or planted potatoes, cabbage, and peppers. He also advised other people about growing things, so it was apparently something of some interest to him and explained his adept handling of planting, weeding, and picking vegetables.

The young man seemed to try to briefly record everything religiously. He was exacting about amounts of money for every little thing as well as the details of what forms he had to file in his attorney work—a very detailed person. The diary obviously served to keep track of his expenses and his work for clients as well as describing his social life, his purchases, and anything else he did. He mentioned who he wrote and who wrote him—and he wrote his father in Alabama dutifully. As to the gambling, he not only told what specific game he played—monte and faro were favorites—but exactly how much he won or lost. If he owed money, he wrote it down, the same if someone owed him. If he paid a debt, he also wrote that down. Lots of people he knew died—it seemed someone was always dying, and he reported what they died from. He sat up with the corpses, as was the tradition of the day, and went to a lot of funerals. Cholera was killing people at the time. Lori gleaned from the diary based on his recordings of deaths that Buck was lucky he lived long enough to get to the Alamo. Old Texas was a tough place.

He told who was coming into town and who was traveling through. He was obviously in demand as an attorney and doing well. He could write—and well—in English, and, albeit clumsily, in Spanish, in a time and place where most people could not write at all. Travis was extremely industrious. It may have been a sin, but he worked all 7 days each week. He rode a mule to get to a nearby town until he got a horse. Often, when he had to go somewhere else, he stayed overnight. Things were that much slower back then. He stayed overnight somewhere one night because his horse got sick.

He was always having clothes mended, and he also had more made than most men likely did at the time. He bought fabric for shirts on a Sunday and gave it to a Mrs. Huff to make the shirts for him, to be done by the next Wednesday—in pre-sewing machine days! She finished the shirts and charged him $2.50 for two of them. He wrote "exorbitant!" regarding

251

the price. Even accounting for inflation, Lori, knowing just how hard these shirts were to make, thought he was a bit unfair to Mrs. Huff. On "28 November," he made a long list of fabric and notion purchases for a coat, vest, pants, and more shirts and bought two pairs of flannel drawers and socks. He dropped the fabric off at the tailor's, and he was supposed to have the completed items in 4 weeks. He referenced his favorite style of pants—the tight-fitting pantaloons, including a pair in red, which must have been an attention getter in old San Felipe. On "29 January" of 1834, he bought a white hat, very possibly the one he was still wearing. He had boots made, and he paid someone named Alex to clean his boots. Travis reported if he got a shave and haircut. He bought a lot of paper and candles. He reported on the weather. He was always having to swim creeks to get somewhere. He actually made a raft in an attempt to cross a creek on "21 December," but he failed that day, getting across the next.

And, of course, he wrote those raunchy descriptions of his conquests in Spanish. On "7 November," he noted that he had sex with someone named Susana, and that she was number 59—he actually counted! The fact is that Travis counted everything. He apparently suffered an inability to get what he paid for with one prostitute on "21 February" of 1834! He had started courting Rebecca Cummings at this point, and their relationship involved all-night stays. On "13 March" of that year, he gave Rebecca a breast pin, and she gave him a lock of her hair. The next day, she gave him a ring, presumably the famous cat's eye ring now at the Alamo. He recorded numerous instances of buying vials of "medicina." In addition to paying for sex, both the money he put out and paying in the form of the venereal disease he contracted, he also made some somewhat more above-board attempts with the ladies. He wooed a "Miss H," bringing her cologne water and cinnamon, but, alas, she married someone else, and he went to the wedding.

Not surprising at all to Lori was his entry for "24 November," where, among other things, he noted "got Coffee at Durst's paid 68 ¾ cts." So he had always liked coffee. He was stubborn and determined and would not give in, something for which he would pay dearly at the Alamo. On "9 March" of 1834, he was headed to Rebecca's place on Mill Creek. He famously said that the water was "all swimming & prairie so boggy—could not go—*The first time I ever turned back in my life.*" By March, things were going pretty well with Rebecca, and he admitted he showed her a letter about the conduct of his estranged wife, Rosanna, which he apparently thought damning. Travis clearly did not think that what was good for the goose was good for the gander. He attempted at least one more sexual encounter with a prostitute at this time, and he was suffering badly from the venereal disease and drinking vials of calomel regularly. He dutifully reported how

252

much he paid for both the sex and the medicine. There was some up-and-down with Rebecca, until he finally noted on "31 May" of 1834 that "L-v-e triumphed over slander &c—staid all night at C.'s." He did buy books, candy, and shoes for children among other things. He gave children spare change. Maybe it was because of his own little son. The boy, who was brought to Texas when Rosanna and Travis formally decided to split, lived at the home of Travis' friend David Ayers. Travis last swung by and saw his son in February 1836, on his way to the Alamo. He definitely put himself out for children.

The revisionist historians who blasted him so badly complained about Travis' reading of Sir Walter Scott and other Romantic era novels. He was a voracious reader, and it was the Romantic era, so he was rather stuck with what was out there. However, he also read histories and anything else he could get his hands on, including one book that was appropriate for a young South Carolinian, *Yankee Among the Nullifiers*. On December 29, he noted, without elaboration, "Hell among the women about party." He did like to use the word Hell. He bought whiskey for Indians and to take to parties for other people, but Buck didn't drink, one of the few sins in which he did not heartily indulge. He noted whenever he had "fun." The guy turned down invitations to a number of weddings, but he never seemed to miss a ball or fandango. All in all, he came off as a rather lonely young man who was trying to keep constantly busy so that the loneliness did not get to him. As Lori finally closed the book on Buck's earlier life with his June 26 entry, she fell asleep, her cheek resting on his little book. It was 3 a.m.

Everyone, including Buck, had been up and guzzling coffee for hours on Saturday morning, but no Lori. Vicky's patience was at an end, largely because Elena was stalling putting breakfast out until Lori appeared. Finally, Vicky took matters into her own hands, knocking softly first, then, when she did not get an answer, opening the door and heading to her sister, who was still asleep, head on the diary. She shook her.

"You OK? It's 10:00. Everyone's waiting breakfast for you."

Lori raised her head sleepily. Her hair was sticking out rather wildly.

"What's this?" Vicky asked, pulling the little book that had been under Lori's head toward her.

"Uh, nothing—I was just up reading late last night—that's why I was so sleepy—sorry," Lori said groggily. She reached for the book but was too dazed from sleep to react as quickly as Vicky.

Vicky had closed the opened book. *Diary of William Barret Travis?* You've got to be kidding! Buck left a personal diary, and YOU are reading it?" Vicky was astounded.

"Uh, yes—this thing was published long after the Alamo. Apparently his law partner saved it from being burned. Bob Gordon had a copy and loaned it to me."

"Did you finish it?"

Lori nodded, "Yeah—about 3 in the morning."

"No wonder you slept in—must have been a good read. Still the same old Buck?"

"Yeah, I wish I could keep it. It gives a little more background to kind of explain why he's the way he is, but, yes, same old Buck. I wanted to read it because folks who don't like him in history circles are using it to badmouth him. He did confess his greatest sins to his diary—and there were some whoppers. He would have been smart to just not put his whole life down on paper, but that's a part of who he is . . . ."

"I assume you still love him?" Vicky interrupted.

"Oh yeah, I still love him! But don't you tell him I read his innermost thoughts, OK?"

"I'll think about it," Vicky said with an evil grin. "Now you better get dressed, or we are going to go ahead and eat. Buck drank most of the coffee already."

Lori put the little book under her pillow before she left the room. She would return it to Bob when she next saw him on Monday.


Although William Barret Travis wrote his diary for someone young—himself, at age 24, he did not write it for a 9-year-old. Vicky did not know, nor would she have particularly cared had she known. She waited until Lori and Buck dressed up in Alamo garb and left for a reenactor demo program at the Shrine that Saturday afternoon, then promptly searched Lori's room. She knew the purse was a possibility, but she had already missed that, as Lori took it with her when she left. Considering that Lori had been reading the book in bed, that was the obvious place to look. Lori had made a number of white and yellow decorative pillows to place over her yellow rose embroidered bedspread. Vicky tossed the small mountain of pillows, finally getting down to the genuine bed pillows—and there was Buck's book. She looked around quickly, then hurried with her treasure to her room. The rest of the family had gone their separate ways, and Vicky was supposed to be picked up to go to a friend's house. She feigned a sniffle and called her friend and got out of that, then settled down to read the diary.

Unlike Lori, who had read some of the editor's notes to figure out who was who, Vicky, who was not known for her patience, concentrated on what Buck wrote—that made the reading go much faster. She was at the top of her class in school, excelling particularly in reading, and had been taking Spanish since first grade, so Buck's amorous adventures in that language were not a problem for her. In fact, neither were the content and details of what he was describing. Her mom had already had "the talk" with her, as if that mattered anyway, as the kids in school were all rather well versed on the so-called taboo subject of sex. Her green eyes widened when she hit the Spanish portions, but she basically reacted the same way Lori had—Buck seemed to be a rather sad and lonely young man who kept crazy busy to push out the loneliness. Although he clearly would not be too welcome in any church except one unless he changed his lifestyle, he was serious and diligent about his work, really gravitated toward young people, and was thoughtful, industrious, and intelligent. She was actually sad when she finished the diary. Vicky closed the little volume and put her hand on it, thinking it was a precious window into Buck's previous life. His rather lurid escapades made her smile, not damaging his reputation at all in her eyes. She wished she could keep the book—the same reaction that Lori had confessed to her, when she closed it on June of 1834. She put it back under the pillow, placing all of the other pillows back as they were, just in time. Ten minutes later, Elena walked in the door laden with groceries.

"Vicky, you're back?" she said when she saw her.

"Uh, well, actually, Chloe had something else come up—so we canceled," Vicky replied nonchalantly.

"I've got more groceries in the car," her mom said.

Vicky, a smile on her face, ran to fetch them.

255

Luisa was disappointed. A tremendous amount of effort, working every network available to her, had gone into the rally. And it had brought the results she had hoped for—thousands of participants. And Travis showed up and waved his sword and opened his mouth. He unwittingly did his part to further her cause. And the plan for Carlos to tranquilize him to get him to shut up and come down from the roof was a good one, except for the fact that no one figured on him falling off of the damn thing. He was standing close to the edge, to the right side of the famous arch. She or Carlos, or both, should have thought of the possibility. The colonel had figuratively landed on his feet, although he didn't literally, so lesson learned about shooting people off of buildings. But it had forced the end of the rally, created more sympathy for the defender cause, and caused her to have to start over thinking about another way to make Hispanic voices heard. When it turned out that the colonel's injuries were minor, the authorities determined that downplaying the whole episode rather than fanning the flames between the Hispanic activists and Travis' adherents, made the most sense. Carlos was charged with a misdemeanor, and Luisa only got a warning.

There was news floating around that the President of the United States might be coming to San Antonio. It seemed like the last place in the world he would come except for the draw of the town's large military contingent. He would surely talk about his wall, and the colonel would defend his. She would begin planning for the contingency. Hard to imagine it, but a presidential visit might be an answer to a prayer. Presidential visits were not often publicly announced far in the future for security reasons, so she needed to get everything set up, ready to go, in case they were on, in the next few days. She bellowed to Angelo, who came running, a slight smile on his face. He would be busy the next week.

Bob had finally tripped over that old, ripped-up ottoman in his office. The piece was something that had originally been in his house. As was the case with just about all of the oddball collection consuming every square inch of his office, Bob had brought it there because he could not part with it for some reason known only to and appreciated by him. It had been further beaten up when used as part of the colonel's defenses against the Mexican foe. The ottoman was on casters, and when Bob ran into it, the thing rolled, and he lost his balance and crashed over it. The unhappy result of the fall was that he was on crutches for a week, which meant that he was operating out of a tiny room on the main floor until he could manage the stairs. He also could not drive, which required Leslie to drop him off each day. Leslie would stop in the traffic just long enough to drop Bob along busy Houston Street and then hurry on to his own job. At 5:00, Bob had to walk back to Houston and wait for Leslie to get there, or, if he had already come by, for him to circle around again for pickup. The traffic was so heavy at rush hour that he figured no one would be paying any attention, and he had no choice until the cast came off. This particular day, it was raining, not a little shower, but monsoon rain had set in for the duration. It was late in the afternoon, almost time to quit work, and Bob dreaded the long walk to wait for Leslie. With the crutches, he could not manage an umbrella.

Lori had thought about the dilemma. She discreetly came in the little room he was using as an office, softly shutting the door behind her.

"Bob, would you like me to go with you—take an umbrella?" she offered.

He made a face. "I really don't want to attract any attention," he replied, twisting his mouth in a look that said "I'm not sure what to do."

"Well, I'll be glad to do it if you like. Just buzz me when you're ready to leave if you want. It's pretty bad out there—picked up this mail just now." She handed him a few damp envelopes.

Bob was a nice guy, but he was a creature of comfort. He would not have made a good Alamo defender for a number of reasons, but one of those was that he did not like roughing it. Lori had figured that out long ago, and she finished up what she was working on quickly in anticipation of his call. Sure enough, at 5:02, the phone rang. She got her things and ran upstairs with Bob's golf umbrella at the ready. She held the door for her boss, alerting him to Bella's quick dart into the building, her fur drenched, and out they went, the enormous umbrella covering both of them amply.

Buck didn't have an umbrella. In his day, ladies in big cities carried decorative parasols, but folks pretty much toughed it out and got wet in inclement weather. He headed out of his office in the long barracks and toward the gift shop to meet Lori for the trip home, as usual. As he walked toward the building, the rain was coming down in sheets, making it hard to see anything clearly. But he did notice two people walking toward the front of the church—slowly. One, a woman with yellow-blonde hair, was definitely Lori, and the other had to be Bob as he thought he saw crutches and knew Bob was being picked up by someone. He followed them at a distance as they passed the church, turned into the plaza, and headed toward the north wall, the rain lashing his face as he trailed them. The couple reached Houston and stood, the traffic whizzing by and rain off the cars splashing them mercilessly. In the end, Bob's umbrella did little good. They were staring ahead, obviously looking for Bob's ride's car, and they did not see Travis heading their direction. Buck hung back a bit. Finally, a white car stopped, and Bob got in carefully, Lori holding his crutches to make it easier, then opening the back door and throwing them in the backseat. While she did that, Leslie leaned over and gave Bob a little kiss. Buck stared for a moment, then quickly headed back the way he came.

Vicky was worried. She loved Buck, but she loved Lori more than anyone else in the world. Although the two of them apparently didn't totally see it, or at least always act as would have been expected if they did, it was quite clear to Vicky that they were seriously in love. But Vicky kept thinking about Buck's lost love, Rebecca, the girl who gave him his Alamo ring. Although he reported dutifully to his diary that he had slowed the rest of his busy love life when Rebecca came on the scene, he certainly had not abandoned it. Clearly, from his writings, he was in a physical relationship with Rebecca. He had promised her an understanding, the idea being he would marry her once his divorce was final, but that never happened. Lori had said that the divorce did not go through until Buck was heading to the Alamo. He probably never knew when it was final. And who knew what really happened back east with his wife? Both partners pointed fingers at the other. He had really screwed up his love life, always putting his desire to have a good time ahead of any other considerations. Opportunities for that kind of thing in his present life were almost nil, at least currently. But it worried her that he might view Lori the same way he had Rebecca, numero uno but not the only game in town. She hated to bring it up to him, but she felt she must to protect Lori, whom Vicky perceived as rather clueless and not particularly adept at watching out for herself.

A rare opportunity presented itself the next day, as Len was off playing Spanish guitar, as usual, her parents were at work, and Lori had gone in to the Alamo but left Buck at home, there being no military adventures or reenactor demos on the horizon that day. School was out. He was sitting in the backyard, dressed in his modern clothes, reading a book, as she came out the door.

"Buck?"

He looked up, turning his head toward her.

258

"Vicky! I thought everyone had gone somewhere. It was so quiet, I just thought I would come out here and read for a while," he replied with a sort of sad little smile.

"It's awfully hot to sit out here and read," she observed.

But Buck did not mind. Air conditioning was nice, but he had gotten along without it for years.

"Think you can tear yourself away from—what is that?" she glanced at the front of the book, "The story of the Alamo? I would think there's not a lot of suspense for you in that one?"

"Surely can," he replied, putting the book on his lap and giving her his full attention.

Vicky almost lost her nerve. This was going to be delicate and difficult. But she persevered.

"Buck, I've got to ask you something. You know how much I care about you—I'm crazy about you," she started.

A worried look crossed his face, as he thought for a minute that she might say she was in love with him, but she went on.

"But I want to ask you about Lori."

He relaxed slightly and gave a little laugh. "What about Lori?"

Vicky soldiered on. "Uh, well, Lori is the most special person in the world to me. Even though I'm younger, I sometimes feel that she doesn't look out for herself as well as she should—misses some things. So I feel it's my duty," she chose that word duty deliberately as she knew what it meant to him, "to kind of, you know, protect her."

"From what?" he asked.

"Now don't take this the wrong way," Vicky replied, "but maybe from you?"

He looked devastated. "I don't understand," he said sadly, looking down at his book, as he did not want to look at Vicky.

259

She steeled herself with determination to go on. "Buck, Lori got a copy of your diary from Bob and read the whole thing—late at night after everyone else was asleep. That's why she was so tired Saturday and didn't get up until 10:00."

He stared at her, not comprehending what this could have to do with him endangering Lori and how and why Lori wanted to read the diary, and even more strange—how Vicky was involved.

He gave a barely audible "Yes?"

"Well, she had been up until 3 in the morning finishing it. I asked her if it changed anything about her view of you, and she said not at all. In fact, her words were 'same old Buck,'" Vicky continued, not mentioning that she had prompted that description, Lori only parroting it in response. "And she told me she still loves you and that she wished she could keep your little book."

"I'm glad to hear that," he said hesitantly.

"But she did give me a few details, and I decided I needed to see for myself. She left it under a pillow, and I found it and read it."

He closed his eyes and put his hand over his face, his head hanging down, but he didn't say anything.

She continued. "Actually, I ended up with the same reaction she had. All it does is give some background as to why you are the way you are—does not make me love you any less at all. And some of it is so sweet—the way you did so many thoughtful things for people, especially kids. But . . . ."

He glanced up at her for just a moment. Her green eyes were round with excitement, and he quickly looked down again.

"The love life part—I'm worried for Lori. I know you will hate me and likely avoid me forever, and I can hardly stand to think about that, but I can't let Lori be another Rebecca—where there could be, sometime, . . . others?" her inflection rose at the end as she stared at Buck.

He was still looking down, toward his book, but he wasn't looking at it. He wiped a tear from his cheek and finally looked at Vicky. She was certainly wise beyond most 9-year-olds.

260

"Come sit by me, Vicky," he said gently, giving her a hug as she got up and came to him.

"I have really messed up my life over the years, no doubt about it. And I'm not that old, although I suspect I seem old to you. I had a bad marriage, debts I couldn't pay, and I did run off to Texas. When I got here, I lied to get in. I was what I'm hearing everyone call an illegal alien these days, only now it's the Mexicans who are doing it. It's all true. Charlie was still in Alabama with my wife at the time, and," he looked down again and wiped away another tear, "honestly, I had no one. I'm not making excuses, but it just sort of all happened. That doesn't make it right, but lots of folks lived that way in that time. Of course, I wish y'all had not read the journal, at least without telling me first. But I've heard about it from all kinds of hostile folks I don't know as it seems to be in wide circulation. So I shouldn't be too surprised that it would eventually come up among the people I care about more than anyone else."

Vicky was beginning to feel guilty, was getting the same vibes she had when she had asked Buck about his little son. Maybe she was too headstrong.

His eyes met hers. "You are a brave advocate for your sister, a most admirable trait in my view. Yes, I can see, based on my past history, why you would be concerned. All I can tell you is that I love Lori more than anyone else in the world. I do not even look at other women . . . ."

"Not even me?" Vicky tried to lighten it up slightly.

He gave her another hug. "Well, excepting you, of course. But, no, honestly, although it brings back sad, ancient memories to think about Rebecca, and she was a wonderful girl, that relationship was more—what shall I say?" He searched for the right word. "Volatile—we had lots of ups and downs, and she had a fiery temper. I never knew after I rode all the way out to her place, sometimes in a flood, to see her what my reception was going to be like. With Lori, it's not like that at all. We just fit together. I think that if there really is any purpose in my coming back, it may have been for me to meet her."

At this point, both of them had teared up.

Vicky put her arms around him. "The prosecution rests," she declared. "I promise I will not ever tell Lori about this conversation."

# THE TRINITY

Mary and Lyle Jones were taking the table out of the van for a second book signing as Buck walked by on his way to see Lori. He had not been aware that this event was on the day's schedule, likely a deliberate oversight on Bob's part after the disaster the first time. The first book signing, despite the confrontation with Travis, or possibly because of it since the colonel basically proved he was insane and provided unintentional support for Jones' thesis, did net quite a few sales, and Bob had encouraged Jones to come back again. The colonel tipped his hat to Mary and waved but kept going. The truce between Jones and Travis rested uneasily upon the two not seeing much of each other, and both of them knew it.

Jones stared after him, then quietly remarked to his wife, "I hope he's gotten some new pants since the last time!"

Buck ran down the stairs just as Lori was getting up to go out to get the mail.

"Let's stop in on Morena," he suggested.

"You're awful, Buck! Do you really enjoy seeing Morena, or do you just want her fudge?" Lori laughed.

"Well, kind of . . . both," he responded. "Come on!"

Morena was scurrying around the shop, straightening things and moving a few t-shirts that customers had put on the wrong rack. When she saw them, she waved, the bracelets jangling.

"You just missed Col. Bowie and Congressman Crockett," she informed them. "They're doing a presentation for the kids today. Kids just can't get enough of Davy's cap."

"You say they're still here and going to be?" Buck asked her.

Morena nodded, and he went on. "I've got an idea. I don't seem to do so well on offense, confronting folks on my own by waving my sword at them. And I suppose I can't depend on you to make me another pair of pants if I get into it with Jones again?" He turned to Lori.

She shook her head in the negative, adding, "Honestly, Buck, you're not so great on defense, either."

"We'll use a different strategy this time—intimidation. Your Bowie impersonator has got him down perfectly, and that little old knife he's got says a whole lot without a word being spoken. The congressman is not as intimidating, but, if nothing else, he can talk your ear off and divert the conversation from bashing the defenders to wrestling alligators. All I have to do is arrange it and stand back and watch!"

"You're the commander," Lori laughed.

"Before you prepare for battle, sir, would you like a piece of fudge?" Morena asked with a smile.

"Yes, ma'am!" came the quick reply.

The rendezvous with the kids was not until later in the afternoon, but Dave and Mitch had decided to make a day of defending the Alamo since they had to dress as Saints Davy and Jim anyway. Dave had taken off the hot fur cap as the weather was warming for what would be a blistering day. He was standing, talking with his counterpart, when the commanding officer strolled up. Travis tipped his hat to the two.

"Good morning, y'all!" he greeted them. "I understand that your program is this afternoon?"

"Good morning, to you, sir," the congressman responded in his twangy voice, placing the coon back on his head. "Yes, we're free for any assignments you might have in mind up until mid-afternoon."

Travis grinned. "Perfect! Actually, I do have something in mind, but I believe it will require all three of us to carry it off."

Mitch, as Bowie, had unsheathed the knife and was looking at it, moving it back and forth as the sun glinted off of it.

"I hope, Col. Bowie, that your intentions with that thing are honorable?" the South Carolinian noted in his drawl.

"All depends, Col. Travis," Bowie said, still moving the knife back and forth in the sunlight and with his lips curled in a rather sinister little smile.

Davy was laughing at the two rather disagreeable and hostile colonels. "Well, sir," he asked, turning to Travis, "What do you have in mind?"

"That fellow who had the book signing several weeks ago and caused me so much trouble is back at it again, setting up as we speak," Travis responded.

"Actually, Colonel, I kind of appreciate him. As I heard the story, he sort of put you in proper perspective. I heard your most prominent feature was on full display," Bowie said calmly, still moving the knife back and forth.

Travis glared at him but went on. "Anyway, what I would like y'all to do is show up as they're getting started with the book signing and make your presence known. And," he turned to Bowie, "Colonel, for what it is worth, although I seem to be the professor's favorite target, he had some choice words for you, as well, as I recollect."

Mary and Lyle had everything set up. It took a little longer than before because there were no students in attendance this time around. They were at the same location, set to hook any tourist who displayed the least bit of interest, Jones ready at the first opportunity to begin his monologue regarding the personal failings and foibles of the Alamo's Big Three. Buck stood off to the side and back, somewhat behind a tree, where he could hear but not be in the professor's line of sight. Jones was standing in front of his table, looking toward the plaza. Finally, a Hispanic man came up with his young son, saying something about having had an ancestor in Santa Anna's army and how proud he was of that fact. He asked Jones how come everyone just sort of naturally assumed that the attacking army constituted the forces of darkness, while the beleaguered defenders were the forces of light. Jones was off and running. Travis headed for Davy and Jim, who were conversing in front of the gift shop. He motioned them forward.

"War's started," Buck said as he reached them. "Some Mexican fellow just asked how come they're always given short shrift. It's time to move in!"

Davy picked up Old Betsy, which he had leaned against a tree. The fact was that Crockett didn't really take the famous gun to the Alamo, but run-of-the-mill tourists didn't know that. Bowie and Crockett sauntered up to where Jones and the man with the little boy were talking. They made a point of standing a little ways back but clearly in Jones' view. The professor was unloading his version of the Alamo on the man who asked the question, while the child, clearly bored to death, fidgeted.

"There's simply no justification for 'good' versus 'bad' in this thing. From my research, I have pretty much concluded that all of the Texian leaders, as well as Santa Anna and most of his generals, although the generals had to do as told, were unsavory characters. The Alamo commander, Travis, was a real piece of work. He couldn't do anything right in his life and always seemed to be running from failure but not as fast as he was creating new fixes for himself with his impulsive and fanatic approach to everything. I put much of the blame for what happened on him. He was only 26, an incredibly immature 26. Some 91 of the garrison members were older, 14 the same age, and 59 a little younger. That's of the ones whose ages we know. Bowie was older and more seasoned, arguably a better leader, even when roaring drunk, which he was much of the time. That really just means that the roughnecks populating the fort were more likely to listen to him than the uptight and prickly Travis. Bowie should have been sentenced to life in prison for the crimes he committed . . . ."

At that point, Bowie and Crockett moved forward, Bowie playing with the knife, and the movement caught Jones' eye. His voice got a nervous edge, but he continued.

"Bowie was not only a slave trader, but he was violating the Slave Trade Act enacted by Congress in 1807, which banned importing slaves, via work with the pirate Jean Lafitte of Battle of New Orleans fame, pulling a scheme that got the slaves in the country and sold to Bowie through fake transactions, and then on to new buyers in the South."

At this, Bowie moved closer, Crockett following him. The knife was clearly out in the open. Travis, having moved into line where he could see and be seen, but further back than the other two, had a malicious smile on his face.

Jones pressed on, nervously. "If the slave importation scheme weren't bad enough, Bowie was also setting up and executing fraudulent land deals right and left in Louisiana and Arkansas involving thousands of acres. When the Americans got hot on his trail, he headed to Texas and sucked up to the Mexicans, even marrying the daughter of a prominent citizen of Bexar—old San Antonio, in order to . . . ."

"Now hold on there just a minute," a gruff voice interrupted Jones.

265

He turned slightly to see the glittering knife, Bowie still playing with it, turning it, right in front of Jones' stomach.

"Sir, I would suggest that you might be wise to avoid personal attacks on someone that you cannot prove," Bowie said in a calm but deadly tone, an even, cold stare on his face as he continued turning the vicious knife back and forth in his hand.

Travis was laughing as he came forward to stand not far behind Bowie. He stood there with his arms crossed, a smug smile on his face. Crockett moved up next to Bowie, and the child quit his fidgeting and asked Davy about his cap. The congressman was, as always with little ones, pleased to oblige. Other children in the crowd started to head for Crockett.

"Uh, sorry," was all Jones could say, staring at the knife.

He knew it was not really Bowie, but the impression was so good that it was easy to forget that. More practically, the guy obviously was a Bowie fan, and he had that big, threatening knife and did not seem at all squeamish about it. Jones tried to go on, moving away from the delicate subject of Bowie's young wife, who had died of cholera a couple of years before the Alamo fight.

"Yes, all three of the Texian leaders were really losers, as were so many of the Americans who went to Texas in those days. Hopefully, we're breaking down some of that old Trinity thing, at least trying to. I'm not professing to know what God does and does not want in general, but I am certain that St. Peter turned down Travis and Bowie when they got to the pearly gates—probably slammed the door in their faces. In fact, they were bad enough that the Devil may not have even wanted them."

Bowie stepped forward, the knife now held steady in his right hand, blade forward. "Obviously, sir, you are rather dense. I am going to tell you one more time—a bit firmly—that you need to shut your trap instead of denigrating folks. I don't know where you are from, but, in the South, we expect folks to be more polite than that. Do you think you understand what I'm saying?" He twirled the knife in his hand once for effect.

Davy had finished talking with the first little boy, although a mob of children still tailed him. He moved up next to Jim, the long rifle in his hand.

"What the colonel says is true, sir. A gentleman does not talk so ungenerously about other folks when he really doesn't know them—or

266

usually even when he does," the good-natured frontiersman chimed in.

Their leader finally stepped up right behind them, and he had the sword unsheathed at this point, although he had no intention of charging over the table with it this time.

Jones was nothing if not persistent, although he was perspiring heavily at this point, and not just from the sun beating down overhead. He did not notice Travis behind Bowie as he was focused on the big knife, so he turned to bashing the commander, knowing that, at least historically, Bowie was not exactly a Travis fan.

"Let me try to explain myself from a little different angle," he began. "I'm not trying to slander anyone—just giving facts. Unlike Bowie, Travis left a paper trail, including the famous letters from the Alamo. And I'll admit, his one positive is that he was a good writer. But it's the rest of his paper trail that is damning—that infamous diary, where he laid out all of his numerous sexual exploits and the fact that he was paying for them with drinking a toxic cure for his venereal disease that was making him crazy."

To Jones' unpleasant surprise, Bowie moved closer with the knife. "Now look, fella, this is the third time I've had to warn you." He took another step so that the knife was no more than a foot from Jones' gut.

"But, Colonel, I was always under the impression that you didn't much care for Col. Travis . . . ," the professor started.

Bowie cut him off. "I know Col. Travis, and so I have a right to my opinion of the man. I have a sneaking suspicion that you don't—certainly don't recall seeing you around Bexar or in the Alamo. Now this is the last time I'm going to say it—shut up!"

Jones backed away several steps, hitting his table and knocking a few books off the top of the stack as he did. Mary reached down for the books. Crockett was gathering children to the side of the table and telling them about his fight with several wildcats—at one time. Travis was standing rigidly, his left hand gripping the sword and a smirk on his face. And Bowie stood there glowering.

Jones finally got the message. He continued selling books, sitting at his table and answering questions from the public. But there would be no more pontificating about the cardinal sins of Saints Davy, Jim, and William and which, if any of them, might be in Hell.

267

As Travis left to head toward his office, he called out to Jones, "If the Devil won't let me in Hell, at least I won't have to spend the hereafter with you!"

"May 5? You're sure about that," Luisa stared at Angelo in amazement. "I knew this president wasn't the brightest bulb, but really?"

"Yeah, May 5. I couldn't believe it, either," he said. "I guess he knows what Cinco de Mayo is? There's not much time to plan. It's going to be a quick in and out. They fly him in, and he comes to the Alamo. The governor will be there and some other dignitaries, and you know Travis will be there. The President will give his speech, and then he's whisked off and out of town. That's the way they usually do these things. Of course, security is really ramped up when the President comes to any event."

"Well, I think we're going to have to go with stealth again. They'll be better prepared this time for two reasons. First, the fact that the President is coming, and second, our botched effort before. I think we need to use the same basic approach—no chanting or singing—quiet people just filing out of small streets at a distance, feeding into the larger roads, all heading silently toward the Alamo. One other difference between this time and last time—there will already be a crowd of people there to see the President. Some will no doubt want to hear him rant about his wall. Others will be protesting it. I'm hopeful that I can scoop up most of those for our effort ahead of the game. They'll have some of the roads coming in here blocked off. Timing is going to have to be perfect. We need to be converging on the Alamo about the time the President's plane has landed. The goal is for everyone to be in place immediately after he reaches the Alamo but while the preliminary speakers are talking. Otherwise, there's not enough time to get there before he's through. They're going to have to walk fast."

"Yeah. Of course, the governor will say some words, and some of the other politicians, and I bet Travis will get up and yell 'Victory or Death' and ask everyone to honor his brave command, but this president doesn't usually give really long speeches, so we really are going to have to move the people forward fast," Angelo agreed.

Bob had gotten some of his stuff back in his desk, but it was hopeless. It came nowhere near fitting before, and he was actually wondering if someone had thrown some of someone else's stuff in his office when all the furniture was commandeered for the fortifications. He had finally given up and shoved the excess against the baseboards in a little fortification of its own, all around the room. The few things he actually needed to do his job either weren't there or were buried under so much stuff that he would never find them. He was fumbling around in the desk drawers, looking for his favorite pen, which he had looked for every day since the "battle," to no avail, except for the week he was wearing the cast. It had become a daily morning ritual—always fruitless. There was a knock on the open door, and he looked up. It was Travis.

"Sir, do you have a moment?" the colonel asked.

"Sure, Colonel, I'd ask you to sit down, but, as you can see, the chairs are piled with stuff. What can I do for you?"

Travis looked around, amazed. He was quite content with his little table, candle, paper, quill, and ink. How could someone need, or stand, all this stuff? But he was too polite to ask why Bob's office was such a horror. He glanced over toward Lori's cubbyhole. She wasn't there, but he closed the door anyway, just in case she returned.

He began in a rush: "I know Lori read a copy of my journal. It's kind of complicated. Vicky found her asleep, face down resting on the book. I'm not sure what that says about my writing ability, but she told Vicky that she wished she could keep it. Vicky then purloined it from Lori's room and read it herself. I feel bad about that as there are some things in there that really shouldn't be seen by a 9-year-old girl, but it's done now. She seems pretty mature for her age. I understand that you loaned the copy to Lori. If they really did print copies, which is still hard for me to imagine but obviously true as I've heard from just about everyone about it, do you know where I could buy one for Lori? And, if they printed copies, it must have been from my handwritten copy. I'd like to have it back if I could."

Bob was laughing. "Somehow, when Lori asked to borrow it, I knew something like this would happen. I didn't know quite how—should have figured Vicky would have something to do with it. That kid is precocious in the extreme."

"She's a sweet child. She means well with everything she does. She goes ahead with her instincts, and it just doesn't quite come out the way she thinks it will all the time."

"Yeah, like someone else I know—a little headstrong and impetuous!"

269

Travis knew Bob was talking about him, but he couldn't deny it. There had been too many instances of it to ignore, so he just smiled sweetly.

"Listen, Colonel, you can see this place." Bob swept his arm around. "When I find the diary, it's yours, in more ways than one, of course. It should be a little easier to spot than some things as this mess was pretty much in place before she borrowed it." He glanced around. "I thought I put it on that table in the corner."

Bob still had a boot on his foot, but he was able to get around without too much trouble. He got up and hobbled over to the table, Travis looking over his shoulder as Bob shuffled through the stuff piled high. Buck spied his name on a small black book.

He pointed. "Is that it?"

"Certainly is. Here, son—it's yours." Bob handed him the book.

"Sir, I do make a salary here now. I will be happy to pay you for it."

Bob waved him off. "I might make some people pay me for it, but I can't see charging the author for his book! I believe the University of Texas has the original. If you like, I'll check with them. Anything that's yours is pretty much considered sacred in Texas, like your ring here, because so few identified items survived the Alamo. Although various state entities have title to your few surviving possessions as someone who ended up with them either donated or sold them to the state, I would think that you should be able to get anything back that's yours. I'll call them today."

"Thank you, sir," the colonel said quietly. "Even though I guess everyone in Texas has read it by now, the diary is rather personal to me. As to the ring, I'm still thinking about that. I know what I would like to do with it, but it's sort of mixed up. I'll let it stay where it is just a little bit longer if that's all right with you?"

"Colonel, why don't you call me Bob instead of sir or Mr. Gordon? And, yes, it's perfectly OK to leave the ring on display right now. I'm sure the public will be grateful to you for it."

"Sir—I mean Bob, it's all right if you call me Buck," Travis replied with a little smile.

"Deal," Bob responded.

270

Travis opened the door and glanced toward Lori's space—still not there. He headed straight for Morena. She was in the corner near the fudge counter. He waved to her and called her name.

"Let me guess, Colonel. You want a piece of fudge?"

"Well, I do, but, actually, I need your help with something else first." He gave her a pleading look.

"I'll see what I can do. What do you need?" she asked, smiling.

He looked around to be sure Lori wasn't somewhere in the shop, then held out the little book. In a low voice, barely above a whisper, he told her an abbreviated version of Lori and Vicky reading it and Bob giving it to him so he could give it to Lori. He did not tell Morena anything about his entries, hoping she had not read it.

"Do you have a pretty ribbon I could tie around it? And maybe a sack I could put it in so she won't see it before I give it to her? I'm sorry to trouble you with this," he apologized.

Morena smiled and gave him a little hug. "That's so sweet of you. I think I may have just the ticket—follow me."

She led him to the back of the cashier counter, on the other side of the hustle and bustle of people checking out. She reached down and pulled out a rather beaten-up large heavy box from under the counter. Inside were a few small gift boxes, tissue paper, scissors, tape, and other odds and ends.

"We don't wrap for customers, but every now and then there is a piece of ribbon and we throw it in this box and save it—for occasions just like this."

She was scrounging through a rather beaten-up small cardboard box filled with ribbons that was among the contents of the large box.

"Occasions just like this?" the serious young man responded. "How often do you have someone come in and ask for a ribbon for something he didn't buy here and that is actually something he wrote and is giving as a gift to a lady?" he asked.

Morena laughed at him. "Oh, every day," she said nonchalantly. "Here—do you see a ribbon you would like for Lori?"

271

"The wide yellow one, if that's all right?" He pulled on a pretty lemon-yellow ribbon. "I helped Lori paint a room at her house—never had done anything like that before. We didn't bother to paint," he paused. "She told me that yellow is her favorite color, and we painted the room a color she said was 'Yellow Rose'"

"That sounds perfect," Morena said. She pulled out the ribbon. "Here, Colonel, it's yours, for your Yellow Rose!" She handed him a plastic Alamo gift shop bag as well. "Now come over to the fudge counter with me."

It was quitting time at the Alamo. Bob hobbled out and over to Houston, still hesitant to drive, although it was his left foot in the boot. Buck walked from the long barracks to the front of the gift shop, waiting for Lori, as usual.

"What's in the bag?" she asked immediately upon seeing him.

"Uh, nothing special," he responded without elaboration.

Lori knew not to ask too many questions—it was probably something relating to 1836, she thought.

Once in the car, and as she started to put the key in the ignition, he handed her the bag.

"It's for you," he said softly. "I'm not at all sure why you like it, but I have it on good authority that you do."

She put the key in her lap and took the bag. The little black book that had been her companion for several late nights was tied in a yellow silk ribbon. She stared at him, then reached over and hugged him, giving him a kiss.

"But how did you . . . ?" she paused. "Vicky, right?"

He nodded. "But don't be upset with her—I'm glad she told me. The fact that you cared enough about my life to read it means everything to me," he said softly. "I love you, Lori—you are my Yellow Rose."

Buck had made it unscathed through the Battle of Flowers Parade at Fiesta, San Antonio's spring event. Just as important, he had made it

272

through the event without killing anyone else. He stood front and center on a gorgeous float featuring a floral Alamo church. El Presidente had to hoof it, no horse this time, marching with a handful of his soldados, fortunately at some distance back from the colonel. Buck did not see him, and thus peace and flowers reigned. The festival dated from 1891 and was originally intended to honor the memory of the colonel and his men. On that long-ago first Fiesta day, local ladies in decorated carriages threw flowers at each other, hence the parade name. With the Alamo's hero intact and avoiding a confrontation, through no fault of his own, Lori and Bob breathed a big sigh of relief.

Lyle Jones knew who was behind the confrontation with "Bowie" and "Crockett." At the very end of the unpleasant encounter, he had seen Travis standing there behind the other two with that little smirk on his face, but he would have known had the colonel not been there. And then the crazy fool had the nerve to make that smart comment about Hell. He had to hand it to Travis. He really had not realized the Alamo commander could think straight long enough to do something that took planning instead of engaging in instantaneous and usually foolhardy reaction. The colonel had paid Jones back handsomely for the earlier book signing event, and now Jones wanted to settle the score once and for all. He had pretty much given his word to Bob and Lori that he did not want Travis dead and did not want to harm him, but he did want to put him in his place and stop all of this 1836 business. He needed to force the issue and make Travis admit that 1836 was dead and gone. Maybe that would unclutter the young man's mind if anything would. Jones intended to force Travis to surrender the Alamo to the Mexicans. Although the professor was not in the least interested in reenacting the battle, he did know a few of the reenactors via mutual interest in history. He picked up the phone and called Vincente Montoya.

"You were wondering if I could do what?" Vincente asked him. "You've got to be kidding."

"No, really, Vincente, I'm dead serious," Lyle said calmly. "You've got the uniform—can't imagine the cost of having another one like it produced. I am envisioning Santa Anna, with a convincing number of soldados . . . ."

"You know you're not going to get anywhere near 4,000," Vincente interrupted.

"I don't need anywhere near that many. If it's a surprise, unlike that ridiculous stunt with the school kids from Chihuahua, there's only one defender, not 180 or even the Alamo staff with their rolling pins and pop

273

guns," Lyle continued. "He's not going to have time to be counting—just need to make it look convincing. Have them swarm in quickly, surround him, treat him a bit rough, and demand his surrender."

"Lyle, trust me, it's not going to work. He won't surrender. He'll repeat the 'I shall never surrender or retreat' line. I get the part about not surrendering, but I never could figure out why he declared that he wouldn't retreat. Like where could he go?"

"Yeah, I always wondered about that one, too. A lot of bravado and just not too much thought behind it. I still say the mercury had gotten to him," Lyle laughed.

Montoya continued, "And probably yell 'Victory or Death.' He's got a one-track mind on this. Honestly, I've already done battle with him—on March 6. I ended up spread out on that huge cactus on the Alamo grounds. No thanks. I actually kind of enjoy the colonel when he's not in Alamo mode—would prefer to keep it that way and keep me out of the succulents, if you get my drift. If you can find someone else who wants to battle Travis at the Alamo, and he can fit into my Santa Anna suit, I'll be glad to loan it, but that's as far as I want to go."

"Can you recommend anyone about your size who might be willing to do it?" Lyle asked.

Vincente thought for a moment. "Try Luis Estrada. After the March 6 event, he told me that he had, as he put it, 'had it up to here with the crazy defender,' but I don't know if he will really want to tangle with him. He very well might enjoy getting to wear the Santa Anna headdress and uniform coat, though. He's really into Mexican army clothing of the period, far more than I am. And he has a better view of Santa Anna as a general than I do."

Jones was in luck. Estrada was more than happy to assume the generalship of the Mexican Army. He thought he could summon around 40 soldados who could come up with uniforms convincing enough if he really worked at it. This was far fewer than the force that actually attacked the fort, but Travis was one out of 180. It would hopefully be enough, particularly if they charged in a hurry, before Travis could get his bearings, if, indeed, he ever had them. Estrada suggested a Monday. The staff would be there, but that seemed to be the lowest tourist count day. He made a few phone calls and called Jones back. He thought he could get the troops in line in 5 days—the next Monday.

274

FANDANGO

Lori had started work on the last piece of the reproduction uniform—and the hardest—the blue tailcoat, but her dull rose dress was getting so worn that it was in need of repair. She was toying with the idea of making another reenactor frock, in pale yellow cotton lawn if she could find it, for some of the little dressier events, to the extent anything at the Alamo could be called dressy, after she finished Buck's coat. But for now, she would have to mend the rose dress, and she would look rather worse for wear standing next to her beau in his bloodstained coat. Another trip to see Cathy Johnson was in order. Both Buck and Lori were home. It was her day off, and the colonel had no pressing military matters to attend to. She asked him if he wanted to help her pick out fabric for a new dress, and, although he shrugged with disinterest, he consented to go as the only alternative was reading another Alamo book. Fortunately, considering their last trip to the shop, Vicky was otherwise occupied with her friend Chloe. Much to Lori's relief, Buck wore his modern clothes for the excursion across town.

When they walked in, Cathy did not recognize Buck until she got a good look at his face. His hair was combed down over the gunshot wound per Vicky's previous advice, and Lori had used the concealer on the sword slash.

"How's the uniform coming?" she asked, wondering, once she did figure out that Lori's companion was the colonel, if the 1836 clothes had come apart.

"Great," Lori responded. "I've done the vest and pants—am about halfway through the coat. All is looking good if you can call 1836 men's fashions good."

He made a face. "I kind of like the styles."

"Cathy, I'm here for me today, not the colonel," Lori said. "My old rose dress is wearing out, so I may look at something not too expensive and sort of durable—maybe a quilting cotton, soft but not too thin. But what I really want is something for an Alamo party dress . . . ."

"Alamo party dress?" Cathy laughed. "Somehow I just don't think of the words 'Alamo' and 'party' together for some reason!"

"I didn't mean it quite that way," Lori smiled. "I see what you mean."

Buck had a stricken look on his face.

"I should have said an 1836 style dressier dress. If I could have any color my heart desired, I would pick yellow, not too fancy as we're still on the frontier, but something one could wear to a fandango," she said, turning to Travis and giving a sly smile.

"That sounds a whole lot better," he added. Buck liked fandangos.

"Come over here," Cathy directed them. She headed to a row of the ladies' reenacting and quilting fabrics, going past the calicos to a few more delicate fabrics on the far end. "How about this?" She pulled out a delicate, frothy-looking pale lemon lawn.

"Oh, it's heavenly!" was all Lori could say.

She felt the soft fabric, almost silky in its fineness. It was rather expensive, but it was 54", so it would go much further than the usual 45" cotton bolts. She knew she had to have it. She had already picked out an 1830's pattern on eBay but was waiting to see what fabric options were available before actually ordering it.

"So how long do you think it will take to make this?" Buck asked tentatively.

"Well, Col. Travis, I have to finish your uniform coat first, and those things are not easy to make," she laughed. "But I can usually do a dress in about a week if I have evenings free to work on it."

"So when can we have the fandango?" he asked. Lori smiled. Cathy laughed.

"OK, Buck, I'll get with the Texian Association folks. In fact, you're their commander—you can do it while I'm sewing if you like, and we'll have a fandango on the lawn out back of the church, or, if that's too morbid for you, we can do it at the house in the backyard."

"If we do it at the house and Bowie comes, he'll get drunk and fall in the pool," Buck responded.

276

"Sounds like a fun party," Cathy noted.

Lori took a few moments and searched through the more durable cotton bolts, finally settling on a blue one with a large print, that hallmark of the 1830's in fabric, and purchased it as well. She would still mend her rose dress. It would always be special to her as she was wearing it when Buck was found, and there had been so many events with him where she wore it. Maybe the blue dress would allow her to preserve the rose one.

Luis Estrada was admiring himself in the mirror. He made a dapper General Santa Anna—actually looked much more like the original than did Vincente. He adjusted the ridiculous hat and admired himself again. He had rounded up all of the Mexican side reenactors he could find, close to 40 in all, counting those Tomas had been able to drum up. It was time to take the Alamo. This time, only El Presidente, Tomas, and Ciro would be on horseback. Unfortunately, there would be no *Deguello*, as Andres flatly refused to have anything to do with the Alamo battle. Luis removed the enormous hat and headed for his car. Tomas had arranged for bringing the horses. He and another friend had trucks to haul the trailers. With no permit for this unofficial event, the drivers paused long enough to unload the horses, with plans to pick them up once the event was over. The troops had carpooled, and many of them were standing in the vicinity of the Menger, not wanting to possibly tip off Col. Travis. It was 9:00, time for the colonel to be at work, but the tourists were just beginning to come in, still sparse. Luis pulled into the parking lot, got out, placed his hat on his head, checked his sword, and straightened his uniform coat, then marched over to where his troops were assembling. He had thought to give the Alamo Rangers a heads up that there would be a small and very brief Mexican "attack" that morning, making up an excuse that it was being filmed for a documentary. Tomas and another man were just bringing up the horses.

"Everybody here?" the commander asked.

Tomas looked around. "I can't tell for sure, but," he glanced at his watch, "they should be. It's certainly a large enough force to overwhelm one defender!"

"Then, let's attack the Alamo!" Luis commanded. He mounted his horse, and Tomas and Ciro followed suit. Tomas lined the troops up in attacking columns.

The general yelled, "Adelante!" and the Mexican army moved forward at a run into the plaza and toward the old church. The few tourists present quickly got out of the way. The troops were screaming "Viva Mexico! Viva Santa Anna!" as they ran.

The colonel, working in his dim little office, heard something and opened the door. He heard the vivas and saw men rushing forward at a distance. Travis quickly unsheathed his sword, grabbed his hat and put it on, and ran out the door toward the oncoming throng. His worst nightmares were confirmed. Mexican troops in 1836 uniforms were charging his direction. There was no one else to help him defend the place. All he could do was stand ready with the sword and fight off as many as he could before they overwhelmed him. He had a fleeting thought of Lori and the fact that he knew this would really be the end, and they were on him. He swung the sword at the first men to reach him. They had rifles but did not fire. He swung the sword again, slashing the arm of one man, who cried out, but other soldados had come around his rear to where he was completely surrounded. Someone grabbed the sword from his hand and flung it on the ground. Two more men wrestled with Travis and finally tied his hands behind his back.

Luis rode up, smug and confident. "I am weary of dealing with you, Senor Travis. You have been a problem for me for 181 years. It is time to end it."

He gave Travis a stern, penetrating stare. It was clear from the rather stricken look on Travis' face that he did not remember Estrada from the March 6 encounter. Of course, Luis looked very different since his promotion to commander-in-chief.

Luis continued, "As you can see, we have you completely surrounded. You have no troops this time. You will surrender the Alamo to me."

"Never! I will die before I surrender to you," Travis shouted in Santa Anna's face.

"I think you will surrender, Colonel," Luis said calmly.

"Go ahead. Kill me. I don't care. I will never surrender!" Travis shot back.

Luis raised his eyebrows but went on, in a steady voice. "Colonel, I do not intend to kill you. For one thing, it seems to do no good as you have a way of coming back. However, I do intend to take you in chains to Mexico City and show you off as a trophy of war there. I will put you to work in public view toiling on a rock pile or digging ditches. If you do not accomplish your work diligently enough to meet my standards, you will be chastised . . . ."

"What?" Travis shouted.

"Whipped, Colonel, whipped. And your sentence will be for life. You are a young man, but, if you survive the brutal conditions I have in mind for you, you will live many years breaking up rocks, good, loyal, upstanding Mexican citizens strolling by and pointing and staring at you and saying, 'Wasn't that the young American fool who would not give up the Alamo? We got it anyway in the end.'"

At this point, the Alamo rangers, Bob, and several other staff members, as well as the tourists, were watching from a distance. No one dared to interfere, hoping this would be as brief as Luis had promised, although Elbert called for law enforcement backup.

Travis looked stunned at El Presidente's words.

"Well, Colonel, how about it? Surrender the fort to me!"

"No! Never! I will not surrender regardless of what . . . ." Travis turned deathly white and collapsed.

General Santa Anna and his troops stood around staring down at the unconscious man, not sure what to do in this unexpected situation.

"Stop this! I don't know what's going on, but I demand that you stop whatever you are doing!" a female voice was shouting. Lori pushed and shoved her way through the soldados and knelt, pulling Buck toward her. "Get out of here, all of you! My gosh, hasn't he been hurt enough? Look at the scars," she yelled as loud as she could. Then turning her face in fury toward Santa Anna, she screamed, "Go home! Get out of here! I mean it!"

"We were only trying to scare him," Luis admitted meekly.

"Scare him? Why?" Lori asked.

"Someone who is tired of Travis' antics, honestly, lots of people are tired of him, asked us to stage the attack to freak him out into surrendering the place—figured that might end his 1836 fixation," Luis confessed.

"Someone asked you to set him up?" Lori asked. "You had better tell me who it is," she demanded.

"All right, I don't want to take responsibility for it. I just enjoy the costume. Professor Jones. He thought forcing him to surrender would stop the colonel's sword waving and yelling Victory or Death," Luis explained.

"That fool!" Lori exclaimed. "He may be a brilliant historian, but he doesn't know Buck. He will not surrender no matter what—will die first."

El Presidente was not intimidated by the colonel, but Lori in her fury was a whole different matter. He tipped his enormous feathered hat to her and ordered his troops off. As Santa Anna and his soldados headed toward the Menger, Lori untied Buck's hands and placed his head in her lap. He was still white as a sheet, eyes closed. She held him close, wondering as she had the last time, whether these incidents and his propensity toward fainting would ever end. He was a long time coming to this time. He obviously really did think the Mexicans were attacking the fort, just as in 1836. It certainly gave every appearance of it from his vantage point. When he finally opened his eyes, he saw Lori's face peering down toward his.

"Lori?" he said in a whisper.

"Yes, Buck, I'm here. You did see Mexican soldiers this time—no high school kids. Actually, they were reenactors, but you could not have known. Professor Jones got the Mexican reenactors to stage the attack to force you to surrender. He thought that would stop the incidents that seem to come out of your determination to defend the place."

He was very weak, but he shook his head slightly. "No, Lori, no matter what, I will never surrender."

She put her head down next to his. "I know that, Buck—believe me, I know that."

Lori had mended her rose dress so that it was presentable for demos, and she was almost through with Buck's coat—had only the buttons and

280

buttonholes left to go. But the coat required a total of 20 buttons, so that was no small matter. Men had button overload in the old days. She was eager to finish the coat so that she could start her yellow dress, but it was hard to find the time. She was in her old dress, patched up, waiting for Buck to finish tying on his sash and buckling on his sword, for their ride in to the Alamo. Bob had informed her at quitting time the day before that the President would be paying them a visit in 3 days. It was very short notice, and he wanted to meet with everyone on staff first thing the next day to prepare for the event.

They got there right at 8:30, Bob having called the meeting a little early in order to be through by the time the tourists showed up. The President and his entourage would basically only be standing in front of the church for the obvious photo-op advantage it provided—no need to worry about them exploring offices. Bob asked Ed to be sure that the grounds looked extra neat, mowed, edged, and blown, and for everyone to be prepared for security details to check out personnel and all space in the compound before the President's arrival. Unfortunately, as the colonel could have confirmed, the Alamo was not built for security. It did not take the feds long to show up. That afternoon, security agents appeared, seemingly checking every bush and trash can on the grounds. They apologized, at least most of them, but entered private offices, checking everything, desk drawers included. When the security agent reached Bob's office, he just stood and stared.

"I know what you're thinking," Bob laughed. "Actually, if you want to take some of my stuff out and detonate it, that's fine with me—would be doing me a favor."

The agent gave a grim little smile but proceeded on automatic to go through the pile of stuff. This was only an initial run-through. There would be another one right before the President's arrival. A woman was assigned the long barracks sector, and she knocked on Buck's closed door. He opened it, and she jumped slightly.

"Excuse me, I didn't mean to startle you," he said politely.

"Sorry, it's so dark in here—I thought you were some kind of apparition," she responded, her eyes adjusting to the gloom.

"I kind of am," he responded sadly. "I don't know how much you know about the Alamo, but I made headlines recently—they dug me up," he explained.

281

"Oh yeah, I did hear something about that," she stared at him. "You certainly look like you've been through the battle," she said uncharitably, noting his face and the coat. "Anyway, with the President coming, I have to check out every room."

She pulled out a flashlight to augment the little candle and checked every crevice. The colonel's little writing desk was basically just a table, so the upshot was that checking his space, although dimly lit, was far easier than the work the other agent had with Bob.

Lori finished the new coat that night. It was a perfect fit, about as close as anything could be to Buck's original, without all that blood. To get the full effect, Lori used the concealer on his cheek, and, with his hat covering the gunshot wound and in the new and improved 1836 clothes, he did look the part of a dashing Texian military officer. He would debut the new coat in public for the presidential visit, continuing to use the old one for days when he had to sit in the dirt to plant vegetables or anything else likely to make a mess. Buck had calculated that this would likely be the night Lori finished and, right before the end of the workday, he ran by the gift shop to buy fudge. He was in luck. A sign out front advertised "Hope you have a Serious Sweet Tooth, Buy two, get one free" underneath a design showing the Lone Star with two crossed swords underneath it. He bought two boxes for Lori and got his free box for the family to share.

Cinco de Mayo had arrived, and so did the President of the United States. The quick visit to the Alamo was the only thing the leader of the free world had on his San Antonio agenda. The same battery of federal agents who had turned everything over several times to be sure the Alamo compound was safe had just completed their final check. Unobtrusive barriers that were nothing like what the colonel put up when the Mexican students invaded the place kept the tourists out, as did swarms of Secret Service and law enforcement officers. Many of the Alamo staff had chosen to take the day off rather than deal with the mess, especially those who had strong feelings against the idea of the President's wall to keep out illegals. Lori wished she could have taken off, but, instead, she found herself going in early—thankfully in regular clothes and actually dressed up slightly for the occasion. She had no choice. She was the colonel's transportation, and he did have to be there. The dashing Alamo commander, in his "new" 1836 uniform, was excited about meeting the President, not knowing anything about him but having been told about his wall concept, which, needless to say, appealed to Travis.

Luisa planned to be there, too. Everything was set. She doubted she would have a crowd as large as the one at the earlier rally, simply because some people who experienced the fail the first time would be jaded and not want to do it again. Although the displeasure with the President's wall idea would add to Luisa's ranks, the logistics of getting thousands of people close enough to the Alamo to make a difference with the security in place for a presidential visit was daunting at best. They would go as far as they could—or until the police turned tear gas or water cannons on them. She glanced at her watch. People should already be slowly moving out of small streets, where buses had staged, in groups of five or six, heading for feeder roads and forming larger groups, to head to larger feeder roads, all converging on the Alamo. As before, there were no signs, and they would be silent—no singing or chants. Angelo walked in.

"Ready to go?" he asked. "We don't want to get stuck back in the crowd somewhere."

"Good point! Yes, I think we're ready." She grabbed her enormous, battered old purse, and they headed out of the tiny La Voz headquarters and started walking briskly toward the old mission.

Most of the reenactors stayed away from the presidential visit because, generally, the fewer people, the easier it was to control the crowd for the security people. However, for local color, Dave and Mitch had been asked to reprise their roles as Crockett and Bowie. They would not have speaking parts as all eyes would be on the President and his likely brief speech. Their leader, however, had been asked to say a few words before the governor introduced the President. Lori was amazed. Buck did not seem to be flustered in the slightest at the prospect. He was so detached from modern politics, and the only person in the country who did not know who this President is and have a strong opinion of him one way or the other, that he was really clueless as to the nuances implicit in simply being a part of the event. Crowds were converging on the plaza as close to the barricades as they could get, and there were helicopters flying overhead. Just like in the old movies only with much more modern weapons, men were stationed on the edge of the top of the church, as well as on the roofs of the other buildings. Lori hoped no one fell off this time. At least Buck was on the ground.

The "pro" and "anti" protesters had been assigned turf by security. Those gathered in the "anti" area were not Luisa's people. Because of her efforts, there were relatively few "anti" people in their assigned space. The almost exclusively Anglo "pro" demonstrators and fans were packed in their area, cheering their man even though he had not yet arrived. With the helicopters circling constantly, Lori figured Air Force One must have landed at the airport. The motorcade was likely heading in on the freeway. Andres and Len's high school band had been given the honor of playing for the President. Both boys played multiple instruments. In band, Andres played trombone and Len trumpet. At present, the band was playing Lori's favorite, "The Yellow Rose of Texas." There were seats for the dignitaries who would attend—various members of Congress, state legislators, the mayor, and the like. She had been given instructions that she could sit in the far back row if there was room available. Otherwise, she would have to stand behind it. Buck, on the other hand, had been given directions regarding a prominent place on the first row, as he would have to walk to the microphone and speak. "Bowie" and "Crockett" were to stand in back and off to each side of the podium for effect. The security folks had even checked out Old Betsy to make sure there was no chance of the old gun taking out the new President.

Buck had on his sword belt, but, at least for now, the sword was sheathed. Lori hoped it would stay that way. She was getting weary, shifting her weight from one foot to the other, the high heels uncomfortable, already tired of this before it even started. The band finished the "Yellow Rose" and started on "The Eyes of Texas," always, she thought, an odd subject for a song. Crowds were continuing to increase, but most of those who wanted to see the President were already in place. In fact, it seemed odd that people were continuing to stream in at such a heavy pace so close to the ceremony. Lori looked at her watch. It was 10:00. The President was scheduled to give his address at 10:30.

As she looked up, she saw what had to be the front of the motorcade. Houston had been blocked off, and the black cars were stopping there. She could see just a little of it from her vantage point. It was time to get in place, behind that last chair. Buck had already walked to the first row and was shaking hands with various political dignitaries, still seeming perfectly at ease. She figured he probably would have become President of the Republic of Texas or a Texas senator had he lived the first time.

Luisa was smiling. Angelo was feeding her details. He was in constant contact via cell phone with the various coordinators. Although some streets were blocked completely off, they were still moving forward, getting very, very close to the Alamo. Luisa and Angelo were in the first rank of their column, and they were slightly ahead of the other columns converging on the place. In fact, they could see the already-gathered crowds ahead of them. Angelo was pointing out the general direction of "reserved spots" for protesters, and, since that area was the closest accessible place left, they headed directly to that point. This was a good spot, although most of Luisa's legions would be much further back. They had an excellent view of the church and the people involved in the program.

"There's Travis," Angelo pointed out the colonel.

"Doesn't look like he's got the sword out, yet," Luisa laughed.

"Want to bet on whether he waves it?" Angelo dared her.

"No thanks. I know the answer to that one! Wouldn't it be funny if he got all excited and accidentally stabbed the President with that thing?" she replied.

Someone gave Buck and the other front-row people a cue that it was time to sit down. The motorcade had stopped, and Texas' U.S. Senators were just walking up to take their seats in the first row. The band was still playing, now "America the Beautiful," as a swarm of people, with the tall President in the center, started making their way from what would have been the north wall toward the church. The security people parted enough that cameras could get a clear view of the President as he came forward. "America the Beautiful" came to a close, and the high school band started "Hail to the Chief." When the President reached the rostrum, he shook hands with all the front row folks. He spent more time with Buck than most of the others, although this President and the Alamo commander had nothing in common except for their mutual fixation about walls. A congressman—Lori had seen him on the news before but could not place him—opened the program. Someone had to do it, although the fact was no one was listening to him as they wanted to get to the main course.

Luisa was in place, Angelo beside her. More and more silent people, largely a Hispanic crowd, but with a number of African Americans and many young Anglos, were streaming up behind Luisa and Angelo. Angelo was fumbling with a small battery-operated microphone while Luisa looked at her army coming steadily forward, more and more of them crowding any space where people could stand. The security people were looking too, some pointing and with lots of cell phone activity.

Folks in the crowd started paying a little more attention as the congressman was winding down on his little speech.

"Ladies and gentlemen, I think everyone has heard that the President

285

wants to build a wall along the border to stop illegal immigrants from coming into this country in violation of our laws and rules . . . ."

The "pro" crowd started cheering wildly.

"And it's true—I expect we'll be hearing more about that in just a few minutes. But first, we have a true American hero, a young man who gave everything defending the walls here at the Alamo in the name of freedom and liberty. I suspect that everyone has heard by now that Col. William Barret Travis, commander of the Texan forces at the Alamo on March 6, 1836, was found in a recent archaeological dig and was still living. He survived brain surgery and is here today to help welcome the President to San Antonio. Ladies and gentlemen, it is my profound pleasure to introduce Col. Travis!"

All the Anglos making up the "pro" side shouted and cheered and whooped for their brave hero.

Angelo leaned over to Luisa and said, "Fine thing that the President is here to talk about his wall to keep illegals out, and they've got the first illegal alien on the stage giving a speech!"

Luisa raised her eyebrows and nodded.

Buck calmly walked to the podium and stared at the enormous crowd and began his short address.

"Thank you, sir, for that warm introduction. The governor graciously returned me to my post here, even though I did not prevail in 1836, so, in my capacity as the officer in charge, I would like to extend a true Texian welcome to all of you—and sir," he turned and gave his little bow to the President, "most especially, to you. I think I know what the Alamo means—what it stands for—to most of you, and I am absolutely positive as to what it means to me. My brave garrison laid down their lives for freedom—freedom that was authorized, then pulled away by an arrogant and evil dictator in a country that did not value or understand American freedom. Honestly, horrible as it was, I would do it again if I had to."

The "pro" folks gave him another ovation.

"Let's hope that we never have to do that. As it is, in this second chance at life, I will walk through it with hideous scars from a sadistic and vicious foe who mutilated their victims after slaughtering all of them under

286

a blood-red flag of no quarter. I did defend my wall, as best as I could with the disparity of forces involved, and now our President wants to build a wall to keep these same people who do not value our freedom and our laws out of this country. I believe we must do this for the sake of everything we hold dear. I would like to introduce a man who shares these views regarding the value of our freedom and liberty, the governor of the Great State of Texas, but, first . . . .'

"Here he goes," Luisa said with a laugh.

Travis pulled out the sword, waved it over his head, and shouted, "Victory or Death!"

The "pro" forces yelled, hooted, and hollered as the governor came forward to shake hands with Travis and provide the crowd with another brief little speech, culminating in introducing the President.

Finally, as the President came to the podium in front of the Alamo on Cinco de Mayo, Luisa gave her signal. Thousands of voices, in unison, shouted, over and over, "Viva Mexicano Americanos! Ninguna pared." The President tried to talk, to no avail. The dull din of the legion of voices made it impossible for anyone to be heard. The leader of the free world stood there, a slightly bewildered look on his face, hoping the vivas would die down. But they did not. The senators and congressmen were staring at each other, unsure what to do. Luisa's followers were far too many for security to run them off. Travis went up to the podium, whispered something to the President, who stood back, and the colonel yelled into the microphone and waved the sword, all to no avail. His appearance bolstered the crowd's determination to continue, steadily, the low, rumbling, metronomic chant.

The time for the President to begin his speech had long passed, and the crowd showed no sign of letting up. One of the President's aides conversed with him, pointing to his watch. The President nodded. The speech and the entire program should have been over by now. The President turned to leave. Travis realized what was going on, but he had no understanding of presidential timetables. He went to the commander-in-chief one more time, personally urging him to stay and wait them out, but the President had had enough. He shook hands with the Alamo commander, then, with his entourage in tow, headed toward the north wall. Travis had a chagrined look on his face. He stood at the podium and glared at the protesters, who did not vary their chant, continuing steadily to repeat, "Viva Mexicano Americanos! Ninguna pared." As the motorcade began a slow move away from the Alamo, Luisa's legion cheered wildly. The colonel, still at the podium and a stricken look on his face, sheathed his sword and headed to his office in disgust, Lori not far behind him.

Luisa and Angelo turned to each other and smiled.

May 6 was a Saturday but not just any Saturday. It was, in the parlance used by Alamo reenactors, "First Saturday," the day each month where the 1836-era reenactors came out in force on the Alamo grounds in back of the old church, demonstrating use of firearms, medical procedures, cooking, mapping, surveying, and anything else from the era at which someone in the reenacting corps was proficient. It also showcased the colorful and unique clothing worn by the folks of the 1830's. In fact, the entire weekend was to be full of reenactor activities this month. The Texians had already set up tents in the back of the complex at their usual location, almost a mini military camp. It was early yet, not quite 9:00 opening time.

Jorge Lavaca was slightly nervous, frustrated at the late start, and definitely already warm in his wool soldado uniform. The Mexican army reenactors would set up their own camp this Saturday, a tradition usually left to the province of their erstwhile enemies alone as, historically, the site was not too welcoming to Santa Anna's forces. But the Mexican-American reenactors felt it was important to make their presence known on the grounds of the old mission. After all, it was a Spanish mission, and Santa Anna, despite his many faults, was the victor in the famous battle, whether or not the Texians wanted to admit to the truth. Jorge was embarrassed that the "enemy" was already completely settled in, while the forces of Santa Anna had not even reached the site yet, except for himself. Jorge, who was a captain in Santa Anna's modern-day army, was trying to find whoever was in charge to fix the exact point to set up camp, preferably not too near the Texians. He had not gotten much help from the ranger as he entered the gate to the side of the church, the lawman not having the slightest idea which reenactors were to be posted where. Jorge headed past the buildings and, a somewhat queasy feeling arising in his stomach, toward the enemy camp, hoping someone there could point him to either the right location or someone who could locate the spot for him.

"Amigo! Can we help you find something?" Dave, in his Crockett outfit, called to the enemy soldier in an amiable tone.

Other Texians were staring, their countenances not particularly friendly. Crockett's greeting caught Mitch's attention, and he stopped

288

looking at his knife and stared at the Mexican officer.

"Yes, you know we're setting up camp somewhere, but I need to find whoever is in charge around here to give me the exact location so I can tell the guys . . . ." Jorge started.

"Whoever is in charge? Right over there," Mitch, in his gruff Bowie impersonation, interrupted, pointing in the general direction. "The gentleman you need to talk with just walked that way about 5 minutes ago. He will tell you exactly where to go. He's a tall redhead wearing a blue coat and white pants—can't miss him," he added, trying to maintain his serious mien as he said it.

Jorge thanked them and headed in the direction pointed out by Jim Bowie. He felt increased relief with each step he took heading away from the Texian camp. It did not take long to reach the very back of the complex, where the plantings gave way to the shed standing guard over the drink machines. Jorge stopped in his tracks as he saw a trio hovered over something slightly in front of the shed. One man, in a Texian reenactor outfit, obviously his suggested contact, was lying on his stomach, his arm extended forward, holding the point of a sword, opposite the usual handling of the weapon, and pushing the sword into what appeared to be a hole. A blonde woman dressed in 1836 garb and a Tejano reenactor were bending down, staring into the hole. The man in the blue coat pulled the sword out of the hole and looked up at the other two.

"Lori, do you have a string or something we can tie to the sword to attract her?" he asked the woman.

She nodded and reached into the pocket of her frontier dress. She had a piece of ribbon she had intended to pull around her hair. He gave her the sword, and she tied the ribbon around the grip, then gave it back to him. He shoved it, again grip first, back into the hole. Jorge continued to stare, knowing this was not a usual part of the Texian reenactor presentations.

"I see her! She's heading toward me," the man on the ground said calmly to his companions.

He ever so slowly pulled the sword toward him, luring whatever it was in his direction. Finally, a blur of patchwork fur flew from the hole and into the lush shrubbery, just missing the man's face.

"Bella! You certainly gave us a time!" the woman shouted after what was clearly a cat.

The man with the sword yelled, "For God's sake, put something over the hole! We don't want to have to do that again!"

He got up, brushed himself off, then untied the woman's ribbon and returned it to her. The Tejano, having placed a large, holey limestone rock over the opening, was now staring ahead, toward the Mexican soldier. The other two turned to see what he was looking at. Jorge took one step forward with the intent of introducing himself to the man in the blue coat, but that was as far as he got. Buck swung the sword and charged toward Jorge, waving the weapon.

"Get off the Alamo grounds right NOW! Go to Hell! There will be no Mexican troops on this sacred ground where you murdered and mutilated my command! Victory or Death!" he yelled.

Jorge took off, the Texian colonel chasing him, shouting one threat after another and waving the sword, all the way. As they passed the Texian camp, Buck's men cheered their valiant leader, who was at another "Go to Hell" as he passed. Bowie was laughing at the Mexican soldier's plight.

"I warned that Mexican that the man in charge would tell him exactly where to go," he said. "That's what he gets for asking for whoever is in charge of this place."

When Captain Lavaca reported to El Presidente, who was not Vincente Montoya this go-around, conveying the unsurprising news that the real Col. Travis was in command of the Alamo and would not hear of a Mexican soldado setting foot in his shrine, the Generalissimo was not happy. But there was nothing the Mexicans could do unless they wanted to appeal to the governor, and it was clear that would be a dead end. A hasty call was placed to the mayor's office, and permission was quickly granted for the Mexican Army to set up camp on Alamo Plaza, right outside the compressed sacred ground. The Alamo's commander was furious, railing to anyone who would listen that the property outside the current compound, on which Santa Anna sat, was also Alamo ground—where men in his garrison, including himself, fought, bled, died, and were mutilated by the evil dictator and his army of murderers. Most people, including the colonel's reenactor troops, let Travis' histrionics go in one ear and out the other, but that did not stop the colonel from making his opinion known. Santa Anna, meanwhile, was adding to his "army," bringing in more soldado units, as had been the case in 1836.

290

Anthony Robbins was dressed in torn tan trousers, a dirty white shirt, a grimy vest, and shoes that were coming apart, appropriate attire for a slave stuck in the Alamo in 1836. He had made a point of avoiding his "master," the crazy colonel, not ever stating to the man that he was supposed to be Joe, the colonel's servant.

"I wish we had some way to blast them off the plaza!" the flame-haired fanatic shouted to Bowie and Crockett.

"Want me to take some pot shots at them with Old Betsy, Colonel?" the amiable Crockett offered with a grin.

Travis smiled in anticipation, but Bowie cut short his euphoria. "Buck, you know we can't actually kill them—it's not REALLY 1836," he cautioned the younger man, noting that strange look on Travis' face that came over him when he seemed to be in his other world.

Travis made a disagreeable face.

"Sir," a voice called out timorously to the commander, "How about a water cannon? That would blast them out of there but not actually hurt anyone."

The colonel turned toward the voice and stared with flashing eyes. He had never acknowledged the young black man's existence before. Anthony, wishing he had just kept his mouth shut, averted his eyes from the fiery commander.

"Boy, what is a water cannon?" Travis demanded, his eyes still fixed on Anthony.

Anthony summoned the courage to speak. "Sir, it's mounted on a truck and acts kind of like a real cannon, only it shoots out a really strong stream of water that will knock folks back but doesn't actually harm them. I can contact someone who has access to one, and we can borrow it. We could have it brought in through the employee entrance at night, aim it at the plaza, and let Santa Anna have it!"

The smile returned to the commander's face. "You actually know where we can get one?"

Anthony nodded. "Yes sir, I do. If you say the word, I'll be glad to arrange to borrow it." He never volunteered how on earth he knew

291

someone with access to a water cannon.

"Yes, as soon as possible—immediately—anything to get them off that sacred ground!" came the impatient reply.

While Santa Anna and his men slumbered, Anthony and his friend with the water cannon pulled up with the contraption on a truck, inched through the gate and up the pathway toward the front of the complex, and attached it to a hydrant. They positioned the weapon slightly to the side of the church but inside the compound gates, the barrel aimed toward the enemy troops on the plaza. When the Mexicans began to stir at dawn, the weapon was pulled in front of the gate and Col. Travis ordered "Joe" and his friend to let the enemy have it. Soon Spanish curses rang through the air. The colonel, not slightly concerned about the forthcoming water bill as he had no clue how that kind of thing worked, ordered the two men to keep firing throughout the day. The Mexicans moved as far to the back of the plaza as they could, but there was no complete protection if they were to hold their ground.

Finally, that night, the Generalissimo had had enough. He also had all of his reinforcements, just as in 1836. He ordered his men, led by Jorge Lavaca, to go around the Alamo complex and scale the relatively low wall at the back of the compound, come forward through the grounds, round up the defenders, and take the water cannon. It worked perfectly. The defenders, sound asleep, never knew what hit them, all of them suddenly finding angry and damp Mexican soldados standing over them with real bayonets, although everyone—or almost everyone—knew they would not use them. When they reached Travis, several men surrounded him, worried about an erratic reaction. One man roused the groggy commander, while the others aimed bayonets in his direction, but not too close.

"Colonel, you are our prisoner," Jorge announced to the still half-asleep Travis.

"Huh? What?" Travis started. Then it set in. "No! I will never submit to being your prisoner!" he shouted.

The men with the bayonets just stood there.

"Colonel, you will surrender the Alamo to us immediately," Jorge demanded sternly.

"Over my dead body!" came the answer.

292

Several of the soldados exchanged glances with looks indicating they were tempted to take him up on it.

At that point, the Alamo Rangers, who had called for backup, swarmed the reenactors, ordering everyone to stand down. They directed the Mexicans back to their camp and the water cannon sent back to wherever it had come from. Travis was yelling about the Mexicans being on sacred soil, and it took Bowie and Crockett to calm him down and shut him up. After bidding his friend with the water cannon adieu, Anthony's lips curled into a smile. The colonel was insane, that was clear, but now Anthony felt he could dare to tell his "master" that he was Joe, and that he was a Texian.

The Yellow Rose of Texas stared in the full-length mirror. She was ready for the big night. Finally, after all the pseudo-Alamo battles, cooking and planting demos in the dirt, and picking up Buck when he passed out, something "fun," as he liked to say was finally at hand. She had only finished the simple but gorgeous 1830's party dress the previous evening, barely in time. The frothy creation, in the delicate lemon lawn that almost pretended to be silk, had a full, gathered skirt that came to the ankle. Hem lengths were slightly shorter in the 1830's than they would be in the Victorian era. The bodice featured a pleated, crisscross drape affair in front and the wide gathered sleeves popular in the first half of the 1830's. Lori had pinned some silk yellow rose buds in her blonde hair. Her parents had been not only gracious, but enthusiastic about having the fandango at the house, although they did not dress up. Buck had simply not been able to get his head wrapped around the idea of a dance party on the Alamo grounds where his garrison had been slaughtered, and Lori appreciated that. Elena, Vicky, and Lori had been preparing hors d'oeuvres and desserts all day. Davy Crockett's fiddle and Andres and Len, in street clothes, on guitar would provide the music.

Most of the guests were members of the reenacting community. Dave and Mitch came in costume as did Raul. Vincente and Rosalia did, too, but Vincente wisely presented a Tejano impression, with Rosalia in a gorgeous silk Spanish senora dress and mantilla. Morena was there, her only nod to 1836 being the purple-gray shawl she wore at the March 6 ceremony. She had Melia and Tom in tow. Melia was in short shorts, a tight tank top, and flip-flops, Tom in jeans and a t-shirt—no Alamo clothes for them. Melia had mostly come for the opportunity to observe Travis and see what nutty stunt he might pull.

293

Bob had approached Lori the day before the event, finally getting up the nerve to ask about Leslie. Lori shrugged and said, "No big deal." He had wrestled with the decision as it was basically coming out to all the people he knew at work, but he felt it was time. She laughed as she remembered Bob asking if he thought Bowie would knife him or Travis would run him through with the sword. The Alamo, by its very nature, attracted tough he-man types. She assured him that it would be OK, then discreetly clued in the reenactors, who, to a man, seemed not to care. That was the easy part. She sat Buck down and told him, watching a stunned look cross his face. Although Old Texas was rampant with sexual escapades, Buck being a chief contributor, they tended to be heterosexual, or else the homosexuals had the sense not to commit their activities to a diary. He was familiar with the concept of homosexuality, having stumbled across it among all of that reading he did by candlelight. But he had never known anyone who was an admitted homosexual—until now. He confessed to Lori that he had seen the strange kiss between Bob and the man driving the white car on that rainy day and wondered about it. But Bob had been kind to him, especially with regard to overlooking the destruction of the pigsty for the sake of fortifying the Alamo and Bob's gift to Buck of the diary copy, and Buck did not want to pry. He admitted to Lori that he thought it was odd but then shrugged and said that, although strange and something he could not understand anyone wanting to do, it was part of that freedom for which he fought so hard.

The party was on. Davy was playing for the crowd, and couples were dancing on the patio. Bowie, standing next to where Davy was fiddling, had a bottle of something, probably Tequila, and was drinking straight from it, not bothering with a glass. John Williams, portraying Bonham now that he was out of a job as Travis, was there, sans horse, as the colonel would not be giving him any letters for a courier run tonight. He made a better Bonham than Travis, regardless of what Bonham actually looked like, as Williams clearly did not look like Travis. He did have the same thick South Carolina drawl, and it was funny to hear the two converse—almost a language of its own. Vicky, in jeans and a t-shirt, was dancing with one of the Tejano reenactors. Bob was dancing some sort of variant on the twist with Leslie, who was a thin middle-aged man with reddish blonde hair, a high forehead, and glasses. Melia, in her tiny denim cutoffs and tank top, was partnered with Tom, dancing current style to the old music, as they had no clue how to do historic dances. All the while, she was praying that the crazy colonel would not ask her for a dance. Anthony, as Joe, was circulating among the guests with a platter of hors d'oeuvres. Buck was standing next to the bar, but he did not have a glass in his hand. He was decked out in the new uniform, as handsome as a mutilated Alamo defender could be. One of the criticisms in revisionist literature made fun of Buck because of a diary entry regarding his purchase of pumps, men's shoes for evening wear in the Romantic period. It was another target for folks who did not like him, especially as the current usage of the term is restricted to women's high heels. On this occasion, the colonel, who no longer had any pumps, was wearing boots with his uniform.

Lori had deliberately delayed her entrance until everyone else was there, in place. She normally did not seek to attract attention, but the dress was so pretty and there was someone she desperately wanted to notice that in the world of 1836 she could be something other than a muddy farm girl. She opened the French doors onto the large patio. Crockett was on "Believe Me If All Those Endearing Young Charms," an apropos song written by Thomas Moore to show his badly scarred smallpox victim wife that he still loved her. Several guests heard the door and looked. Buck turned and stared. He knew Lori was pretty, but they had always been so closely engaged in some work project or health or military crisis that he had not spent too much time thinking about it. He didn't move—just kept staring, as she gracefully headed straight for him. When she reached him, he pulled her to him, saying softly in her ear, "Lori, you truly are my beautiful Yellow Rose," then gave her a kiss. The attendees, most of whom had been able to see this relationship more clearly than the two participants for a long time, clapped as the couple embraced.

Bowie, his speech slightly slurred, held up his bottle and proposed a toast to "Colonel Travis and his Yellow Rose!" He leaned back, took a swig, lost his balance, and fell in the pool, taking Davy and his fiddle with him.

While Raul and Vincente were helping Bowie and Crockett climb out of the pool, Andres and Len provided some Spanish guitar music, and a new round of dancing began. Buck asked Lori for the first dance. The congressman shook out his wet fiddle, then headed for some liquid refreshment. Bowie procured another bottle, again not bothering with a glass. Teetotaler Buck was not interested in the liquor. He was totally focused on Lori, and they shared all the dances. Soon Davy was back in action with his damp fiddle. They swirled to "Spanish Waltz," "Green Grow the Lilacs," "Will You Come to the Bower," "Bloom is on the Rye," "Rise Gentle Moon," "Flowers of Edinburg," "Welcome Here Again," and a reprisal of Buck's favorite, "Rosin the Beau." Not surprisingly, he was an adept dancer at old-time dancing. After the lively "Turkey in the Straw" and "Clare de Kitchen," the still dripping congressman played the sweet but sad "Long, Long Ago," as Buck and Lori swirled gracefully. Now she knew why Buck liked fandangos.

# BAPTISM

In his mind, Lyle Jones was seeing dollar signs as well as converts to his revisionist cause. He had weighed everything thoroughly and decided that he could milk the book signing routine one more time at the Alamo. Sales had been brisk at both of his previous efforts. A part of him wished that Travis would be on vacation—a concept unknown to the trapped defenders of 1836. But the colonel's antics, annoying and a bit scary as they were, attracted would-be purchasers as he unwittingly provided free entertainment and shock advertising for Jones. Long-suffering Mary was placing stacks of books on the ground on plastic at one side of the table, with a sales-ready small batch on the table. There were still no students, they having made themselves scarce after that first signing where Travis came across the table at the professor with the sword.

Anthony's water cannon had made a lasting impression on Travis. The colonel had already observed the Jones' van, with which he was now intimately familiar. Ed was trimming the shrubs on the Alamo grounds. Travis walked over to him.

"What can I do for you, sir?" Ed preempted the colonel as he saw Travis was getting ready to ask him something.

"When we did the seed planting, I got water for the new seeds by lowering a bucket into the acequia. A child asked me how come I didn't just get water out of the hose. Where is this hose?"

Ed gave him a perplexed look. He wondered what the crazy colonel had in mind this time, but he kept that thought to himself.

"Right this way, sir."

He led Travis to a spigot on the outside of the gift shop building. Attached to it was a long, curled up hose.

"You just turn this," Ed demonstrated, "And the water runs through the hose and out."

Travis studied it for a moment, twisted his mouth, then said, "I don't think that will be long enough. Do you have a longer one?"

"How long do you need? I can attach several of them together if you like. Also, there's a sprayer nozzle that can be attached to the end—makes it easier to adjust the amount of the spray. A fine spray is good for more delicate plants."

"Perfect! Yes, if you could round up several and put them together for me, I would appreciate it," Travis replied.

"How soon do you need it?" Ed asked.

"Could you do it right now?"

Ed dropped his trimmer and set to work snaking together a truly long hose for the colonel.

The books were stacked neatly, Mary had gone off to check out the latest at Morena's shop, and Lyle Jones was conversing with a man who had flipped through a copy of the book. Jones began his harangue about how awful folks in the 1830's were—on both sides.

"I'm not trying to beat my own drum, but, honestly, you will find some facts in here," he pointed to a copy of his book, "that other historians either did not find, or, shall I say, candidly, maybe chose not to find. It's all documented in the bibliography. As outlandish as some of stuff is—some of these guys were, quite frankly, kind of weird . . . ."

Travis did not wait for Jones to tell the man just how weird the colonel was. He was tired of being verbally pummeled by the professor. The spigot was already on full throttle, and Travis had moved to within striking distance with his hose train. He pressed the lever about midway down on the spray nozzle, opening the flood, and let Jones and his books have it. An unfortunate victim was the man who was asking about the book, but maybe he deserved it just for being interested. The colonel was not satisfied with a light shower. He rained water on Lyle Jones and destroyed considerable inventory—a bonus. Jones, soaking wet, stared at the plume of water coming toward him. He could just barely see Travis' unique clothing in back of the spray.

"Colonel," he yelled. "So help me God, I'm going to kill you deader than Santa Anna did if you don't stop interfering with my perfectly legal business! You just destroyed hundreds of dollars of inventory as well as making another scene!"

He shook his fist at Travis and started walking toward him through the spray. Travis pressed the trigger further, dousing Jones even more.

"Professor, as you can see, Santa Anna damaged me, but he did not kill me," the colonel shouted back. "You once said I got what I deserved at the Alamo. Well, you, sir, deserve far more than just this, but it does seem to be working right nicely!" he laughed.

Jones shook his fist again, swore at Travis, then turned around and stomped back to his ruined books. He tried to squeeze the excess water out of his sopping jacket. The colonel finally turned off the spray and simply stood and glared with a smirk on his face, then turned and dragged Ed's hose back to the spigot.

When Mary finished chatting with Morena and headed to the book table, there was water everywhere. There were no customers. There was no salable inventory. When she reached her fuming and dripping husband, all she could muster was, "What happened?"

"Crazy William Barret Travis—that's what happened," he growled.

Bob was still uneasy about the "Press Conference with General Santa Anna," but he had not felt he could nix it and risk seeming partial to the Texians. The "general," Luis Estrada in Vincente's uniform, was straightening his ornate jacket. He had the enormous bicorn hat, but he was not wearing it, as this performance was inside a small room at the left side of the long barracks, where a short film on the battle was usually shown. El Presidente was seated in a comfortable chair with several rows of benches facing him—meant for and usually filled with tourists watching the film. This time there were tourists crowding around, but a few real news people and a number of Alamo aficionados and scholars had claimed most of the seats. Bob stood at the podium, nodded to the general and introduced him, thanking him for coming all the way up from Mexico City for this event. The general, in turn, graciously thanked the Alamo for asking him to return to the scene of his victory. A few tourists stared at each other at this, but no one said anything. To no one's surprise, the first question, from a woman near the right end in the front row, was:

"General, in hindsight, do you see any way that all of this bloodshed

298

could have been averted?"

The general gave an elegant bow to the woman. "Senora, oh that I wish that had been the case! Sadly, we on the Mexican side have been painted as brutes and savages in this fight for Tejas. We are a generous, friendly, and welcoming people. The fact that we allowed people from everywhere to come and settle in our country, paying a pittance for land on which to establish themselves—and overlooking, to a degree, illegalities such as ignoring our state faith and bringing in slaves, which is against our collective conscience, shows our welcoming spirit. Unfortunately, some bad citizens were not satisfied with cheap land and waiving of the rules. They wanted to wrest a part of our country from Mexico—make it part of the United States of the North or a separate country. This was too much. This we could not abide. Therefore, we were forced to take action."

The woman raised her hand. "A follow-up, General, if you please?" she asked.

Santa Anna nodded with a charming smile, and she went on. "But did you have to massacre the Alamo garrison?" she asked point blank.

The general lowered his head slightly. "I much regret that action had to be taken," he said slowly. Luis was a good actor. "I believe, had the immigrants taken some simple actions earlier in the controversy, we might not have reached the point of the Alamo fight. For 4 years, the small group of bad citizens and land pirates fomented rebellion. Granted, many settlers, such as Senor Austin, fought this threat to peace, at least initially. But there were some who kept at it.

"Senor Travis, who later commanded at the Alamo and refused our offer to let him surrender, comes to mind. This young man had been stirring up trouble, creating incidents since 1832. We arrested him that year, but he did not learn his lesson. He actively advocated open rebellion, and he led a group of rebels commandeering a ship and forcing surrender of a Mexican garrison in 1835. We demanded that the settlers turn him over—put a price on his head, but he fled, and they protected him. Had we been able to collect and place Travis and the other ringleaders before a firing squad, it is possible we could have made clear to the colonists that insurrection would not be tolerated. Maybe we never would have gotten to the Alamo situation. The loss of life in the battle is to be regretted, although the elimination and burning of the enemy soldiers was a necessity." He paused, then, following the traditional story, added, "At least, thankfully, when we did reach the Alamo, we finally disposed of Travis, and I get some satisfaction at the thought of the buzzards picking at his roasted remains."

"The Hell you did, you lying, evil fiend from Satan!"

With the sword in his face, Luis summoned the courage to ask, "Eres inmortal?"

The audience laughed, but it was no laughing matter to Buck. He had the point of the sword at the general's throat.

"I ought to pin you against the wall for those comments!" the infuriated colonel shouted. "And I think I will!"

Two men grabbed Travis before he could plunge the sword into Luis' neck. The colonel promptly fainted.

Santa Anna gazed down on his adversary. "Senors y Senoras, I regret to say I think this press conference is over," the general stated the obvious, breathing a sigh of relief. Then, reverting to his native tongue, "Gracias por venir. Les deseo lo mejor en el trato con su joven comandante. No podia hacer nada con el. Tal vez puedas!"

Luisa was still savoring her victory over the President of the United States. Her legion had made news all over the country with their chant of thousands making it impossible for the President to be heard. But that did not help the local issue most on her mind—the crazy colonel. Two huge demonstrations were enough, for now anyway, but she had another idea.

"Angelo? Are you busy?" she shouted.

Her assistant came running. "Actually, no. I was tracking Hispanic political activities on the news. Nothing much going right now."

"I may have figured out how to take care of the Travis problem," Luisa informed him.

"Another rally? Do you think folks will really turn out a third time?" he asked.

"No, I don't, and that's obviously not going to be effective for this, anyway. The goal is to remove Travis," she answered.

"Remove him? You mean like use a real bullet this time?"

Luisa laughed. "No, I told you before, I wouldn't do that. He doesn't deserve that. But he really is off. I heard a report from a friend who heard from a friend, so you can't be sure it's true, but it sounds like him. He turned a water hose on a professor selling books the other day just because the professor has a very negative view of Travis in the revolution, wrote to that effect, and was telling his customers so. A news clip this morning showed him with the sword at the throat of a Santa Anna impersonator. It was some program billing itself as a press conference with the general. I am thinking about finding a friendly judge who could issue orders for involuntary admission to a mental health facility."

Angelo was still laughing at the vision of the colonel with his hose. "Perfect! That zeroes in on Travis without involving anyone else—takes him out of the Alamo to stop fueling whatever extra attention they get because of him and takes that dangerous sword out of his hands." Angelo beamed at his boss. "Want me to look up judges and find one who may be amenable?"

She nodded. "Oh, and one more thing—just to be sure what we do is as current as possible, do you have a source for a friend and a couple of soldado outfits? I was thinking you could see if you can trigger a sword response—but, by all means, be careful if you do!"

Angelo smiled. "Yes, I think that can be arranged."

Later that afternoon, Angelo, in his hot and uncomfortable Mexican infantryman outfit, borrowed through connections with Luis Estrada, strode toward the old church with his best friend, Jose Salinas, identically attired. Jose was rather clueless about what was going on but thought it might be entertaining and so had agreed to the stunt. Angelo had proven to Luisa long ago that he would do just about anything for the cause, but this was his first ever dress up event. Knowing nothing about military protocol or activities of the 1830's except what he hurriedly read on the Internet in preparation for his performance, he was a bit nervous. It didn't take long to locate the colonel. Travis had just left his office and was heading toward the church when he saw the enemy soldiers.

"Halt! Get out of here immediately!" he shouted, running toward them as they caught his eye. He reached for the sword.

"Watch out! He knows how to use that thing!" Angelo hurriedly

301

warned Jose.

"You didn't tell me about that part!" his stunned friend said in alarm.

The colonel was at them. He took one swipe, more as incentive for the Mexicans to leave than to cause any damage.

"I mean it! Leave now or you will regret it. There are to be no Mexican troops at the Alamo!" Travis yelled, his face showing his agitation.

"You must be Col. Travis?" Angelo queried hesitantly, although it was obvious who the man was.

"Yes! I'm Col. Travis, and I'm in command here . . . ."

Jose looked around, and seeing no other defenders, with temerity mixed with mirth in his voice, interrupted, "In command of what?"

That didn't stop the colonel. "Maybe you didn't hear, but the governor placed me back in command of the Alamo. I am ordering you to leave immediately!"

The two "Mexican soldiers" stared at each other, not too sure what to do now. Angelo ad libbed it.

"Sir, we are the advance guard of General Santa Anna's forces. We will not leave, and we will take your position!" he tried to sound military.

"Victory or Death!" Travis yelled, swinging the sword at them and just missing Angelo.

Jose, who was stockier than his friend, grabbed the colonel by the shoulders, and the sword came free, falling to the ground. Travis was in a rage, shouting for them to leave and that they were defiling the sacred ground where his command was murdered.

"Yeah," Jose said to Angelo. "I'll be honest, at first I didn't get this, but I see what you mean. He really is crazy."

Travis was still yelling, and some of the tourists were staring, staying back somewhat from the scene. Finally, the colonel turned very pale, then collapsed.

"Let's get out of here!" Angelo advised Jose. "Walk fast and keep it orderly, but we need to head on out."

Buck was standing with "Bowie" and "Crockett" in front of the church when a patrol car pulled up. Police didn't have to worry about permits. Two officers got out of the car and walked toward the Big Three.

"Is one of you William Barret Travis?" the officer who had been driving asked.

"Yes, I'm Col. Travis," Buck replied.

"Colonel, first, I am honored to meet you—I'd like to shake your hand," the policeman said, stepping toward Travis.

Buck held out his hand, and the other officer asked if he could shake the commander's hand as well.

The officer who had driven stepped back, his voice rather unsteady, and said, "Colonel, I can't tell you how much I hate to do this, but we have been tasked with bringing you in as a result of a court order requiring you to submit to a mental health evaluation."

Travis looked stricken, but he had no idea what the man was talking about, only that it couldn't be good.

"A what?" he asked, all he could bring himself to say.

"Someone who is concerned about safety issues with all the sword-waving incidents has petitioned the court to have you declared mentally ill and placed in an institution where they help with that kind of thing," the officer tried to explain.

Bowie and Crockett stared, unbelieving. Buck pulled the sword from the scabbard and pointed it at the officers.

"Colonel, please, that is just the kind of action that led to this and that will not help you get past this incident," the officer pled with him.

Travis swung the sword at him, the other officer grabbed the colonel from the back, and they wrested the weapon from him. Travis' white hat fell to the ground.

"I'm truly sorry, sir, but we have to do this," the first officer told Buck with sincere regret in his voice as they led him, arms pinned behind his back and yelling to Bowie and Crockett to get help, to the police car, shielding his head as they put him in back and headed off.

Davy picked up the hat and the sword, and, with Bowie, headed for Lori and Bob. But no one knew where the police had taken their commanding officer.

The car stopped at the receiving door at the psychiatric building at the hospital where Buck had been taken when he was found at the dig and numerous times since. The two officers, one on each side, led him in.

"Got a petition for mental health evaluation for possible involuntary admission to the facility," the driver told the woman at the desk.

"I see," she said slowly, looking at Buck's odd clothing. "And who do you think you are?" she asked him.

"I'm Col. Travis—I have to get back to the Alamo," he practically shouted at her.

"Uh huh," she nodded.

The officer stepped in. "No, ma'am, he REALLY IS Col. Travis. You did read about that in the news, surely? Everyone knows about it."

"Oh, yeah, I do remember that." She stared at the angry countenance on the ravaged face. "So what did you do, Colonel, that landed you here?"

"I don't know. I do not understand any of this. I have to get back to my post!" he shouted.

"Luisa Montoya, the lady who led the two big rallies recently, petitioned to have the colonel declared insane because of all his sword waving," the officer explained.

She shrugged. "All right, we'll do what we have to do under the law."

She called someone in the back, and a burly nurse no shorter than 6 and 1/2 feet came up, rather roughly pushing the angry colonel to the back.

304

Travis was placed in a tiny room, the big nurse ordering him to lie on the examining table. He said a doctor would soon be in for his initial evaluation, then closed the door. Buck heard the door lock as the man left. Shortly thereafter, a small, older man with wire-rimmed glasses and a balding pate unlocked the door and came in.

"I'm Dr. Rogers," the man introduced himself. "I understand you are the hero of the Alamo, Col. Travis?" he asked.

"Yes, I'm Col. Travis, but my status at the Alamo does not seem to help me here," Buck said angrily to the doctor.

"I'm truly sorry, Colonel. None of us want this to be happening. But they've got a court order, so we have to go through the motions. My hope is that we can get everything checked out and send you back to your post in a few days at most. But you have to work with us to make that happen."

Travis made a face, but he didn't say anything.

"We're going to do some brain scans. There's no doubt you have some abnormalities due to your wound. We got your test results from when they did your surgery. The fainting that you are prone to is part of that. I want to see if anything else shows up," the doctor explained.

"But I thought they already did all of that after they operated on me?" Travis said in frustration. "I don't understand."

"I know you don't, Colonel. I'm not sure I do. But the gist of all this is that the anti-Alamo people . . . ."

"Mexicans!" the colonel cut in.

"Well, Hispanics who don't much care for the Alamo story, yes, I've got to agree with you on that one," the doctor admitted. "But they came up with the court order as a way to get you out of the Alamo and out of sight. They used the numerous incidents that have made the news where you took after someone, usually Hispanic, with your sword as grounds for the request to the court. So keep that in mind for the future. Think before grabbing the sword as it could land you in trouble with your enemies," the doctor advised.

"I have to defend the Alamo from these people. The cannon don't work, I have no troops—all I've got left is my sword!" the colonel yelled.

305

"Colonel, calm down! This is exactly what they're talking about," the doctor urged in a gentle voice. "Honestly, I don't think most of the people you went after—certainly not the two Mexican government officials who met Mr. Gordon about some artifact, the cadets who were met with your hastily thrown up defenses, or Professor Jones—were really going to storm the Alamo and kill everyone. You do know that, don't you?"

Travis stared at him. "Yes, I guess I do when I think about it. But what about folks who are dressed like Santa Anna and his soldados? How am I supposed to know?"

"I think this is where the real problem is coming in," the doctor noted. "You do have some difficulty shifting between your life in 1836, really just the battle, and present day. The Mexican army, under whoever their head general is down there now, is not going to march up here and storm the fort."

"But that's what we thought in 1836—or at least we didn't think they would get here as fast as they did—and look what happened!" Travis was getting worked up again.

"I don't know how to explain it to you. It's a 181-year disconnect. But I promise you it just can't and won't happen. Things aren't done that way with large land armies in today's military. It's all different. You really do have nothing to fear in that regard. There will be protest groups like Luisa Montoya led twice. That kind of thing is a fact of life all over this country these days, but not a true army with cannon and rifles. With Mexican government officials, protesters, tourists who happen to be from Mexico, or even Mexican-side reenactors at the fort, you need to find a way to let it go."

"But the Mexicans killed my entire garrison—murdered them, then mutilated them—look at me if you want to see what that looks like, then insulted them by burning them."

"I know," the doctor said with true sympathy. "I honestly can't know how terribly hard it must be for you, sir. But you have got to try to get straight that it was Santa Anna—and he's long gone—and his men who did this to you and your command, not anyone now. There will be people who do not like you—like this Luisa Montoya, but there's not a large army that intends to attack the Alamo and kill everyone there. Do you understand me at all?"

306

"Sort of," Buck murmured. "I will try to be more discerning regarding the Mexicans, but I don't think I can ever forgive and forget . . . ."

"No one would ever expect that, Colonel. Texas will never forgive and forget what happened to you," the doctor replied. "Now, let me order the brain scan tests. You just rest here for a few minutes. It won't take long, then we'll move you into a room. I'm guessing this whole thing will take about 48 to 96 hours if it plays out the way they usually do. Then, hopefully, we can get you back to the Alamo."

After the tests, Travis was led to another tiny room, painted stark white and with no windows. The only furnishings were a cot, a small counter and sink attached to the wall, and a toilet. It was basically a cell. He lay down on the cot, and the big nurse locked the door behind him as he left. Buck saw no one until a meal was brought on a tray and set on the counter by a silent staff member. Travis turned to look, but he did not get up. The same routine occurred, like clockwork, the next morning, noon, and evening. The trays sat untouched.

Finally, the next morning, Dr. Rogers unlocked the door and came in. Travis didn't even turn. He just lay facing the wall.

"Colonel, I understand you are not eating?" the man asked. Travis ignored him. "Sir, we'll have to put you on fluids if this keeps up. It's not making matters any easier. You've got to eat," he advised.

Travis finally, weakly, turned over to face the doctor. "Go away. You have won. You have defeated me as I am powerless to do anything in this awful place. But you cannot control me—I am going to be with my garrison. Now get out of here!"

He tried to sound determined, but he was so weak that it did not come out quite that way. He attempted to turn back toward the wall but was not strong enough to make the movement. The doctor came over to him and sat on the edge of the bed.

"Colonel, please. We do not want to hurt you in any way. We want you back at the Alamo. But there are things you have to do—to play the game, so to speak, for us to get to that point . . . ."

"I don't play games," came the angry response.

"Yes, I've pretty much figured that one out, Colonel," the doctor

307

laughed. "But I'm going to order that you be put on fluids. We're not going to have the brave hero of the Alamo die in this little room because of some confusion and misunderstandings. It will be uncomfortable for you, and I'll pretty much guarantee you won't like it, but it's a necessary step to keep you functioning until we can get you out of here."

Five minutes later, the burly nurse and a black man nearly the same size arrived and took the weak Alamo commander by the arms down the hall. He was placed on another bed. One man held him in place, the colonel trying futilely to fight but too weak to do much, as restraints were placed on him so that he would not pull the tubing loose when he was hooked up to the fluids. Travis did yell in protest—until he fainted.

"I like him much better when he's unconscious," the burly nurse said to his colleague.

"Yeah, I can see why," came the answer.

Travis did not remember the trip back to his tiny room. All he knew was that he was back on the cot in the claustrophobic space. As before, all he could do was lie there. In the early evening, a silent staff member brought the tray as usual, and the colonel never even turned to acknowledge the act. He prayed to the God he hoped was really there that this would end soon and that he would be at peace, with his men, away from all the sadistic and cruel foes who tormented him. Finally, he fell asleep.

Buck was jarred awake when the nurse and his sidekick appeared over him. He hadn't even heard the door unlock and the two men come in.

"Time for a bath—it's been almost 3 days," the nurse said in a gruff voice. "And we need to get some clean clothes on you."

"I have no other clothes. I am fine. Leave me alone," the colonel replied angrily.

"Orders are orders—you know that being a military man," the nurse threw in his face.

The two grabbed him by his shoulders and led him down the hall again, this time to some sort of a communal shower—Buck had never seen anything like it before. They sat him down on a bench.

"Now get undressed or we'll do it for you," the big nurse commanded.

"No, I tell you I will not submit to this. Take me back to my room NOW!" Travis shouted.

Without a word, the large black man took hold of Travis while the other man started untying the sash. The yells were futile. Buck soon found himself with wet hair, in a hospital gown, lying on his cot. Tears streamed down his ruined face. How long would this go on before God freed him from this prison?

There was another silent entry and untouched food tray, as Buck lay in despair, weak and sick, and hoping for the end. Finally, Dr. Rogers appeared again. Buck did not acknowledge him.

"Colonel, are you strong enough to turn toward me?" the doctor asked kindly.

"Go to Hell!" came the reply, weak but the anger unmistakable.

The doctor laughed. "I would hate to have been one of Santa Anna's men!" he exclaimed. "You don't give up, do you?"

The Alamo commander finally turned over slowly, hatred showing on his pale face, but he just glared at the doctor, not saying anything.

"Well, Colonel, maybe this will lighten your mood a little—we're at the end of the 96-hour period. And even better, the state challenged the court order and won. You are free to go back to defending your post," the doctor announced with a little smile.

Buck was not through with him. "So you held me against my will and tortured me for 4 days, only to now let me go free? Why?" he demanded.

"Unfortunately, that's the way the court system works," the doctor said. "Our hands were tied. We had to just ride it out, although I was pretty sure all along that the greatest hero in Texas history would not be declared incurably insane and consigned to life in an institution. Texas simply wouldn't stand for it. Although, I'll have to confess, I do think you're a little unbalanced, but maybe you have to be to deal with Santa Anna. Anyway, you can go."

"How do I get back? I do not drive one of those cars, you know."

"Yes, I do know. We'll have the police take you back same as they got you here," the doctor explained. "We need to get you dressed . . . ."

"I don't know what they did with my clothes," Travis interrupted. "They took them from me when they bathed me—haven't seen them since."

"I'll take care of that right now, and we'll get you up and out of here."

An hour later, the still somewhat angry colonel was whisked out of the building and into a patrol car for the short ride back to the Alamo.

Someone spotted the cop car as it rolled up, and the word was out to Bob and Lori via cell immediately. They rushed to the scene. As the officers got the unsteady colonel out of the back seat and standing upright, Lori rushed to him, holding onto him.

"Buck, are you OK? We've been worried sick—had no idea where you were!" she exclaimed, tears streaming down her face.

Buck tried to take a step away from the car and fell, Lori and Bob keeping him from hitting the pavement.

"He's extremely weak—was apparently very defiant the entire time he was at the mental health unit. He was picked up pursuant to a court order to examine him for involuntary treatment. He kept refusing to eat and yelling threats to the staff," one of the officers clued them in.

"Yeah, defiance is who he is. I think I know a short-term remedy for the weakness—don't think there is a fix for the defiance," Lori said, envisioning Buck's reactions. The police got in their car and headed out, and Lori and Bob guided the weak colonel toward Morena's fudge counter.

Dave and Mitch were setting up for another of their frequent demos featuring Crockett's and Bowie's frontiersman skills. The two, being the most famous names in Alamo lore, attracted the biggest crowds of any of the numerous demonstrations of 1836 life at the old mission. Lori was standing in the front of the crowd, slightly to the right, dressed in her frontier dress, as she had cooked cactus about an hour before.

As Davy was about finished showing the crowd the loading process for Old Betsy, one of the spectators shouted, "Say, aren't there three of you guys on top?"

Crockett and Bowie both looked in his direction. Bowie answered him.

"You must be referring to Col. Travis? He's around here somewhere—probably writing more of those damn letters pleading for help. But his weapon of choice is that sword—the one he drew the line with!"

Many in the crowd, having either taken a guided tour or seen the IMAX movie, at least made the connection and laughed.

"Now, folks, let me tell you what we're gonna do," Crockett started. "Have you heard the tale of William Tell, that fella who shot an apple off his son's head with an arrow?"

Some in the crowd nodded or said something in the affirmative. Others just stared.

Davy went on: "We're gonna do something kinda on that order, only I'm gonna use my tomahawk to take an apple off of someone's head," he said in his twangy voice. The frontiersman did not tell his audience that the tomahawk was a stage prop, rubber and painted to look like the real thing.

"I volunteer to put the apple on my head!" one teen, about 15, interrupted, waving his arm to get Crockett's attention, as his horrified mother moved toward him.

"Sorry, son, but there's regulations against it, as I understand," Davy apologized to him. "We've gotta have someone from our 1836 folks," he

311

explained, meaning the reenactors.

The mother looked relieved, and the boy looked disappointed and stepped back one step but still eagerly stared toward Crockett, who was panning the crowd, looking for Texian Association members.

"Say, Juan, how about it? Can I take an apple off your head?" Crockett called to Raul, who was in his Juan Seguin getup, standing off to the side under a pecan tree.

"No, Senor, I think I will decline your kind offer," Seguin replied with a smile. "I would like to keep my hair today."

Crockett started his search anew. Finally, his gaze settled on Lori, as she was the only other person in the area dressed in 1836 garb.

"Ma'am—Miss Clayton, I normally wouldn't ask this of a lady, but seeing as there's no one else available . . . ," he started hesitantly.

"There's Col. Bowie," Lori quickly replied, pointing to the knife-fighter.

"He's got to show these folks what to do with a knife . . . ."

Some of the people in the crowd laughed. The commander walked up at that moment.

"What's going on?" he asked simply.

"Colonel, glad to see you," Davy greeted Travis. "I just asked Miss Clayton if she would mind me taking an apple off the top of her head with my tomahawk here." He showed the weapon to the colonel.

"She will not consent to that!" Travis replied quickly.

"Now Buck, I don't mind, really," Lori said. "The congressman never misses . . . ."

Travis cut her off. "I am in command here, and I absolutely forbid it!" Buck said in his commander voice. "Why didn't you ask Bowie?" he added, aiming an annoyed look at Crockett.

"That's what Miss Clayton asked, but Col. Bowie will be following me immediately with a demonstration regarding his knife," Crockett explained.

Lori and Buck exchanged puzzled glances.

"And you are insinuating what?" Buck asked.

"Nothing at all, sir. Just letting you know that Col. Bowie has another job to perform." Somewhat desperate for a volunteer and persistent to boot, Crockett continued: "Sir, I hate to be presumptuous, but would you consent to volunteer?"

Folks in the crowd were snickering.

"Might as well," Bowie interjected, looking at his knife. "Colonel Travis already has one hole in his head."

Another round of laughter ensued from the audience. Travis gave him an angry glare, but he turned to Crockett.

"All right, then, if it will get this whole thing over with, I'll do it." He took off the planter hat and handed it to a worried Lori.

"Buck, you don't need another hole in your head—they might not be able to fix you a second time! Don't do it!" she pled.

"I thought you said the congressman never misses?" he reminded her. "No, I'm confident he can hit the apple," Buck replied with no trace of fear in his voice.

"Guess we need to get an apple—forgot that part," Crockett said, to laughs from the audience. Bowie shook his head, still looking at his knife.

"I feel like I'm aiding and abetting, but I'll get one—think there's a big bowl of them in the kitchen," Lori said, starting in that direction.

"Get a green one if there are any," Crockett called to her.

She stopped and stared at him. "Why?"

"Under the circumstances, with this volunteer, green will be easier to see than red," he replied.

Travis never flinched. Bowie laughed.

313

Lori was back in a few minutes, and Crockett directed Travis to where he wanted him to stand, then placed Lori's green apple on the red hair. The colonel stood stiffly as if at attention. Davy stood directly in front of Travis. He judged the distance carefully, staring at the red hair with the green apple perched on top. Travis was still ramrod straight. Crockett calculated once more, then threw the hawk. The apple flew behind Travis' head. The colonel came forward to congratulate Crockett for not killing him, and the crowd cheered.

Bowie turned to the frontiersman, saying in a voice loud enough for all to hear: "Too bad you're so good, Crockett. Would've been kind of nice for Travis to have a matched pair!"

Lori and Buck walked away from the Crockett & Bowie Show. An impromptu concert was going on down the walkway, one costumed man playing a rather beaten-up old fiddle, the other, in a fine tenor voice, singing along to the tune of the "Yellow Rose of Texas":

> "He's Moses Rose of Texas
> And today nobody knows
> He's the one who left the Alamo
> The night before the foe
> Came storming up across the walls
> And killed the men inside
> But Moses Rose of Texas
> Is the one who never died.
>
> "When gallant Colonel Travis
> Drew a line down in the sand,
> Everyone stepped over
> But one solitary man.
> They called him Rose the Coward,
> And they called him Yellow Rose,
> But it takes brav'ry to stand alone,
> As God Almighty knows.
>
> "He said, 'I'm not a coward,
> I just think it isn't right,
> For me to throw my life away,
> In someone else's fight.
> I have no quarrel with the Mexicans,
> Nor with the Texians, too.'
> So Moses Rose of Texas,

314

He bade the men adieu.

"Whenever you're up against it,
Pressure from your peers,
A challenge to your manhood,
Or frightened by the jeers,
Remember that discretion
Is valor's better part,
And let the life of Moses Rose
Put courage in your heart.

"So shed a tear for Travis,
And Davy Crockett, too,
And cry for old Jim Bowie,
They saw the battle through.
But when you're finished weeping,
And you're finished with your wail,
Then give a grin for Moses Rose
Who lived to tell the tale!"

Lori and Buck stood staring. At first Buck had a disagreeable look on his face. But he pretty quickly picked up on the tongue-in-cheek recounting of the story, mocking the one man who had headed out when presented with Travis' challenge to the garrison. A crowd had gathered, and many of them recognized the colonel from the apple performance or otherwise. At the end of the song, the spectators turned to Travis and cheered, saluting the brave young commander who had asked his men to die with him.

Bob had avoided telling Buck about Hispanic Heritage Day, always eventually intending to say something but not quite being able to get the words out, then shifting it to the back of his mind. Now it was here, and he had procrastinated to the point where it was too late. The event was starting, and Travis was on campus, presumably scratching out something with that quill in his dark little hovel of an office. The program details were a bit sketchy. The goal was implicit in the name of the event—to highlight Hispanic lives and contributions over the long history of the old Mission San Antonio de Valero and focus on that aspect of the Alamo. Folks in costume as friars, Native Americans, and Spanish soldiers of the 18th Century were out in force on the Alamo grounds, strolling across the lush grass, some doing demonstrations of an even earlier time than Lori's demos.

Although the colonel might not like it, Bob was not too worried about

315

this aspect of the day. The anticipated conclusion, however, was another matter. As a wrap-up to Hispanic activity over the Alamo timeline, someone had the bright idea of bringing in El Presidente and his little army to play *El Deguello* and march, or, in the case of Santa Anna, ride, into the fortress. Not having any defenders available to kill and maim would hopefully make this look more peaceful than March 6, and the colorful uniforms, huge hats, and spectacular horses with their accoutrements were sure to be a crowd pleaser. But Bob was worried that not quite everyone on the Alamo grounds would be pleased. He tried to persuade Lori to take the day off and take the colonel somewhere, but she had work to do. The fact was that it had reached a point where Buck wanted to be where Lori was, and he always wanted to be at the Alamo. Vincente had hesitantly agreed to reprise his March 6 Santa Anna role when asked, but he warned Bob that he must keep the colonel away or he would ruin the closing ceremony. Throughout the day, while friars from the College of Santa Cruz de Queretaro prayed and the Native Americans cooked cactus in much the same way pioneer Lori would in the next century, the colonel mostly kept to himself. He did take one stroll across the grounds, seemingly looking for something or someone, then headed back to his office. So far, so good.

Vincente was adjusting his enormous hat. He had pretty much ordered Andres to don his bugler uniform one more time and, with a new bugle paid for by his dad, join the procession and play *El Deguello*, as he was the only musically inclined member of Vincente's entourage. Ciro was there for moral support and because he liked dressing up as a Mexican soldado. The general's staff—Enrique, Tomas, and Luis, were there as well, and a few regular soldados on foot. The general and his staff on horseback slowly came in front of the church, Andres nervously sounding "slit throat." The few soldados on foot followed the horsemen. With Andres sounding *El Deguello*, and the largely Hispanic crowd cheering, no one heard the door fly open in the long barracks and the opposition, sword in the air, coming at a run. Travis was shouting, waving the sword dramatically, and ordering the Mexican army to leave the premises. Lori, in her ragged old rose dress, casually walked out of the gift shop on break and stopped, frozen, staring.

"Oh no, here we go again," Enrique said to Vincente.

"I guess pepper night at Ramale's wasn't enough to overcome his base instincts with regard to Santa Anna!" Vincente laughed.

But the colonel was heading straight at them, sword in the air.

"How long until he yells 'Victory or Death'?" Enrique queried as the

Mexicans calmly awaited the Texian foe.

General Santa Anna pulled up his sleeve to reveal a thoroughly modern watch. "Probably right about now," he laughed.

"Victory or Death! Leave immediately, or I promise you, you will face the latter!" yelled the angry colonel. Vincente and Enrique turned to each other, raised their eyebrows, and smiled.

Andres was trying desperately to ignore the frenzied Texian and concentrate on his music. He knew this would happen and had so wished his dad had not forced him to come. Ciro had a smirk on his face. The staff officers were laughing, as were some of the soldados.

Travis reached the horsemen and took a swipe at Vincente's mount. The horse seemed a bit spooked, maybe remembering the unpleasant episode in March. Still yelling, the colonel ran toward the back of the animal, waving the sword.

"Oh, no, Colonel, I'm wise to that one," Vincente said in Spanish, quickly turning his horse and blocking the colonel from stabbing it in the rear. El Presidente decided to try a new tactic. Trying to show no fear, he dismounted in the face of the enemy, his staff at the ready to intervene if the Texian got too close.

"Colonel, is it too much to ask that we have one day to commemorate Hispanic culture in this place . . . ?"

"Yes! There should not be any Hispanic anything in this place. It is a sepulcher—a shrine to the brave Texian defenders. I will not have it defaced by those who murdered and mutilated and incinerated my command!" Travis shouted.

The colonel was so worked up that it was clear he was not seeing Vincente but truly was faced with Santa Anna. Vincente saw the strange look on Travis' face and knew he was off in that other world, but he did not know how to bring him back to reality. Vincente took a step toward the infuriated colonel, but Travis did not back down. Instead, he came at Vincente at a run, the sword swinging wildly. Travis was on Vincente with the sword, just barely missing him with one swing. El Presidente, his huge hat falling off, ingloriously took off. His troops stared as the enraged Travis chased him across the plaza, yelling "Victory or Death" and various broken-Spanish curses to Mexicans in general and Santa Anna in particular.

The crowd and incoming tourists stood back as the overdressed general ran as fast as his middle-aged legs could carry him with the sword-wielding young Texian right behind him, shouting one threat after another. Lori ran after them, truly concerned that someone was going to get hurt this time. Buck was totally out of control and in 1836, and Vincente was actually in danger if Buck could catch up with him.

They ran toward the north wall, Vincente taking a quick look for traffic but never really hesitating in crossing the street, just missing getting hit by a truck. Buck was right behind him. Still not used to traffic, he did not look, so concentrated was he on destroying Santa Anna. He was lucky. Lori, bringing up the rear, glanced at the traffic, then ran into the street. In the bright overhead glare of the sun, she did not see one oncoming car. It grazed her, the wheel catching on her long skirt and dragging her forward a few feet before pulling free. She cried out. The driver stopped, and other drivers, realizing something had happened, stopped their vehicles. Buck heard the cry and turned, then saw Lori sitting in the street. He lowered the sword, about faced, and ran to her. Vincente heard something, then saw that his pursuer was now going the other direction and that there was something in the road. He ran to see what had happened.

Buck was kneeling at Lori's side. She looked up at him, tears in her eyes. She was holding her ankle and crying slightly, assuring him quietly that she was OK. Vincente was now standing there.

"I'll call an ambulance," he said, fumbling in the pocket inside his ornate and heavily embroidered general's tunic. "Lori, are you sure you are all right?" he asked. She nodded.

"No, can't we just take her in the car?" Buck pleaded. "I don't want to wait for an ambulance. We need to take her now!" he said, not fully understanding the value of medical transport.

Buck very carefully picked up Lori, gathering her torn skirt. She let out a little cry. The traffic on Houston was still stopped, drivers treated to the unlikely sight of the rival Battle of the Alamo commanding officers working together trying to help Lori.

Vincente asked her again if she was OK.

"I'm OK, really, just my ankle hurts," Lori told them.

"Vincente, will you drive us?" Buck turned to El Presidente, his face

318

one big worry.

A stunned Vincente, who had just fished out the phone, replied with a smile, "Do you REALLY want General Santa Anna to take you to the hospital, Colonel? I bet that's the first and only time Col. Travis ever asked for help from the Generalissimo," he quipped. "But, yes, let's get off the street and to the car."

"Yes! I'd ask the Devil himself—guess I just did. We need to get help for Lori!"

Lori laughed through her tears. In a choice between battle with Santa Anna in 1836 and helping her now, he had chosen her. Buck slowly started across the plaza with his precious burden. The horse trailer was hitched to Vincente's truck, so they crammed into Lori's car for the ride to the hospital, Lori in the front passenger side with the seat all the way back, and Buck cramped and sitting sideways in the backseat.

Not 10 minutes later, Buck may actually have been right for once—it was as fast or faster than an ambulance would have been, they were there. Buck carried Lori in the emergency room door and gently placed her in a waiting room chair, then marched up to the desk, followed by Vincente.

"My lady has been in a car accident . . . on Houston Street—she needs looking after," he said in his quaint way.

"You're from the Alamo," the desk clerk stared at him with a deadpan look. "What is it that you people DO over there that's always getting you over here?"

He just stared at her blankly. Vincente grinned but didn't say anything.

When Lori was called back for examination, Buck lifted her from her chair. Vincente followed. The nurse just stared.

"Hello, ma'am. I'm General Santa Anna, and these are my long-time friends, Col. William Barret Travis and his lady friend, Miss Lori Clayton," Vincente introduced everyone.

"I think I'm going to ask if I can move to the night shift," the stunned woman replied. "This job is beginning to get to me. Now come again?"

Vincente laughed. "We've come from the Alamo—do reenactments there. That's why we're all dressed up like this—except for him," he pointed to Buck. "He's really from the Alamo. Y'all helped bring him back so to speak," he elaborated.

The woman was nodding, her eyebrows raised, at this point. "You know, the psychiatric ward is to the left. Take the elevator, and go to the third floor—there's a connector," she pointed, but with a smile. "Now, seriously, what can we do for you?" she turned to Lori, still in Buck's arms.

"I think I broke my ankle," Lori said softly. "It hurts, but, otherwise, I'm fine."

"I'm almost afraid to ask this question, but how did you do it?" the nurse queried.

"Uh, the short answer is that I got hit by a car . . . ." Lori hesitated.

"I'm assuming there's a story behind this?" the woman asked.

"Yeah, there is. Colonel Travis was chasing General Santa Anna off the Alamo grounds, and I was running after them to stop the colonel from killing the general with his sword. We all ran across Houston Street. They made it. I didn't."

The nurse was shaking her head and staring. She pointed. "Like I said, the psychiatric ward is to the left and up to the third floor."

But she did lead Buck to a hospital bed, where he gently set Lori down. The nurse took a look at Lori's swollen left ankle.

"Yes, you've done something to it—either a really bad sprain or a break. I'm sure the doctor will want to do X-rays. He'll be in shortly," she said with a little smile.

The emergency room doctor was a small Filipino man, middle-aged. When he walked into the cubicle, he gave the same stare that the other hospital staff had given. He tried to ignore the military men, looking only at Lori.

"And ma'am, what seems to be the problem?"

"I was grazed by a car on Houston Street. The wheel caught my dress, and I was dragged a little. Everything feels fine except my ankle got turned.

It hurts and is kind of swollen," she explained.

The doctor looked at her. The dirty frontier dress was shoved up above her lower legs, the torn part of the skirt hanging down over the edge of the bed. One ankle clearly was much larger than the other. The man ordered X-rays as the nurse had predicted, and the rival commanders from the Battle of the Alamo sat down to wait.

A half-hour later, they wheeled Lori back in, the doctor arriving shortly and pronouncing that she did, indeed, have a minor fracture at the ankle. She would have to wear a boot. Since it was her left ankle, if she was careful, she would be able to drive after a couple days of rest. He ordered her boot, and she was wheeled off while the military sat for another wait. Finally, Lori was wheeled back in the room. She was given the option of crutches or a knee scooter for the first week. She chose the crutches. Buck lifted her and carried her to the car, Lori having phoned to tell her family what had happened and that someone would have to meet them at the Alamo so that Vincente could get his truck and the Claytons could get Lori's car home. Robert and Elena were on their way, with Vicky riding shotgun.

"You know, the last time this happened, it was pepper night at Ramale's. Just so happens it is tonight. Anyone want to go?" Vincente asked when Robert, Elena, and Vicky arrived.

"You're on," Buck answered quickly before anyone else had a chance to say anything.

"Lori, are you up to it?" Vincente asked.

"I'm in a torn-to-pieces 1836 outfit and have a boot on my foot, but, if you don't think anyone will stare too much, yeah," she replied.

"I think it will be OK," Vincente laughed. "They may give you a look or two, but I was thinking we could all go straight from here. With the colonel and myself looking the way we do, I don't think you have much to worry about! I called Enrique, and he got Tomas to take care of the horses, so I don't have to deal about that. I'm going to give Rosalia a call and see if she wants to meet us there."

"Lori, don't worry about folks staring—you're a whole lot more appealing to look at than we are!" Buck added.

She smiled sweetly, all the while tying the torn piece of the dress hem in a knot so it would not drag the floor.

Rosalia said she would meet them, and she came with Juana in tow.

This evening, in addition to the usual jalapeno contest, there was an extra—someone had brought in some Carolina Reapers, the hottest pepper on the Scoville scale. Vincente knew this was in the offing, and the name of the pepper just seemed to suit the South Carolinian Travis. Vincente did not know whether he wanted to try eating one of these things—or possibly more. But it would be fun to dare the colonel to see how he would react. From the reputation this pepper had—and the numerous YouTube videos showing the agony of folks eating them, it might be that the Reaper would finally do in the Palmetto State native. Considering the colonel's rash nature, Vincente would have to be careful that Travis did not go overboard on a dare and fall victim to a pepper when Santa Anna could not kill him.

This contest worked differently from the one involving plates of jalapenos. Each contestant got 60 seconds to consume as many of the evil peppers as possible. The ugly little red peppers were not normal pepper shape. They actually looked like the Devil's own version of a pepper. Each contestant had to wear latex gloves to keep from burning his or her hands when picking up the vicious peppers. After the 60 seconds were up, the contestant had to wait 60 more incredibly painful seconds before downing some milk or shooting spray whipped cream into the mouth to mute the flaming effect of the peppers. In Vincente's party, only he—because he had come up with the idea—and Travis were willing to give it a go. Vincente figured that trying to swallow as much of the pepper whole as possible might be the best strategy. But when the plate of peppers was put in front of him, he discerned quickly that they were not something you could swallow without chewing. Buck was oblivious to it all. There had been no serious plant breeding to increase pepper heat exponentially in his day, the upshot being he didn't know what he was doing.

Buck pulled one of the chairs set up for the jalapeno contest back from the table and against the wall for Lori and helped her get seated. He then stepped forward to join Vincente in the climactic reprise to the Battle of the Alamo. No other patrons took up the challenge. As the server brought small bowls, each with three peppers—a starter batch, and latex gloves, for the opposing commanders, everyone in the restaurant was watching. The crowd pretty much divided by ethnicity, each group rooting for its Alamo leader. This matchup—and this pepper—made the jalapeno contest pale in comparison. The clueless colonel followed the lead of El Presidente and put

322

on the strange gloves, not because he understood what the peppers would likely do to his skin but because he assumed it was some silly Mexican tradition related to the contest. As soon as he had the gloves on, he grabbed a pepper and popped it into his mouth. Vincente, observing a rule that Travis never seemed to grasp, in 1836 or now, that discretion often really is the better part of valor, waited to see if his foe would expire without Vincente having to make a commitment at all. He stared with a wry grin on his face as Travis chewed and downed the pepper quickly, then grabbed another one and did the same, before reaching for a third. As the colonel chewed on the last pepper, the searing heat began to kick in. His face turned the color of his hair. He now had to wait 60 seconds to be sure the peppers stayed down before declaring victory. They did, and so did Buck. He promptly passed out, his face hitting the table and knocking the little bowl flying to the ground. Vincente, seeing what he would have to do to even equal the competition, surrendered to his adversary without taking a shot, shoving his bowl and its contents to the far end of the table. The crowd laughed. The server took the bowl and was back in a minute with a can of Redi-Whip. He handed it to El Presidente, who lifted the colonel's head and tried to open his mouth slightly, shooting a stream of the milky substance into it, making a mess. Travis started to come to, his face still red and eyes watering, and the crowd cheered.

"Well, Colonel, which is it, Victory or Death?" El Presidente asked with a laugh.

Travis tried to focus on him. "Both," he replied with a gasp, then put his head back down on the table.

## 1836 AND 2017

Buck was in his dim little office, scratching out replies to letters that had come addressed to him as commander of the Alamo. He actually had lots of correspondence, largely because people around the country who collected signatures figured out pretty quickly that this was a way to get his. Outside, there was a misty rain falling—had been that way all day. Buck had just dipped his quill in the ink when there was a knock at the door. It was Bob.

"I've got some good news for you. State agencies never act quickly—that's government for you . . . ."

Buck interrupted. "Believe me, I know. The sitting around and discussing exactly how and when to declare independence kept anyone from coming to our aid, as near as I can piece it together. They should have gone ahead and done that earlier since it's what we were fighting for," he replied sadly.

"Well, this is on a little happier note than that, but it is related. The university folks weren't happy about having to do it, but they are going to turn over your original diary," Bob announced.

"Really?" Buck replied. "I wasn't sure how they would handle it if someone in the family really sold or gave my things to the state—certainly creates a legal argument as to who really owns them."

"They did caution that the diary is very fragile and valuable—that you might not want to just put it on your desk here and leave it," Bob explained. "Subject to weather, like our rain today, and the possibility of theft, they do have a point. You may want to think about that. If there is a way that you can have access to it—and anything else of yours that we can have returned to you, while, at the same time, taking archival precautions to preserve them, that would be the best of all worlds."

Buck had a puzzled look on his face.

Bob explained, "They use all kinds of methods to preserve old documents and artifacts these days—keeping them cool and dry, under low

324

light, acid-free. I know none of that makes much sense to you. Honestly, I don't know how a lot of it works, either, but it does preserve items better than just leaving them on a desk or storing them in an old trunk somewhere. That and to prevent theft are why we have Crockett's gun and the other items on display here under glass in low light. It would be a good idea to come up with something before we actually take the items from archival protection. Like I said, you might want to think about it. Oh, and your letter to the "People of Texas & all Americans in the world"—the state archives bowed up their backs some but admitted that you certainly have a claim on that—still working that one out."

"Why can't we just bring these things to the Alamo and put them in cases here where I can access them if I wish?" Buck cut in.

"That's a great compromise if it suits you," Bob replied. "Fact is, the Land Office has begged for permanent return of the letter to the Alamo for years, but archives has steadfastly refused until now. We explored the logistics of housing the letter here, but they never would consider it—keep it in some super-secure vault in Austin. They would likely be much more agreeable to keeping it here now. We would have to build appropriate and secure cases for the items—especially that letter."

"Of all the places the letter could be, this is certainly the most appropriate," Buck interrupted, a dead serious look on his face. "I wrote it because of our situation here!"

"I'll call them again and tell them if you think that's how you would like to settle it?"

"Yes, if there is anything that belongs here at the Alamo—besides me—it is my letter," Buck firmly replied.

"I believe archives also has your family Bible—will mention that. Unfortunately, your lieutenant colonel commission is in Mexico, part of the spoils of war. I don't think you're going to see that one again since you took a swipe at the Mexican government guys with your sword. A private collector may have your sword belt, and he's allowing the Alamo to display some of his collection, but we need space to show it."

Buck interrupted. "If it is my sword belt, I would definitely like to have it back!"

Bob continued. "You will be able to yea or nay that one quickly. I'm

325

sure something can be worked out if it is yours. We also have a little poetry book that was apparently something from your childhood—you wrote your name in it. And I know we talked about this once already, but there's your ring, too. We can do something about that. Have you thought any more about it?" Bob asked gently.

"Yes . . . yes, I have," Buck replied slowly. "I know this may sound sort of odd, since Rebecca gave it to me, but . . . I would really like for Lori to have it . . . I would like to make a special gift of it to her . . . ."

Bob smiled. He could see where the colonel was going with this, yet it was obvious the young man was having trouble enunciating it to someone other than Lori.

"I don't think it's odd at all. In fact, I've been kind of wondering how long it was going to take you, quite honestly," Bob laughed.

"Well, to be truthful, I've been hesitant about asking," Buck confided. "Lori is such a beautiful and gentle girl, and she is so capable at everything she does. It doesn't seem right to saddle her with someone from the past who will likely never be able to do all the things a man from now could do for her . . . ." He stopped, lowering his head.

"Son, Lori loves you. If that's not evident, I don't know what is," Bob responded. "Now look at me."

Buck raised his head and faced Bob. "I can't drive one of those cars—and with my propensity for fainting, it doesn't seem like it would be a good idea . . . ."

"I don't think true love is based on driving a car!" Bob laughed. "No, I don't think that's something you should learn as it would be dangerous. And there will be some other things related to your injuries as well, but you have a good job with good pay, you certainly have status and reputation, and outright fame. Don't sell yourself short, Colonel, just because you are from 1836!"

"But, at least to my way of thinking, a man protects his lady and does everything for her—if we . . . if . . . she would even have me, it would be the reverse. That's just not the way we did things . . . ."

"In 1836." Bob finished the sentence for him. "Buck, it's not 1836 now. Everything is different. Women do as much as men, although I

326

suspect Lori likes your solicitations and protection such as when you stopped chasing General Santa Anna and came back to her and picked her up and carried her away from the accident. You do more than you think you do."

"And my appearance—I've heard people say I look like something that would scare small children with my face torn up like this," Buck gave his next excuse.

"I think Lori is pretty used to your looks at this point," Bob noted. "She actually told me not long after you were revived that she thought you were 'cute for a mutilated Alamo defender' or something like that. I really don't think she's seeing the scars when she looks at you. My observation has always been that she is proud to be seen with you—although, in some venues, maybe not in the 1836 outfit all the time!"

"She has been awfully tolerant. I really don't deserve her with all of my failings on the romantic front. But all I see now is Lori. I don't think on Rebecca or the women I listed in the diary—any of that. I know y'all laugh at me for sometimes seeming like I'm stuck in 1836. And I am, suspect I always will be militarily—I owe that to my men. But that old love life is a thing of the far past. All I think about, all I want, is for Lori to love me. I am going to ask her and hope against hope that she might be willing to share her life with someone so . . . different from her world."

"Buck, Lori should be finishing up with her fried cactus right about now." Bob glanced at his watch. "If I were you, I would consider heading over that way."

Lori was hot and sweaty and still wearing the boot, which did not help her 1836 impression. The heavily mended long skirt of the old dress pretty much covered it, and she was to the point where she was able to walk without the crutches. One thing about it, in its present condition, the dress probably looked like an original. She sat down wearily on her little wooden stool in back of the dilapidated table, wiping her hand across her brow, her damp hair hanging around her face. She looked up as she heard someone coming behind her.

Buck smiled. He had a couple pieces of the fudge and handed her one. He stared at Lori, beautiful as an 1830's pioneer girl could possibly be in her ragged dress.

"A lot better than fried cactus!" she said, the delicious candy melting in

327

her mouth.

"Lori, I realize this is not the most romantic setting in the world . . . ."

"You mean a battlefield where everyone got slaughtered and I have just finished a hot and sweaty demo in this dirty and torn old dress isn't romantic?" she interrupted with a little laugh, then wiped an errant strand of dripping hair out of her face and took another bite of fudge.

"Certainly not," he responded. "But, honestly, it assuredly has been the venue for the two of us getting to know each other. It has a very special meaning for me for that reason beyond the less pleasant reason that draws and keeps me here," he said earnestly.

She looked into his serious eyes and took another bite of fudge.

"Lori, I've alluded to it now and then, but fact is I love you more than anyone or anything in the world—this one or my other one. I know I have a lot of limitations, and that you could do a lot better than a scarred soldier from long ago who will never be able to drive you anywhere but whom I can promise will always try to protect and defend . . . if you would consider . . . I am asking you to marry me!"

She had finished the fudge. She threw her arms around him. "Yes, defend," she said softly. "Defend me, Buck! Yes, yes."

They embraced for what seemed an eternity, at least to the passing tourists who stared at the reenactor couple in their goofy frontier clothes.

"I have something I want to give you, but I have to work on the details for freeing it up, first," he told her. "I hope you won't mind its origins, as that was the one thing that troubled me a bit about it. But it is from my time so would be appropriate in that respect," he said. "It's my cat's eye ring. Bob said that the Land Office will release it to me if you will wear it."

Lori was crying tears of happiness as he held her again. The tourists kept staring at the odd young couple as they walked by. Lori and Buck finally turned from their embrace as a youthful tour guide and his charges passed them. The young man pointed toward them, not skipping a beat:

"Some of you may have heard about the racy journal kept by the Alamo's commander, Col. Travis. Looks like those two are reenacting a page from the colonel's diary!"

As Bob stepped into Lori's cubbyhole, she looked up from her computer screen.

"You wanted to see me?" he asked.

"Yeah, I have a little news . . . ." she replied, a slight smile on her face.

"Does it have anything to do with Buck?"

"He told you, right?" Lori asked.

Bob nodded. "I'm so happy for you. You know, Buck came to me—worried that the time warp made him somehow deficient and that you would not accept him. I assured him that was not what love is based on, and I obviously guessed right?"

She nodded. "Yeah, he said something apologizing for not being able to drive a car and for the scars on his face—poor thing. If he only could see himself the way I see him . . . ."

"Well, we'll have to work on that," Bob answered. "I've been meaning to talk with you about this for a couple of weeks. I've got an idea that might help with the sword-waving incidents and maybe move him forward a bit from 1836. Although, I'll admit, and I suspect you agree, we never want to totally obfuscate that as it simply is who Buck is."

"Needless to say, I'm in favor of anything that would move him forward, but how?" she asked.

Bob pulled up a chair. "I think one of the problems—not the only one, by any means, is that the colonel has a so-called job here as commander, but he has no one and nothing to command. We all know the Mexicans are not really coming again—even if he doesn't, and he has no real military duties. I include him in preliminary planning for national guard ceremonies, that kind of thing, but other than that, all he does is go in that dim little office and write replies to his fans with his quill. Buck may be clueless about much of the modern world, but I bet even he realizes it's not a real job. In other words, we need to find a way to really keep him busy."

"Yeah, I know, but what can a guy from 181 years ago do? He doesn't know how to use a computer, and, although I think he's certainly intelligent

329

enough to learn, I really can't quite see . . . ." She didn't end her thought.

"Yeah, I agree. I've been trying to think of things where he could actually be helpful. You're right, he is very bright and a quick study—just too impulsive and totally clueless about modern society and technology. And I don't think those things are going to change radically, certainly the first one. But he does have a couple of skills that might be of some actual benefit, in addition to the value of having a genuine defender on the premises," Bob said.

"Like what?" Lori asked.

"The writing talent. If we could turn that to something other than just bashing Mexicans and asking for help for the beleaguered garrison, it might really help promote the place."

Lori laughed.

Bob continued, "Based on those famous letters, he's very good with propaganda, advertising, promotional material, etc. He knows how to turn a phrase and get attention from his readers. The other possibility that might be of some use would be to have him read through our contracts and related documents, not to really finalize them but to give us a little feedback before we deal with the folks in Austin. I checked with the State Bar of Texas on his status. The bar had never had a question like Travis' status before, of course. They're cautious about allowing someone who really is not qualified to practice. But he's technically an experienced attorney, not to mention the little thing of the hero status. They told me they would grandfather him and make him a member automatically—and waive dues and continuing legal education requirements. But we really need to watch his actions, as he will be liable for any inappropriate attorney activity as would be any member of the bar."

"You think a lawyer who basically worked on piddling debt cases and minor theft issues 181 years ago is going to know anything about the complex legal shenanigans that go on now? Remember the case about the stolen chamber pot that he referenced in his diary," Lori noted.

Bob smiled. "Not really. I don't think he would really be competent to practice in today's world, and the learning curve might be impossible with such a large number of years gone by. But there are some things that attorneys, by their very training, know to look for. They have a different outlook from us normal people . . . ."

Lori laughed. "Yeah, I can see that. Well, if you want to sit him down and put him to work, I think it's a great idea. But remember—he's technically the boss, so be careful how you word it. Maybe more a plea for his expertise or help rather than telling him you have a job for him."

"Believe me, I already thought about that one. I know he's sensitive about his position commanding the place. I think I can finesse it. I'm hopeful it might result in a happier colonel and a more peaceful work environment!"

Lori smiled at him. "Hope it works, for all our sakes. I'll encourage him once he's got some assignments! Goodness knows, I've tried to keep him out of trouble by involving him in some of the demos, but we can only plant so many vegetables and cook so much cactus. He needs more than that! Based on the diary, he likes to stay constantly busy. He has to live in this world now, and I think his life would be more meaningful and relevant if he felt he was more a part of the present and contributing something. And it might keep him away from people like Lyle Jones or the Mexican soldados when they come around."

"Lori, you're going to marry this guy. I don't think I have to tell you that Buck will wave that sword if his adversaries come calling," Bob replied.

Bob's phone rang, and he rushed around the corner to pick up, Lori following.

"Social Security? Yes, I'm Bob Gordon. I'm with the Alamo," Bob responded.

He was contorting his face and smiling at Lori as someone at the other end of the phone was talking. He hit the speaker feature.

" . . . someone employed there with what has to be some faulty information—an 1809 date of birth, for example, but there is no phone listed for him. We're trying to find out what is going on and get the errors corrected."

Bob and Lori were laughing, and the Social Security Administration worker surely could hear them.

"You're talking about William Barret Travis," Bob replied.

"Let me go back to that screen," the voice on the other end responded.

"Yeah, a Mr. Travis in San Antonio, Texas. Does he work for you?"

Bob tried to control his voice. "This is the Alamo . . . ," he started.

"What's that? I know there's an Alamodome where they play college Final Four basketball games," the voice replied.

"The historic mission church where they had the big battle in 1836 with the Mexicans—surely you've heard of it?" Bob asked incredulously.

"Uh, no, never heard of that one," came the reply. "Never was much into history. They don't teach much of that these days."

"No, apparently they don't," Bob replied. "Well, it's famous, and not just in Texas. This is not incredibly relevant to the Social Security Administration in general, but it is to this case. Bottom line, around 180 Texans trapped in the fort, which contained the old church, held off a Mexican army of 4,000 for 13 days. The Mexicans finally overran the place and slaughtered all the Texans. It's the biggest historical event in Texas, and you know that's saying something. The Texan commander was found in an archaeological dig and revived. That's Col. Travis, the man with the 1809 birth date—it's perfectly legit. He's actually my boss. The governor of the state put him back in charge of the place."

There was dead silence on the other end of the phone for a long enough time that Bob and Lori thought the agent had either expired or hung up, when he finally responded.

"Let me get this straight—this William Travis is some guy from 1809 who was dug up from the past, and the date is correct? And he works at a place called the Alamo, which you can confirm is in San Antonio, Texas?"

"That's it," Bob said simply.

"Can you give me Mr. Travis' phone number and email?"

"Like I said, he's was born in 1809 and fought in the 1836 battle. He doesn't have a phone and doesn't even know what email is. I doubt that's likely to change."

"OK, you learn something new every day. That's probably more than I wanted to know and all I need. I'll just note no phone or email by his name. Thanks!" the agent replied, hanging up.

Bob and Lori just looked at each other.

Lori got up to go.

"One more thing," Bob stopped her. "Remember how I said we were going to start you off half-time but wanted to work it up to full-time?"

"Now that you mention it, yes!" she replied. "Honestly, the hours have been so crazy ever since Buck came back, and there's been so much going on, that I hadn't thought about it too much—figured you would tell me when the time comes."

"Well, if you are interested, I think the time is here," Bob replied. "Alamo tourism is actually up—you know who I attribute that to!" he laughed.

"Yeah, I think I do."

"The renovations that are starting are going to require more work on our end, and someone is going to need to work with the colonel regarding any ideas he may come up with to promote the place. I really do think we can guide him toward being useful in that regard, but somebody is going to have to get his thoughts from quill and parchment to the computer!"

She laughed. "Yeah, I see your point. Quite honestly, there's nobody I'd rather work with!"


"Vicky, we're going to see Cathy Johnson," Lori told her sister in a slightly commanding tone.

"Huh? You're getting kind of bossy. Is Col. Travis' commander thing rubbing off on you? You know I don't like that reenactor stuff or looking for fabric for the clothes—unless of course, Buck is going?" She softened a bit at the end, hoping the dreamboat colonel would come with them.

"No, Buck is not going this time—just the two of us girls," Lori replied.

The green eyes got huge. "Why?" Vicky asked suspiciously.

"Because I'm going to make you a reenactor frontier dress," Lori replied seriously.

"Lori, I love you, and I love Buck, but I don't want to be an 1830's anything," Vicky responded. "It's just not my thing—you know that!"

"Yes, I do, but this time, you're going to have to just suck it up and do it," Lori told her with a smile.

Vicky was eyeing her with a knowing look. "Don't tell me, finally, y'all are going to get married?" she blurted out.

"Yep, we certainly are—and it's going to be an 1836 wedding. You have to be the bridesmaid, so you have to wear an appropriate dress!"

Vicky was hugging Lori. "That puts a totally different spin on it. I've been wondering if this was ever going to happen," she told her sister. "That's the best news in the world!"

Once released from Vicky's stranglehold, Lori told her, "I want you to wear blue."

"I don't really even like blue," Vicky complained.

"Well, let me put it this way. Besides the fact that it's my wedding, there's someone else who always wears blue, and it goes really, really well with red hair!"

Vicky was silent for a minute, pondering Lori's words. "All right, then. I surrender! Let's go to the fabric store." Vicky gave in. "What are you going to wear?"

"Well, fact is that white wedding dresses came into vogue with Queen Victoria. She became queen in 1837 and married in 1840, so we missed her by a few years. Although I did wear it to the fandango, I'm going to wear my yellow dress. I think it will be perfect!—pretty but simple as befits Texas in the 1830's."

"So do I. That thing is gorgeous. If I have to do this, will mine be kind of pretty like that?"

"Yes, that's what I hope. Cathy had several colors in that heavenly lawn—can't recall what she had in blue if anything. But that's what I want to get if so. Your dress will be very similar to mine but with short sleeves.

Younger ladies tended to wear them back in the day," she explained.

"And I'm guessing Buck will be the commander of the Alamo?" Vicky asked.

"Of course—the new version of the clothes that I made. He does it for almost everything else, and he will really have to dress the part for this!" Lori replied serenely.

"First time I think I can recall you sounding thrilled about that uniform," the observant Vicky replied. "Let's go ahead and go so we can get it over with and get back."


"Some professor is giving an impromptu lecture on the sex life of the Alamo's commander—I heard a little of it as I walked by. Come on! Maybe history can be interesting after all!" a young man called excitedly to his girlfriend, who had an annoyed look on her face and had obviously been waiting for him to return from somewhere.

He said it loudly enough that it caught the attention of others as well, and a number of them moved toward a much larger than usual crowd for an author selling books. Lyle Jones had sold out of his first printing. Of course, he lost a number of those copies to Travis and his hose. The professor had a second edition printed and was hawking them at his usual spot. He had not intended to speak at length on the colonel's love life this day, but a man who had read the book and asked him to autograph it queried if Travis had something wrong with him to be so obsessed with sex. Jones found it impossible to just say "yes," "no," or "I don't know," and used the question as a springboard to cover each and every one of the diary entries in Espanol tracking the colonel's romantic escapades. The fact was that sex sells, including history books.

"Although Travis was the messiah of liberty, freedom, and revolution, he was expert at several of the seven deadly sins. Of those, he worked the hardest at lust. He was a captive to his promiscuity. It's a lack of responsibility and can be the result of a search for love, companionship, and security gone awry. It was a game for him—the thrill of the hunt and the catch, once achieved, over and on to the next. If a woman pushed him for marriage, he headed the other direction. I was curious about it and ran Travis as he presented himself in the diary by a psychologist friend. She could not be sure, of course, but she said the symptoms described could

335

indicate sexualized behavior, narcissism, a controlling personality, or even high-functioning autism. Studies indicate that the severely afflicted, and Travis certainly was, are never satisfied, and these people are characterized by impatience, isolation, and loneliness.

"Travis was no-good Southern white trash who proudly paraded his string of women through his risqué diary. Our hero would seek out sexual comfort any way he could find it. He wooed the higher-class single ladies. Men outnumbered women 10 to 1 on the frontier, and the ladies didn't remain single long. Dressed to the nines and with perfume in his red hair, the handsome and dashing young man would dangle temptation in the form of gifts to whatever young lady—or ladies—he was attempting to impress. But, regardless of his efforts, and a long list of conquests painstakingly spelled out by the young Don Juan, the ladies always ended up marrying someone else. To his credit, Travis would sometimes attend their weddings, maybe hoping they had lady friends he could meet. But he also crawled along the dark underbelly of the sex world, paying Hispanic prostitutes or slave girls for their services. Truth is that young Travis was always looking for an opportunity. And he really did keep score, counting his conquests meticulously. The young man found it convenient to have a wife back in Alabama, as it kept the females at bay when he did not want to make a commitment—which was pretty much all the time. He had quite a reputation, and I suspect this is why he had trouble latching onto a reputable belle he deemed worthy of his own somewhat over-inflated opinion of himself."

The crowd laughed. Buck and Lori walked up just in time to hear this. He motioned her to stand over to the side and act as if they were paying no attention, just talking with each other. They definitely stood out in the crowd with their 1836 clothes, but there were several other reenactors, including Crockett and Bowie, on the far side of the gathering, as well.

Lori whispered to Buck, "What are you going to do?"

"I didn't wear my sword, but, honestly, that didn't work so well when I tried it before, anyway," he answered softly. "Let's see how bad it gets."

"Personally, I already think it's gotten pretty bad," she rejoined. "Maybe we should just walk away?"

"I don't walk away," he came back quickly.

"Yeah, I know." She smiled as she said it.

336

Jones was continuing his monologue: "Travis finally met a woman for whom he seemed to truly have some feelings, Rebecca Cummings. She lived at Mill Creek, way out from town, and helped run an inn owned by her brother. It was a long ride out there, and Travis and Rebecca seemed to have had a kind of stormy relationship. He would go all the way out there only to find she was angry about something one time, and the next they would be spending the night in each other's arms joyfully. He slowed but did not stop his catting around. He paid a visit to a whore, a couple of acquaintances found out about it—makes you wonder what THEY were doing—and they squealed to Rebecca, who then gave Travis the cold shoulder. He got mad at the friends. On another visit to a house of ill repute after he met Rebecca, Travis found himself unable to perform his part of the bargain—maybe out of guilt, but he paid the woman something anyway. And he recorded every bit of it as well as his persistent venereal disease and calomel—mercury—treatments. It's really all rather comical."

A number of Jones' listeners were laughing.

"Rebecca obviously was not a pillar of propriety, either—for her day. The two did exchange what we would now probably treat as engagement gifts. She gave him the famous cat's eye ring in the case in the Alamo church. He gave her a pin. The extant diary ends, and there's a gap of a year and a half where we know he was still continuing to visit her because he wrote several letters from Mill Creek, but he was still married to Rosanna. The divorce came through right before he was killed at the Alamo. Who knows whether he would really have married Rebecca, and, if he had, whether it would have lasted any longer than his first marriage, which was a disaster." Jones wrapped up his discourse.

The professor glanced to his left and, out of the corner of his eye, spotted Buck and Lori. He turned back to his audience.

"In fairness, there's someone here who has a stake in all of this and may want to weigh in on it. I'm assuming most everyone has heard about an Alamo defender being unearthed at an archaeological dig a few months ago? He survived brain surgery and works here at the Alamo."

Jones turned to his left again and called out, "Colonel, I'm sure you heard some of this. Is there anything you want to say?"

"Come on," Buck gestured to Lori, taking her hand and leading her to Jones' table. Lori, embarrassed beyond words, had to practically be dragged.

"Good afternoon to all of y'all!" Travis panned the crowd, tipping his hat, an attempted smile on his face. "I'm afraid I can't deny what Professor Jones has said, as putting it all down in my journal seemed like a good idea at the time, although it clearly does not in retrospect. That said, here's my answer."

Buck swept off his hat, pulled Lori to him, and gave her a long kiss, putting his arm around her. When he finally let go, he turned back to the crowd.

"We got engaged 2 days ago. From now on, Lori's the only lady for me!"

Everyone applauded, including Jones. The professor turned to Lori.

"Miss Clayton, congratulations on a feat that seemed unattainable. General Santa Anna and all the ladies in frontier Texas tried to capture the elusive Mr. Travis—the general and the ladies having different motives, of course. You have succeeded where they could not!"


"A wedding at the Alamo? You've got to be kidding. It's small, dark, depressing, and there's that little thing of all those dead soldiers," the voice on the other end of the line said.

"Yeah, Joe, I know all that. They're not sure they want to do it, but it came up and they wanted to know if the option is a possibility," Bob asked.

The man at the General Land Office was silent for a minute, then replied. "Honestly, I think there's a prohibition on it—that folks kind of know not to even ask. I don't think we've ever had that request before. If so, it must have been turned down. I'll check on it, but I bet they haven't had a wedding there since it was a mission church, and I really don't know if they had any then. The place is synonymous with the 1836 massacre, so I can't believe anyone would find that appealing and want to remember their wedding in that context."

Although the Land Office employee couldn't see him, Bob shook his head. "Fact is, the bride thought it would be appropriate for this couple. They met here and both of them work here. The groom is focused on the death and gore. I imagine he will win in the end, but they wanted to know if the regulations prohibit it with the Shrine status and all. I thought there was

338

a rule against it, but I can't put my finger on it. Some of our files went missing with that little stunt where Col. Travis dumped the contents and hauled all the office furniture out to fortify the place against the Mexican high school cadets."

Joe laughed. "Yeah—I remember reading about that one. He's a little off, but it was funny. I'll have to check on the rules. You know the governor recommissioned it as a military installation. I kind of doubt that would have any impact . . . ."

"Well, Joe, it might in this case," Bob replied. "Colonel Travis has asked Lori Clayton, who works here and does lots of history demos on the grounds, to marry him. She was standing there when the archaeologists dug him up, and she's been there for him through thick and thin and all the sword waving, 'Victory or Death,' and controversy. She wants to get married in the chapel. He's concerned that would be showing disrespect to his garrison. Regardless of where they do it, this is not going to be the usual wedding."

"Wow. I get it. Well, if there's a regulation against it—honestly, there should be, I think we could probably make an exception for this one, but I'll check it out. I think it's probably Texas sacrilege, but I really do think our brave hero is unbalanced, if you want the truth. That said, I think he's right on this one. But, considering his track record, I suspect she will win and it will be at the Alamo if we can authorize it."

Bob laughed. "Yeah, considering his track record, you may be right."


Young Felipe Esparza looked in the mirror. He had donned his soldado uniform at the request of the Alamo folks for a presentation regarding Mexican uniforms worn at the battle. Felipe was relieved that he didn't have to say anything. He was basically just a live mannequin demonstrating what was worn in those long-ago times. He had his Brown Bess rifle—unloaded, and stood at attention, gazing at himself in the mirror. All was in order. Felipe enjoyed the reenactments but not the controversy and continued animosity that came out of some of these things, far worse lately. He had seen Col. Travis in action, waving his sword at the "enemy," which he knew, in the colonel's damaged mind, included him. However, he did not hate the young commander from so long ago, knowing the colonel had severe injuries from the Mexican ball to his head. Felipe was in an atypical position as to his "take" on the whole thing. He came from a split

339

family, unusual in the case of the Alamo battle since most of the defenders were Anglos, but something that would be very common a generation later in America's Civil War. The Esparza family featured brothers who fought against each other in the famous battle, one dying for the Texian cause. Felipe headed for his car and the fort.

As Felipe approached the old fortress, he looked around. He was 10 minutes early. The little presentation was to start at 11:00. Tourists were milling around. It was hot, as it almost always seemed to be, and he was beginning to sweat, glad that he was not a real soldier from 1836 as he would not have wanted to wear the heavy clothes folks from those days endured even in summer. He strolled toward the gift shop. Morena Alejandro knew everybody, and everybody knew her. He figured the presentation would be at the long barracks as that was where most of the exhibits were set up. He popped his head in and said hello to the sales manager, got a piece of Deguello fudge for his efforts, and confirmed the direction he needed to go and headed that way.

"Halt! You will be killed if you do not leave immediately!"

Felipe knew who it was before he even turned, a frozen look on his face. The colonel, waving the sword, was running toward him. There was an open door behind him. Travis stopped as he got to Felipe, pointing the weapon at him.

"There are to be no Mexicans in the Alamo. Get out immediately or I will put YOU to the sword in retribution for what you evil scum did to my command!" the infuriated officer yelled.

"Colonel Travis, please, let me explain . . . ," Felipe started hesitantly. Tourists were gathering to watch the latest show.

"There are no exceptions. You are a Mexican soldado—you killed and mutilated my garrison!" Travis yelled.

"No sir, honestly, I am not a soldado—I'm here for a demonstration. I was asked to dress up like this so that tourists could see what Mexican soldiers wore during the battle," Felipe explained. He went on, "Sir, I cannot tell you how much I respect your courage and determination . . . ."

Travis had turned very pale. He held his arm out slightly, as if to catch himself, then fell to the ground. The tourists continued to gather, standing back slightly.

340

Felipe dropped his gun and knelt by Travis, checking his pulse and holding his head. He had seen the scars at a distance, but this was his first close-up look at the ravaged face. He was overwhelmed with sadness for the Texian leader. Finally, after a couple of minutes, Travis began to stir. When he opened his eyes and looked up to see a Mexican soldado looking down at him, he jerked slightly, trying to sit up.

"Colonel, please, it's OK," Felipe said in a soothing tone. "I promise you, as I said before, I am not really a soldado. I did have a relative in Santa Anna's army, but his brother was in your command—Gregorio Esparza."

Travis stared at him. He remembered Gregorio well. Before the colonel could possibly start talking and go "off" again, Felipe helped him to a sitting position, then put his arm around the shoulders of the "enemy" leader.

"Sir, please, I know it must be incredibly difficult, but I want you to know that there are many people of Mexican heritage who do admire your bravery and commitment to Texan and American liberty and freedom"—he referenced the colonel's core beliefs—"and who do work to 'Remember the Alamo' and the sacrifice here. You know, of course there is pride with us as to our heritage just as there is for you with yours, but there are very few people who honor Santa Anna because of his cruelty. When you see a Hispanic face, please do not assume it is an admirer of Santa Anna—they are very rare. May I help you up?" he asked gently.

As Felipe steadied the colonel and got him to his feet, the increasing crowd was staring.

"Sir," Felipe said hopefully, "I would be so honored if you would shake my hand?" He put his hand out.

Travis, still wavering a bit and a slightly bewildered look on his face, gazed at the young Mexican soldier, hesitated a moment, then finally stared straight into Felipe's eyes and extended his hand.

"Thank you for your kindness," he said softly. "I never would have thought . . . ." he didn't continue.

The tourists cheered wildly as the Texian commander and the Mexican soldado shook hands. Then, to the astonishment of all, Felipe reached for the colonel's shoulders, in a hug, the colonel instinctively responding. Lori headed out of the gift shop building and toward the demonstration just in time to witness a sight she had been sure she would never see.

The Texians were not always as kind to their leader. Buck walked toward the back of the complex, where the reenactors had set up several tents, including a long one, under which sat a number of tourists. A couple of gentlemen in 1836 garb were providing a demonstration of what comprised a soldier's kit in the 1830's, as well as an explanation of the rather primitive and downright scary medical equipment of the day, including a leech jar with its occupants. Another reenactor, standing slightly to the side and in front of the tent, was expositing as to his views on the command situation in the Alamo. He was a large, middle-aged man, decked out in a broad-brimmed hat, the obligatory side whiskers, beige pants held up by suspenders, and a seedy-looking 1830's coat. His voice definitely carried, and he was clearly in character as one of Bowie's volunteers. Travis stood inside the edge of the tent, in back of the man. The Bowie adherent was so passionate for his man that he had attracted quite some attention, and he brought back some unpleasant memories for Buck. The speaker, thumbs tucked in the sides of his waistband and elbows out, kept speechifying in his take on the vernacular of an Alamo soldier:

"Now, that thar Jim Bowie is a man. He's a leader by God. If we're really goin' to try to hold this broken-down, no-good excuse for a fort, he's the fella to do it, not that uppity young fool who's not dry behind the ears and is always writin' them high falutin' letters no one kin understand and sendin' 'em off with all them couriers we can't afford to lose. Young Travis is no doubt itchin' to get out of here so he can scout out some ladies to add to his conquests—Katy bar the door and be sure you get your womenfolk inside first when Mr. Travis comes around! Colonel Bowie wouldn't engage in that nonsense. And he doesn't strut around in them town clothes with his nose in the air. He'll mix it up with the best of 'em, get right in it. I kinda wonder whether Col. Travis, despite his non-stop fancy talk about dyin' for Texas, will really come through when Santy Anny gets off his duff and does decide to come over these here walls!"

The tent swayed, then came down. The panicky tourists seated for the presentation pushed at and wrangled with the fabric, heading toward daylight. The leech jar fell from the table, and the worms headed out, too. Some of the other reenactors ran to the scene, quickly and carefully making sure all of the kids and everyone else got out, taking up the ropes and pegs and folding the canvas. At the front right corner lay a sword, a white hat, and, partially shrouded by the fallen tent, Buck. He had fainted, taking the tent with him. One of the other reenactors glanced toward the tent, then turned to the man who had been pontificating.

"Hope you enjoyed your career as a reenactor, George. Looks to me

342

like it just ended! I think you were entitled to your opinion up until that last remark, but whatever you think of young Travis, he followed up all that 'fancy talk' and then some when the time came."

The Bowie fan glanced over to where a couple of other men had picked up Travis and were trying to get him to come to.

"Yeah, but I was portraying a Bowie man when Bowie was still well enough to command—and before we knew what Travis had in him."

"I know, but those scars tell the tale, and you have to take that into account. I'd suggest you get on over there and apologize pronto, and hope to God that the colonel really does feel he needs every man—except for the ones he sent as couriers, of course," the other man smiled at the discomfited George.

The unhappy Bowie man headed toward the commander, who was just coming to. Travis just stared at him. George squatted on his haunches next to where the colonel was sitting.

"Guess you heard all that, sir?" the Bowie man asked sheepishly.

"Yes sir, I did. You're entitled to your views, soldier—that freedom is what we're fighting for," came the response. "I don't care what you think of me, except I do want you to know that those words were not just words. They were my most heartfelt beliefs—and still are. I think you can see that I meant what I said!"

"Yes sir, I can see," George said, staring into the ravaged face at Travis' fiery eyes. "I'm sorry, sir. I suspect you won't be needing my . . . ."

Travis cut him off. "We need every man, God knows. Talk about my clothes or my age—or, I'd prefer not in a public forum—but it's up to you, even my love life, all you want, soldier. Like I said, I don't care. But you will remain a soldier under my command, and I do expect you to follow my orders. And, if we are attacked, I expect you to follow my example! That will be all," the colonel, his voice strengthening, replied with a fierce look.

"Yes sir!" George stood, giving a salute, which the colonel returned.

## ALARM BELL AT THE ALAMO

The fire alarm was blaring at the Hipolito F. Garcia Federal Building across Houston Street from the Alamo: "There has been an emergency in the building. All personnel leave by the nearest exit" in a canned voice, repeating over and over, grating and loud enough to force cynical workers to get up from their seats because they couldn't stand to continue listening to it. The people poured out of the large structure, fortunately in orderly fashion, most obviously thinking it was truly just a fire drill, joking and laughing as they headed away from the building, getting out of a little work for a short while. But the number of police cars streaming toward the structure indicated it might be something more.

With all the ruckus going on, the Alamo staff congregated on their grounds, staring in the direction of the north wall. Their commander went further. He sprinted toward his original command post, starting to cross Houston, heading against the tide as the office workers were streaming from the front and side doors going the other direction. He had never experienced a fire alarm, so, as with so many other things, he was clueless. As always, and even with a possible crisis in the offing, folks streaming toward the Alamo, when they got a look at the colonel's colorful and unique outfit, stared.

Travis was soon stopped by a police officer. Police had barricaded Houston Street. No traffic was getting through, and there were police cars lining the street, two lanes thick, one each way, with more coming. Bob and Lori, standing on the plaza next to the Alamo grounds but within sight of the colonel, saw him waving his arm, sans sword—although he was wearing it, apparently agitated. The police officer was pointing back toward the Alamo rather sternly in response, likely having heard of some of the colonel's crazy antics and not having time for any of that in a real crisis. For once, the commander followed someone else's command, turning and moving with the flow of office workers who were pouring onto the plaza. Police swarmed the place, pushing the tourists and office workers to the far end of the front of the church property and beyond toward the Menger Hotel. The Alamo Rangers, supplemented by city police, ringed the old church and the perimeter of the compound to secure it, something that was not actually practical to protect the site in the event of a bomb going off. Incoming tourists were blocked from coming into the Alamo compound.

344

Police officers soon directed the Alamo staff to a hopefully safe area, and the entire compound was secured. The colonel stepped forward, arguing with the police captain in charge, pointing toward the Alamo church and insisting that he must stay and defend it, and, if need be, die at his post. Melia, in line with the other employees, was laughing hysterically at the commander's dramatic gestures. The captain did not want anyone to die that day, including the willing colonel, and he barked an order at the higher ranked officer. Travis again pointed toward the church, shouting at the officer. Finally, the captain, who had no time for a hero who wanted to repeat his feat of heroism, ordered a couple of his officers to take the Alamo commander by each arm and place him with the other mission staff members. Rather rudely shoved into line by the officers, the angry and embarrassed Col. Travis stood with his "troops," bewildered as to what was going on. Melia gave a thumbs up signal toward the police, and Tom, who was standing with her, smiled.

Finally, near the end of the federal building workday, several explosions could be heard. Travis again walked forward, this time angrily expressing his concern to the police officer keeping the mission employees corralled, but, as before, his hero status did not matter in this instance. The officer either would not tell him anything or did not know and gruffly ordered him back to where the staff members were standing. Travis refused and started to pull the sword from the scabbard, at which point, as before, two officers grabbed his arms and dragged him back in line with his staff, warning him he had better stay put this time. The colonel swore something under his breath at them, then, at a run, charged toward the church, unsheathing the sword and waving it, yelling his catchphrase "Victory or Death!" Melia dissolved in laughter, and some of the other staff members followed suit. Morena, standing next to Lori and Bob, shook her head sadly and whispered something to Lori, who was staring wide-eyed. The captain quickly ordered his men to apprehend and detain the Alamo commander, who had reached the front doors of the church and stood there, sword at the ready. He took a swipe at the officers as they converged on him. The police had their weapons at their sides, although it was clear to all involved, except likely Travis, that no Texas law enforcement officer would actually shoot the famed hero of the Alamo. Several of the officers distracted the colonel enough that he looked toward them while another man rushed him from behind, grabbing his arms and pulling them behind him, the sword falling to the ground. The officers, one of whom picked up the sword, in a body, escorted the infuriated colonel, his arms pinned behind his back, to where his staff, many of whom were trying to suppress laughter, were waiting. After what seemed an eternity but was really not that long, the word spread that a couple of suspicious packages had been found, triggering a bomb threat alarm. Law enforcement had detonated them, hence the explosions, finding nothing dangerous. The still-angry colonel and his men—and women, were released to go back to their duties. Melia was still laughing. The world had definitely changed since 1836. Although much of it was better, some of it was not.

The gift shop was packed. Saturday afternoons tended to be the worst, at least in the eyes of Melia and Tom. They were working the fudge counter, Melia handling the register and Tom appropriating the fudge per customers' directions. Melia was tired and dying for the afternoon to be over.

"I am so tired of this place!" she complained.

"You're just a volunteer—quit," Tom said without looking at her as he reached for a box of the Crockett fudge for a fat lady and her little girl and thinking the woman was likely to get even bigger if she ate this stuff.

"I can't—it's my community service requirement for school," Melia grumbled.

"Yeah. Honestly, I never quite figured out why they count this as community service!" Tom laughed.

"Well, we DO cater to the mentally compromised," she replied.

"Huh?" Tom finally turned to look at her, having handed off the fudge to the fat woman and the beaming child.

"Travis. He really is insane, and we have to handle the crazy fool with kid gloves because he's famous and the governor—he's another crazy, but at least he doesn't look weird—put him back in charge of the place to reward him for the most colossal failure and disaster in history," she explained. "Go figure!"

Tom shrugged. "Guess I never quite thought about it like that, or, quite frankly, that much, period. He's basically just another reenactor to me, although I know he really was there," Tom replied, now picking out three boxes of the Bowie fudge for a man and his wife.

"Thank God he doesn't work the fudge counter," Melia continued. "He would certainly turn off customers. All that dried blood on the ridiculous old outfit. And it's coming apart at the seams. And he should

346

have tried plastic surgery or something on his face—it's just ghoulish."

"He can't help it," Tom replied calmly, glad for a brief break from the rush of customers.

"He could help the uniform and probably improve the face. While that's awful to look at, the sword waving and yelling 'Victory or Death' is just too much. It's making a laughingstock out of this place. He's supposed to be in charge, but he's a deranged fool who is eventually going to hurt someone as he's totally out of control. He's one who definitely should have been burned. Then he could be a past hero without being a present problem!"

The display stand backed against the column to the left of the fudge counter suddenly gave way, all of the merchandise crashing to the floor with it. Morena, on the other side of the shop, ran toward the collapsed display.

"Is everyone all right?" she called anxiously, looking around at the customers, who had backed away from the accident but circled around it, curious.

"Yes, ma'am," one man in a cowboy hat responded, "Except, I think you lost one of your reenactors!" He pointed.

Morena looked down. The display stand was not heavy. Miraculously, it only contained folded t-shirts and Davy coonskin caps, nothing breakable. But it was lying on top of the colonel, who had obviously fainted and hit the stand going down. The man in the cowboy hat lifted the stand and helped Morena get Travis face up.

"Colonel, can you hear me? Are you OK?" Morena asked.

His eyes were closed. She checked his pulse, and it seemed strong. It was clearly just another fainting incident. She saw no new scrapes or bruises.

"I gotta get out of here!" Melia said in a panicked voice to Tom. "Can you handle the fudge alone?"

Before he could answer, Melia, fear in her eyes, came around the corner and ran from the shop.

Morena explained who Travis was to the gathered shoppers. Finally, he began to come to, and she ordered him to stay seated on the floor until he was less light-headed. Customers began to come forward, wanting to meet him and shake his hand. The slightly dizzy Alamo commander tried to accommodate them. When Buck felt like standing, Morena called Tom to come over and help him get up. Tom did her bidding, then raced behind the counter as he had a line of customers.

"Where's Melia?" Morena asked.

"Uh, she seemed to get kind of upset—asked if I could handle it alone and headed out, not really giving me a chance to answer," he said, not wanting to convey the gist of Melia's complaint about Travis to his supervisor.

"OK, I'll go try to find her," Morena said. "Can you work the fudge counter alone?"

"I can pick out boxes of fudge—I'm pretty good at that!" Buck offered.

Morena looked pleased. "By all means, Colonel. That would be a great help!" she replied.

Tom seemed nonplussed by the idea of his new partner, so, while he worked the register, Buck located the customer choices.

After about 15 minutes, he finally got a request that stymied him: "I'll have the Deguello," a clearly nearsighted woman stated after spending what seemed like an eternity perusing the options

"Are you sure? You know what it's named for, don't you?" Buck asked gently.

"Yeah—something about the bugle call and that red flag of no quarter? I'm not too crazy about that, but chocolate gives me migraines," the woman replied. "Someone told me this one is vanilla."

"That it is," Buck acknowledged. "However, it's not the only non-chocolate option available. I'm not trying to brag on myself, but I can promise you there is a better choice," he offered.

She looked askance at him. He did look like a rather strange reenactor, and what he was doing working the fudge counter God only knew. Buck

348

pointed to the orange fudge.

"Do you like orange flavoring?" he asked, still pointing to a variety at the end of the counter.

She nodded. "Yes, yes I do—guess I didn't see that one since it's on the end." She squinted through her glasses. "William B. Travis—named for the commander, I suppose?"

Buck gave a big smile. "Yes ma'am! I'm Col. Travis," he introduced himself. "I would be honored if you made that selection!"

She stared at him and gave a little laugh, but she had a warm look on her face.

"I heard about that in the news! Well, Colonel, I am honored to meet you, and yes, by all means, I will try your fudge!—two boxes, please!"

"I believe we're having a special—buy two, get one free," he replied, looking at Tom for confirmation. Tom nodded.

While the two guys continued hawking fudge, and the colonel made a couple more "saves" to avoid the red flag, Morena went in search of Melia. She found her in the women's restroom at the back of the complex, crying. At the sight of Morena, Melia looked distraught and worried.

"Guess I'm going to lose my job," she said flatly, trying not to tear up again.

"No, Melia. Not at all. But what happened?" Morena asked gently.

"To pass the time, I was giving Tom my thoughts on just how weird Travis is when the display stand went down. I had no clue that he was standing there—guess he heard everything I said."

Morena observed that Melia's tone and look did not seem to convey compassion for the colonel, only fear for herself.

"You think whatever you said about him made him faint?" Morena stayed calm.

"Yeah. I might faint if someone said that about me, not knowing I could hear," Melia admitted. "I said he is deranged, that he looks weird,

349

and—this may be what caused him to go over—that had he been burned like the rest of them, he could be a past hero without being a present problem. I really do believe that."

"Oh, Melia!" Morena groaned, "I wish you hadn't!" She thought for a moment, then remembered. "Melia, didn't you tell me your little sister has Down's?"

"Verdad? Yeah, she does," Melia said with a shrug. "But what does that have to do with the colonel and the display cabinet?"

"Everything," Morena answered calmly.

Melia stared at her, puzzled. "I don't get where you're going," she admitted.

"I've heard you mention over and over how much you love Verdad," Morena answered.

"I don't think I've ever heard you say anything negative about her, and, yet, people with Down's are certainly different," Morena explained.

"You're comparing Verdad with the colonel?" Melia asked incredulously. "They're nothing alike."

"I'm sure they're not," Morena laughed. "But both of them are not what I guess could be called mainstream . . . ."

Melia cut her off. "There are lots of people with Down's. There's only one colonel, and he's a big problem."

"True, there are more folks with Down's than living Alamo defenders. But in both cases the individuals cannot help the issues they have. It's unkind to judge them or be cruel to them just because they are different." She was giving Melia a steady stare.

Melia waited a long time before answering, looking directly at Morena. "Yeah, I kind of see that. I'm sure the colonel was traumatized and had a hideous experience in the battle. Lori told me she made a no-blood copy of the coat, but he apparently saves it for special occasions. Too bad, as that would help a little. I'll try not to be so unkind to him, but I'm still going to laugh at his antics—can't help it," she admitted.

Morena counseled her, "Just remember that he's a person with feelings, too—just like Verdad, like you, and like me. I laughed, too, when I saw the *Express-News* picture of all the furniture lined up in defense of the Alamo, but not to his face. Try not to ridicule him for things he can't help. He does have a brain injury."

"I really had no idea he was standing behind that column, but I did lay it on pretty thick. I guess I owe him an apology?" Melia confessed hesitantly.

"I'm sure he's aware you're not crazy about him. I doubt he expects one, but it certainly would be a nice gesture," Morena suggested.

"OK. I think I can live through that," Melia answered.

As Morena and Melia got back to the shop, the tourists were still swarming. They headed for the candy counter, where Tom and Buck were doing a brisk business, the colonel still successful at warding off any would-be Deguello purchasers. A young Hispanic man and his little son were at the counter, pointing at the Deguello fudge.

"I would like one box of that, Senor," the man looked up at Travis.

The colonel gave his usual spiel providing customers with a history lesson as to what the name of the red-tinted fudge meant.

"Senor, my great-great-great-grandfather was on General Santa Anna's staff!" The man beamed with pride while his little boy just stared at the candy and shifted his feet.

Travis looked stunned for a second, but quickly resumed his composure. "I'm so sorry for you," he said in a low tone one usually reserved for conveyance of the news of a family death.

The customer stared at him, bewildered, then, taking a closer look at the "store clerk," asked gently: "Are you the gentleman they dug up here a couple months ago—Col. Travis, I believe?"

"Yes, yes I am," the colonel said quietly. "I guess you can see why I do try to encourage patrons to pick any of the other varieties, considering what that name signifies to me," he added, his countenance downcast.

The customer smiled. "While I am proud of my heritage, I do respect

351

your bravery, Colonel, and your sentiments. I think we will go with the Crockett variety after all—it looks intriguing with the nuts and raisins!"

"Thank you, sir," the colonel replied, making his little bow, then quickly getting the fudge for the man and his son.

During this exchange even more customers had come up, the long line of folks wanting a fudge snack or a gift for someone else snaking through the shop. Travis started to help the next customer. Melia stared at the sight. The smiling young man was dishing up boxes of fudge with gusto, clearly enjoying being useful. She had to admit that his attitude toward the job seemed much better than her own. She waited until the line shortened to one customer, then called to him.

"Colonel, got a minute?"

He looked up, asked Tom if he could handle it alone, got an affirmative nod, and headed to Melia.

"I'm sorry I said those awful things about you," she said directly, staring straight at him. "I really don't quite know how to take you," she admitted. "But, regardless, what I did was reprehensible. I'm asking your forgiveness," she said, having a hard time producing those words.

He smiled at her. "Forgiveness granted," he replied. "I know I stand out in a crowd, and that it does seem rather odd, but I'm afraid that's just who I am—nothing much I can do about it. And I will offer no apologies for defending this place—that is my core. But I promise you—no hard feelings." He smiled again, a very winning smile despite the ravaged face.

"Deal, Colonel," Melia replied. "I probably will laugh again if you put me on the defense line with my rolling pin at the ready," she admitted, "but I am sorry for what I said—especially the part about wishing you had been burned." She looked down.

He had a sad, sweet smile on his face. "All forgiven. I think I understand," he said, then glancing up and pointing to the fudge counter, he noted, "Look at the line!"

"The one you drew?" Melia couldn't resist.

"No, the one formed at the fudge counter!"

Both of them raced to Tom's aid. Morena smiled.

"I know they said they couldn't get all the rust off of that old sword, but do you think there's any more they could do to try?" Lori asked Bob.

"Considering everything that's gone on here since Buck started waving that thing around, I wish it would disintegrate from rust," Bob laughed. "What brought this on?"

"Wedding cake," she replied, making a face.

"Come again?"

"He wants to use that thing to cut the wedding cake. I would like it to be a little more sanitized if there's really any chance of that happening. I can't quite get over the idea that we will be cutting my wedding cake with something he plunged into Mexican soldiers' bodies in 1836—makes me a little sickish to think about it," Lori said, but with a laugh.

"You want to know what I really think?" Bob asked.

She nodded. "Yeah, I do. Bob, honestly, you have been the voice of wisdom and reason all along since this whole extraordinary saga started."

He smiled at her. "I think both of you need to compromise. I suspect that's easier for you than for him."

Lori nodded. "I'm pretty sure you're right on that one."

"I know you said something about getting married here because it's where you met. And I get that—the two of you have spent a tremendous amount of time here together. And the meeting itself was certainly not the way two people destined to fall in love usually find each other. But fact is, he's right. It's the sight of the most gruesome battle in American history—no survivors on the American side—until now. And you are asking that one survivor to get married where he saw all of his comrades killed and where he suffered grievous and permanent injuries himself. I think Buck loves you enough that he will do it if you press him hard enough, although he does get really stubborn about anything involving the Alamo. But I would have the wedding somewhere else, maybe your parents' gorgeous backyard. As to the sword, it's kind of gotten to be a joke around

353

town with all the incidents, and it's not sanitary. He should wear it as part of his getup. I'm assuming you are doing an 1836 theme?"

She nodded with a smile. "Oh yes—wasn't any other choice for this one."

He smiled. "That's what I thought. Buck ought to keep that thing sheathed as part of his uniform. The reenactors could do something—I guess most of them don't have swords? Sort of like what the modern military does for a commissioned officer's wedding, where they line up and hold the swords above, points toward each other, and the couple walks through. If the colonel commands enough officer reenactors, that would be a nice touch if you want to do a sword thing."

Lori laughed. "I can't believe we're really talking about this!"

"I'm curious—what about your dad? How is he handling this?"

"He's not one for dressing up and play-acting. He doesn't care if other people do it, but he's not buying into it. When I told him about the theme, he said something along the lines of 'I'm not wearing some dead raccoon on my head to give away my daughter!' He will be in a tux, or, more likely—and I think appropriate, his uniform. My mom doesn't play 1836, either, nor Len. Vicky gave me a hard time about it, but she has to dress up since she's the bridesmaid."

Bob was laughing. "Are any of your Mexican friends invited? I can't quite see General Santa Anna?"

"I think we're going to try to avoid the general's presence as I can't envision getting through the ceremony intact if Buck feels obliged to run the general off with that sword right as we're getting ready to say our vows!"

"Well, there is a difference if you have the wedding at the house," Bob observed.

"Like what?—if he sees a Santa Anna costume, you know he will charge the man."

"Maybe not if it's not on the Alamo grounds," Bob rejoined.

"I think Buck is like a bull seeing the red cape when it comes to Santa

Anna. No doubt, it's worse on the Alamo grounds, but I bet he will react to that anywhere. I don't want the wedding spoiled by it—will clue in Vincente and encourage his Tejano impression instead for this one!"

"Well, you probably already figured this out, but Leslie and I aren't dressing up. We both realize that our relationship, while the most special thing in the world to us, is simply not suited to the 1830's!"

Lori smiled. "Well, you never know, as long as folks didn't spread every detail in a tell-all diary as one person we know did with his sex life!" she reminded him with a laugh.

"Yeah, but back then and in a place as rough and tough as frontier Texas, I think a gay person, if there were any, would be wise to be very, very careful about even a hint. A gay version of the Travis diary could get you strung up in a hurry!"

"I totally agree. He was so explicit in that thing that I think I should thank my lucky stars that someone didn't find it and come after him for his transgressions. Don't worry, there are lots of people coming who are not going to be operating in 1836."

"I suspect all but one of the people coming, regardless of how they're dressed, aren't going to be operating in 1836," Bob replied.

Lori looked at Bob seriously. "I think—maybe I'm wrong about this, but I do think that he will be in the present for this one. When I got hit by the car and he stopped chasing Vincente—to Buck it truly was Santa Anna—you could tell from that look he gets—and turned to me, I knew for sure. Poor Buck is always going to have some issues what with the surgery, the hideous Alamo experience, and the time warp. And, who knows, maybe there is a tinge of truth to what Lyle Jones and Jeff Long and the others have said about the mercury treatments. But when he stopped chasing Santa Anna to come to my aid, I knew how very much he loved ME. He was able to force himself into the present and realized that there were some things, and, more importantly, some people in this present world more important than chasing old ghosts, even if those old ghosts loomed so large in his experience that they pretty much inundated it. He will always be frail and fragile, and I don't doubt that there will be more sword incidents. But I do know that he cares more about me more than anything—even fighting with Santa Anna to honor his dead command."

Lori wiped a tear from her cheek. Bob handed her a box of tissues.

"We've come a long way in a relatively short time with the commander of the Alamo. I'm not a religious person—at least in the traditional sense, but I do believe there are purposes for things. And I think there was a purpose in all of this from the moment the students started unearthing the heel of the first boot. I think you're right and going into this relationship with your head on straight. It will always be a little different—and certainly interesting, but I think it's going to work out OK. Love does triumph over all as Buck wrote in the diary so long ago," Bob said with a sweet smile.

Bob was seriously thinking about taking marriage counselor training. Not one hour after his talk with Lori regarding the upcoming wedding, the groom showed up in his office.

"Getting nervous yet, Colonel?" Bob asked with a slight laugh.

"No, I'm not. I am convinced this is why I am here instead of in my other world," Buck said quietly, a serious look on his face. "But I've got to ask you, has there been any movement on getting the ring out of the case? I understand it will likely have to be sized, and I have no clue where to go or how to do that."

"Actually, yes, the Land Office has consented—heard from them near closing time yesterday. They really couldn't say no, but it's hard to get a government agency to let go of something once they have it in their clutches. I think we can remove it any time you like."

"Lori and I talked about it. I asked her if she would like it as an engagement gift, to be followed by something else as a wedding ring, as it really does not look like what any bride would have for her wedding. But you know Lori. She is so down-to-earth and not mindful of having to follow all of the traditions. She said she wanted it for her wedding ring. Back in the day, the man usually did not have a wedding ring. It was permissible, but not everyone did. Maybe this doesn't seem like enough? But it seems appropriate for what I'll admit is our rather unusual situation."

Bob smiled at him. "Yes, Buck, I can see where Lori is coming from, and I'm sure she is telling you straight from the heart what she wants. It is most appropriate. I think we can have it removed from the case anytime you want. I would like both of you to be here. I know a good jeweler. Leslie and I use them. And I'm sure your bride would be happy to drive you there so they can size it for you."

"One more thing—will I need a copy of the divorce decree from Alabama to submit here to remarry?" Buck asked.

"You're the lawyer," Bob laughed.

"Normally, I think I would," Buck replied. "But it's obvious that Rosanna is long dead—even had the decree not gone through. I honestly did not know the status, although, of course, I knew she had filed, when I headed to the Alamo, but I understand I became a free man on January 9, 1836, per an act of the state legislature. I would hope a copy of the decree was filed in the records in Monroe County, Alabama, where we lived and where she continued to live and filed for divorce long after I left for Texas. I also have been told that she remarried—to an old acquaintance of mine—very quickly, a little over a month after the divorce was final, I guess about the time . . . ." He didn't finish the sentence.

Bob saw a sad look crossing Travis' face. Rosanna's timing had certainly been awful, even though she could not have known of the tragic events already in play in far-off Texas. And she certainly did not wait around to remarry, making obvious the fact that she was already attracted to husband no. 2 before there was a divorce from husband no. 1. That said, the Don Juan of the Alamo certainly couldn't point any fingers.

"Well, if you think there's any chance you might need it, you could write for a copy," Bob replied. "I suspect they will know who you are immediately. Tell them the impending wedding is soon and ask them to expedite it. Or you could get with Lori and send an email if you want to move it faster," Bob suggested.

"A what?" Buck asked.

"Email—it's sending a note to someone on the computer. You type it out on the keyboard, then hit a button and it sends it straight to the recipient immediately," Bob explained. "Everyone does it all the time now."

"This is rather personal. I think I'll just use my quill," Buck replied, making a slight face. "Of course, I reckon it's possible the address may not be the same as it was in 1836?" he thought out loud.

Bob turned to his computer screen. "I can get that for you in a hurry," he offered. "What did you say, Monroe County, Alabama?"

Buck nodded. Bob pressed some buttons on the strange keyboard. He stared at the information that came up on the screen, typed a little more and looked at another screen, then grabbed a newfangled pen and wrote the address on a piece of paper, handing it to the colonel so that he could write his 1836 style letter to the modern-day court officials.

The herds were moving slowly through the old church as they did every day, the men congregating around Davy's rifle and guesstimating what he could and could not hit at how many yards with the heavy old gun. Bob had thought about waiting until after closing time to open the case containing the ring for Buck and Lori, but then it would be too late to get to the jeweler that day. So the three of them pushed through the crowds, Elbert and Jaime with them. As they got to the cases containing the relics, Elbert went ahead, clearing some space in front of the case containing the cat's eye ring. Jaime blocked traffic from the back. Bob had a key, and Elbert disarmed the alarm as Bob deftly put the key in and retrieved the famous ring and handed it to Buck. He held it in his hand a moment, staring at it, determined to think only of its future, not 1836, then turned to Lori and slipped it on her finger. It was a little large—would have to be resized, but she stared at it, then at Buck, quickly moved the ring to her middle finger, where it was just the right size, and put her arms around her Alamo hero. The crowd, most of whom had heard of the colonel's return to life and knew who he was from the clothing and scars, broke the rules about silence in the church as he embraced Lori and kissed her.

The clerk at the jewelry store stared. Bob had thought to give them a quick call and a heads-up that some unusual customers would be coming in late in the afternoon to have an unusual ring sized. But the warning couldn't quite encompass the appearance of the male half of the young couple as Buck opened the door for Lori and followed her inside. The chic young woman behind the counter continued to stare as they walked toward her.

"Uh, may . . . I . . . help you?" she stuttered, eyes wide at the sight of the young man with the damaged face, odd costume, and clanking sword at his side. Lori, whose schedule at work had not included cooking anything weird this day, looked perfectly normal in a blue top and jeans.

"We need to have a ring sized," Buck said simply.

The clerk was still staring—even more so now that the colonel was right in front of the counter. Lori removed the ring from her middle finger and handed it to the young woman, who almost dropped it as she was having a difficult time concentrating.

"It's very old," Lori said reverently. "It's from the Alamo battle."

The clerk was still staring. "Under the circumstances, that kind of makes sense," she said softly, still looking at Travis. "Just curious—I hate to pry, but what's going on? Someone from over there did call and say I would have customers tied to the place coming over to have a ring sized, but that's all he said."

Buck looked at Lori and smiled. The woman was still staring.

"This is Col. Travis—commander of the Alamo—at the 1836 battle. Did you hear about finding him?" Lori raised her eyebrows in question.

"Yeah. I think just about everyone heard something about an Alamo defender being found," the woman replied, finally looking at Lori. "So you're really from way back then?" she renewed her stare at Buck.

"Yes ma'am, I am," he said quietly, looking directly at her. "But I have been given this wonderful second opportunity—and met Lori, who has helped guide me into the present, although I'm still not too good at navigating your new world. We're going to be married. The ring is mine, from 1836. I would like to have it sized for Lori's left hand. I'll admit right off that it does not look like the usual wedding ring, but that's the intent."

The woman looked at the ring, affirming what he had already told her. "Your ring?" she looked up at him.

He nodded.

"Yeah, it doesn't look like an ordinary wedding ring at all," she said as she turned it over, then looked directly at the stone. "It's a bit beaten up."

"That's OK," Lori said quickly. "After all, for God's sake, it's been through a battle 181 years ago. I think it's the most wonderful ring in the world." Her eyes were focused on Buck.

The clerk shrugged. "It's a personal choice," she said. "Certainly will be unique," she added, her look taking in the colonel as if including him in the comment as well.

She sized Lori's finger, wrote something down on a ticket, placed the antique ring in a little envelope with the ticket attached to it, detached a perforated stub from the ticket and handed it to Buck, and asked them if picking it up in a week would be convenient.

"Yes, that will be fine if you are sure you will have it ready by then. The wedding is in 2 weeks," Buck said.

"This time of year, repairs go pretty quickly. I'm confident that it will be ready for you in a week," the clerk replied.

"One more thing," Lori added. "I'm sure you have a safe? This ring has tremendous value—to us, of course, but the historical value has to be considered as well. Could you keep it in the safe for us?"

"Yes, definitely. If it's been around 181 years and is tied to the battle, we certainly don't want the liability of someone walking off with it," the saleswoman replied. "This wedding should be quite an event," she added, again staring at Buck.

"It will be a little different from the cookie-cutter weddings you see all the time—we're trying to mesh the 1830's with the present since that's the heart of the story, so to speak," Lori said, her eyes on Buck, who had a little smile on his face. "Thank you. We'll see you in a week."

The chic young woman continued to stare at the tall young man in his funny clothes as he held the door for Lori and they exited the store.

The clerk of court's office work was slowing down on Friday afternoon. It was the end of the long week, and it was also rural Monroe County, Alabama, where things moved at a more leisurely pace than in the big cities.

Alice Bensen had worked there for 31 years—her entire career. Her dad had been a local attorney, and, although she had no inclination to go to law school, she was familiar with the court system. The clerk's office just seemed like a natural place for her to fix her career. And so she had.

"Say, Miss Alice, I just got the mail. Didn't you tell me you're kin to Col. Travis of the Alamo?" a young black woman popped her head in the door of Alice's office.

360

"Yes, Ruby, I am. Why?" the older woman responded.

"Well, in today's mail," she shuffled through it, "there's an antique-looking letter on some kind of special paper and written in funny ink and handwriting addressed to the clerk of the court from a Col. Travis at the Alamo in San Antonio. But hasn't he been dead for like over 100 years?" Ruby asked, a puzzled look on her face. "Must be some kind of joke," she added.

Alice laughed. "Actually 181 years, but they did an archaeological dig out there and found his body. He was sort of in a state of suspended animation, I guess. He was barely alive and they were able to revive him. I was out there last month and made a point of going by to meet him—nice young man, rather old-fashioned as you would expect, considering. We've written back and forth a few times since. He writes with an old-fashioned quill pen—rather quaint! That's how come the funny ink," she replied.

Ruby handed her the letter. "Can't imagine what he would want from the clerk's office here," she said in a puzzled tone, shaking her head.

Alice opened the envelope. Ruby, curious, continued to stand there.

Alice laughed. "He's leaving nothing to chance! The colonel had an unhappy marriage here in Monroe County, and, after he headed to Texas to get away from that situation and a pile of debts, his wife filed for divorce. The decree came down too late for him to find out about it before Santa Anna stormed the Alamo and killed everyone. Now it looks as if our young colonel is going to tie the knot with Lori Clayton. I met her, too—delightful, sweet young girl. The colonel wants a copy of the ancient divorce decree just to be sure!"

"But, Miss Alice, isn't his ex-wife DEAD?" Ruby asked, her eyes wide.

"Yeah," Alice replied, "But they may require anyone who has been divorced to produce proof out there—many states do," she said. "Of course, this possibility regarding the amount of time that has gone by has never come up before and wouldn't be accounted for in the law!"

"Want me to search the old divorce records and find it for you?" the eager young woman asked. "I'm kind of curious to see it."

"Surely!" Alice replied. "That would be a big help, as I'd really like to get the rest of this stuff off my desk this afternoon. The divorce should be in early 1836. I don't know the exact date, but I know it was shortly before the Alamo was stormed—that was March 6." Alice scanned the letter again. "He gives January 9. Sounds like the wedding will be fairly soon from the tone of urgency in his letter!"

Bob knocked at Buck's closed office door, the colonel calling out "Come in," as usual.

"What can I do for you?" Buck asked as Bob tried to adjust his eyes to the dim light.

"Buck, I'm thinking you could help us out with our contracts if you feel comfortable with it," he started.

"If you mean from a legal standpoint, it's possible things might have changed some," the colonel cautioned.

"Yes, I know that. In fact, there was a trend among the states long after the Alamo battle to require lawyers to become members of newly constituted state bar associations. I called the Texas organization and told them about your situation. They were quick to say they would grandfather you in and waive dues and so forth due to your status as a state hero," Bob explained.

"I don't expect any special privileges," Buck replied quickly.

"I know, but I thought it was a nice gesture—think I'd take them up on it if I were you," Bob suggested. "I don't know that I'd hang out a shingle—and there's no need as you've got a great job here, I bet for life if you want it. However, I would appreciate a look at our current contracts, not with an eye to rewriting them in total but just to see if you see anything obvious from an attorney standpoint that us non-attorneys might miss. I honestly think y'all think a little differently, even if your legal world was rather different from the present. I made copies of a couple of the contracts in hopes you would take a look. There are more if you feel you are accomplishing anything."

"Surely, if you think it will be of any possible benefit to the Alamo," the colonel agreed. "I can just note any suggestions on these copies?"

Bob nodded. "Yes, please, and let me have them once you're done.

The deadline for submittal is 2 months from now, so you have plenty of time to peruse them. I'll then forward them to the General Land Office—all our stuff goes through them. Fact is, they pretty much use standard contracts without taking into account any deviations that might be helpful for a unique organization such as the Alamo. That's where I'm hoping you can do us a favor—maybe tailor anything you notice to our specific needs. They will at least take notice of anything you find."

The young lawyer smiled. Someone finally wanted him to do something besides dress in uniform and give speeches at ceremonies or help with demonstrations.

"Oh, and one other thing—I think Lori is going to be showing you a few things on her computer screen. Don't worry if you do not care to learn how to use it—it's just that's where the information is. She needs some help with the list of the known defenders that we maintain. There are a lot of gaps. I realize that, as commander, you probably won't know everything about everyone, but I'm betting you will be able to clear up some of the discrepancies or missing information. If, when she shows you the list, you start noticing things, we'll print it out so you can update it as well."

"Y'all are finally putting me to work!" the young man blurted out. "I appreciate that, I truly do. It's nice to feel needed. Without a Mexican army to fight—and God only knows I do not want one, I have kind of wondered what I'm supposed to do around here."

Bob smiled. "As we think of more things where you can help, we'll let you know. We're going to be doing some promotional and inspirational activities, and I know you have skills in that area based on your famous letters. As you know, the staff is so small here that anything anyone can contribute makes for a better Alamo."

"I'm all for that. Anything to keep the memory of my men and the flame of liberty that this place represents alive!" the colonel said earnestly, determination in his eyes.

## THE TEXIAN AND HIS YELLOW ROSE

Raul, dressed as Seguin, caught up with Lori.

"Hey, I was talking with a few of the association folks, and we've got a new idea for a cooking demo."

"Uh . . . like what?" Lori asked hesitantly.

"Rattlesnake!" he replied, a strangely eager look on his face.

"I'm not catching it," she replied quickly.

"No problem there—Ol' Davy is going to do that. He and Bowie are going on some kind of snake hunt. If you're willing, they'll bring in a fresh snake for you to chop up and cook on Wednesday after the hunt!" Raul actually sounded excited. It was obviously a guy thing.

"Tell me, Raul, is this in place of cactus or intended to go with it?" she asked.

"Whichever you think is best—just thought it would be something a little different."

"Certainly will. But, yeah, I'm up for it if they bring the snake. I'm assuming the congressman will skin it for me?"

"I'll be sure and tell him—or, better yet, I'll get him to bring it with the skin still on and give a skinning demo before you cook it," Raul replied.

"Oh, yes, that will definitely make folks' mouths water," Lori said as she envisioned the clearly unappetizing sight. "Were you thinking of fried snake 'bites' so to speak or rattler chili?" she continued.

"Wow! Rattler chili sounds awesome if you could do it!"

"Well, no beans, of course, and we can just throw the chunks in a big pot with some tomatoes, peppers, and onions, if that will cover it?" she asked.

364

"Say, who is this 'we'?" Raul had picked up the scary pronoun in her reply.

"Don't worry, not you. I have someone else in mind who can help me cut up the snake if need be," she replied with a grin. "Don't go mentioning this to anyone right yet, you hear?"

It was 2:30 on Wednesday afternoon, and Buck had just left the gift shop—and the latest strange look from Melia, armed with an entire box of fudge. Lori stopped setting up for her demo for a moment as she saw the candy. He set the box on her ancient little table and opened it.

"You're not going to eat that whole chunk are you?" she asked.

"No, I'm going to cut a piece for each of us," came the response. "I figured we might want more than just one piece."

"Oh no, let me guess . . . ." she started.

Buck whipped the sword out of its scabbard and neatly sliced two large pieces of fudge, one for each of them, handed her a piece, and then grabbed his piece. She thought about where the sword had been—and what it had been used for, but she quickly got over that at the thought of the delicious candy.

"Want any more?" he asked, already having downed his.

She was still chewing, but she nodded in the affirmative. Out came the sword, and he sliced off two more generous pieces.

"You know, there's not much left," he noted, looking at the candy remaining in the box. "Let's just go ahead and finish it off!"

He took one more swipe and split the remainder of the fudge in two pieces, handing Lori, who had her mouth full of the candy, one last piece, then finally returned the weapon to its scabbard.

"Although I'm a little squeamish about where that sword has been," Lori told him, her mouth still full, "it is a better use for it than your usual."

Both of them were licking their fingers after their last bites of candy.

365

Raul knew from his conversation with Lori the other day that she had something in mind, and he made a point to be standing a short way off in the distance as she prepared for her presentation. Lori was still in the forlorn old rose dress, the huge rip in the skirt from the accident mended but obvious. There had been no time to even think about starting on the blue print replacement what with having to make Vicky's dress for the wedding.

Crockett and Bowie strolled up, Crockett with a large burlap sack in his right hand and Bowie with his perennial scowl on his face and the vicious knife in his belt. Lori cleared the rickety little table, putting her large wooden bowl, full of cut-up vegetables for the chili, on the ground, her paring knife in it.

Crockett put his sack up to the table, turned it upside down, and out fell not one, but three large, live rattlers, two hitting the table and the third bouncing and falling to the ground, still moving. The brave commander of the Alamo jumped back, lost his balance, and fell on his rear end, his hat flying in back of him. Lori was already at a little distance, but she added a little more quickly. Raul, from his safe position ensconced behind a pecan tree, was laughing. Bowie swiftly took the heads off of one of the rattlers on the table and the one that hit the ground with his knife. The other one was left for the congressman's demo. Crockett had it contained with a knife held at the base of the head. Bob would have had an apoplexy had he known about this event. The congressman and the knife-fighter roared with laughter. Even Lori could not suppress a laugh. The horrified and embarrassed colonel, his face beet-red, picked himself up, grabbed the hat and put it on his head, and tried to dust himself off. He still hung back slightly.

"Why the Hell do you need THREE of them?" Travis shouted.

"I kinda like my chili meaty," the congressman said with a toothy grin.

"What the Hell?" was all Travis could muster as he glared at Saints Davy and Jim.

"When we told Raul that we were going to a snake shoot, he said he thought a snake dinner would make an interesting demo. Problem is, for a connoisseur, at least, they taste best fresh," the congressman explained seriously. Bowie just stood there, a sinister look on his face.

"Snake dinner?" the South Carolina gentleman replied in revulsion.

"You've got to be kidding!"

"No, sir. We eat it all the time," Crockett responded calmly. "It's right tasty once you get past the thought of what you're eating! Tastes like chicken. Your lady here has been gracious enough to volunteer to cook it for us." He turned to Lori.

Travis gave her a disconcerted look.

"Uh, that's where you come in, Buck," she joined in. "I want you to chop them up for me."

"Sounds like a job for Col. Bowie. He's got the equipment," Travis quickly replied, looking at the big knife.

"You don't need anything like this," Bowie said, patting his weapon, "To cut up a little ol' rattler. Colonel, that little paring knife Miss Clayton's got down there in that bowl will do just fine—or, if you feel you need a little more distance, use your sword. You go ahead. I wouldn't want to take the honor away from you, you being the commander and all!" he added, pointing to the knife in the bowl.

Travis looked at the snake Crockett had in front of him. "It's still got the head and skin on it!" the disgusted lawyer responded.

"The congressman will take care of that little issue in a jiffy," Bowie said, turning to Crockett, who had at the ready a knife close to the size of Bowie's, with which he was holding in place the one still live and dangerous snake. With his other hand, he grabbed Old Betsy and stomped the head of the rattler to death with the butt of the gun, quickly and adeptly, then started to lop off the head with his knife.

He explained as he worked, "See how the fangs popped out? He's history. You gotta continue cutting through 'til the head's completely off—can be a bit tough because you're cutting through the spine. You just lop that ol' head off, then might want to wait a bit until it's through wiggling around if that happens to bother you any. But that can go on for a while, so I usually like to go ahead. Then you take a-hold of the skin where the head was, slit it, put your finger in the slit, grab onto the skin and pull it right down—should just kind of peel off and turn inside out." He whacked off the rattles at the tail end and stuffed them in a pocket, stating, "For folks who are into that kind of thing, it helps you keep score."

367

Lori tried desperately not to laugh at that last remark. Travis looked stricken.

Crockett had finished with the first snake and pushed it to the side of the table, going ahead and starting on the second. Bowie had speared the snake that fell to the ground with his knife and flipped it onto the table. The headless serpents were continuing to writhe and squirm, blood from where the heads had been joined to the bodies spilling out on Lori's table.

Travis was turning pale. "And what did you say you want me to do?" he asked Lori nervously.

Bowie answered for her. "Well, Colonel, after the congressman gets them skinned, you want to take out the entrails from the belly. They're all packed together in a sac, so you can just take it all out together. Don't let it break or it will stink to high heaven—not that I'm familiar with that place. Be sure you get that long artery that goes the length of the body. Just pull all that reddish goo out from stem to stern. What's left will be the spine with the meat on it—that's all there is to a snake! You just rinse and clean any membranes out in water, being sure that your container is deep enough so the snake can't wiggle out if it's still fresh enough that it's lively."

Lori added, "Then you can get the meat off in chunks—if they're cut small enough, they won't move. I want small pieces for the chili," she said calmly.

Travis hit the ground in a dead faint.

Bowie and Crockett came around the table and lifted their limp leader off the ground and placed him in Lori's wooden chair. She took out the "goo" and dunked the first snake in a bucket of water, and was chopping up snake meat to place in her Dutch oven set over a nice fire. She put the meat in first, browning it, and stirring with a long wooden spoon, then added salt, pepper, and garlic, and loads of onions, chilies, jalapenos, habaneros, a couple of tomatoes, and a tomatillo, as well as water from a second bucket. She also added one Carolina Reaper—considering the size of the pot and the contents, the Reaper would not seem as deadly as the evil little peppers did in the contest at Ramale's.

The disgusting part over, the concoction smelled pretty good. Travis was coming around, and he had to admit that. When Lori put the vegetables and water in to cook, it started looking like something someone might consider eating. She had a good fire going. An hour and a half later, a

368

heavenly aroma of peppers, onions, garlic, tomatoes, and snake filled the air. It was getting close to time for dinner, and tourists as well as some of the other reenactors were hanging around. The tourists were out of luck due to the rules prohibiting offering food cooked at the complex to visitors, but the reenactors and staff were lined up to partake. Alamo legends Bowie, Crockett, Seguin, and Bonham, as well as Lori, were digging in. Despite Travis' reputation for always seeming hungry and not too picky, there apparently was a limit. He politely declined, despite the fact that it did smell divine. The preparation had been such a god-awful mess that the fastidious young man simply didn't think he could ingest the concoction. Lori was busy doling out seconds to admirers of her cooking.

"I think I'll head over to the River Walk and get something at the Republic of Texas," Buck said anxiously, turning away from the steaming pot.

"Buck Travis! This is a perfectly genuine Texian dish. Now you set your butt down and I'll get you a bowl!" Lori commanded in true frontier style, somewhat put out at his reticence after all her efforts.

Bowie, Crockett, Seguin, Bonham, and the rest of the troops were trying desperately to suppress laughter and concentrate on their chili. Travis considered the fact that the others had not keeled over, observed the none-too-pleased look on Lori's face, and hesitantly joined the party. Once he tried it, he had to admit that as long as he didn't have to catch, kill, skin, clean, or cook it, rattlesnake was rather tasty.

"Got to have you try the dress on again," Lori told Vicky, holding it out to her. "I want to make any alterations needed to get the fit perfect."

Vicky made a face. "I'm sure it's close enough," she replied with a shrug and a disinterested tone.

Lori threw it at her. "I know you hate this, believe me, but, if you don't want to do it for me, do it for Buck!" She was trying anything to get the stubborn Vicky to cooperate.

"Buck doesn't care whether I'm wearing 1836 stuff or not," Vicky shot back.

"Yeah, you're probably right on that one," Lori responded. "But he does care about this wedding and making it as easy as possible on me," she tried to cajole her little sister.

Vicky made another face, but she took the pale blue lawn dress and tried it on. It was a mini-version of Lori's yellow dress in every way except it was just slightly shorter in the skirt and had short, puffy big sleeves instead of the elbow-length huge sleeves of Lori's original. Vicky stared at herself in Lori's big mirror. She wouldn't admit it for anything, but it was kind of pretty.

"I don't look like me AT ALL—I'm not the puffy, foo-foo type," she proclaimed. "And what are you going to DO to my hair?" she asked in a friendly but slightly suspicious tone.

"Not much—just comb it and maybe stick a white artificial rosebud in it."

"That's a relief!" Vicky replied. "I was afraid you were going to make me put on some kind of wig because I don't have long hair and all those pioneer women did!"

"No, we're not going that far with it—just want your dress to somewhat go with mine. I think it's gorgeous," Lori said, "even if I did make it myself. I bet I know someone else who will think so, too!"

The someone else happened to walk down the hall right at that moment.

"Why, Miss Vicky, you are the epitome of an 1836 Texian belle!" Buck bowed as he said it.

Vicky screwed up her face, grabbed a book on the Alamo that was sitting on Lori's bed, and threw it toward the colonel. He ducked, and it sailed just over the top of his head.

The media were circling the quiet neighborhood where the Clayton family lived, casing the place for the big event the next day. Somehow, as is their wont regarding a potential story, they had found out that Texas' greatest living hero was going to be married there. Buck had finally won one. Lori had caved to his concerns about a wedding at the Alamo, despite the fact that Bob had obtained a waiver to the ban had the couple really wanted to push it. So an outdoor ceremony in the expansive backyard was in the works. In a show of compromise, the colonel had agreed to wear his sword but not eat with it, much to Lori's relief. She had gotten with Raul, and he rounded up enough "officers" from the organization to perform the sword ceremony for their commander at his wedding.

Elena, Lori, and Vicky had spent the entire day in the kitchen, making fancy cookies and pecan brownies for the reception. Buck was in his t-shirt and jeans, saving the "new" old uniform, which Lori had taken to the cleaners—and the same strange clerk who had been there when she took the bloody clothes months ago. Len mowed the yard, and Buck was trying his hand with the hedge clippers, cleaning things up around the yard. Lori had finalized Vicky's dress and found a few tiny white rosebuds for her to wear in her hair. The eclectic combination of the past and present allowed for a reality of anything goes for this event. Several of the media types had singled out the house and actually come up and knocked on the door or rung the bell, which the Claytons ignored. One van, complete with camera crew, pulled up in the driveway and parked until Major Clayton ran them off. Not long after the major chased off the van, Rosalia, Juana, and Margarita showed up with more "goodies" for the reception.

Rosalia had a huge, beautiful plate heaped with round, bite-sized cookies rolled in confectioner's sugar. "Don't tell him they're MEXICAN wedding cookies!" she laughed, as she handed the plate to Elena. The Montoya women pitched in to help the Claytons in the huge kitchen.

"Funny thing about Buck," Lori noted. "Despite all the sword waving when he sees the Mexican troops, he doesn't seem at all hesitant when it comes to Mexican food—or, when I think about it, food in general!"

All the women laughed.

With the Montoyas there to help with the food, Lori headed outside to the backyard, first to give glasses of water to Len and Buck, as it was another scorching day, then to look around at the flowers in the yard. Most would stay right where they were, providing a gorgeous backdrop for the ceremony. But she did need a few for bouquets for Vicky and herself, and something for corsages for her parents, the groom, and Bob, the best man. She wasn't sure whether a corsage on the antique military outfit or her dad's new one was even correct, but she intended to procure them just the same. Fortunately, a gardenia bush was laden with the fragrant white blooms. She would wait until the last minute to pick them, as they turned brown if not fresh or at a touch. The only rose bush in the yard—a climber with yellow

371

blooms, had been planted by Lori as a child years ago. It was now enormous, covering the fence on the side of the house. There were plenty of yellow buds just getting ready to bloom. They would be perfect for Vicky, their mom, and herself. Vicky was her only attendant. The wedding party itself was as small as Lori could arrange, but the guest list was not. All of the Alamo staff and the reenactors were invited. Alice Bensen and her husband were due to get in that night driving from Alabama. Tom Ryan and his class who had unearthed the colonel were invited as well as some of the hospital folks who were involved in Buck's return to the living. Even Lyle and Mary Jones made the list—after Lori had extracted a promise from Lyle that he wouldn't badmouth Buck at his wedding.

The Claytons did not have a church affiliation. Buck did, of course, but his church didn't have a pastor. Finding someone to perform the ceremony turned out to be a little more of a stretch than Lori had originally thought it would be. Finally, Raul solved the problem. He divulged a well-kept secret. Mitch, Col. Bowie of all people, was actually an ordained minister, although not currently practicing. Mitch made a point of not advertising it as it certainly did not fit well with his Alamo persona. When Lori mentioned this to Buck, he balked at it, in fact, flatly denied that it was possible, until Saint Jim showed him his credentials. Buck noted that it was some denomination he had never heard of, certainly not Baptist! Considering that Travis had no other answer to the dilemma, he consented to let his Alamo competitor perform the ceremony.

By 6:00, they had made considerable headway, but there was much yet to be done, although most of it was last minute and would have to be wrapped up late in the afternoon the next day. The wedding was set for 7:30 in the evening, when it would still be hot but hopefully beginning to cool off a little.

Vincente drove up in his old truck with Andres and Ciro in tow. "Say, anyone want to head out to Wingo's for barbeque to celebrate the colonel's last night as a free man?" he practically shouted at the herd of women working frantically in the kitchen.

Elena looked up from the pan of brownies in her hand. "Sounds good to me! I'm getting a bit tired of looking at sweets—don't know about anyone else?" She looked around at her kitchen compatriots.

"Yeah! How about right now!" Vicky yelled, thoroughly sick of the kitchen work. "I'll round up the guys," she offered, heading to the door.

372

Len and Buck were sitting on the back steps to the brick patio, admiring their handiwork. The yard did look gorgeous.

"You guys want to go out for barbeque? Vincente is here, and he just asked," Vicky shouted at them as she opened the French doors.

"We're kind of dirty," Buck called to her. His standards for what constituted "dirty" had gone up since 1836. Len nodded.

"Trust me, they won't care at Wingo's. You've seen it—not exactly fancy," she replied flatly. "You want to go or not? I'm hungry."

The two guys looked at each other. They were hungry, too. Wingo's sounded really, really good, and they followed Vicky inside.

The Montoyas' truck, the junior members of the family in the truck bed, and the Claytons' SUV formed a mini-caravan heading west to the barbeque joint. As they pulled in the dirt parking lot, kicking up a lot of dust, Vincente spotted a small, rather beaten-up Toyota Yaris in a dull beige. The entire back of the car was plastered with various liberal cause bumper stickers as well as one that read "Me No Alamo," the cry the Mexican soldiers gave as the victorious Texians exercised their murderous payback on them at the Battle of San Jacinto. He stared at the vehicle, told himself it wasn't possible, and headed into the restaurant with his family and the Claytons. As usual, there was a wait for seats. His eyes scanned the room. He didn't see anyone he knew. Then he looked at the line ahead of them. Toward the head of the line, there she was—Luisa.

"Pardon me for a minute," he said to Robert, then headed forward.

"Cousin? Is that really you?" he exclaimed as he tapped her on the shoulder.

Luisa turned with a look of embarrassment on her face. The tall young man with her just stared.

"Uh, tell me, cousin, have you changed your views on reactionaries?" Vincente laughed.

"No, not at all," she answered quickly. "I just really wanted some good barbeque!" she laughed, then hugged Vincente. Angelo continued to gawk until Luisa thought to introduce him.

373

"All right, but I can tell you that the reactionaries are here in force tonight—including their fearless leader!" Vincente warned her.

"You've got to be kidding? This is the first time I've set foot in this place in 3 years, and the colonel is here?" she asked.

Vincente nodded. "I'll be right back," he replied, then quickly headed back to his place in line.

A few seconds later, he was back with the tall young redhead in his t-shirt and jeans, the hair combed over the gunshot wound. Angelo stared, his eyes wide behind his glasses. Luisa stared, too. The transformation was remarkable.

"Colonel?" was all she could say.

"You're the lady from the rally—the one who didn't make my list, right?" Buck was direct with her.

Luisa smiled at him. "Yes, I'm the one who didn't make your list!" she laughed. "Let me introduce you to my friend Angelo—I believe the two of you are the same age." She pointed toward the young man with glasses. Buck and Angelo shook hands.

"I am sure you don't want to take advice from a Latina activist," Luisa admitted to Buck, "but that's not going to stop me from giving it. The current clothes and whatever you did to your hair make all the difference in the world, Colonel. I understand, although don't necessarily agree with, your desire to dress in 1836 garb at the Alamo, but I can't tell you how much better you look now. I think it's something to keep in mind when you want to relate to people—not just Hispanics. Anyway, you look great, and I continue to be SO thankful that you were not hurt that day when you fell from the roof!" A genuine smile came over her face. "Take care young Colonel. You have a marvelous second chance most of us never get—use it to the fullest!" she advised.

"Thank you ma'am," he replied quietly, giving her his quaint little bow. "Good to meet you," he acknowledged to Angelo, who replied with the same, and Vincente and Buck headed back to their party.

It was the morning of June 24. The wedding was 11 hours away. The

374

media feeding frenzy was getting out of hand. Buck offered to threaten them at sword point, but the major wisely deterred him, knowing that would just fuel the fire. Robert Clayton pulled out a more modern weapon, his cell phone, and called the police. Within a half an hour, officers had shooed away the most aggressive newshounds and placed blockades at the two approaches to the street.

Once the coast was clear, Robert and Len headed to the cleaners and then to the bakery to pick up the bride's and groom's cakes. They were now just getting out of the SUV with their treasures. The wedding cake had the traditional bride and groom figures on top, surrounded by a ring of fresh yellow rose buds, but the little bride and groom were not the plastic figures usually adorning such cakes. One of the Texian Association members whittled and carved wood as a hobby. He had produced and painted an 1836 wedding cake couple, the man in a blue tailcoat and planter hat and the blonde lady in a long, full yellow dress. The groom's cake, smaller, was the traditional fruit cake, this one iced and with a Texas flag in the middle and decorator frosting swords crossed below the flag. Lori had chosen to ignore the all-morning routine at the hairdresser for herself and Vicky, 1836 ladies not having that option available, although Elena headed in that direction, no time warp impeding her. Vicky was greatly relieved.

Lori took one last look at the flowers in the garden. There were agapanthus aplenty, both white and blue, as well as the numerous yellow roses on her enormous bush. She cut enough flowers for bouquets for Vicky and herself and a corsage for her mom, leaving the gardenia bush alone for now as those flowers had to stay pristine. She tied bunches of the flowers with yellow ribbons and placed them in the refrigerator.

By 7 p.m., the wedding guests were beginning to arrive. Rented white chairs had been arranged beyond the pool in the huge backyard. There was an aisle but no "sides" for the bride's family and for the groom's family. White Chinese lanterns had been hung around the grounds but would not be needed until the reception as it was still light and would be for quite some time.

The 1836 crowd garnered some stares from neighbors and passersby as they began pulling up in sedans and SUVs. One resident couple, walking around the block after dinner as they did religiously each night, were stopped briefly by the police, who quickly let them pass after they pointed out that they lived three houses down.

The man turned to his wife. "They look absurd all dressed up in their

1800's regalia and driving in here in their air-conditioned cars!"

"True, but think what a mess it would be if they all came in on horseback," she replied with a laugh.

Mitch, as Colonel Bowie, had shown up early. After all, he would perform the ceremony for his erstwhile competitor at the Alamo. He was wearing the same brown coat and pants and dark olive silk vest, and his brown felt gambler hat, that he usually wore to Alamo events. But he had his clothes cleaned and brushed so that they looked less rustic, and, in 19th Century style, the knife-fighter looked downright debonair. Dave, as Congressman Crockett, had obviously pulled out his old Washington, D.C., duds, as he was dressed in a tailcoat in black, beige pants, and a white shirt with cravat and red vest, thankfully not one of the hideous concoctions on the order of the one in the Alamo display case. He had combed the longish dark hair and certainly looked neater than in his buckskins, but no one would confuse the frontiersman with Beau Brummell. Crockett had his fiddle with him, and, indeed, was seated and beginning to play old tunes, beginning with the graceful "Spanish Waltz." Anthony Robbins, dressed elegantly in a black tailcoat and fully into his "Joe" role, was directing the guests as they came in. Raul and Vincente both were turned out in full ornamented Tejano dress costume. Rosalia was in her beautiful garnet silk dress and mantilla, and Juana and Margarita each wore simpler versions of that outfit. Juana had a gorgeous Spanish fan and was using it to advantage in the heat. The Texian Association reenactors and their ladies were beginning to stream in, all in their 1836 Sunday best. The officers of the Alamo garrison "regular" troops were in their "uniforms" and with their swords ready for that part of the ceremony.

Morena had Melia and Tom in tow, as usual. None of them opted for the 1836 look. Morena had on a long mauve silk top over coordinated silk palazzo pants, and plentiful jewelry, including her trademark bracelets. Melia was in a hot pink short-short dress and Tom in a sports shirt and jeans. The Bensens pulled in along the long block in a late model Cadillac sedan—in Crimson Tide red with "Roll Tide" stickers on the back. Alice was in a simple navy dress. Her husband, new to all of this and staring intently at all of the costumes, was plainly attired in a sport coat and pants. Bob had to wear a suit. He chose a not-quite navy blue in an attempt to somewhat coordinate with the colonel's blue coat as he was Buck's best man. Leslie wore a navy suit.

As Davy started playing "Rose of Allendale," the incoming guests were milling around. The dashing and handsome Col. Travis, in full Southern planter costume of blue tailcoat, white pants, yellow vest, and red sash—the new and improved version, compliments of his bride, Lori's concealer dulling the sword slash on his face, and wearing his white hat and his sword, strode toward Col. Bowie. Bowie, twirling his knife, did not see Travis coming.

"Good evening, Colonel!" Buck greeted the knife-fighter.

Bowie sheathed the knife. "And to you, Colonel! Are you ready for the next big adventure in your life?" he asked with a laugh.

"By all means! Honestly, it's the best thing that's ever happened to me!"

Bowie stared at him. "In your case, you realize that's not a high bar!"

Travis laughed, but he had a semi-sad look on his face. "Yes, I'm afraid you are right on that one—but this is more happiness than I ever thought possible." His demeanor brightened. "One question I do have for you, though—do you actually possess a Bible, and are you going to use it?" He raised his eyebrows in question.

Bowie laughed. "Well, yes, I've got a pocket Bible, but I thought we were going to go light on the religion?"

"Yes, by all means. I still want it as simple and bare bones as possible, and so does Lori, except for the music from the congressman, of course."

"I thought you came from a distinguished Baptist preacher's family, you know, the teetotaler thing and all," Bowie noted. "What gives?"

"My uncle, yes," Travis responded. "But, alas, as you know, I'm afraid the only major sin in which I have not heavily indulged is drinking. I encouraged and promoted religion in my earlier existence, and, deep down, I guess you could say I'm a believer. And I certainly have nothing against it, but fact is that it has never been my focus!"

"Me neither," Mitch replied in character, ignoring the little fact that he was the only one on the premises authorized to perform a wedding.

"The understatement of the century—make that two different centuries," the Alamo commander responded with a smile. "You know Lyle Jones is actually coming, don't you?"

"Nothing like asking all of your closest friends. Is Santa Anna coming with him?" Bowie inquired sarcastically.

Buck made a face. "I certainly don't like what Jones has said about any of us, although I apparently have him to credit for finding me when I did give up hope. That's why he was invited, that and the fact that his wife is a kind lady. But, bad as he can be, he's no Santa Anna."

Bowie looked at him seriously. "Colonel, that is one thing on which we can heartily agree!"

Travis thought for a minute, then added: "I wonder how Jones would react if you did pull out a Bible. After all, he's quite convinced that we're going to Hell—or maybe already went there but are so bad the Devil won't let us in!"

Vicky was, as Buck had said, "the epitome of an 1836 Texian belle" in her beautiful pale blue dress. Lori pinned three tiny white rosebuds in the side of her sister's short red hair.

"The dress is beautiful—for that kind of thing," Vicky told Lori, "But I've never felt so ridiculous in my life!"

"Suck it up little sister," Lori laughed. "It's the only time you will ever have to do this. And don't worry about it—there will be more 1836 folks present than modern day."

"Yeah, kind of like Halloween come early," Vicky shot back.

"Remember what you said when we first started talking about Buck coming here to live—not really all that long ago?" Lori reminisced.

"Yeah, I do—put him in a rocking chair on the porch on Halloween night to scare the kids with his scars and the silly uniform," she said. "I still feel guilty about that because he can't help the scars. As to the uniform, it just is plain goofy, and I still stand by that part of it, although I would never want to subject him to ridicule. I'm so glad you're getting married—now he can be another brother—a strangely dressed one!"

"Give it up, Vicky," Lori feigned exasperation. She went on to admit, "Yeah, honestly, I still think the outfit is sort of goofy, too—definitely in some totally non-Alamo settings, but it's certainly part of who Buck is. Love him, love the uniform, I guess."

"Not me!" Vicky shook her head in defiance.

"Could you do something for me?" Lori asked. "I need gardenias cut for Dad, Buck, and Bob to wear as corsages—and a pin for each—probably need to go ahead and get those on them," she said. "Be careful not to touch the blooms as they'll turn brown, you know. And we'll need Mom's corsage and our bouquets from the fridge. It's getting close to time."

"Yeah, I know. Sure—I'll do it right now." Vicky headed off to cut the flowers and find the recipients.

Lori looked at herself in the mirror. Of course, she had worn the pretty yellow dress at the fandango. She still felt beautiful in it. In 1836, there was no rule requiring a bride's dress to be something newly bought—or made—for the wedding. She pinned her little yellow rosebuds in her long blonde hair done up in 1830's style—no veil—just keeping it simple as appropriate for the Texas frontier.

Elena stepped in the doorway. She was in an elegant pale blue silk crepe dress, accenting her red hair and echoing the effect of Vicky's dress.

"Hi Mom," Lori said softly, turning to her. "Y'all have been kind enough not to say anything to me, but I'm pretty sure you never dreamed your child would do anything this . . . uh . . . unconventional?" she said, looking at her mother earnestly. "I hope I haven't worried you too much?"

"Come sit by me a minute, Lori," Elena sat down on the yellow rose bedspread, and Lori sat next to her. "I'll have to confess that never in a million years would I have guessed we would be where we are today," she smiled at her daughter. "But, unique as the whole thing is, it was clearly meant to be. I've watched you grow up rather quickly in these last few months." She brushed away a tear. "I've seen you go through the struggles of the teen years. I know how not getting accepted at UT was such a disappointment, and that it was difficult to find a niche for your true love—history. I can't say how much I appreciate Bob's nurturing you at the Alamo. I've seen you mature and gain a wonderful confidence to go with your talents and desires. And then, what can I say—this special young man from long ago was unearthed with you watching—instead of doing your job cooking that cactus if I remember right?" Elena noted.

Lori gave a little laugh. "Yeah, no one got any fried cactus that day. Some of it was just curiosity. But the idea that someone from the battle was still in one piece. And then, when I felt his pulse, still alive. I don't know how to describe . . . ." Her blue eyes met her mom's green ones.

She continued, "But I know that Dad and you probably hoped your little girl would be more of a success," she looked down slightly, "and marry someone who was and looked . . . uh . . . normal, as well as successful and able to provide for me in the usual sense of the word," she said.

"True love doesn't work that way," Elena replied. "Not that Buck isn't a success . . . ."

Lori cut in, "Well, he certainly wasn't a success at the battle!"

"No, I guess not," Elena laughed. "But, as a human being, he's a bright, talented young man who is very protective of you and dedicated to his beliefs—noble character traits. And he has a good job and income, something all parents hope for in a daughter's husband!"

"Yeah, but I'm sure you're worried about the effects of the brain injury and the fact that I'll have to deal with that . . . and the stares at his scars . . . and the outfit!"

"Lori, there's always something with everyone—including everyone you love," Elena replied. "I do wish Buck could retreat a bit from the old battle, but I also remember he said he would not retreat—think it's on the mug? It's all just a part of who he is. And, although we need to work together, all of us, to help him navigate the present—and I think he has already made headway on that end, he wouldn't be Buck without his 1836 roots. When you told me about him stopping the pursuit of Vincente when you were hit—after all of those confrontations with the so-called Mexican troops, I knew this relationship was meant to be, that he truly did love you above all else, despite the injuries and trauma from long ago. And that makes it all OK. As to his looks, he's a very handsome guy. It is certainly most obvious when he's in modern clothes, but if you live in Texas and are the commander of the Alamo, the outfit is simply going to be a part of the job—and part of Buck. Seems to me you have become immune to the stares—I think we all have! Quite frankly, at this point, we really can't imagine our young colonel not being a member of the family!"

Lori hugged her.

Vicky had tracked down everyone who needed a corsage, and the

380

current and 1836 military uniforms were now adorned with them, regardless of whether it met regulations or not, as well as Bob's blue suit and Elena's blue crepe dress. All of the guests had assembled, and Crockett was on the tail end of the beautiful old Welsh tune, "The Ash Grove."

Elena and Len were on the front row. Buck, his planter hat removed, and Bob were standing in front of them, slightly to the side of the Reverend Bowie, who had removed his hat as well as the vicious knife for the ceremony. Vicky, with her agapanthus and rosebud bouquet, followed by Lori, on her father's arm, were just inside the French doors leading out to the backyard. Crockett started playing a slightly slower than the usual tempo "Yellow Rose of Texas" as the doors opened and Vicky headed toward the reverend, trying desperately to keep measured steps instead of her usual fast clip. Behind her, Lori, in her beautiful lemon-colored dress, headed slowly down the aisle with the major.

As they got to the front of the assembly, 2017 Major Clayton handed off his daughter to 1836 Colonel Travis, and the couple stood in front of the reverend as the "Yellow Rose" wound down and Bowie began the brief and simple service.

"As I think all of y'all know, we are gathered here this evening to join a rather unique young couple in holy matrimony." Bowie emphasized the word 'holy,' drawing muffled laughter from the assembled congregation. Buck and Lori smiled at each other.

The officiant continued. "I haven't done a wedding in a while." More laughter came from the audience.

"But these two people are among my favorites—well, one of them, anyway." Guests continued to laugh softly as Bowie stared at Travis.

"Seriously, this is truly a wonderful occasion and one I think all of us saw coming, except possibly the bride and groom! Anyway, I guess we're at that point where I need to ask if there's anyone who objects to these two folks being wed?" Bowie looked around at the guests. "Looks like we're all right there. Good thing we didn't invite Santa Anna!"

He continued with a smile. "So let's get on with it. William Barret Travis, do you take this woman to be your lawfully wedded wife, to have and to hold, from this day forward, for better or worse, richer or poorer, in sickness and health, to love and cherish till death do you part?" he stared at Buck.

Buck answered, per their decision to emphasize the vows, repeating all the words instead of a simple "I do," and looking down at Lori: "I William Barret Travis, take Lori Clayton to be my lawfully wedded wife, to have and to hold, from this day forward, for better or worse, richer or poorer, in sickness or in health, to love and cherish 'til death do us part. And hereto I pledge to you my faithfulness."

Buck had not told Lori about the last pledge, but after all of the talk about his diary over the time they had known each other, he wanted to settle the record once and for all. She brushed away a tear as she smiled at him.

"Lorelei Ravenel Clayton, do you take this man to be your lawfully wedded husband, to have and to hold, from this day forward, for better or worse, richer or poorer, in sickness or in health, to love and cherish till death do you part?" Bowie turned to Lori.

"My gosh, I didn't know that Lori's real name was THAT!" Melia blurted out. Everyone turned and stared at her. She looked mortified, thinking to herself that must be the way the colonel felt all the time.

Bowie quickly saved the situation. "Lori?" he said softly.

"Yes, I Lorelei Ravenel Clayton take William Barret Travis to be my lawfully wedded husband, to have and to hold, from this day forward, for better or worse, richer or poorer, in sickness or in health, to love and cherish 'til death do us part!" She beamed with happiness.

"Then, it's official—I pronounce y'all man and wife. 1836 is now joined with 2017. Buck, you may kiss your bride! Looks like we have a match made in heaven, even if the groom doesn't fit too well there!"

Crockett had started in on "Long, Long Ago."

"You know what, Buck?" Lori said softly, looking up at him.

"I just know I've never been anywhere near as happy in my life—either of them—than I am right this minute," he replied.

"Well, I, for one, hope that folks in Hell can still see and hear through their agony!" she said.

"Huh? That's a strange thought for our wedding!" he replied. "What made you think of that?"

"I'm hoping that El Presidente is watching in his torment right now, his defeat—at least as concerns you—complete!" she said.

"My kind of lady!" Buck replied, hugging her. "I believe this is the first time you ever focused on Santa Anna while he was the furthest thing from my mind!"

Made in the USA
Columbia, SC
14 December 2018